KU-176-365

Rosie Goodwin has worked in social services for many years. She has three children, and lives in Nuneaton with her husband, Trevor, and their three dogs.

Praise for Rosie Goodwin:

'A touching and tender story . . . tremendously uplifting and life-affirming. A feel-good read that tugs at the heart strings' *Historical Novels Review*

'A gifted writer . . . Not only is Goodwin's character-isation and dialogue compelling, but her descriptive writing is a joy' *Nottingham Evening Post*

'A heart-throbber of a story from Goodwin that puts many other so-called emotional blockbusters in the shade' *Northern Echo*

'Goodwin is a fabulous writer . . . she reels the reader in surprisingly quickly and her style involves lots of twists and turns that are in no way predictable'
Worcester Evening News

'Goodwin is a born author' *Lancashire Evening Telegraph*

'Rosie is the real thing – a writer who has something to say and knows how to say it' Gilda O'Neill

'Rosie is a born storyteller – she'll make you cry, she'll make you laugh, but most of all you'll care for her characters and lose yourself in her story' Jeannie Johnson

By Rosie Goodwin and available from Headline

The Bad Apple
No One's Girl
Dancing Till Midnight
Moonlight and Ashes
Forsaken
Our Little Secret
Crying Shame
Yesterday's Shadows
The Boy from Nowhere
A Rose Among Thorns

Tilly Trotter's Legacy
The Mallen Secret
The Sand Dancer

Rosie Goodwin

The Boy from Nowhere

headline

Copyright © 2009 Rosemarie Yates

The right of Rosemarie Yates to be identified as the Author of
the Work has been asserted by her in accordance with
the Copyright, Designs and Patents Act 1988.

First published in Great Britain in 2009
by HEADLINE PUBLISHING GROUP

First published in paperback in 2009
by HEADLINE PUBLISHING GROUP

1

Apart from any use permitted under UK copyright law, this
publication may only be reproduced, stored, or transmitted, in
any form, or by any means, with prior permission in writing of
the publishers or, in the case of reprographic production, in
accordance with the terms of licences issued by the
Copyright Licensing Agency.

All characters in this publication are fictitious
and any resemblance to real persons, living or dead,
is purely coincidental.

Cataloguing in Publication Data is available from the British Library

ISBN 978 0 7553 4228 0

Typeset in Bembo by Palimpsest Book Production Limited,
Grangemouth, Stirlingshire

Printed and bound in Great Britain by
CPI Mackays, Chatham ME5 8TD

Headline's policy is to use papers that are natural, renewable and recyclable products and
made from wood grown in sustainable forests. The logging and manufacturing processes are
expected to conform to the environmental regulations of the country of origin.

HEADLINE PUBLISHING GROUP
An Hachette UK Company
338 Euston Road
London NW1 3BH

www.headline.co.uk
www.hachette.co.uk

Dedication

Doreen Margaret Goodwin 1932–2008

Alfred Arthur Goodwin 1927–2008

This book is for my lovely mum, who lost her brave
fight on 11 October 2008. You were a true star, Mum.
I miss your shoulder to cry on and having you just a
phone call away more than I can say.

Also for my dear dad, who followed Mum on 14 December
2008. You were so brave, Dad, and I am so proud of you. I
miss your invaluable advice and all the laughter we shared.

To lose you both just nine weeks apart was heartbreaking,
but thank you for always being there for me. You were the
best and I will love and miss you both for ever.

I know now that the saying is true, *God only takes the best.*

Acknowledgements

First of all, many thanks to Penny and David for all the help with research for this book. I hope you'll enjoy it!

And as always, thanks to Flora, Kate, Maura, Jane, Joan and the wonderful team at Headline for all their support.

Sonia Land, my agent, and Leila, Gaia and everyone at Sheil Land.

To my wonderful husband and children, who have kept me going through a dark time with their love.

And lastly, an enormous thank you to all my lovely readers, who have kept me strong over the last difficult months, following the deaths of my beloved mum and dad. Your cards and messages meant the world to me.

Prologue

Nuneaton, October 1983

The child lying at the bottom of the stairs was unnaturally still, and as her mother stared down at her, her stomach turned over. She was no doctor, but this time she could tell that the injuries were really serious. All three of her children were on the at risk register, and the Social Services department had warned her that one more suspicious incident could result in them all being taken off her and put into care. Now panic began to set in.

'What are we gonna do?' she asked her partner fearfully.

Kevin Darley dragged on the cigarette dangling from the corner of his mouth before muttering, 'Well, we ain't got much choice in the matter, 'ave we? We'll 'ave to call an ambulance.'

When Kay started to cry, Kevin's lips curled back from his teeth and he exploded, 'I *told* yer you'd go too far one o' these days, yer silly cow!'

She took her eyes from the child just long enough to glance at him. He was immaculately dressed as usual. A designer T-shirt beneath a smart linen jacket while she and the children walked about in ill-fitting clothes. It was no wonder she lost her cool with him from time to time. She admitted to having a terrible temper, but it was always her or one of the children who came off the worst when she gave way to her tantrums, so she wondered why she couldn't control them. Still, it was too late to worry about that now. She would have to ring an ambulance and suffer the consequences.

With shaking fingers she lifted the phone and dialled 999. Then, turning to Alexander, her four-year-old son, who was staring up at her with fear shining in his eyes, she raised a finger to her lips.

'Remember, Alex, you mustn't say a word,' she cautioned, and the child nodded solemnly with a wisdom far beyond his tender years.

July 1984

'So what you're tellin' me is, you're goin' to take me kids off me?'

'I'm afraid that's about the long and the short of it, Kay. The department will be going to court next week for a freeing order, and once that is obtained they'll all be placed for adoption.' The social worker hesitated before continuing, 'I'm sure this won't come as a complete surprise to you. You *must* have known that this latest injury to Natasha would be reported to us by the hospital?'

'I've told you . . . it were an accident, she fell down the stairs,' Kay Slater retorted sullenly as she moved the wad of chewing gum in her mouth from one cheek to the other.

Mary Ingles wearily wiped her greying fringe out of her eyes. There could be no arguing with the panel's decision. Over the last twelve months, either one or another of Kay's three children had been repeatedly attending the hospital, and each time, Kay had insisted that their injuries were purely accidental; even the cigarette burn on Alexander's leg. He had run into it, she said.

The children had already been on the at risk register when Mary took over the case, and during the year she had been working with the family, she had offered every bit of support she could think of. *Fat lot of good that did!* she thought to herself now as she looked across the desk at Kay. And yet for all that she couldn't help but feel sorry for her. Although she was the mother of a four-year-old son and twin girls of two, Kay Slater was still only nineteen years old and looked as if she needed parenting herself. Small and thin, she could easily have been taken for a fifteen year old, although what she lacked in size she more than made up for in volume when she opened her mouth. Foul language usually punctuated every sentence she uttered, and she could be heard from one end of the Social Services department to another when she let rip, which was a fairly regular occurrence.

Today, however, Kay was unusually quiet. Mary supposed that was to be expected. After all, it wasn't every day you were told that you were about to lose your children. All three of them had been taken off Kay some months before and placed into foster care, following Natasha's dreadful fall. It had resulted in the child being left with brain damage, though to what extent still remained to be known. One thing was for sure. The child would never be the same again and all because of this young woman's temper. Kay had been lucky to get away with it; due to insufficient evidence, the courts had had no choice but to conclude that it had been an unfortunate accident.

Kay had screamed and cried on the day they went to her flat to take the children from her, but now she seemed to have settled into a dull acceptance of the situation. 'How long will it be . . . before they go, I mean?' she asked tentatively.

'That I couldn't tell you.' Mary dropped her eyes. 'It could be some months yet, but now that the panel have reached their decision, I fear there's very little chance of the court going against it.'

Kay raised a grimy fingernail to brush her bleached frizzed hair from her forehead. Her clothes were filthy and even with the desk between them, Mary could smell the unwashed stench that emanated from the girl. She was wearing brightly coloured striped leg-warmers and one of the shortest mini-skirts Mary had ever seen. Her feet were encased in high platform shoes.

Since going to live with foster-carers, the twin girls, Lauren and Natasha, had thrived; they had gained weight and Lauren was even beginning to say little words. But the same unfortunately could not be said for Alexander, a withdrawn child who shied away from any affection his carers tried to show him. During the times that Mary had visited the foster family, she had noticed that he seemed to be far older than his years and said little, preferring to sit in a corner and watch what was going on.

Kay's relationship with her latest partner, Kevin, who was the father of the twins, was a volatile one. He had put Kay herself into hospital so many times during the period that Mary had worked with the family that she had lost count, but Kay had always steadfastly refused to bring charges against him. Thankfully, however, he had always seemed to be surprisingly gentle with the children, which Mary supposed was just as well. The poor little mites had enough to endure, with a mother who could fly off the handle at the least provocation. Nevertheless, despite Kay's temper it was obvious how much she and the children loved each other.

Mary had no idea who Alex's father was, but from what she could gather from the enormous file that was teetering precariously on the desk in front of her, he had been just one in a long line of disastrous relationships. Kay seemed to attract the wrong sort of men like a magnet, not that she would admit to it, of course. For now at least, the sun seemed to rise and set with Kevin Darley for Kay, and she would not hear a bad word said against him.

A heavy silence had settled on the room, and hoping to end this painful interview, Mary said, 'Is there anything else you'd like to ask, Kay?'

'Yeah, I would as a matter o' fact. Will I still be allowed to see me kids once they go for adoption?'

'I think there's very little chance of that.' Mary swallowed as she saw the colour drain from Kay's face. 'You will still be allowed to have supervised access visits until we have the full care order, but then I'm afraid they'll probably be moving on. You will be allowed to say goodbye to them, of course.'

'Oh, thanks a fuckin' *bunch*,' Kay ground out as she rose to her feet, then leaning across the desk she hissed, 'I bet you're really enjoyin' this, ain't you? Thinkin' it serves the rotten cow right!'

'Actually, I think this is hurting me almost as much as it must be hurting you,' Mary told her honestly. 'I'm a mother myself, not just a social worker, and I can assure you this is the part of the job I hate.'

'Huh! An' you expect me to believe that, do you? Why, you're all hand in glove, the whole fuckin' lot o' you! Why you had to interfere in the first place I'll never know. *All* kids have accidents, don't they? So why did you have to pick on *my* family?'

Kay's voice was rising dangerously now, and hoping to prevent a scene, Mary crossed to the door and held it open as she said, 'I think you need some time alone, Kay, to come to terms with what I've just told you. Just remember, I'm at the end of the phone if there's anything I can do for you.'

Snatching up her shoulder bag, Kay flung herself towards the open door with a face like a thundercloud. 'I reckon you've done enough, don't you?' she snarled as she swept past Mary. 'You can have a good laugh at me now, can't you? You've won.'

Mary closed the door behind her, then retreating to her desk, she let the tears she had held back throughout the difficult meeting finally slide down her cheeks. It was then that she made her decision. As soon as this case was sorted she would retire. Spend some time in her garden and more time with her grandchildren. She had seen enough heartache in this job to last her a lifetime.

PART ONE

Chapter One

November 1984

The bungalow at the back of the Social Services department in Edmund Street was the meeting place for children in care who had visiting access with their parents, and it was there that Mary Ingles was now driving Kay Slater to say goodbye to her children. She had been dreading this farewell all day, but now that the time had come she knew deep down that she would be glad to get it over with, although she could only begin to imagine how Kay must be feeling.

The girl was slumped at her side in the passenger seat puffing furiously on a cigarette, her eyes straight ahead and a resentful expression on her face. Over the last months there had been endless court cases, conferences and meetings. Even though Kay had got away with Natasha's fall through lack of evidence, the decision still stood that the children should go for adoption, and suitable families had now been located for all three of them. Normally, Mary would have tried to find a family that was prepared to take all three siblings together, but because of the children's very individual needs it had been decided to place them with three separate families.

She had expected Kevin to come with Kay today; he was the twins' father, after all, but when she picked the young woman up from her flat and enquired if he would be coming, Kay had merely shrugged her shoulders and told her that he wasn't fussed.

Wasn't fussed! Mary found it incredible that a father wouldn't wish to say goodbye to his own children, but then she had seen enough during her years as a social worker that she had now got to the stage where nothing truly surprised her.

'Are you feeling all right?' she asked softly, as she took her eyes from the road just long enough to glance at Kay's pale face.

'What the bleedin' 'ell do you think?' Kay shot back ungraciously. 'You're takin' me to see me kids for the last time an' you're thick enough to ask am I all right! *O' course* I ain't all right, but what do *you* fuckin' care!'

They were travelling along Edmund Street now, and Mary wisely lapsed into silence as she turned the car into Harry Street and the car park of the Social Services department.

'Right then, shall we go and get this over with?'

Kay glared at her before clambering out of the car and slamming the door behind her. After tossing her cigarette on to the tarmac she ground it out with the heel of her shoe then, without waiting for Mary, she strode towards the bungalow.

Mary sighed heavily and, after locking the car door, quietly followed her.

The second that Kay set foot through the door of the bungalow, Alexander's little face lit up brighter than a ray of sunshine and he came hurtling from the play room to fling himself into her arms.

'*Mummy, Mummy!*'

''Ello, sweet'eart.' Kay returned his embrace and once again the little finger of unease that she always experienced when she saw Kay with her children sprang to life in Mary's stomach. The children appeared to love their mother despite the physical abuse and cruelty they had suffered at her hands. But then, the old saying had been proven to be true time and time again during her career. Blood certainly was thicker than water, and no matter how their parents treated them, most children remained unswervingly loyal to them.

Alexander was staring up at her adoringly now, and as Kay swiped a thick lock of dark hair back from his forehead she asked gently, 'You all right, are you?'

He nodded and, taking her hand, he tugged her into the play room where Lauren and Natasha were sitting on the carpet surrounded by toys. Lauren was chattering happily away to Polly, her rag doll, who was her constant companion. She was a fairly ordinary doll as far as rag dolls went, apart from the fact that she had one blue eye and one brown eye. In all the time that Mary had been working with the family, she had never seen Lauren without her. Natasha, meanwhile, was staring off blankly into space, just as she had since the night of the accident.

Mary's heart went out to the child. She was a pretty little thing, totally unlike her twin in both looks and nature. Natasha was small and delicate with baby blond hair and blue eyes, whilst Lauren was taller and sturdier with dark hair and laughing grey eyes. Neither of the girls showed much interest in the fact that their mother had arrived, which was just as well because Alex was monopolising her now.

'I come home now, Mummy?' As his deep dark eyes stared hopefully up at his mother, Mary's heart sank. This was going to be even more painful than she had anticipated.

'I'll . . . er . . . be in the kitchen if you need me,' she muttered as she scuttled away.

Once in the small kitchenette, she hastily opened the window and, after fumbling in her bag, she withdrew a packet of cigarettes and lit one with shaking fingers. It was a habit she had been trying to break for months but right at that moment she felt the need for one. She was leaning against the sink when the door opened and Lorna Craine, her much younger colleague, joined her.

'You all right?' she asked, looking at Mary's strained face.

'As all right as I can be.' Mary flicked ash out of the window and said quietly, 'Alex isn't making it easy, is he?'

'No, but then he's old enough to understand a little of what's happening, isn't he? I've no doubt once we've got today over with and he's with his new family, he'll settle in time. The Andersons seem to be a lovely couple. You did well to find them – I'm sure he'll be fine.'

'Mm, well, let's just hope you're right.' Mary gazed at a crack in the ceiling as Lorna frowned.

'What is it exactly that's troubling you?' she probed.

Mary shrugged. 'I don't know. It's just . . . something doesn't feel *right*. After all the times Kay's put that child in hospital, you'd think he'd be frightened of her, wouldn't you? Yet he always seems so thrilled to see her.'

'Huh! Isn't that usually the case?' Lorna snorted derisively. 'Still, after today he can start to move on. I'm sure the Andersons will adore him. It would be hard not to. He's a gorgeous little boy, isn't he? I could take him home myself, to be honest – if I wanted kids, that is. Fancy having a social worker who doesn't even want kids, eh? I think I've gone into the wrong profession.'

'You will want them one day, when you meet the right person,' Mary assured her, and when Lorna chuckled, Mary smiled at her fondly. She and Lorna were as different as chalk from cheese and yet they had got on like a house on fire ever since Lorna had joined the Harry Street team fresh from university the year before. 'Yes, they are a nice couple,' Mary now admitted. 'We couldn't have wished for a better place for him. The Andersons are childless so I've no doubt they'll spoil him rotten. He'll certainly lack for nothing and their home is very comfortable, right by the sea in Devon. They're already talking about getting him into a private school next year too.'

'There you are then. What are you worrying about?' Lorna flashed her an encouraging smile. 'You've found great places for the other two as well, from what I can see of it. There's Natasha all set to go off and live in Yorkshire with a doctor and his wife, and Lauren about to go and live in what amounts to a mini-mansion. You've excelled yourself, so come on, let's get back in there and make this last meeting as good as we can for all of them, eh?'

Mary smiled weakly, then flicking her cigarette end out of the window she smoothed her skirt over her plump legs and followed Lorna back into the meeting room.

Natasha was still sitting in the same place but Lauren was now busily building a house with brightly coloured bricks, helped along by her mother and brother.

'That's lovely, Lauren.' Kay smiled as she sat back on her heels to admire the building. It was then that Alex flew into a towering rage as he kicked out, sending the bricks flying in all directions.

'It was *me* that built it, Mummy,' he gasped, red-faced with temper, then before Kay could respond he flung himself on to her lap and began to sob uncontrollably.

Sally Wootton, the carer he had been staying with and who had taken him there, rushed forward to try and placate the child, but he kicked out at her savagely.

'Don't want *you*, want *Mummy*,' he screamed as Kay stroked his hair and held him protectively against her.

Mary gulped deep in her throat before turning and heading for the kitchen again. She thought it was high time she made everyone a drink while Alex calmed down a little.

When she returned some minutes later, balancing a tray in her hand, she found him still sitting on his mother's lap with his thumb jammed in his mouth.

After placing the tray on a small table she then tentatively held out a plastic beaker of lemonade to him. 'Look, Alex, it's your favourite drink,' she coaxed, but he lashed out, sending the beaker and the drink splashing all over the place. 'Don't want it!' he declared petulantly.

Lorna glanced at Mary and shrugging, the woman turned to serve the drinks to the other people present. By now it was more than obvious that all Alex wanted was his mother, the one person he would not be allowed to have after today.

At last, the hour was over and it was time for goodbyes. Kay kissed first Lauren and then Natasha, and the girls smiled, not understanding the finality of it all. But Alex seemed to sense that this was a different parting to the previous ones when his mother had visited him at his foster-carer's home, and he clung on to her leg like a leech as tears poured silently down the young woman's cheeks. There was no sign of the arrogant foul-mouthed girl that Mary had been forced to endure over the last months. Before her now was a heartbroken young mother who must say her final goodbyes to her children.

'I . . . I'm so sorry,' Kay sobbed, as the two solemn-faced foster-mums took the little girls' hands and silently led them away. And now there was only Alex who was crying brokenheartedly as she knelt to his level and took his chin tenderly in her hand.

'You're going to be OK,' she assured him. 'Mary has found you lovely people to live with right by the seaside. Won't that be smashin', eh?'

'Don't want to live by the sea! Want to live with *you*!' the livid-faced child insisted as he clung on to her for all he was worth.

'An' you will again, one day,' Kay promised him. 'I'll come an' fetch you, just you wait an' see. I'll come an' fetch you, an' we'll be together again. I promise.'

Mary almost choked as she witnessed the raw pain in the young woman's eyes, then with an enormous effort, Kay managed to prise her son's hands away and now she thrust him towards Mary, kicking and screaming, as she suddenly made for the door.

'Kay, wait,' Mary implored her, as she struggled to keep hold of Alex who seemed to have developed the strength of ten children. 'I'll run you home if you hold on.'

Eyes straight ahead, Kay walked blindly past her and all Mary could do was watch helplessly.

Kevin was sitting in a chair watching snooker on the television when Kay entered their flat some time later, and for the first time since their relationship had begun, her eyes did not immediately go to him. Instead, she stood in the doorway as her eyes slowly roved around the dingy room. It was as if she was seeing it for the very first time, the dirty curtains, threadbare carpet, sagging settee and nicotine-stained walls. She and her children had been forced to live in this squalor, sometimes wondering where their next meal would be coming from, while Kevin swanked around in designer clothes. Mary had been right, after all. The children would be better off with new families, people who would give them all the things that she had never been able to. Only then did her eyes settle on Kevin. He had a can of lager in one hand and a cigarette dangling from the other. His long legs were sprawled out in front of him and Kay noticed that he hadn't shaved. But then he wouldn't bother until the pubs opened, then it would be a quick dash to the bathroom to make himself handsome for his latest conquest. Oh, she knew he had other women, she'd always known, but up until now she'd been prepared to turn a blind eye to his bits on the side because he always came home to her.

Standing just inside the doorway she watched him until he glanced at her before barking, 'Oh, yer back then. Well, get me another can o' lager, would yer, an' make yerself useful fer a change.'

Her head wagged from side to side. He hadn't even asked how the meeting had gone. How the children were. How *she* was. The rose-coloured glasses she had always viewed him through slipped away and she saw him for what he really was: a no-good waster who would never amount to anything, who would never care for anyone but himself.

The tears had dried now. Kay was sure she would never cry again; she had used all her tears up and her heart was empty. Crossing to the kitchen, she walked slowly to the fridge, then after taking out a can of lager she moved to the cutlery drawer and stared down into it for a moment.

Seconds later she was back in the lounge and he took the drink she held out to him without a word of thanks. She let him take a long swallow before raising the bread-knife and bringing it slashing towards his chest with every ounce of strength she possessed. A brief look of shock flared in his eyes as he stared up at her, then dark blood began to bubble from his lips and he slipped lifeless to the side as the lager spread in a golden pool across his Levi jeans.

There, it was done. She smiled with satisfaction, then her heart contracted with pain. Kevin's suffering had ended within seconds; he was lucky – hers would go on for a whole lifetime.

Chapter Two

Mary shivered as she locked her car and hurried into Harry Street Social Services department. She was suffering from a severe case of Monday morning blues, not helped by the weather, which had suddenly turned bitterly cold. The tarmac on the car park was white all over and the grass that bordered it was standing to attention with hoar frost.

I'll try and take it easy today, she promised herself as she slithered across the slippery surface and entered the building. She went into the front office to put her name on the board, only to see her colleagues clustered about a newspaper that was open on one of the desks.

'Mary.' Lorna beckoned her over. 'Have you seen last Saturday's newspaper?'

Mary shook her head. She lived in Sibson, a small village on the outskirts of Nuneaton, and rarely got to see a local newspaper apart from when she was in work if someone left one lying about.

'You'd better look at this then,' Lorna urged. 'It seems that straight after the meeting with the children on Friday, Kay Slater went back to her flat and stabbed Kevin.'

'Good God! Is he badly hurt?' Mary's shock was apparent as she gripped the edge of the desk.

'Huh! It's worse than that, she's killed him. They've got her in custody.'

Mary tried to take in what Lorna was telling her. Why would

Kay do that? The young woman had thought that Kevin was the best thing since sliced bread. But then if she'd gone off on one of her drinking binges she'd probably not know what she was doing. It had usually been after one of these lapses when the children had been injured. Mary sat down heavily on the nearest chair as a picture of the children flashed in front of her eyes. Poor little devils; perhaps it was just as well there were new homes lined up for them all. No doubt the courts would lock Kay up and throw away the key now. And yet still something didn't feel quite right . . . On the Friday before, as Kay had spent her last minutes with her children, Mary had glimpsed her inner pain and seen beneath the brash front the girl presented to the world to the gentle heart within. Kay herself had come from a very dysfunctional family and had been through the care system since an early age. She had suffered one placement breakdown after another because the foster-carers couldn't cope with her challenging behaviour, until eventually she had ended up in a small children's home in Manor Road. The staff there had done their best for her, to give them credit, but it was already too late for Kay by that time. The barriers had been put in place by then and no one had been able to get through them. Apart from Kevin, that was, and now he was lost to her too.

That poor kid, Mary found herself thinking. She never stood a chance really.

'Mary, are you off with the fairies or what?' Lorna's voice interrupted her thoughts. 'I asked if you'd like me to make you a cup of tea. You certainly look as if you could use one. You've gone as white as a ghost.'

'What? Oh yes, that would be lovely, thanks.' Mary flashed Lorna a bemused smile. 'I'll have it in my office if you don't mind bringing it through.'

Lorna watched with concern as Mary rose and chalked her name on the board before heading off to her own office. 'I think it's safe to say that bit of news has fair taken the wind out of her sails, don't you?' she commented wryly to the others.

Stella, who was at the reception desk, nodded in agreement as Lorna hurried away down the tiled corridor to the kitchen without waiting for an answer.

Minutes later, she tapped at Mary's door.

'Come in.'

Lorna entered the room and placed the mug of tea on Mary's desk before perching on the edge of it and looking at the older woman with concern. 'Feeling better, are you?' she enquired. 'I'm sorry I dropped the news on you like that. I wasn't thinking. It was bound to affect you after all the work you've put in with Kay and her family.'

'It's all right.' Mary looked at her over the rim of her gold-framed glasses. 'I suppose we should just thank our lucky stars that we got the children away when we did, otherwise it might have been one of them.'

'Mm.' Lorna tapped her chin thoughtfully, but after a few moments she stood straight again and with an apologetic smile headed back towards the door. 'You'll have to excuse me. I've got a mountain of paperwork to get through then I've two home visits to make. Are you quite sure you're OK?'

'Perfectly,' Mary assured her. 'I've got phone calls of my own to do. I'm hoping to get all three of the Slater children to their adoptive families before Christmas. There doesn't seem to be any point in delaying – especially after what's happened. At least then I can stop worrying about them.'

Lorna nodded in agreement as she closed the door behind her and slipped away.

Alone again, Mary dropped her pen and stared around her office. Until Social Services had converted it into offices, the building had been a children's home, and sometimes, especially if she was forced to work late at night, Mary would swear she could hear laughter and tears. It was as if the very walls of the place were impregnated with the souls of the children who had once lived there. The building retained many of its original features: the high ceilings still boasted ornate plaster cornices, and the original sash cord windows were also still in place. Many of the staff complained that the building needed completely updating, but Mary found it charming and strangely cosy, even with the creaking floorboards and the clanking pipes.

As her thoughts turned back to the Slater children she frowned and, lifting a pencil, she chewed on the end of it. She had phoned Sally, Alex's carer, shortly before heading for home for the weekend on the previous Friday, and Sally had informed her that he had been inconsolable ever since being torn from his mother's arms earlier in the afternoon. Mary's heart ached for the poor little chap. All she could hope for now was that he would settle once he got to a new environment and a brand new family.

A smile lifted the corners of her mouth as she thought of Jacob and June Anderson and their immaculate home in Puddlesea in Devon. She had met with them frequently over the last months and hoped that Alex would find a loving home with them. Admittedly, June was a little on the quiet side – it seemed as if she wouldn't say boo to a goose – but Jacob, an outgoing man who taught at a school on the way to Barnstaple, more than made up for that and was constantly chattering. The couple were keen to have Alex home with them as soon as possible now.

Mary had worried initially that the Andersons seemed a little too old to be taking on a child, but they had appeared to be the most suitable of the three couples who had come forward to offer Alex a home, so she hoped that she had made the right choice. Their house was very nice and the room they had since prepared for Alex was fit for a prince. They were comfortably off financially, and Mary had no doubt that Alex would want for nothing, least of all love – something he seemed to have been sadly lacking, despite his unswerving devotion to his mother.

The home she had found for Lauren was much closer – in fact, almost on the doorstep. The little girl would be going to live in Feathermill Lodge, a beautiful old farmhouse on the outskirts of

Nuneaton. Set in five acres of ground, it was a wonderful place for a child to be brought up in, with rolling lawns for her to play on and twisting corridors inside the house where she could romp to her heart's content when the weather wasn't good enough for her to be playing outside. Her new parents would be Penny and David Daventry. David was an accountant who worked from home, and Penny was a former nurse who had given up work and was content to stay at home. Originally, Mary's only concern was the couple's close proximity to Nuneaton, but after reading of what Kay had done today, Mary realised it would no longer be a problem. It was highly unlikely that Kay would walk free for many years to come, and by then, Lauren would no doubt have grown up and forgotten all about her first mother. The Daventrys also had parenting skills to their credit, though their two children, Heather and Aiden, were now away at university.

It was finding a suitable home for Natasha that had caused Mary the most concern as it was still unknown to what extent her brain damage would manifest itself. That was why Mary had been so delighted when she was first introduced to Gail and Joseph Salisbury. A childless couple in their late twenties, they were not at all concerned about taking on a child who might prove to be a challenge in the years to come. Better still, Joseph – or Joe as he preferred to be called – was a doctor, who had his own surgery in North Yorkshire where Gail acted as his receptionist. Mary had fallen in love with their home on her very first visit. The picturesque village of Hockley Vale was right in the heart of the Brontë country. It was full of little cobbled streets and twisting lanes, with chocolate-box thatched cottages and a quaint little church. It was in one of these cottages that Natasha would live. Although nothing like as grand as the houses her brother and sister would be going to, the Salisburys' cottage was quaint and inviting. It had low-beamed ceilings and a huge inglenook fireplace in the lounge, and Mary could picture the child curled up in front of it on a cold winter's night. Gail was a bubbly, happy-go-lucky sort of person, whilst her husband was a quiet man whose face lit up every time he so much as looked at his attractive young wife.

All in all, Mary was happy with the three different choices of parents for the children, not that the choice had been wholly hers, of course. There had been endless meetings and numerous people involved in the final decisions for the children's futures, but now Mary felt that all three of them would be going to good loving homes.

All that remained now was to arrange when the couples would like to take the children. First, the couples would all be invited to the foster-homes where the children were staying, in order to spend time with them and get to know them a little. Then, when Mary felt that the children were ready, she personally would accompany them to their new homes.

Pulling the prospective adopters' phone numbers towards her, she first rang Alex's new parents. It looked as if it was going to be yet another long morning.

Chapter Three

'So it's all set for next week then, is it?' Lorna enquired as she peered over the rim of her mug in the staff room. She and Mary were enjoying a well-earned break, the first of the day, and Lorna was keen to be updated on what was happening with the Slater children.

Mary nodded as she glanced towards the window where the first flakes of snow were just beginning to fall. 'Yes, I've decided to move Natasha first. I was planning on it being Alex, but his foster-mum tells me he's still being very difficult and asking for his mother. I thought I'd give him a little more time to settle and perhaps move the twins first.'

'Sounds wise to me.' Lorna suddenly leaned forward to ask with concern, 'Would you like me to come with you? You're looking a bit peaky lately. I've no doubt the boss would allow it if I asked.'

Mary seemed to consider her question before eventually replying, 'Actually, I'd like that if you're quite sure you wouldn't mind. I've got very involved with this case and just between you and me, I won't be sorry when the children are all placed with their new families and I can close the file. I think it's beginning to get to me a bit. I keep thinking of Kay locked up in prison and how awful it must be for her. I mean . . . I know she deserves to be there, but her whole life has fallen apart, hasn't it? What state of mind must she have been in, to kill her partner?'

'Mm, I know what you mean.' Lorna stared thoughtfully off into space for a moment before sighing loudly and placing her mug on the rickety coffee-table. 'The thing is though, Mary, you can't take the worries of the world on your shoulders. You did everything within your power to help her, and now it's up to the courts to decide what her punishment should be. You've just got to concentrate on getting the children happily settled. What day were you thinking of taking Natasha? And are you going to try to do it all in one day? It's a long journey up to Hockley Vale and back.'

'I thought I might book into a bed and breakfast,' Mary replied. 'You're quite right. It would be pushing it to try and get there and back without a proper rest.'

Lorna grinned now as she replied, 'Then in that case, it's a shame it's not the summertime. A bit of a break and a few hours on the moors could be just what the doctor ordered, judging by the look of you. Still, I dare say there will be a pub where we can while away a few hours in the evening – that's if the Salisburys don't live in the back of beyond.'

'Oh, I'm sure we'll find somewhere,' Mary assured her with a smile. 'Hockley Vale is a lovely place; I know you'll like it. I certainly wouldn't mind retiring there, I don't mind telling you. It's like stepping back in time and the Salisburys' cottage is just beautiful. Like something out of a magazine.'

'In that case I'd better go and square it with the boss,' Lorna told her, and with a final smile she left the room, leaving Mary to finish her tea in peace.

On the following Monday morning, Mary and Lorna loaded Natasha's bags into the boot of Mary's car before heading back into the carer's house in William Street where Natasha had been staying. Lesley, her foster-mum, had tears in her eyes as she buttoned the little girl's coat.

'I'm going to really miss this one,' she confided as she cuddled the child to her. 'She's such a lovely child. I just hope things work out for her now.'

'I'm sure they will,' Mary told her. 'You've met the Salisburys and I'm sure you'll agree we couldn't have found a better couple for her. They can hardly wait to have her home now. I've no doubt Gail will be waiting on the doorstep chewing her nails by the time we get there.'

Lesley smiled, knowing that Mary was right. The Salisburys were a lovely couple but it was always hard when it was time for a little one to move on, especially one as beautiful as Natasha. Children were much like social workers. You got good ones and you got bad ones, and she knew with Mary and Natasha she'd had the best of both.

'Well, I've got a bit of good news for you before you go,' she now gleefully informed Mary. 'When I got her up this morning, she said "Mamma" as clear as a bell. I thought she said it the other night but couldn't be sure. Let's hope it's a good sign, eh?'

'Absolutely.' Mary scooped the little girl up into her arms and headed for the street, where Lorna was waiting for her with the back door of the car open.

There were lots of hugs and kisses and more than a few tears from Lesley as Mary looked on before saying, 'Thanks for all you've done for her over the last months, Lesley. You've been a real star.'

Lesley sniffed loudly and then she stood and waved them away before shivering and hurrying back indoors out of the snow.

It was 125 miles to Hockley Vale and the journey should have taken them no more than two and a half hours, but the weather conditions were so bad that it took almost five hours with two stops on the way. The first was in Nottingham, where Lorna took Natasha to the toilet and got them all a hot drink in a café. The second stop was in Huddersfield, where they rested for a while and had lunch. By then Mary was looking slightly frazzled and had the beginnings of a headache throbbing behind her eyes. The roads were like a skating rink and she had to concentrate so hard on her driving that she was grateful that Lorna had volunteered to come along with her to keep her eye on Natasha. Not that the child was much trouble. She simply sat staring silently out of the window until eventually she dropped into a doze.

At last they saw the sign for Keighley, and Mary sighed with relief. The snow was coming down heavier than ever now and she was just thankful that she wasn't going to have to drive back today. Gail had kindly offered to let Lorna and herself stay at the cottage for the night before they headed back to Nuneaton, but Mary was aware that they would just have been in the way. After all, it wasn't every day you gained a daughter, and she had no doubt that Gail and Joe would want to spend time alone with the little girl, once the paperwork was out of the way, of course.

'Isn't that the station where they filmed *The Railway Children*?' Lorna asked as they drove through one village.

'Yes, it is,' Mary said. 'There's a lot to do round here. Not far away is the Georgian parsonage where the Brontë sisters lived. I believe you can go around it at certain times of the year, though I doubt it would be open to the public in this weather. And then, of course, the moors surround all these villages. This whole area really is the most beautiful place in the summer.'

'I can well believe it.' Lorna sighed enviously as she eyed the picturesque cottages they were driving past and thought of her own little one-bedroomed flat.

Mary chuckled as if she could read her thoughts. 'Anything worth having is worth waiting for,' she pointed out. 'You're only young with your whole life in front of you. You might just meet some handsome millionaire who'll buy you anything you want.'

'Huh! I think the chances of that are fairly slim.' Lorna peeped over the seat at Natasha who was still curled up under a blanket fast asleep before turning her attention back to the cottages they were passing, now they had finally entered the village of Hockley Vale.

Mary was right: this place *was* like a little corner of heaven, particularly under its snug white covering of snow. Although it was only just past three o'clock in the afternoon, the light had already gone from the day, and lamps were shining from the little leaded windows of the dwellings, spewing a myriad of colours into the twisting streets.

After a time, Mary sighed with relief as she drew the car to a stop outside a cottage whose front door opened directly on to the cobblestoned pavement. The sign above the stout oak door read *Beehive Cottage*.

'This is it.' She glanced at the sleeping Natasha and smiled, but before she had a chance to say any more, the cottage door suddenly flew open and an attractive young woman with long fair hair tied back in a ponytail rushed out to meet them with an excited smile on her face.

'Oh Mary, I've been so worried about you having to travel in this weather,' she gushed; however, it wasn't Mary she was looking at but the child on the back seat.

Mary climbed out of the car and stretched painfully as Lorna got out of the other side and hurried round the car to join her.

'I was beginning to think you wouldn't make it,' Gail told them.

Mary shook her head. 'I wouldn't have let you down even if we'd been under ten foot of snow,' she laughed. 'I know how much you've been looking forward to this day, though I have to admit, I'm glad I don't have to make the return journey until tomorrow. But anyway, that's enough about that. We're here safe and sound now, so how about we wake the little madam up and get her inside out of the cold, eh? I've no doubt she'll be bursting to use the toilet and longing for a drink by now. It seems an awful long time since lunchtime.' Without waiting for Gail's response, she opened the rear door of the car, lifted the little bundle, still wrapped warmly in the blanket, and placed the child in Gail's arms.

Joe, her husband, had come to join them on the pavement and he beamed from ear to ear as he saw the look on his wife's face. He, better than anyone, knew how much she had longed for this day. He had watched her break her heart month after month when she realised that she wasn't pregnant yet again. He had accompanied

27

her on so many hospital appointments that he had long since lost count, and with each disappointment his heart had broken a little too.

In truth, it had always been Gail who had longed for a child more than him. As long as he had his wife, Dr Joe Salisbury didn't really need anyone else. But even so, his love for her was such that he would have done anything to please her, and when she had finally realised that she would never bear a child of her own and had suggested adoption, he had gone along with it gladly. And now it was finally happening. Gail was carrying their child into their home, and he was sure he had never seen her so happy. She had fallen in love with Natasha the very first time they had visited her in Nuneaton, and she had barely spoken of anything else ever since.

His arm snaked about his wife's waist and as they disappeared out of the snow, Mary and Lorna exchanged a satisfied glance. It looked like this was one little girl they wouldn't have to worry about in future, for sure.

When they followed close on the couple's heels and entered the cottage, Lorna gasped. It had looked quite small from the outside, but inside it was spacious and inviting. They stepped directly into a large lounge where a huge log fire was burning cheerily in an enormous inglenook fireplace. The flames were reflecting on highly polished horse brasses which hung on the heavy beam that served as a mantelshelf, and Lorna was surprised to see that the room seemed to be bulging with antiques. Gail herself was a trendy-looking person, so the décor of the cottage came as something of a surprise to her. Two large settees covered in brightly coloured floral chintz stood at either side of the fireplace and behind them were various elaborately carved mahogany cabinets that were full of what looked like very expensive silver and china. Chintz curtains with matching frilled pelmets hung at the small leaded windows, and Lorna had a sense of stepping back in time. She herself liked more modern furniture, but even so the room was so tastefully decorated that she couldn't help but be impressed with it.

She was still looking around when Natasha suddenly yawned and stretched and looked up at the woman who was to become her new mother. And it was then that the strangest thing happened, for she smiled, something she hadn't done for many months.

Mary felt a large lump forming in her throat. Both Gail and Joe were cooing and whispering endearments to the child, and she seemed to be responding to them, which Mary hoped was a good sign.

'Goodness me, I've completely forgotten my manners,' Joe said apologetically, as he dragged his attention away from Natasha. 'Why don't you ladies come through to the kitchen – you must be dying for a hot drink. Gail has everything ready for you. I'm sure she'll join us when she's got Natasha's coat and bonnet off.'

He ushered them towards a door in a far wall and once again Lorna was shocked when she entered a large kitchen, which took her breath away. In the centre of the room was a large scrubbed pine table that matched the many units that were fitted around the walls. A Belfast sink stood below a kitchen window that was framed with fresh-looking gingham curtains, and beyond the window was a garden that Lorna felt was more like a field. In the centre was the most gigantic cherry tree she had ever seen, and behind that stood a row of old beehives that she guessed had given the cottage its name.

As she gazed from the window she commented, 'Goodness me, I wouldn't like to have to mow that lot.'

Joe chuckled good-naturedly as he placed the kettle on the hob to boil. 'Actually, I quite enjoy gardening, which is just as well as we have almost an acre. It's not all laid to garden though. We have a paddock and a stable out there and Gail has already invested in a pony for Natasha to ride when she's a little older. We've been doing our homework and were assured that riding is very therapeutic for children like Natasha.'

As he spoke, a black and white Cavalier King Charles spaniel suddenly lurched out of a basket and began to lick Mary's hand as his tail flicked from side to side.

'Oh, that's Charlie.' Joe introduced him with a grin. 'I think he'll be another playmate for Tasha. He's very fond of children and extremely good-natured.'

'I rather gathered that,' Mary grinned, as she stroked his silky fur. She was feeling better about this placement by the minute. Joe and Gail seemed to have thought of everything that a child could need. It was then that Gail led Natasha into the room and after lifting her she seated her at the kitchen table.

There was a large Victoria sponge and a plateful of homemade biscuits in pride of place in the centre of the table, and as Natasha's eyes settled on them they lit up greedily.

Gail chuckled with delight as she bent to the child's level. 'Which would you like first?' she asked fondly, and when Natasha licked her lips she instantly loaded a large slice of cake oozing jam and cream and two biscuits on to her plate. The little girl tucked into her treat as Gail served everyone else, keeping an indulgent eye on the child all the time.

The snack was a surprisingly merry affair and by the time it was done, Natasha was covered in jam and cream.

'Why don't you show Mary and Lorna Natasha's room, dear?' Gail suggested as she began to wipe Natasha's face gently with a flannel, which was no mean feat as all the child's interest was now centred on Charlie, who she was struggling to get down to. 'I'm sure they'd like to see it now it's all finished.'

'Of course.' Joe rose from the table and Mary and Lorna followed him up a dog-legged staircase that led from an inner hall to the first floor. This too had beamed ceilings and a thick carpet that their feet sank into. Soon they found themselves on a long landing from which led a number of doors and once again Lorna was amazed at the size of the place.

Joe stopped outside one of the doors and flung it open, and when Lorna and Mary entered the room they both exclaimed aloud at how pretty it was. Three walls had been painted in a soft lilac colour, and the wall behind the bed was papered with a design of fairies in sparkling dresses all the colours of the rainbow. Lilac curtains hung at the window and there was a deep-pile purple carpet on the floor that matched the pretty bedspread.

Crossing to a tall pine wardrobe that matched the chests of drawers and bedside cabinets, he opened the door and they saw that it was full of new clothes that had all been carefully chosen for Natasha. There were pretty dresses and tiny jeans, warm jumpers and coats. Folded on the shelves were pyjamas and a dressing-gown as well as a large selection of underwear. A big cuddly teddy bear was propped against the pillow on the bed, and an overflowing toy box stood in one corner. On another wall were shelves full of gaily illustrated storybooks.

'My goodness me.' Mary looked around in amazement, trying to take it all in. It was a room fit for a little princess. 'You *have* been busy. You seem to have thought of everything. And we still have all her things to bring in from the car. Speaking of which, I suppose we ought to do that and then think about getting the paperwork done. We can get out of your hair then. It's been a long day for Natasha and I've no doubt you're ready for some time to yourselves before you settle her down for the night.'

Soon they had loaded all Natasha's things out of the car into the hallway and had all the necessary signatures on the paperwork. Natasha was stumbling awkwardly around the room chasing Charlie, whose tail was wagging furiously with delight at his newfound playmate.

'Oh dear, I rather think they're going to be partners in crime,' Mary commented as she watched their antics with amusement. She had never seen Natasha so happy, and it did her heart good to see her so animated.

'I think you could be right,' Joe agreed, as his arm slid around Gail's shoulders.

'We'll be staying at the King's Head in the High Street tonight, should you need us for anything,' Mary informed them, but the couple shook their heads in unison.

'I'm sure we won't. I think we'll be too busy enjoying our new daughter,' Gail told her with sparkling eyes. 'Thank you, Mary, for all you've done. I never dreamed I'd end up with such a lovely daughter. I'll never be able to thank you enough.'

'You don't have to thank me – I'm just doing my job. And don't forget, I'm right at the end of the phone if you're worried about anything, and I'll be back to see how things are going in a few weeks' time.' Mary then shook the couple's hands warmly before turning and heading for the door. She was feeling very emotional and would be glad to get away now.

Once she and Lorna were seated in the car she looked towards the cottage where Joe and Gail were waving to them with their arms protectively about Natasha, who was standing between them. They made a pretty picture.

'They look like a family already, don't they?' Lorna sighed happily and, blinking back the tears, Mary nodded in agreement as she started the car and pulled away from the kerb.

Chapter Four

'I can't believe it's December already,' Lorna complained as she pulled a pile of paperwork towards her across the desk. 'I haven't even started my Christmas shopping yet. How are you doing with yours?'

'About the same as you,' Mary replied with a wry smile. 'And I don't see myself even thinking about it either until I've got Lauren and Alex settled.'

'Aw well, that should be all sorted by the end of next week and then you can switch off from it all hopefully. Have you heard how Natasha is doing?'

'Absolutely fine, thank goodness. I rang Gail last Friday and she was still bubbling. They haven't had a single tear so far and they seem to be totally doting on her.'

Lorna chuckled. 'I'm not surprised. That's one lucky little girl, if you were to ask me – her past apart, of course. I think they'll adore her. Do you still want me to come with you on Wednesday when you take Lauren to Feathermill Lodge?'

'It would be a great help if you could,' Mary told her as she tapped her pencil on the edge of the desk.

Lorna grinned. 'You know, I wouldn't mind you leaving me there an' all, from what you've told me about it,' she sighed. 'What a lovely place for a child to be brought up in, except for the ghosts, I mean. You did say it was haunted, didn't you?'

'According to Penny Daventry it is.' Mary nodded. 'And not just by one ghost either. Apparently there's about five or six of them in different parts of the house. But then it is a very old house, so I suppose it's seen a lot of history.'

'Ugh!' Lorna shuddered at the thought before asking curiously, 'Have you ever seen any of them during your visits?'

'I can't say that I have to be honest, though I will admit there have been a few times when I've had the strangest feeling that I was being watched. Penny showed me all round the house when I first went there, and in one bedroom I felt so weak that I had to sit down for a moment. There's a four-poster bed in that room and Penny reckons that guests who have stayed in there have reported seeing an elderly man standing crying at the side of it. Apparently, Penny sees him all the time. He's dressed in Quaker-style clothes, a long black coat and bow tie, and she was told that his wife was supposed to have died in that room during childbirth.'

'So couldn't she get someone in to exorcise him or something?'

Mary laughed, 'Oh no, she wouldn't do that. To Penny, the ghosts are part of the family. She told me very early on during her assessment that she has what she called "The Sight".'

'What, you mean she's a medium or a psychic or something?'

'That's what I asked her initially, but apparently they are something entirely different. Penny can't forecast what's going to happen or what has happened in the past. She can just see ghosts, as her grandmother did before her. And she doesn't see them as wispy apparitions either. To her they are as solid as you or me.'

Lorna was intrigued now and perching on the edge of the desk she asked, 'Exactly how old is the house?'

'Feathermill is actually located on the site of Queen Boadicea's last battle, and if I remember rightly I think Penny said it was built in 1881 by Captain Townsend who owned Caldecote Hall. Before that, the quarry owned the land it's built on and there was a dwelling there dating back to 1305. There used to be a well in the kitchen that's covered over now, and there's also another one that is still visible out in the garden by the chicken-house. Right up until the sixties it was a dairy farm and the original milking stalls are still in the outbuildings. There's also a separate stall where the bull was stabled as well as another two barns out in the courtyard. One of them used to be a blacksmith's and the other was the laundry.'

Lorna was totally engrossed in what Mary was telling her, but suddenly glancing at the clock she hopped off the edge of the desk and exclaimed, 'Crikey, I'm supposed to be doing a home visit in ten minutes' time! I could listen to you all day but I'm afraid the rest of the history lesson will have to wait for another time, else the boss will have my guts for garters.' With that she wobbled out of the room on her platform shoes, leaving Mary with a broad grin on her face. Lorna was such a lovely girl. Mary sometimes wondered how their friendship had ever evolved. To all intents and purposes they had absolutely nothing in common and yet they had got on famously ever since the day Lorna had arrived. There was at least thirty years between them and they didn't share the same tastes in clothes or music. Mary tended to be a home bird when she wasn't at work, content to potter about her small garden and spend time with her grandchildren, even more so since she had been widowed three years before, while Lorna had an endless stream of boyfriends, each one of whom was going to be the one she wanted to spend the rest of her life with – for at least a week.

Mary grinned as she turned her attention to the endless reports waiting to be written. It wouldn't be long now and hopefully Lauren would be happily settled in her new home too.

'Right then, madam, let's get you into the car, eh?' As Mary scooped Lauren into her arms, her foster-mum planted a last affectionate kiss on her cheek.

'It's going to be very quiet without this little livewire rampaging about the place,' she commented with a trace of sadness in her voice.

'Huh! I doubt that very much, Sheila,' Mary chuckled as she headed for the door. 'I'd bet a pound to a penny you'll have another little one here before you know it. We always seem to have children coming into care at this time of year, don't we?'

'Yes, we do,' Sheila agreed. 'More's the pity for the poor little mites. Still, at least I won't have to worry about this one. Penny and David seem to be a lovely couple and I've a feeling she's going to be spoiled rotten.'

'Let's hope you're right.' They were outside on the pavement of Earl's Road now, where Lorna was busily loading Lauren's cases into the boot of the car.

In no time at all, the little girl was safely tucked on to the back seat with her precious rag doll Polly wrapped tightly in her arms. Lorna and Mary waved as they pulled away. Thankfully, it hadn't snowed for some days now, although it was still bitterly cold. What snow had fallen had turned to slush, and the roads were slippery despite the fact that the council cart had been out gritting since early morning.

'Ah well, at least we haven't got far to go today,' Lorna said optimistically. Feathermill Lodge was almost halfway between Nuneaton and the neighbouring town of Atherstone. Soon they were going cautiously through Hartshill and once they had crossed the Clock Bridge, Mary pointed ahead.

'Feathermill Lane is over there,' she said. 'We go right just before the railway bridge and it's on our left. I have to say you could miss the lane if you blinked. It took me a couple of attempts to find it when I first came out to assess the Daventrys.'

Lorna turned to smile at Lauren, who was cuddling her rag dolly and staring out of the car window with interest. 'She's a pretty little thing, isn't she?' she said thoughtfully, and Mary nodded in agreement.

'She certainly is; in fact, all three of the children are attractive. Not that we can see that much of Lauren today. Sheila has her wrapped up fit for the North Pole.'

'Mm, you're right. I think it was hard for her to say goodbye, if you were to ask me. I often wonder how carers feel when the kids move on.'

'I should think they breathe a big sigh of relief with some of the children they have to care for,' Mary answered truthfully. 'They're not all as sweet as the Slater children. In fact, some of the teenagers can be very difficult. They've seen too much by the time they come into care and they've put the barriers up. Hopefully, these three are all young enough to forget what's gone before and start a new life. I certainly think the twins are. It's Alex I'm most concerned about. Apparently he hasn't settled at all since that final visit with his mum. Sally says he spends most of the time in the front window waiting for her to come and fetch him.'

Lorna frowned. 'He doesn't know what's happened to Kevin then, and that his mum is in prison?'

Mary shook her head. 'No, he doesn't. There's no point in telling him. He's far too young to understand and he wasn't going to have any more contact with her anyway. To tell the truth, I find it really strange that he's so devoted to her after the way she treated him and the twins. You'd think he'd be glad to be away from her, wouldn't you? But then this is something we see time and time again in this job. No matter what the parents do to them or how badly they are treated, most children still have an allegiance to them. All we can do now is hope that once he's placed with his new family he'll forget all about his birth mother in time. He is only a little lad, after all. Ah, here's Feathermill Lane now.'

As she spoke, she turned the corner into a country lane and Lorna looked ahead with interest, waiting for her first glimpse of the Lodge. At the end of the lane they came to two tall wrought-iron gates and Lorna got out to open them. Once Mary had driven through them she shut them again and hopped back into the car – and now she could see the house ahead of them. She gasped with amazement. It was a truly beautiful house, maintaining many of its Victorian features.

'Blimey, this is *some* pad,' she said admiringly, as she stared across the manicured lawns to a large lake on which a variety of ducks were swimming. It was more like a small stately home than a farmhouse, and Lorna guessed that it must be worth a small fortune.

Mary had phoned Penny and David shortly before setting off to pick Lauren up from Sheila's, and now as she drove into the courtyard the couple hurried out to meet them with two enormous black Labradors frolicking about their feet.

Mary parked the car next to the stable in the courtyard, and before she had even had time to get out, Penny and David were standing staring through the car window at Lauren with wide smiles on their faces.

Mary gently lifted the toddler from the back seat and deposited her into Penny's waiting arms. The child clung to her as she gazed fearfully at the two enormous dogs but Penny quickly told her, 'Don't be frightened of them, sweetheart. The big one is Harry and the other one is Belle. I'm sure you're all going to be great friends and get into all sorts of mischief. They want to play with you – look. That's why they're wagging their tails.'

Lauren still looked somewhat uncertain and continued to cling to Penny, much to the woman's obvious delight. 'Come on,' she encouraged the small group as she hitched Lauren into a more comfortable position on her hip. 'I'll make some tea and I've got some homemade scones fresh out of the Aga in the kitchen. I know you're not supposed to eat things like that between meals, but this is a special day, isn't it?'

Mary stifled a sigh of satisfaction as Penny set off in the direction of the kitchen clutching her precious bundle. It looked like this was going to be yet another successful placement. Mary had instantly taken to Penny and David on the very first assessment visit she had made to them. They were in their early forties and by their own admittance were rattling around like two peas in a pod in the Lodge since their own two children had left home. That was why they had decided to adopt. Throughout the assessment it had become obvious that they would be perfect for Lauren. It appeared that they had done a fine job of bringing their own two children up, and when they spoke of them, which was frequently, they glowed with pride. On top of that they seemed to have all the patience in the world.

Fair-haired and of medium build, Penny had a kind face that seemed to be constantly smiling, especially when she looked at David, her husband. He was a gentle giant of a man, with dark hair and twinkling eyes. He also had a keen sense of humour and was forever cracking jokes. Mary felt that this would help Lauren. After all, the way she saw it the poor little scrap had had very little to smile at in her young life up to now and she was sure that David would be like a tonic to her.

She and Lorna exchanged a happy look as they followed Penny and David into an enormous kitchen and the warmth instantly wrapped itself around them like a blanket. There was a wicker basket in the corner next to a large Aga and inside it a big tabby cat was tending to a litter of tiny kittens. Lorna was once more amazed. The kitchen alone was almost as large as the whole of her flat put together. An enormous table flanked by eight sturdy chairs stood against one wall, and a matching dresser, which was loaded with colourful china, stood next to it.

A large island loaded with cakes and scones fresh from the oven was situated in the centre of the room and the air smelled of baking and furniture polish. Lauren's eyes lit up like beacons at the sight of so many treats, and Penny placed a cake in her hand and smiled indulgently as she wrestled with the buttons on her coat.

As Mary located the necessary paperwork and spread it out on the table, Penny poured them steaming hot cups of tea. Lauren eyed Harry and Belle cautiously.

'Don't worry, they wouldn't hurt a fly,' Penny assured Mary, who was watching closely, and sure enough, within minutes the child had crossed to them and tentatively stretched out her hand to stroke them. From that second on, her fear of the great black dogs fled and in no time at all they were all rolling around the floor together as Lauren giggled uncontrollably.

'Want wee wee!' the child suddenly declared a short time later, when Mary and Penny had almost finished the paperwork. Sheila, her foster-mum, had been working very hard during the time that

Lauren had stayed with her to get her potty-trained, and it seemed now that all her patience and hard work was finally paying off.

Penny excused herself and hurried away with Lauren in her arms and David, who had noticed Lorna's eyes straying about the place asked, 'Would you like to have a look around while we wait for them to come back?'

'I'd love to,' Lorna answered without hesitation, and so the tour began.

First, David showed her into a lounge that made her eyes pop. It was enormous, with huge sash-cord windows that looked out across the rolling lawns down to the lake. They were draped with heavily fringed swags and tails that framed gold damask silk curtains, and the furniture was like something she had only ever seen in magazines and stately homes. The walls were covered in expensive-looking red flock wallpaper that contrasted well with the curtains and the matching wall-to-wall carpet. Elegant chaise longues and ornately carved mahogany cabinets full of fine china lined the room, and heavy gilt-framed oil paintings of bygone times graced the walls. An enormous marble fireplace, in which a huge log fire was blazing, stood on the central wall. Above it was suspended the biggest mirror she had ever seen, and the flames bounced off a glittering crystal chandelier that hung from a carved ceiling rose in the centre of the room.

Once again, Lorna felt as if she had stepped back in time as she gazed around her. Penny and David had obviously spared no expense when renovating the house, and she had to admit that they had done a remarkable job of it. She also wondered how long it could remain looking so immaculate now that a little one would be rampaging around it, but then pushed the thought aside. From what she had seen up to now, the house would come second to the new arrival, which was just as it should be.

David then led the women into the dining room, which was just as immaculate as the lounge. The centre of this room was taken up by an enormous, gleaming mahogany table surrounded by a matching set of eight chairs. Silver candelabras were dotted along its length, and Lorna could imagine dining there, looking out of the window at the picturesque grounds, with a large glass of excellent wine in her hand. Mary had told her that Penny was a superb cook and she had no doubt that Lauren would thrive here with the wide open spaces to play in and good homemade food.

The upstairs was as impressive as the downstairs, although Lorna found herself glancing across her shoulder for a sight of the ghosts that supposedly haunted the building. Each room had its own co-ordinated colour scheme, and no attention to detail had been spared. Feathermill was more than twice the size of the charming cottage that Natasha had gone to live in with the Salisburys, and she thought what a shame it was that the twins couldn't have been placed together; there was more than enough room here for at least a dozen children. But then she knew that Mary had put a lot of time and effort into finding the very best possible placements for each of the girls, and felt sure that they would both be happy with their new families.

The room the Daventrys had prepared for Lauren was stunning, every little girl's dream, all done out in candy pink with frills and flounces everywhere you looked. Heavy pink curtains hung at the window, which looked directly out on to the lake, and above the bed, a delicate voile canopy was suspended that matched the beribboned and heavily embroidered bedspread. Lauren, however, seemed totally uninterested in the décor and was much more intent on playing with the dolls and teddies that Penny and David had waiting for her. So much so in fact that she could only be tempted back downstairs with an enormous teddy bear under one arm and a dolly tucked firmly beneath the other, as well as her rag doll, Polly, who went everywhere with her.

They were then all shown into another lounge that Penny and David favoured during the day. This was much smaller and not quite so luxuriously furnished as the rest of the house, but warm and cosy all the same. A large television stood in one corner and Torvill and

Dean were on the screen, skating gracefully around a rink, a fact that soon caught and held Lauren's attention.

'Well,' Mary said, her eyes tight on Lauren, 'I think that's about it. We've done all the paperwork and Lauren seems quite happy, so is there anything else you'd like to ask me before we go?'

Penny and David both shook their heads in unison.

'In that case, I suppose Lorna and I ought to be going and leaving you all to get better acquainted. Do remember I'm only at the end of the phone should you need me, and of course, I will be paying a visit before Christmas to see how Lauren is settling in.'

'I have a feeling we're going to be just fine,' Penny answered as she smiled at Lauren indulgently.

Mary felt a warm glow in the pit of her stomach. If she wasn't very much mistaken, this little girl had really dropped on her feet here. Both she and Lorna put their coats on and gathered their bags together before striding to the door where Mary paused to say, 'Goodbye then, Lauren. Be a good girl, won't you?'

Lauren was so enthralled with Torvill and Dean's performance that she didn't even look up. Mary took this as another good sign and after shaking Penny and David's outstretched hands she and Lorna left the family alone and hurried out to the car in the bitingly cold wind.

'That's another gold star to you,' Lorna commented, as Mary reversed the car and drove out of the courtyard. 'Penny and David are so kind, and what a lovely place for a child to grow up in. I think you can safely say that's another one you won't have to worry about.'

'Let's hope you're right,' Mary replied. 'But only time will tell. I wonder if Alex's move will go as smoothly when I take him to Puddlesea?'

'Have you got a date for that yet?' Lorna asked, as she dragged her eyes away from the beautiful grounds, noticing for the first time the River Anker, which ran alongside the perimeter of the garden beyond the lake.

'Yes, he'll be going the week after next.'

'Mm, well, as you say, fingers crossed that his move goes well too.'

Mary nodded in agreement but deep down she had grave doubts that it would. Alex was taking the loss of his mother far worse than the twins and she could only pray that time would ease his heartache.

Chapter Five

Mary stepped into Sally Wootton's neat semi-detached home on a cold morning in December with Lorna following closely behind, wrapped up in so many layers of clothes that she looked as if she was about to set off for the North Pole.

'Bit nippy out, is it?' Sally asked with a twinkle in her eye.

'Nippy? It's enough to freeze the hairs off a brass monkey,' Lorna rejoined as she held her hands out to the gasfire and shivered. She had always been a sunlover and hated the cold weather.

Mary looked towards where Alex was sitting on the settee with a scowl on his face and his arms firmly crossed across his small chest. He looked more like a disgruntled old man than a small child and her heart went out to him.

'How has he been?' she whispered.

Sally's homely face became solemn. 'Much as you see him now, to be honest. I'm almost having to force-feed him, and he spends most of the time standing in the front window waiting for his mum to come for him. Poor little mite. I've really tried with him but there's just no getting through. It's as if he's shut himself off and he won't let anyone near him.'

Mary could see the stress in Sally's face and correctly guessed that Alex had been giving her a hard time of it.

'Well, we can only hope that a new environment and a fresh start will help. You've certainly done your best, that's a fact. A lot of carers would have been screaming for us to get him out after the way he's been behaving.'

'It's not his fault, he's just screwed up,' Sally replied regretfully. 'Though I have to admit I'm looking forward to a rest. He screams the place down if we stay in and he screams the place down if I try to take him out. I caught him kicking the hell out of the cat the other day, almost as if he were taking his frustrations out on her. And when I tried to stop him he turned on me.' She rolled up the sleeve of her cardigan and Mary saw a large purple bruise spread across her arm. 'He's not sleeping well either,' the concerned carer went on. 'We're lucky if he sleeps for two or three hours a night and when he does it's only out of sheer exhaustion.'

'Oh dear,' Mary said sympathetically. 'Let's hope he behaves a bit better when we get him to Devon.'

'Well, the Andersons have seen how upset he's been on the visits they've made to him,' Sally sensibly pointed out. 'So it's not as if they're going into this with their eyes shut, and they have assured me that they can cope with him. In fact, they seem as keen as ever to go ahead.'

'That's something to be thankful for,' Mary muttered. 'I was afraid they'd change their minds when they saw how disruptive he's being. But then, with a bit of luck, a complete change may be all he needs.'

'I sincerely hope so, else I can't see the placement lasting. No one could put up with this sort of behaviour long-term without cracking themselves.'

Mary frowned; she knew that what Sally was saying was right and at that moment in time wasn't feeling too optimistic at all about Alex's future despite the Andersons' positive attitude.

Pointing to his case, which Sally had placed by the door, she asked Lorna, 'Would you mind loading that into the boot? I'll help Sally get Alex's coat on.'

Lorna smiled good-naturedly as she lifted the case and headed for the door, and now Mary approached Alex and bending to his level she told him gently, 'It's time for us to go now, sweetheart. We're going for a very long ride in the car to see your new mummy and daddy. Won't that be nice?'

'*Not going!* Want *my* mummy!' Alex spat as he tightened his arms across his chest.

Mary and Sally exchanged a worried glance as Sally advanced on him with his coat held out in front of her.

'Now come along, Alex,' she said coaxingly. 'You're going to the seaside. Think how nice it will be, to go for walks on the beach. You'll be able to play there with your bucket and spade when the weather is warmer, and paddle and splash in the waves too.'

'*Not going!*' he repeated stubbornly.

Sally sighed as she passed his coat to Mary. 'Why don't you try?' she suggested.

Mary took the coat and held it out to him. They had tried the softly-softly approach and now she was prepared to be strict if need be. The time was ticking away and they had a four-hour journey ahead of them.

'Now Alex, either you put this on yourself and stop being silly or I shall have to put it on for you,' she scolded.

Something in the tone of her voice made him wriggle towards the edge of the settee and snatch the coat from her. Then, glaring, he thrust his arms into the sleeves and began to button it up. Mary could see that the buttons weren't being done up correctly but decided to ignore the fact for now. At least he was making some effort to leave. She had been dreading having to load him into the car kicking and screaming.

'That's better, what a good boy,' she praised, as he slithered from his seat to stand in front of her.

He stuck his nose in the air and crossed to stand by the door but when Sally went to kneel down beside him, he bowed his head.

'Right then, me boyo.' Her voice was heavy with emotion as she battled to hold back tears. 'You just look after yourself and be happy, eh?' She reached out to stroke his cheek but Alex smacked her away.

Mary rested her hand on his shoulder and edged him further towards the door as she glanced at Sally apologetically. 'It might be better if we just got on our way,' she said softly, and Sally nodded as she followed them out on to the pavement.

There seemed so little she could say now, so she stood silently as Mary fastened Alex into the back seat of the car and hurried round to the front. Lorna clambered into the back with Alex and finally they were ready to go.

Mary inclined her head towards Sally as she started the engine and leaning towards the car window, Sally told them, 'Safe journey. Goodbye, Alex.'

He stared straight ahead, giving no indication that he was even aware of her presence, and the last glimpse Mary had of Sally as she pulled away and glanced in the rearview mirror was of the woman standing dejectedly on the pavement.

Poor soul, she thought to herself. It had been a pretty thankless task looking after Alex and she hoped that the woman would now enjoy a well-earned rest.

In no time at all they were heading towards Coventry, leaving Nuneaton behind them, and Mary wondered if Alex would ever return to the place of his birth. His future was all in the lap of the gods now.

They had gone about fifty miles when Alex began to cry. It was soft hiccupping whimpers for a start, but it soon developed into sobs. Lorna did her best to console him but each time she went near him he slapped her away and howled all the louder.

Mary already had the beginnings of a headache thumping behind her eyes and they weren't even a quarter of the way to their destination yet. She had suspected that placing Alex would be nowhere near as pleasant as delivering Natasha and Lauren to their new homes, and it looked as if her assumption had been right. It was going to be a very long day.

47

By the time they had crossed the Avonmouth Bridge, Alex had worked himself up into a terrible frenzy and Lorna was almost beside herself with worry.

'It's no good,' she shouted above the noise Alex was making. 'I think we're going to have to stop and calm him down, Mary.'

Mary nodded as she glanced in the mirror. 'Fair enough. I'm about ready for a break myself, to be honest. I reckon we must be about halfway there now, so we'll stop at a café and grab some lunch, shall we?'

Lorna looked at Alex doubtfully. He was in such a state that she had a sneaky feeling he wouldn't eat a thing, but she supposed it was worth a try. Shortly afterwards, they pulled into a small road-side café where Mary turned off the engine. 'Oh, I'll be glad to stretch my legs,' she commented as she slid out of the car.

The car park was teeming with lorry drivers and the sky had now darkened to a dull leaden grey.

'I reckon we're in for some more snow,' Mary said fretfully as she sniffed at the air. 'Let's just hope it holds off until we're back home tomorrow.'

'I rather doubt we'll be that lucky,' Lorna grunted in answer as she tried to coax Alex out of the car. He was being as stubborn as a mule and making it as difficult as he could for her, but eventually she manhandled him on to the tarmac and gripped his hand as, protesting loudly, he tried to pull away from her.

'I used to think this kid was as soft as butter but I've certainly changed my mind after today,' she muttered resentfully as she hauled him towards the café. He was still protesting loudly and Lorna felt herself blush with embarrassment at the stares he was attracting.

At last she managed to get him seated at an empty table while Mary went to get them some food. A large man on the next table, who was tucking into a huge pile of bacon sandwiches, winked at him in a friendly fashion. 'Havin' a bad day are yer, son?' he asked.

'Piss off!' Alex responded promptly.

Lorna felt her cheeks burn ever brighter as the man's mouth gaped open in amazement. The child was only knee-high to a grasshopper and she was shocked that he knew such language at his age, but then he would have heard it from his mother and Kevin. Kay was famous for her foul language and had obviously taught Alex well.

'I'm sorry,' she muttered to the man as she glared at Alex, who glared right back.

''S'no skin off my nose,' the man assured her, then he threw back his head and laughed aloud, which thankfully shut Alex up for a few minutes. 'Always as vocal, your little 'un, is he?'

'Oh, he's not mine,' Lorna hastily informed him, just as Mary came back towards them carrying a loaded tray and she was saved from having to say any more.

'Right, the choice was sausage sandwiches, bacon sandwiches or burgers, so I got us one of each. Will that be all right for you, Lorna? I'm afraid the menu was rather limited.' If truth were told, the café was none too clean either, but then she was so glad of a break she was past caring.

'It will do me just fine,' Lorna assured her, then leaning towards Alex she asked, 'Which would you like? You can have first choice.'

'Don't want *none* of it,' he said resentfully as he scowled at her and rocked back in his seat.

Ignoring his outburst, Mary placed two cups of tea on the table and a beaker of juice for the child. 'There you are, dear,' she told him kindly. 'I bet you're thirsty, aren't you?'

'*NO!*' Before she could stop him he lashed out and sent the juice hurtling across the table.

'Oh, Alex, what did you do that for?' Mary asked resignedly as she did her best to mop the mess up with a paper tissue. 'Now behave yourself and eat this.' She placed the burger in front of him but within seconds that had gone the same way as the juice.

'If yer were to ask me, I'd say that little chap 'ud do better fer a bloody good hidin',' the man on the next table commented.

'Well, I *didn't* ask you,' Mary informed him haughtily, and very aware of the stares they were attracting she placed a plateful of sandwiches in front of Lorna and began to eat her own meal with what decorum she could muster.

'What about Alex?' Lorna mouthed.

'Well, you know the old saying, dear, you can lead a horse to water but you can't make it drink. I've no doubt he'll eat and drink when he's thirsty and hungry enough.'

Lorna sipped at the stewed tea, keeping a wary eye on Alex the whole time. And suddenly she found herself wondering if his new family were fully aware of what they were letting themselves in for. At this precise moment in time she certainly didn't envy them. In fact, she could hardly wait to drop him off and be done with it.

The second half of the journey, which took them through Lynton, Tiverton and Ilfracombe, was no better than the first. Alex constantly veered between full-blown tantrums and tearful whimpering until at last he dropped into a fretful doze as they drove through Georgeham.

'Phew, thank goodness for that,' Lorna whispered, fearful of waking him. Her nerves were as taut as piano wires and she was having to fight the urge to throttle him. She had always thought what a lovely little boy he was, but today had certainly changed her opinion of him.

'Do I take it from that comment that you won't be going in for a child of your own in the near future then?' Mary asked teasingly.

'After today I might remain childless for ever,' Lorna quipped. 'I never realised so much noise could come out of such a little person.'

'Well, let's just hope he's tired himself out by the time we reach the Andersons.' It wouldn't make the best first impression if we had to drag him in kicking and screaming, would it?'

Lorna looked out at the beautiful countryside flashing past the car window. She had been so occupied trying to calm Alex down that this was the first chance she had had to see where they were going.

'We're not that far away now,' Mary informed her. 'I reckon about another half an hour and we should be there. Do you think your nerves can stand it?'

'Only if he stays asleep. I've gone right off kids. I'm beginning to think I've gone into the wrong career,' Lorna grumbled.

Mary chuckled as she concentrated on the road ahead while Lorna stared in fascination at the picturesque landscape from the car window. She found herself almost envying Alex. Surely it was every child's dream to live by the sea. They were on the coastal road leading to Puddlesea now and Lorna looked down nervously to where the waves were crashing on to the rocks far below them.

'Er . . . why don't you slow down a bit?' she suggested. 'It looks an awfully long drop down there.'

'Don't panic, I've been driving for thirty years and I've never had an accident yet,' Mary assured her.

Lorna settled back in her seat and tried to take her mind off the steep drop at the side of the road.

Shortly afterwards, Mary pointed ahead. 'Do you see those houses up on top of the hill? Well, that's where we're going.'

Lorna swallowed a sigh of relief. Alex was stirring now and she was glad that they had almost reached their destination before he had the chance to kick off again.

Minutes later, Mary steered the car into the drive of a neat detached house perched high on the clifftop.

'This is it,' she said, as she turned the car engine off. 'We're here.' After arching her aching back she then climbed stiffly out of the car and opened the rear door where Lorna was gently shaking Alex's arm.

'Come on, love. We're home,' she told him as he knuckled the sleep from his eyes and stretched. Just for a second his eyes lit up, but then his face crumpled again.

'This ain't home. Where's my mummy?' he demanded.

Deciding that it would be pointless to argue with him, Lorna merely slid him across the seat into Mary's waiting arms. She had expected the Andersons to be waiting for them but as yet they hadn't put in an appearance. They're probably at the back of the house and haven't heard us arrive, she told herself before striding resolutely towards the front door.

Lorna meanwhile was studying the front of the house. It was a lovely place, she had to admit, yet somehow it lacked the charm and character of the twin's new homes. It's probably because it's a fairly new build, she thought, but I dare say it will be really nice inside and it's certainly in a fantastic position.

She hurried forward to stand at Mary's side while her colleague rang the doorbell, and seconds later they heard footsteps in the hallway. A small, mousy-looking woman answered the door and smiled at them. Lorna was immediately put in mind of a very staid schoolmistress, thanks to the tweed skirt, twinset and row of pearls. Mary had told her that June Anderson was only in her forties and yet the way she was dressed and her manner made her appear years older. 'Ah, you've arrived then. Do come in,' she invited them as she held the door wide.

Lorna frowned, finding it rather strange that the woman had addressed them rather than the child that they were delivering to her. The couples that the twins had gone to had been almost beside themselves with excitement on their arrival, yet this woman was as cool as a cucumber and barely glanced at Alex. As they stepped past her into a long hallway she gestured towards a door to their right.

'Do go in and make yourselves comfortable,' she told them politely. 'I'll just go and get Mrs Dickinson to make you a hot drink. I'm sure you'll all be ready for one after your long journey. Jacob will join you in a second. He's working in his study at present.'

Lorna looked slightly bewildered. *Working in his study?* She would have expected him to be hovering on the doorstep waiting for his new son to arrive, but then she supposed that different people handled things in different ways. It wouldn't do if everyone were the same, as her mother was fond of saying.

'Who's Mrs Dickinson?' she hissed at Mary the second the woman had left the room.

'She's their daily,' Mary whispered back as she stood Alex on the floor at the side of her. 'I met her during the assessment visit and from what I can remember, she's a lovely person. Salt of the earth.'

Alex was already inching towards the window, where he stood staring out across the sea.

Mary smiled. 'Well, it appears he approves of the view if nothing else,' she commented.

Lorna nodded as she glanced about the room. The walls were a soft cream colour as was the fitted carpet. The three-piece suite looked expensive but was a drab tan colour that matched the plain curtains that framed the windows. There were no knick-knacks anywhere and Lorna thought how dull and uninviting it looked. It had nothing of the grandeur of Feathermill Lodge, or the old-fashioned charm of Beehive Cottage. It was sterile, more like a show house than a home that was lived in, but then she was sure that Alex would change all that. Within weeks there would be toys scattered everywhere, and Alex would have put his stamp on the place as children had a habit of doing.

It was then that June Anderson came back into the room, closely followed by her husband, who appeared to be the exact opposite of his wife in nature, for while she seemed timid and mousy, he was larger than life.

'Why, hello again, Mrs Ingles,' he greeted Mary, and after shaking her hand warmly he inclined his head to Lorna and instantly joined Alex at the window where he knelt to his level.

'How are you, my lad?' he asked jovially. 'We've been so looking forward to you arriving. I bet you can't tell me where you've travelled from, can you?'

The look Alex cast him was filled with pure disdain. 'I've come from *nowhere*,' he answered flatly.

Jacob looked slightly taken aback but quickly regaining his composure he answered, 'Oh, I'm sure that can't be true. Everyone comes from somewhere. But this will be your new home from now on, and I'm sure we're going to have some grand times together. Now why don't you come away from the window and have some of Mrs Dickinson's delicious homemade cake? I guarantee it will be the best you've ever tasted. And then we'll show you your bedroom.'

'Don't *want* to see my bedroom. I'm waiting by the window till my mummy comes to fetch me,' Alex declared sulkily.

An embarrassed silence settled on the room, eventually broken by Jacob when he made yet another attempt at getting through to the child. 'Then if you want to stand there, why don't we get your coat off, eh? You'll be far too hot if you keep it on.' He reached out to undo the buttons on Alex's coat but before he had even touched them, Alex lashed out furiously.

'Get away from me!' he spat. 'I don't want to take my coat off. I'm *not* staying here, I'm going back home to my mummy.'

'Perhaps it would be better if we all had some tea,' Mary suggested tactfully.

'Er . . . yes – yes, of course.' Jacob straightened and hurried over to the settee where June was nervously wringing her hands. Mary sighed. Things had not got off to a good start at all. Not that she had expected them to go well, if she were to be honest with herself. She had been dreading this day for weeks and felt a measure of relief now that her part in it was almost over. She'd been half-expecting a phone call from the Andersons saying that they'd changed their minds about the adoption after seeing how Alex had behaved towards them on their visits to Nuneaton, although they had maintained a positive attitude throughout.

It was then that the door banged open and a plump elderly lady with a kindly face bustled into the room carrying an enormous tray.

'So the little 'un's arrived then, has he?' She beamed at Alex as if no one else was in the room, and after depositing the tray on a small table she crossed to him and bending to him asked in her rich Lancashire voice, 'So, 'ave yer got room fer some o' me cake then, lovie? I've made yer a nice glass o' juice an' all.'

Alex solemnly shook his head as tears trembled on his lashes, and Mrs Dickinson smiled as she ruffled his mop of thick dark hair.

'That's all right then. Yer bound to feel a bit strange. You just stay there an' we'll get yer somethin' to eat an' drink when yer feel ready fer it, eh?'

Alex nodded as she rose stiffly and crossed back to the table where she proceeded to pour the tea into delicate china cups and saucers.

'It'll be nice to have a little 'un in the house,' she commented to no one in particular. 'Like a bloody morgue, this place is.' She then handed the drinks round and when everyone was served she nodded at June, winked at Alex and bustled back the way she had come. As she watched her go, Mary had the strangest feeling that Alex would find an ally in Mrs Dickinson.

June was looking slightly embarrassed after the housekeeper's comment, while Jacob was looking considerably annoyed, but once again, Mary fought to break the uncomfortable silence when she said, 'I'm afraid there are rather a lot of forms to sign, so shall we get on with it? From the look of that sky, it could start to snow at any minute, so I'm quite keen to get to the hotel.'

As they all glanced towards the window they saw that Mary was right. The wind had dropped and the sky was a ghostly grey colour.

'Of course.' June placed her cup down and she and Mary then retired to a large table in the corner of the room to do the necessary paperwork. For no reason that she could explain, Lorna was feeling agitated and kept glancing at the clock.

'I'll take the tray back through to the kitchen to Mrs Dickinson, shall I?' Without waiting for an answer, Lorna quickly collected the dirty crockery and headed for the door, glad to escape the tense atmosphere. Once the door was closed behind her she hovered uncertainly as she realised that she had no idea where the kitchen was. Deciding that it was likely to be at the back of the house, she went in that direction and within minutes had located Mrs Dickinson, who was busily chopping vegetables for the evening meal at the kitchen table.

'Oh, bless yer, love. Yer didn't need to do that.' She nodded over her shoulder towards the sink and after depositing the tray on the draining board, Lorna pulled out a chair and joined her at the table.

'I was glad of an excuse to escape, to be honest. Things seem to be a little strained in there at the moment.'

'Huh! Things are *always* strained in this place.' Mrs Dickinson clamped her mouth shut as she realised that she was talking out of turn. Lorna frowned at her curiously.

'Tek no notice o' me,' the older woman apologised. 'My old man, Harry, was allus tellin' me as me gob will get me hung one o' these days. It's just the mister, he's a bit of an odd 'un, if yer know what I mean. Now Miss June, she's a lovely girl. Heart as big as a bucket, she has. I've no doubt she'll love that little boy.'

'What exactly do you mean when you say Jacob is odd?' Lorna questioned, and the woman's hands became still as she stared towards the window.

'Well . . . he ain't violent or nothin' like that. But the thing is, Miss June is a nervy type as you've probably noticed, an' I reckon it's 'cos she's here on her own so much. He's always off gallivantin' some place or another. He runs the Scouts group down in the village an' if he ain't there he's at work or off on some other jaunt or another.'

'Oh, I see. In that case why doesn't June get herself a little job to keep her occupied?'

'I reckon she'd love to, but the mister is the old-fashioned sort. He thinks a woman's place is in the home. She ain't allus been like this though. I worked for her mother down in the vicarage when June were just a nipper before her parents passed away, God bless their souls. Did yer know her dad were the parson?' Without waiting for an answer, the old woman rambled on, 'A right little livewire Miss June were in them days. It's only since she married the mister that she's took to keepin' herself to herself. Still, mebbe things will change now the little 'un's here. Miss June will be taken up carin' fer him, an' happen he'll be just the tonic she needs.'

'Let's hope so.' Lorna was growing more uncomfortable about

this placement by the minute and wondered if she should tell Mary about the conversation she had just had with Mrs Dickinson. But the way she saw it, it would only give her colleague more cause to worry and she was looking drained enough as it was just lately, so she decided she would wait and see how things went for a while.

'Right, I'd better get back in there, I suppose. Thanks for the chat, Mrs Dickinson. I hope I'll see you again sometime.'

The woman smiled as she returned to preparing the vegetables and Lorna entered the hall just as Mary and June were heading for the stairs.

'Ah Lorna, June is just going to show me Alex's room. Would you like to come with us?' Mary invited.

Lorna nodded and tacked on to the back of them as June led the way. Alex's room was lovely, she was forced to admit. It was on the front of the house next to June and Jacob's, and his window had a superb view of the sea. Mary had tried to talk him into going upstairs with them to see it, but at present he was still sulking by the lounge window downstairs. The room had been freshly painted in different shades of blue and there was every toy a little boy could wish for just waiting to be played with. A large train-set took up the space on the floor at the end of the bed next to a huge box of Lego. There were books and cars, and both Lorna and Mary could see that no expense had been spared in trying to make him feel at home. Perhaps their misgivings were unnecessary after all?

'It's terrific.' Mary smiled at June who was anxiously waiting for their reaction. 'I'm sure Alex will love it — *when* you can persuade him away from the window,' she added wryly. 'But now if you've no questions I really think we should be going, if you don't mind.'

'Of course.' And soon they were all back in the spacious lounge where Alex watched resentfully as the two women got wrapped up for the outdoors again.

'Right then, Alex. We have to be going now,' Mary explained as she crossed to stand beside him. 'I shall be coming back to see you in a few weeks' time, but until then you try to be a good boy, eh?'

She had expected him to ignore her as he had for most of the journey there, but to her surprise he suddenly snatched her hand and when she looked down into his eyes she saw that they were brimming with tears.

'Don't want to stay here,' he told her tremulously. 'I want to come back with you.'

There was a lump forming in Mary's throat as she tried to think of words that might comfort him, but they were all lodged inside as she stared at him helplessly.

Jacob instantly took control of the situation. He strode towards them and placed his hand on Alex's shoulder.

'It might be better if you just left now,' he told Mary tactfully. 'Alex will be fine. He just needs time to settle, don't you, son?'

The words had barely left his lips when Alex suddenly swung his sturdy little leg back and landed a resounding kick on Jacob's shin.

'*Ouch!*' The man rubbed his leg then leaning towards the child he hoisted him up into his arms and held on to him tightly. Alex immediately began to kick and scream and now Lorna took Mary's elbow and manhandled her towards the door. June was close behind them and once at the front door she glanced nervously across her shoulder before muttering, 'I'm so sorry about this. As Jacob says, I'm sure he'll calm down once you've gone.'

With her lips set in a grim line, Mary hurried towards the car. And all the time a picture of Alex's little face was flashing before her eyes, for never in her life before had she seen such utter torment and despair in anyone so young. It was a picture that would stay with her for many long years to come.

Chapter Six

'Right then, I'll be off now if yer sure there's nothin' else as you need doing,' Mrs Dickinson said as she poked her head into the lounge. 'I ain't done the washin'-up yet but I'll leave it till mornin', if you don't mind. I was hopin' to get home in time to watch Bob Geldof on the telly. Yer know – Band Aid? He's tryin' to raise money fer the famine in Ethiopia an' they reckon there will be loads o' stars on with him.'

Beyond the window the wind had picked up and the shrubs that grew beneath it were tapping the pane as if they were trying to gain entry into the room. She had just served the meal, a succulent shoulder of lamb accompanied by crisp roast potatoes and a variety of vegetables. Not that the new addition to the family had eaten much, she noted. Even the homemade apple pie and custard had failed to tempt him. Mrs Dickinson had an idea that the Andersons were in for a very bad night.

'You get off,' June urged her. 'I'll see to anything else that needs doing, and thank you.'

As Mrs Dickinson glanced towards Alex her heart went out to him. Since being allowed to leave the table, the boy had gone back to maintaining his position at the window. Jacob had his head buried in a newspaper, and after casting a last surly glance his way the housekeeper left the room to get her hat and coat before beginning the journey to her cottage in the village down below. It had been a long day and she was looking forward to settling down in front of the fire with a glass of Guinness and her feet up on a stool.

In a small hotel in Puddlesea, Mary and Lorna were now relaxing in the bar with a large glass of wine following the evening meal they had just enjoyed in the hotel dining room.

'Phew, I feel as if we've earned this. It hasn't been the easiest of days, has it?' Lorna leaned back in her chair as Mary nodded in agreement.

'You can say that again.' The older woman stared down into her glass with an anxious expression on her face. 'You know, I'm beginning to wonder now if the Andersons were the right choice for Alex, after all. The trouble was, whereas I had any number of choices for the girls, there were only three couples that were really suitable for Alex. Everyone wants younger children when it comes to adoption, and even at his age it narrows the choices.'

'You did the best you could,' Lorna consoled her kindly. 'He might just shock us and settle down and be as right as rain. He has gone through a lot lately, after all, what with being taken away from his mum and being put into care et cetera.'

'I know that, but there was just something . . . Oh, I don't know. Something didn't feel quite right though I can't for the life of me put my finger on what it was. The house is nice, his room was lovely, the Andersons said all the right things . . . yet I felt as if there was something I wasn't picking up on.'

'Well, there's no point fretting about it now,' Lorna pointed out sensibly. 'It will take months for the legal adoption to be finalised, and during that time you will have visited to see how he is getting on. The best thing you can do now is to forget about the Slater children for the time being and concentrate on your other cases. So, are you ready for another drink? As far as I'm concerned this is a night off and I intend to make the most of it. It will be soon enough to think about work again when we set off for the office tomorrow.'

'Yes, all right then. I'll have another glass of wine.' As Mary watched the younger woman head for the bar, she tried to put the picture of Alex's haunted little face from her mind, but no matter how she tried the bad feeling in the pit of her stomach persisted.

At that exact moment in the Andersons' household, June was trying to coax Alex away from the lounge window. She had drawn the curtains against the bitingly cold night in the hope that if he could no longer see out of the window he would come away, but still he stood there stubbornly with his chin drooping on his chest.

Jacob had sat quietly watching her efforts but now he stood up and striding across to the child, he took his small hand firmly in his own. 'Come along, Alex,' he told him shortly. 'I think we've had quite enough of this now. You're falling asleep on your feet and it's high time we got you bathed and into your pyjamas.'

'I'll bath him, dear,' June offered nervously, but he simply cast her a withering look.

'If you can't even coax him away from the window, I hardly think you're going to entice him into the bath, do you? What this young man needs is a firm hand. To know who's boss here and that's exactly what I intend to teach him.'

He began to yank the child across the floor as June chewed on her knuckles. 'In that case, I'll start to unpack his clothes, shall I?'

After springing towards the door she hurried upstairs to Alex's spic-and-span new bedroom where she quickly rifled through his case for his pyjamas, and once she had found them she dashed across the landing to the bathroom. Jacob had the taps running into the bath and was now undressing Alex, who was standing meekly with his head down. Already he had recognised how pointless it would be to try and fight Jacob. He was like a giant in the child's eyes and not such a gentle one as he had first taken him for, if the strict treatment he was administering now was anything to go by.

'I *do not* want any nonsense, is that quite clear?' Jacob informed him sternly.

'Oh, Jacob . . . go gently on him,' June implored. 'He's had a very hard day and everything is strange. He just needs a little time to settle in, that's all.'

Jacob glared at her over his shoulder as he pulled Alex's small trousers down. 'Do you want him to rule us?' he ground out. 'Because if you start to let him get the better of you, that's exactly what he'll do. Now please go and leave this to me.'

Normally, June did as she was told but tonight she hesitated, so with an exasperated sigh, Jacob took her elbow none too gently and ushered her out on to the landing. Then turning about he went back into the room locking the door securely behind him, whilst June stood wringing her hands in alarm outside.

'Now then, young man.' He turned the taps off and turned his attention back to Alex. 'We'll get you washed, shall we?' Without waiting for the child's reply he lifted him under the arms and deposited him none too gently into the steaming water. Alex immediately gasped and made to stand up but Jacob kept a firm hold on his shoulder as he held him in the water.

'It . . . it's too hot,' Alex stuttered but Jacob merely frowned at him.

'Rubbish. Now sit still while I get you clean and don't let me hear you complain again or you'll have a bath in *cold* water tomorrow.'

Trembling, Alex did as he was told as Jacob took up a large flannel and began to soap it. He then proceeded to soap the child all over until finally he got to Alex's most private parts. His mood suddenly softened as the child stiffened beneath him.

'There now, that's nice, isn't it?' He was stroking the little boy gently and Alex stifled a cry. He knew even at his tender age that this wasn't right but was powerless to do anything about it, so he just sat rigid as the strokes became firmer and more painful. Jacob's breathing had become erratic and as panic built in the child he had to stifle a sob. And then suddenly it was over and Jacob's voice was stern again as he lifted his hands from the water and told him, 'That will do for tonight. Now hop out and we'll get you dry.'

Alex almost fell over the side of the bath in his haste to do as he was told. His heart was thumping with fear and at that moment he would gladly have died for just one glimpse of his mother. His skin felt as if it was on fire and was red and mottled but he didn't complain. He just stood compliantly whilst Jacob briskly rubbed him down with a towel before leading him out on to the landing where June was still waiting for him with fear-filled eyes.

Jacob pushed Alex towards her before saying, 'Go and get him tucked in. And don't stand for any nonsense from him. We may as well start as we mean to go on.'

Nodding numbly, she whisked Alex along the thickly carpeted landing while Jacob headed downstairs in the direction of his study. He would probably be ensconced in there for the rest of the night now and she would be left to retire to bed to wait for him to join her – *if* he joined her, that was. Nine times out of ten he chose to sleep in the small single room at the end of the landing, saying that he hadn't liked to disturb her in case she was asleep. She glanced at his retreating back wistfully before moving Alex along.

Once in the privacy of his room she shut the door behind her and turned the covers back on his bed while he clambered in.

There were tears in his eyes and her heart went out to him. 'Don't be afraid of Jacob. His bark is much worse than his bite,' she said in a vain attempt to relax him. And it was then that the tears he had so valiantly held back exploded from him like water from a dam.

'I . . . w-want my mummy,' he sobbed. June bent to take him in her arms but he pushed her away with a strength that surprised her.

'Look, Alex. You're going to be fine, I promise,' she soothed as he thrashed his head from side to side. He then burrowed beneath the covers and all she could do was look down on the shaking figure beneath the blankets. Realising that nothing she could say was going to make it any easier for the child for now, she turned despondently and quietly left the room.

★   ★   ★

It was Alex's first Sunday in his new home and June was getting him ready to go to church.

'You'll like it,' she assured him, as she pulled one of his new jumpers over his head, 'and the people who attend are so looking forward to meeting you. Then this afternoon, Jacob is going to take you for a walk along the clifftops. That will be nice, won't it?'

Alex glared at her as she now brushed his thick mop of dark hair in a vain attempt to tame it. Over the last few days his life had begun to fall into a pattern. Each morning, June would get him up and he would have his breakfast in the kitchen with Mrs Dickinson. He liked Mrs Dickinson, and as Jacob had usually left for work by then it was quickly turning into his favourite time of the day. After breakfast he would then be allowed to play with his new toys or trail Mrs Dickinson round the house while she polished and hoovered and did the housework. After lunch, he would then be taken in June's car to do any shopping that needed doing before returning to the house where she would spend time reading to him. But at least a dozen times a day he would wander to the lounge window looking for a sight of his mother. She had said she would come for him, after all, so it would be only a matter of time before she appeared and then he could go home again.

Tomorrow, June had told him they were going to buy a Christmas tree and that once they got it home he could help her to decorate it. Despite the fact that he was determined to hate it here, he was looking forward to that. And then would come the time of day he dreaded. Bathtime. It was the same every night now. Jacob would undress him and pop him into the bath before fondling his private parts. That was the only time he was ever kind to him, but even so, Alex had begun to have nightmares about the way Jacob touched him.

Of course, he was aware that after Christmas his routine would change because June had told him that he would be starting school. She had taken him to see it and Alex was forced to admit that it was a very nice school with a huge hall that also served as the dining room and lots of classrooms leading off it. It was a very small select school for boys and Alex had been surprised to see that no girls attended it. Jacob had told him in no uncertain terms that it would cost a lot of money for him to go there and he expected exemplary behaviour. Alex had no idea what exemplary meant but he had nodded all the same. Jacob was fast becoming a figure to be feared.

June was just slipping his arms into the smart new blazer she had bought him the day before when Jacob strode into the room. 'Get a move on, can't you?' he scolded. 'The service will be half over by the time we get there, the way you mammy-pamper that child. He's quite old enough to dress himself.'

June's reply hovered on her lips but she swallowed it and instead smiled at Alex as she straightened and took his hand. They were almost at the door when Jacob suddenly stopped dead in his tracks and turning to Alex told him, 'Oh yes, just one thing before we leave. I think it's time you started to call June and me Mother and Father now.'

Alex's eyes popped. *Mother and Father?* He already had a mother, though he had never known who his daddy was. He certainly couldn't contemplate ever giving these people those titles.

'*No*,' he stated flatly in his first show of defiance for some days. 'I already 'ave a mummy and she'll be comin' for me soon.'

'My God!' Jacob's disgust was evident in his face. 'It will be a good thing when that damn private school we're sending him to teaches the child how to speak properly.' Then, bending so that he was nose to nose with the child, he ground out, 'You *will* obey me or you'll be sorry. Now say, "*Yes, Father!*"'

Alex's small chin jutted as he stared back at the man defiantly, his lips clamped tightly together as June held her breath.

Suddenly, Jacob took the boy's arm and shook him until his teeth rattled. For a while the boy endured it but then his face crumpled and breathlessly he muttered, 'Yes, Father.'

'That's better.' Jacob released him and straightened his tie as Alex fell back against June's skirts, and then, as if nothing had happened, he said brightly, 'Right, we'd better get off then. We don't want to be late, do we?'

June and Alex exchanged a glance before following him silently from the room. Down in the village as they entered the small church the assembled congregation smiled at them.

'Congratulations on your new son,' a well-dressed woman whispered as Jacob led them to an empty pew. 'He's a fine-looking boy, Mr Anderson.'

'Thank you, Mrs Chadworth.' Jacob puffed his chest out, for all the world the proud new father as June and Alex silently followed him to their seats.

Alex had never been to church before and stood quietly between June and Jacob throughout the service, his eyes constantly lingering on the beautiful stained-glass window above the altar.

Outside, the sky was grey and overcast, yet still the window seemed to glow with a bright light, and he was sure that he had never seen anything quite so pretty. The centre of it consisted of a woman holding a small child in her arms who June later informed him was the baby Jesus.

There was a man standing behind the woman holding a staff and he had a kind face as he stared down at them. Alex found himself wishing that Jacob was kind like the man in the window. Not that it really mattered. His mummy would be coming for him soon and then he would never have to see Jacob again. She might even be waiting for him outside right this very minute. Heartened at the thought, he turned his attention back to the window as the voices of the congregation joined in prayer.

When they got back to the house, June served them a delicious meal which she had prepared earlier that morning. Mrs Dickinson didn't come to the house on Saturday or Sunday and Alex found that he missed her. She didn't talk all posh like June and Jacob, and he didn't have to watch his P's and Q's when she was about. As it turned out, June was as good a cook as Mrs Dickinson, and for the first time since he had arrived, Alex tucked into the roast pork dinner without being nagged.

Once the meal was over, June began to clear the table and Jacob told him, 'Go and get yourself warmly wrapped up. We'll be off for that walk now.'

Alex reluctantly did as he was told, though he would by far have preferred to stay at home with June. He was waiting by the front door for Jacob within minutes and the large man smiled at him approvingly.

'That's a good lad.' As he turned Alex's collar up the boy tried not to flinch away from his touch.

'We won't be too long,' Jacob shouted through to June who was washing up in the kitchen, and then he and Alex stepped through the front door and got into Jacob's car. They drove for a while and then parked in a desolate car park near a small post office. The wind and the spray from the sea immediately took their breath away and Alex wished that he could get back in the car. Even so, he found himself almost running as he tried to keep up with Jacob's giant strides. Alex struggled gamely on, and then, after clambering over a stone stile, the sea suddenly came in sight – and it almost took what was left of Alex's breath away. He had never been to the seaside before and it was more than he could take in. Superb views over Putsborough and Woolacombe Sands as far as Morte Point lay before him and to his young eyes the sea seemed to stretch into for ever. Thankfully, Jacob had paused to admire the view, and seeing the look of awe on Alex's small face, he actually smiled.

'Quite a view, isn't it?' he said.

Alex nodded numbly.

'We get a lot of surfers here in the summer,' Jacob informed himself-importantly, and then, pointing to a trail ahead of them that led up on to the clifftops: 'Up there is what's called the coastal trail. It's also known as the Tarka trail after the book that was written by Henry Williamson. He lived for many years near here in a place called Georgeham and wrote *Tarka the Otter*, though I dare say you won't have heard of it at your age.'

Feeling that Jacob needed no answer, Alex listened attentively, interested in what he was saying despite not wishing to be.

'That big metal gate ahead of us is known as The Kissing Gate,' Jacob continued. 'And some way past that is Baggy Point. It's a favourite place for rock climbers but very dangerous, so you should never go there alone. If you were to fall from Baggy Point you'd stand no chance. You'd die on the rocks below and get swept out to sea. I'll take you there one day, but I think we've gone far enough for today. You look all in.'

Alex's eyes grew huge in his pinched face as he peeped over the cliff edge to the sea thundering on to the rocks below. It was very frightening yet beautiful all at the same time.

'In the summer the place looks entirely different,' Jacob went on to tell him. 'The beaches around here are quite beautiful and I'm sure Mother will let you play there sometimes after school.'

A look of resentment settled over Alex's features. There Jacob went again, calling June 'Mother'. She *wasn't* his mother, and as far as he was concerned, she never would be. His mother was back at home in Nuneaton and soon she would be coming for him as she'd promised.

What pleasure he had gained from the panoramic view was suddenly wiped away and now his small shoulders sagged wearily. He wanted to get back to the house and out of the cold.

Sensing that the child had had enough, Jacob turned on his heel and began to walk back the way they had come, with Alex lagging miserably behind.

June was waiting for them back at the house; Alex could see her staring from the window with a worried frown on her face.

'How far have you been? He looks totally exhausted!' she exclaimed as she rushed to help Alex off with his coat.

Jacob's lip curled with disdain. 'There you go again, spoiling him,' he scolded. 'A good long walk in the fresh air never hurt anybody.

You should try it yourself sometime, then you might not look so washed-out.'

Alex watched the colour rise in June's cheeks. Jacob's comment had obviously hurt her, so why didn't she retaliate? Instead she forced a smile as she told Alex, 'Come through to the kitchen, dear. I've got your tea ready then I'll get you into the bath to warm you up. You look as if you're frozen through.'

'*I'll* bath him,' Jacob informed her curtly. She looked back at him for a moment and, just for a second, Alex thought that she was going to stand up to him – but then taking Alex by the hand, she led him away to the kitchen without a word as the little boy began to dread the bath-time ordeal that lay ahead.

Chapter Seven

It was the first week in January and the lane leading to Feathermill Lodge was covered in a thick blanket of virgin snow as Mary cautiously drove along it. Mary had spent a quiet Christmas with her children and grandchildren but now that she was back at work she was keen to know how the Slater children were faring. She had been in phone contact with their new families and had been assured that both Lauren and Natasha were settling in beautifully. June Anderson had said much the same about Alex, but Mary had found her unconvincing and knew now that she wouldn't rest until she had seen each of the children in the flesh.

After driving into the courtyard of the Lodge she sat for a moment letting the peace of the place wash over her. It was hard to believe that this house was on the edge of a town. Once you turned off the main road, anyone could have believed that they were in the heart of the countryside.

She climbed out of the car and headed for the back door where Belle and Harry met her with their tails wagging ecstatically. Penny admitted her with a smile and after bending to stroke the Labradors' silky black coats, Mary sniffed at the air appreciatively.

'Something smells good,' she remarked as Penny wiped her floury hands on her apron.

'Lauren and I are just making some scones.' She nodded towards the table where Lauren was perched on a chair stirring some mixture in an enormous bowl. Mary burst into laughter. The child was white with flour and a large amount of the cake mix was smeared around her mouth and in her hair.

'She tends to get more over her than into the baking tins,' Penny admitted ruefully. 'But never mind. She does enjoy it.'

'I can see that.' Mary smiled broadly as Lauren glanced up to grin cheekily at Penny, her eyes twinkling with mischief. It was obvious that there was a strong bond between the two, and it did the older woman's heart good to see it.

'Well, I have to say she looks wonderful,' Mary said.

Penny nodded. 'She's a little sweetheart,' she said contentedly. 'David and I can't imagine her not being here now. It's as if she's been here for ever, and she's *so* good. The whole family have fallen in love with her. Heather and Aiden spoil her shamelessly when they come home from university. Even the dogs follow her about like a shadow.'

'That's like music to my ears,' Mary told her, but then lowering her voice she asked, 'Does she ever ask for her mother?'

'I can truthfully say not once.' Penny lifted the kettle and began to fill it at the sink then after placing it to boil on the hob she joined Mary at the table. 'There is just one strange thing though,' she now confided. 'She talks to Sarah all the time.'

'I believe it's rather common for little ones to invent imaginary friends.'

'Oh yes, I know that, but the strange thing is, she always talks to Sarah when she's on the landing – and when David and I first bought the place we were told by the people who owned it at the time that the landing was haunted by a little girl who used to live here. She was the daughter of one of the servants, by all accounts, and she died of scarlet fever. Her name was Sarah and we see her all the time now. Between you and me, I have a feeling that Lauren has The Sight too . . .'

Mary shuddered involuntarily, but not being one to believe in such things she quickly laughed the coincidence off. 'I believe there are hundreds of Sarahs about, right now. It's a very popular name, you know. I've no doubt it's nothing more than coincidence that Lauren came up with it. She's probably heard it somewhere.'

Hearing the scepticism in Mary's voice, Penny shrugged. 'Believe what you will, I personally think Lauren is a very gifted child in more ways than one and she's very receptive too. I myself have seen Sarah on a number of occasions and so has David. She's always dressed the same, in a little blue Victorian-style puffed-sleeved dress with a starched white bibbed apron over the top of it. She's a very mischievous little ghost — in fact, we're always having things go missing and I'm convinced it's Sarah that takes them. She's not the only resident ghost either, as I believe I've told you. Besides Sarah and the old man in the four-poster room we also have another two ghosts that frequent the large parlour. One is an old man who's very friendly and the other is an old woman who sits in a rocking chair but isn't so friendly. Then of course there's George down in the cellar. Now he's a *real* character. Whenever I go down there he'll laugh and inform me, *I'm keepin' out of the way o' them ladies down here!* George is another of Feathermill's friendly ghosts. The last of our ghosts is Grace, who stands in the bedroom overlooking the courtyard.'

Seeing that Mary still looked completely unconvinced, Penny went on, 'Anyway, the only reason I'm telling you all this is to try and get across to you just how bright and receptive Lauren is. As I was saying, I really do believe that she's very forward for her age. Can you believe, David already has her playing "Chopsticks" on the piano and she's only three years old? How incredible is that!' As she spoke she was smiling at Lauren indulgently and Mary knew in that moment that it was time to let the adoption proceed. This little girl had certainly landed on her feet, with ghosts for playmates or not.

She stayed just long enough to enjoy a cup of tea with Penny and then made her way back to the office in a happy frame of mind. Now it was time to see how Natasha was faring.

'So how did the visit to the Daventrys go?' Lorna asked later that day as she passed Mary's open office door.

'Brilliantly.' Mary leaned back in her chair and grinned at Lorna like the cat that had got the cream. 'So well, in fact, that I'm going to recommend the adoption process gets under way. I really don't think we're going to have any troubles in that direction. Lauren seems to be thriving.'

'Great, and is there any news on the other two?'

'I spoke to Gail this morning and I've arranged to visit Natasha next week, though by the sounds of it everything is fine there too. By all accounts they had a wonderful Christmas and Gail says Tasha has put some weight on. They're already doing all sorts of things with her to improve her co-ordination, and Gail insists she's trying to say little words already.'

'That's wonderful.' Lorna glanced across her shoulder and then quickly stepping into Mary's room, she pulled the door to behind her. 'Actually, I've got a bit of news for you too,' she said, solemn now. 'It was in the paper last Friday night. Kay Slater is going to Crown Court the first week in March.'

'Oh, I see.' Mary chewed on her lip. 'I suppose I ought to visit her in prison really. If she were at home I'd be keeping her informed of the children's progress, so I dare say the fact that she's locked up shouldn't stop her knowing how they are settling. I'll make a few phone calls and find out which prison she's in.'

'Ugh! Rather you than me.' Lorna shuddered. 'I've never been in a prison before.'

'*Yet*,' Mary warned her. 'In this job it will be only a matter of time until you have to visit someone.'

Lorna gulped as she walked back into the corridor. 'That's something to look forward to then,' she quipped sarcastically, and Mary grinned before returning to the pile of paperwork that was teetering on her desk.

The snow had turned to slush on the following Wednesday when Mary set off to visit the Salisburys, and she wasn't looking forward to the journey at all. Sadly, Lorna would not be accompanying her this time and so she turned the radio on to pass the time. The news was on and full of the new contraceptive drug that was going to be made available in February. She twiddled with the knobs until she found a music channel and then settled back humming as she headed for the Brontë country.

Despite the despicable weather, the roads were clear and Mary made the journey in good time, drawing up outside Beehive Cottage shortly before lunchtime. The lights inside were shining from the tiny leaded windows and as she made her way to the door she heard laughter coming from inside.

Gail welcomed her like a long-lost friend and quickly ushered her inside out of the cold, keen for her to see the remarkable progress Natasha had made.

The child was playing with her dollies on the hearthrug in front of a blazing log fire that was securely surrounded by an enormous wrought-iron fireguard, and as Mary entered she flashed her a happy smile.

'She's doing so well.' Gail's voice was full of pride. 'One of Joe's doctor friends in Harley Street deals solely with children like Tasha who have suffered brain damage, and he's drawn a programme up for her to follow to help her with her co-ordination. I'm sure it's working already. She goes swimming with Joe and me twice a week and we've got her into the nursery three mornings a week in Keighley so that she can be with other children her own age. She loves going there and has made some little friends already. The other children are so protective of her, even though they're only the same age. It's as if they sense that Tasha needs that extra little bit of help and they almost fight amongst themselves to give it to her. It's quite touching to see.'

'Well, I don't know about Tasha but motherhood certainly seems to be suiting you,' Mary commented.

Gail blushed prettily. 'I don't think I've ever been so happy,' she admitted. 'It's like this great empty hole inside me has been filled. But hark at me rambling on when you've come all this way. I bet you're dying for a drink. Take your coat off and have a chat to Tasha while I go and put the kettle on, eh?' With that she turned about and hurried away as Mary smiled down at the child playing contentedly on the floor.

When she left two hours later after sharing a delicious lunch of homemade soup and fresh-baked bread with the family, Mary had a warm glow inside. Now all she had to do was check on Alex and Kay. At this thought, the warm glow subsided; she shuddered at the prospect of both meetings, neither of which would be as enjoyable as the ones that had taken place so far.

Chapter Eight

As usual, Alex was in the kitchen with Mrs Dickinson. It was the only place in the house where he felt even the remotest bit of happiness, especially since Christmas morning when June had shocked him by presenting him with a beautiful Springer spaniel puppy.

Jacob had not been happy with her choice of present at all, but this time she had stood up to him, insisting that it might help Alex to feel more settled if he had something of his very own to love. On that score she had been right, for since then Alex and Bruno, as he had christened the dog, had been inseparable. Jacob had suffered the animal begrudgingly, provided it stayed within the confines of the kitchen or garden, so since then Alex had had a good excuse to keep out of Jacob's way for much of the time. Just as Mary had hoped, he had also found an ally in Mrs Dickinson and already she was spoiling him, bringing him little treats of chocolate and sweets, which she would smuggle into the house in the pocket of her old coat. Jacob and June were very keen on Alex eating healthily, but the way Mrs Dickinson saw it, a little bit of what you fancied never did anyone any harm, so she felt no guilt at all in supplying Alex with a few tasty titbits now and then. She had an idea that Miss June knew what she was doing but turned a blind eye, and she also had an idea that Miss June would have liked to spoil Alex far more than she was allowed to.

Sometimes, Mrs Dickinson felt like shaking her out of pure frustration. When June was a little girl she had been a happy-go-lucky sort of soul, loved and adored by her parents, the kindly parson and

76

his wife. Then she had grown up and fallen head over heels in love with Jacob and before you could say Jack Robinson they were married. Mrs Dickinson could understand why June had fallen for him. After all, he was a handsome chap, at least on the outside. Inside, as she had learned over the years, he was nothing but a bully. Within months of being married, June had changed almost beyond recognition and now Mrs Dickinson sometimes wondered if she was even afraid of her own shadow. She had hoped that adopting a child would make June stand up to Jacob a little more and give her a purpose in life, but as usual, Jacob had taken over. It was even he who would bath the child each night – not that the little boy seemed too happy with the arrangement. In fact, on the odd evenings when Mrs Dickinson had worked late she had noticed how the child would start to grow nervy as bathtime approached, and when Jacob strode into the kitchen to collect him, Alex would pale to the colour of putty although he always went off with him unresisting. No doubt he had already learned that it would do him no good to do otherwise. In this house Jacob's word was law, and woe betide anyone who tried to dispute it.

Tonight was set to be no different. Mrs Dickinson was putting her coat on to begin the long downhill trudge to her cottage when the kitchen door opened and Jacob appeared.

'Ah, there you are, Alex, I thought I'd find you in here,' he said.

Bruno immediately scooted under the table as Alex visibly paled.

'Come along. It's time for your bath.'

June, who had followed her husband into the kitchen, saw the child's reluctance and said hesitantly, 'Wouldn't you rather I do him tonight, dear? You've had such a long day and you must be tired.'

Jacob looked at her with disdain. 'Tired or not, I am a parent now and as such I have duties that shouldn't be shirked. Never let it be said that I leave all of Alex's care up to you. You have him all day, so the least I can do is take over for a while when I get home from work. Now come along, Alex.'

The child swallowed before joining the man at the door reluctantly.

'Say good night to Mrs Dickinson,' Jacob prompted.

'G . . . g'night,' Alex muttered obediently, and with that the large man took his hand and the two of them left the room.

Mrs Dickinson frowned as she looked at June who was nervously fiddling with the pearls that hung about her neck. 'Don't seem too keen on this bath-time lark, the little 'un don't, do he?'

'Well, I imagine most children dread bath-time,' June said, immediately defending Jacob.

Mrs Dickinson sighed. June must have shit in her eyes if she couldn't see Jacob for what he was. The man was a bully through and through – yet June was still besotted with him and wouldn't hear a bad word said against him.

'Ah well, have it your own way,' she said resignedly. 'But fer what my opinion's worth, there's sommat as ain't right here. Not right by a long shot.'

Bruno had crawled from beneath the table again now and June bent to stroke him so that Mrs Dickinson wouldn't see the tears that had sprung to her eyes. She secretly agreed with the woman but felt powerless to question it. After all, what was so wrong with a father bathing a child anyway?

'I'll be off then.' Mrs Dickinson tied a gaily-patterned headscarf across her tightly permed hair and frowned as she opened the back door and the cold air hit her like a blow in the face. 'God love us, it's enough to cut yer in two out here,' she grumbled. 'G'night, lovie. I'll see yer in the mornin'.'

'Good night, Mrs Dickinson.' As the door closed behind the woman, June bit down on her lip and crossed into the hall where she stared thoughtfully up the stairs.

Alex had started to have nightmares. She had heard him during the night and he didn't seem to be settling at all. Strangely, he seemed much more relaxed when he was alone with Mrs Dickinson and herself, although he still spent long periods standing by the window waiting for his mother to come for him.

On a few occasions she had tried to take him into her arms to comfort him, but up until now all her attempts had been in vain and he had pushed her away. She had hoped that with a child in the house, Jacob and she would become closer and more like a real family, but up until now her hopes had not materialised. Still, she consoled herself, it was early days yet. She turned back to the kitchen where Bruno was waiting to be fed and tried not to think of what would happen if Alex failed to settle.

'There now, in you get, you know what to do.' Jacob turned the bath taps off and turned to Alex, who was shivering uncontrollably. He knew exactly what to expect now and climbed into the bath resignedly as Jacob began to soap the flannel. And then the nightmare began all over again, just as it did almost every single night.

It was as Jacob was roughly fondling him that the child managed to pluck up the courage to say, 'I'm a big boy now, I can do that myself.' He had expected Jacob to shout at him but instead the man chuckled.

'Don't be silly. I'm your father now and this is what fathers do.'

'Oh.' Alex had never considered the possibility that this was normal. All he knew was that each night after the ordeal was over he would lie in bed with his tender parts throbbing painfully. Did this really happen to all little boys then?

'Of course, you must never tell anyone about this,' Jacob told him as his hand moved faster. 'If you do, your mummy will *never* come back for you. This is a secret that all little boys and their daddies keep.'

Alex squirmed uncomfortably as he thought on Jacob's words. The man was doing that funny breathing again now, which was a good sign because it meant that it would soon all be over again for another night.

'Ah, that's better,' Jacob sighed as the child became still. 'We have to have you particularly clean tonight, don't we? Because you're starting your new school tomorrow and next week you'll be six.'

As he moved his hand away Alex sighed with relief, trying hard to ignore the throbbing pain between his legs. And then it was over and he was standing at the side of the bath as Jacob towelled him dry, trying desperately hard not to cry.

Minutes later he was led along the landing to where June was waiting to tuck him into bed.

'Good night, Alex.'

'Good night . . . Father.' The word stuck in his throat but he forced himself to say it, knowing the repercussions that would result if he didn't. He didn't have a father, had never had a father as far as he knew. His mum had told him that his dad had done a bunk even before he was born. All his life, all he had known was a continuous stream of 'uncles' – until Kevin had come on to the scene, that was – and then things had got even worse than they had been before, if that was possible. Now that he knew what fathers did to boys whilst they were in the bath, he wished whole-heartedly that he didn't have one. His hand dropped to the cheeks of his bottom where the bruises were just fading following the last time he had refused to call Jacob 'Father'. It had been three nights ago and June had been clearing the table following the evening meal. Alex had slipped from his seat, intent on visiting Bruno who would be waiting for him in the kitchen, but Jacob had had other ideas.

'I have to go out on business tonight, so come along and we'll get your bath done early and out of the way,' he had said.

Alex had frowned with dismay. The times he spent in the warmth of the kitchen with the black and white dog were the only truly happy ones he had, and he'd been reluctant to miss out on saying good night to Bruno, so he had stared at Jacob defiantly and with a jerk of his chin told him quite clearly, 'No!'

Jacob had gone a funny red colour as June's hand flew to her mouth.

'*What* did you say?' he'd ground out from between clenched teeth. 'When you address me you say *Father*, and you do *not* disobey me! Do you hear?'

Trembling but determined, Alex had stared back at him silently until suddenly Jacob sprang across the room and took him roughly by the arm. 'I think it's time you learned who's the boss in this house, my boy,' he snarled, as he began to drag him towards the door, shaking him until his teeth rattled. Alex had been kicking and screaming by then and June's eyes looked as if they were about to pop out of her head with alarm.

'Jacob, what are you doing? Leave him alone,' she pleaded as she raced towards them, but one glare from her husband stopped her in her tracks.

'*Get out of my way, woman!*'

June jumped back as if she had been scalded as Jacob continued on his way. Alex was crying now, and knowing that she would be unable to help him, June dropped into a chair and buried her face in her hands, sobbing helplessly.

Once upstairs, Jacob had flung him on to the bed and Alex's small body began to shake as he watched the man undo his belt and slide it from the loops in his trousers. He had then suffered the indignation of having his trousers pulled down and having his first good belting. It was something he would never forget, the only good thing being that when it was over and he was forced off into the bathroom, Jacob didn't touch him, only to roughly soap him before yanking him from the water.

Now he quietly followed June into his room where she asked him gently, 'Are you all right, dear?'

He nodded numbly as he climbed into bed and she tucked the covers up under his chin. He noticed that she looked sad, but then he was used to that. June rarely smiled and seemed to jump at the least little thing.

'Is there anything you want?' she asked and Alex had to swallow his reply. He could have said, 'Yes, I want my mummy,' but somehow he knew that it wouldn't do any good, so he simply shook his head, his dark eyes huge in his small face. He had thought of telling her about the bad things that Jacob did to him whilst he was in the bath, but after what the man had told him, he decided not to. Jacob had said his mummy would never come if he ever told anyone what he did to him, so perhaps it would be better to keep it to himself.

June bent and planted a soft kiss on his cheek, which he hastily swiped away, and she sighed sadly before turning and leaving the room.

Alone at last, he looked towards his new school uniform, which was hanging on the wardrobe door all pressed and ready for him to start his new school tomorrow. There were plain grey trousers and black highly polished lace-up shoes, which Alex had no idea how he would manage to do up. Then there was a white shirt, the sort that Jacob wore when he set off for work each day, and a burgundy jumper and blazer of the same colour with a logo stitched to the pocket. He was also going to have to wear a cap, which he knew would be difficult to keep on because of the thickness of his dark curly hair. Still, it won't be for long, he thought. My mum will come soon and then when I go home with her I won't have to wear it.

Thoughts of his mother made him inch towards the edge of the bed and pad silently across to the window where he lifted the corner of the curtain. Perhaps she was waiting for him outside right now? But the only thing he could see from his window was the rolling lawns and beyond them the sea, which looked black and angry in the light of the moon. Sighing deeply, he crossed back to his bed, his shoulders slumped. And there he did what any other small boy would have done under the circumstances; he sobbed as if his heart would break.

'There then.' June stood back to survey him proudly. 'You look absolutely wonderful,' she told him as she straightened his school tie for at least the tenth time.

'Yer can say that again. He looks a right little bobby dazzler,'

Mrs Dickinson agreed. She had come early today especially to see Alex before he went to school, and she smiled at him fondly. The poor little sod, she thought to herself. He looked downright miserable and was it any wonder with that great bully, Jacob, breathing down his neck all the time? The poor child wasn't allowed to act his age but instead had to behave like little Lord Fauntleroy. Mebbe once he got to school he would make some chums and things might take a turn for the better. He certainly looked like he could do with a friend. The only time she ever saw him smile was when he was with Bruno, who was sniffing around him now as if he sensed that Alex was going to leave him.

'Come along then, dear,' June said as she buttoned her coat up. 'It wouldn't do if we were to be late on the first day, now would it?'

Alex looked at Mrs Dickinson helplessly for a moment, but then realising that he had little choice in the matter he patted Bruno and silently followed June out to the car.

The school that Jacob had chosen for him was some five or six miles away. Small and select, it tended to take the children of local business people, none of whom were short of a bob or two. The Headmaster there was a close friend of Jacob's. They were both Scoutmasters of the same group, which June knew would have influenced her husband in his choice of schools. He didn't want his son to attend the school where he himself taught, he had decided. Large metal gates marked the entrance to the school, which was then approached by a long sweeping drive.

Soon, what looked like a small manor house with tall chimneys and many windows that sparkled in the weak morning sun came into view, and Alex watched with interest as posh-looking cars pulled up outside enormous double oak doors, above which hung a sign that read *Borwood Private School for Boys*.

His heart began to thump painfully as June took his hand and led him up three circular stone steps and into the most enormous entrance hall he had ever seen. Boys all dressed the same as him were milling about, and adults with clipboards were pacing here and there. They had scarcely entered the hall when a small man with a large ginger beard and piercingly blue eyes strode towards them.

'Ah, June, I've been looking out for you. So this is young Alexander, is it?' he greeted her affably.

June's chest swelled with pride as she nudged Alex in front of her. 'Yes, it is, Mr Miller. And as we discussed, although the adoption hasn't been finalised yet, Jacob and I thought it would be better if Alex began his school career with his new surname to avoid confusion later on.'

'Of course, of course. That will be no trouble at all, and quite sensible in the circumstances,' he assured her as he licked his thin pink lips, setting his beard wobbling. 'Alexander Anderson it shall be. It has quite a nice ring to it, don't you think?'

As he bent to pat Alex's cap the child glared at him, but ignoring him, Mr Miller turned his attention back to June and told her, 'It might be best if you got off now. I shall see Alex to his classroom personally and ensure that he is settled, so you need have no fear.'

'Thank you.' June now bent to Alex and attempted to kiss his cheek, but he turned his head away as anger surged through him. Why did he have to be called Alexander Anderson? His name was Slater like his mum's.

'Goodbye, dear. Be a good boy now, won't you? I'll be here to meet you at hometime.'

Alex squared his sturdy little shoulders and pointedly looked away, and soon he heard her high heels clip-clopping away across the highly polished parquet floor.

'Come along, Anderson,' Mr Miller now addressed him with a note of authority in his voice. 'You are going to be in Miss Verity's class, so let's get you along there to meet her and your classmates.'

Alex clutched his satchel and followed the man through a labyrinth of winding corridors until presently he stopped in front of a door with glass in the top half of it. 'This will be your classroom,' Mr Miller informed him, and without waiting for a reply he flung the door open and ushered the child in front of him. Alex felt the colour rush into his cheeks as he found himself being studied by a number of curious eyes belonging to boys of various shapes and sizes who were all sitting at small desks laid out neatly in rows.

'Miss Verity, I have your new pupil here for you,' Mr Miller boomed. 'This is Alexander Anderson.'

'No, it ain't. Me name's Alex *Slater*,' Alex piped up hotly.

A titter rippled through the class until Miss Verity rapped the desk in front of her with a wicked-looking cane. As Alex looked towards her he shivered with apprehension. He had thought Miss Verity was a pretty name but there was nothing pretty about this woman. Miss Verity was double the size of Mr Miller and had hairs growing out of her chin, which Alex tried desperately hard not to focus on. Her hair was thin and grey and it looked as if someone had stuck a basin on her head and cut around it. But most of all she was huge, so huge, in fact, that her body seemed to be fighting to get out of the old-fashioned knitted suit she was wearing. It was her eyes that struck the most fear into Alex's heart, however, for they were a dull grey like her hair and as cold as ice.

'Sit there, *Anderson*,' she instructed him with a warning wave of the cane. 'And don't let me hear you speak again unless you are spoken to. Is that quite clear?'

Alex scowled as he slid into the seat she had pointed to, and now she came from around her desk and with a single practised move-ment flicked his cap from his head with the lethal-looking stick. 'I see I shall have to teach you some manners,' she remarked with a cruel glint in her eye. 'Hasn't anyone ever told you that it's rude to wear your cap indoors? Fold it up whilst you are inside and put it into the top pocket of your blazer like the other boys, *if* you please, Master Anderson.'

Alex quickly snatched up the offending cap and after screwing it into a tight ball he jammed it into his pocket. As she turned about and lumbered back towards her desk, Alex stuck his tongue out, causing another ripple of giggles to flow through the class.

With a surprising speed for a woman her size, Miss Verity whipped around but all she saw was Alex staring innocently back at her from huge dark eyes.

'I'm watching you, boy,' she told him ominously – and so Alex's first day at school began.

Chapter Nine

As Mary Ingles stood in the doorway of the visiting room she scanned the sea of faces. The women inmates were all sitting at small tables waiting for their visitors to arrive, but at first glance she could see no sign of Kay Slater. Stern-faced prison officers were standing by each door and Mary had to stop herself from shuddering. She could only imagine how terrible it must be to be incarcerated, and even though during the course of her career she had been forced to make more prison visits than she cared to remember, it never became any easier. Drake Hall Prison in Staffordshire, where Kay had been remanded, was an old building steeped in history. During the Second World War it had been used to provide accommodation for female munitions workers, and then in the 1960s it had become a male open prison, before becoming a female prison in 1974.

The room was dingy and uninviting. Visitors were streaming past her now, heading for their loved ones. Many of the people in the room, visitors and inmates alike, were in tears at the sight of each other. Mary felt a lump forming in her throat as she saw one woman sobbing helplessly as she clung to what Mary supposed was her husband's hand across the scratched table in front of her. Mary forced her eyes to move on past the woman to a small figure huddled over a table behind her and she realised with a little shock that this was Kay Slater. Kay had always been slight of build but now she looked like a little shrunken doll, pathetically small and frail. Mary advanced and when she was standing at the side of the table she said softly, 'Hello, Kay. How are you?'

Kay had been gazing off into space as she rocked to and fro with a vacant expression on her face, but now as she raised her head, Mary gasped in horror. The girl seemed to have aged twenty years. Her eyes were sunken and red-rimmed and her cheeks were hollow. The unflattering prison uniform she was wearing hung off her emaciated body and her hair, which was tied back into a tight ponytail at the back of her head, looked dull and limp.

'Oh, my dear.' Mary was almost speechless as compassion for the girl's plight flooded through her. And there was that uneasy feeling again — the intuition that there was more to this situation than Kay was telling. Of course, she deserved to be here, she had killed her partner. *But why?* Throughout their association, Kay had always been so besotted with Kevin, so why would she kill him when she had just lost her children and he was all she had left? It just didn't make any sense.

Settling herself into the uncomfortable chair facing Kay, Mary tried hard to ignore the muttered conversations and crying that was going on all around them.

'The kids. Are they all right?' Kay asked immediately.

'They're all doing absolutely fine,' Mary assured her. 'But what about you? Has your solicitor been to see you? I believe the date for the trial has been set.'

'I ain't havin' a solicitor,' Kay informed her with none of her former bravado. 'I've pleaded guilty an' that's an end to it. I ain't cared if they lock me up for good an' throw the key away. I've got nothin' left to live for now, have I?'

'But of course you have! You're young with your whole life stretching out in front of you.' Mary was appalled at Kay's attitude. It was as if she had lost the will to live. 'When you get out of here you can start afresh and put the past behind you. I'm sure that a good solicitor could make a good case for you. He could say that what you did was a crime of passion while the balance of your mind was unhinged. You had just said goodbye to your children, after all, so perhaps he could say that it was an accident. That you didn't mean to kill Kevin.'

'But I did mean to kill him,' Kay told her flatly. 'An' if I could go back in time I'd do it all over again.'

Mary leaned across the table towards her and asked, '*Why* did you kill him, Kay? There must be a reason. You don't just stab somebody you love for nothing. If you could tell me, I might be able to help you. I've always felt that there was something not quite right about all this.'

'It doesn't matter any more. Just so long as me kids are OK, I don't care what happens to me. *Are* they happy? Do they ever ask for me?'

Mary sighed as she leaned back in her seat and rubbed her forehead. 'Yes, they're happy,' she replied, as she fought with her frustration. 'And yes, of course they have asked after you, particularly Alex, but that's to be expected. They still have a lot of settling in to do in their new homes. What I can assure you is that they are all getting the very best of care.'

Tears were trembling on Kay's dark lashes, so like Alex's, and now as Mary looked at her more closely, she noticed the marks of a bruise beginning to spread across her left eye.

'How did you get that?' she asked with a frown.

Kay's hand self-consciously rose to her cheeks to swipe away the tears that were now rolling down them. 'Oh, I . . . er . . . slipped in the shower,' she answered chokily.

Mary had a sudden urge to shake her until Kay told her the truth. She knew that she could help her if only Kay would let her, but it seemed that the girl didn't care what happened to her any more.

The young woman suddenly rose and said to Mary, 'Thanks for comin' to tell me how the kids are. I appreciate it. An' . . . well, I'm sorry if I ain't always been the easiest to work with. I ain't never told you this before, an' I must have appeared like a right ungrateful little cow, but you ain't a bad sort for a social worker an' I know your intentions were always good.' She held out a shaky blue-veined hand and as Mary shook it, a warden, who would escort Kay back to her cell, began to walk towards them.

'Bye then, Mary. Don't get puttin' yourself out to come an' see me again. Just make sure that me kids are all right for me, will you?'

'Of course I will.' Mary was openly crying too now. 'Goodbye, my dear . . . and good luck.'

As the warden took Kay's elbow and marched her away, Mary had the most awful feeling that the poor tormented girl would need all the luck she could get.

Chapter Ten

'Don't want to go to school,' Alex mumbled as June held out his blazer.

'Oh, Alex, please don't let's have this again,' she sighed as she prodded one of his arms into the hated garment. Today being Friday would be the last day of his first week at school, and each morning it had been a little more difficult than the day before to get him there. Alex had obviously taken an instant dislike to his teacher, Miss Verity, and June had an inkling that the feeling was mutual. Miss Verity had been very unsympathetic when June had approached her the day before about Alex's reluctance to come to school, and had told her in a very polite way that she was behaving like an over-sensitive mother.

'He'll soon settle in,' she had assured June. 'Some children take to school like ducks to water. Alex is obviously going to be one of those that need a little longer. Just don't pander to him. You must be firm, and when he realises that he has no choice in the matter, he'll soon settle in. Let them know who's boss, eh?'

June had glared at her departing back as she'd waddled off down the corridor dragging a loudly complaining Alex behind her. June had got no sympathy from Jacob either when she told him how difficult Alex was finding it.

'He's testing the water,' he had told her emphatically. 'All children will try it on. You just have to be firm with him. I heartily agree with his teacher on that score.'

'But Jacob, he's had so much change in his life recently,' she'd told him tearfully. 'Perhaps we should have let him settle in more here before we sent him off to school?'

'Rubbish!' Jacob had snapped. 'I've told you before: Alex is a very strong-willed little chap. He'll rule the roost if we let him. We have a battle of wills going on at present, but if we're consistent he'll soon see who's in charge here.'

And now it looked as if there was going to be yet another tantrum. June sighed. Being a parent wasn't turning out to be quite as easy as she had envisaged, and she could only pray that things would get better.

She was slightly heartened when she drew the car to a halt at the bottom of the school steps to see a small boy, who looked to be about Alex's age, waiting for him there.

'Oh, look!' she cried happily. 'There's someone waiting for you. Is he your new friend? What's his name? Perhaps we could invite him to your birthday tea tomorrow?'

Alex looked at her as if she had taken leave of her senses. 'He ain't me friend,' he informed her abruptly. 'An' I don't want him to come to tea.'

Ignoring him, June kept her smile fixed in place as she hurried round to Alex's side of the car and opened the door for him. The boy who had been waiting on the steps instantly came to join them and smiled widely at Alex. His carrot-coloured hair clashed with the burgundy cap and blazer he was wearing. Even so, he was a cheerful little thing with freckles across his broad nose and smiling blue eyes.

'Morning, Alex,' he greeted him.

'A'right, Ginger,' Alex muttered in reply. Despite what he had said to June, Ginger, as he was widely known, was an all-right sort of kid and though he talked posh he wasn't stuck up like a lot of his classmates were. Alex had been teased all week about the way he spoke until now he was almost afraid to open his mouth — except when he was with Ginger, because the other boy seemed to like him as he was. Alex supposed that it was because Ginger got teased too about his freckles and his hair. Even so, he wasn't about to admit to June that he had found a friend. He wasn't going to admit to liking anything about the new life he had been forced into. There wouldn't be any point because when his mum came to take him home he would never see any of them again and he could forget all about the last awful months.

'What's your real name, dear?' June asked the child, and he blushed an unbecoming red as he muttered, 'James Morrison.'

'Well, James, I was saying to Alex here, we're having a little tea-party tomorrow for his birthday and I was wondering if you would like to come. Do you think your mother would allow you to?'

James nodded towards the figure of a woman who was heading towards a gleaming BMW. 'That's my mother,' he informed her, and with a nod at the boys, June hurried after her.

Left to their own devices the two boys stared at each other cautiously before Ginger said, 'I dare say we should be going in then.'

'Yeah, I dare say you're right else we'll have Fatty Verity breathin' down us necks.'

Ginger grinned, showing off a beautiful set of white teeth. Alex was like no one he had ever met before and he liked him enormously. Side by side they trooped into the school.

'There, I think that's about it,' June said with satisfaction as she stood back to admire Alex's birthday tea. A large cake, iced in blue with six candles on it, took pride of place in the centre of the table, and spread around it was an assortment of sandwiches, cakes and small trifles. Could she have known it, it was very similar to the one his foster mum had made him the year before. Balloons were tied up about the room and now all they had to do was wait for Ginger to arrive so that they could begin the party. Alex was outside playing on his new bicycle, with Bruno bounding along at the side of him as he wobbled precariously from one side of the drive to another.

He had been up with the larks, sitting on the stairs anxiously watching the letterbox for a sign of the birthday card that he was sure would come from his mum, but when it hadn't arrived he had been forced to swallow his tears and disappointment when the postman eventually delivered nothing more than formal-looking envelopes addressed to Jacob.

Alex had promised himself that he wouldn't enjoy today, but it had been very hard not to when he had been presented with his gift. He had never owned a bicycle before and was determined to master the art of riding it at the expense of his knees, which were already skinned.

Mrs Dickinson had come in especially today to help Miss June with his birthday tea, though from where she was standing it wasn't going to be much of a party if Alex only had one friend coming.

'Well, he's only been at school for a week and he hasn't really had time to make many friends yet,' June had pointed out when Mrs Dickinson commented on it.

'I dare say yer right,' the older woman agreed, and continued to butter the bread for the sandwiches. Jacob was delighted with Alex's new friend since he had discovered that James's father had his own dental business in Putsborough.

'Ruddy snob,' Mrs Dickinson muttered beneath her breath when she heard him talking to June about it earlier. 'I dare say if the bloke'd been a brickie's labourer he wouldn't have given 'im the time o' day.'

Mrs Dickinson had never had much time for Jacob. In fact, she would have left long ago if it hadn't been for Miss June, even though the money she earned came in very handy. But her dislike of the man had intensified since Alex had come to live with them. There was something not quite right about the way he treated the child; the boy seemed terrified of him. The only time he appeared remotely happy was when he was in the kitchen with her and Bruno. And that was another bone of contention in the household. Jacob hated the dog with a vengeance, and the longer they had him, the worse his hatred became. The poor little mutt would cower under the table the second he heard the bully's voice and had already learned to stay well out of his way. Jacob was always threatening to get rid of him but credit where it was due, Miss June had stood up to him on this point and wouldn't hear of him going. It was just as well, because Mrs Dickinson couldn't imagine how Alex would react if he were to lose the spaniel now.

The housekeeper was forced to admit Alex was a surly little chap, even with her for much of the time, yet occasionally she had caught a glimpse of the fun-loving little boy he might have been if he had been happy, which he certainly wasn't at present. He hated his new school; he made no secret of the fact that he hated living here; he hated Jacob, and for much of the time he seemed to hate June too, though she did do her best for him. The poor woman was desperate for a child to love and Mrs Dickinson could only think that Alex must have come as a sore disappointment to her. He was certainly not the child she had hoped for, who would love her back unconditionally. Still, they could only hope that eventually he would settle down and become a part of the family.

It was as these thoughts were going through her head that a knock came on the door and Jacob himself hurried to answer it. A shiny BMW was parked outside and on the step stood a tall handsome dark-haired man and a little boy with shocking ginger hair who was clutching a gaily wrapped parcel and a card in his hand.

'Ah, Mr Morrison,' Jacob greeted him jovially as he extended his hand. 'And you must be James? Do come in. Alexander is still out trying to get the hang of riding his new bike.'

'I won't come in if you don't mind,' James's father apologised. 'I just thought I'd drop him off for the wife. What time would you like me to pick him up?'

'Would five o'clock be OK?'

'Perfect,' the man assured him and, turning around, he hurried back to his car, leaving Jacob to usher James into the house. He was about to close the door when Alex suddenly appeared and smiled at James shyly.

'You made it then?'

'Yes I did, and I hear you've had a new bike for your birthday. That's brilliant! Can I see it? I already have one and I could teach you to ride it if you like.'

Seeing that Alex had spent more time falling off his new possession than actually riding it he supposed that a little help wouldn't come amiss, so he nodded and Ginger followed him out on to the drive. The next hour was the happiest Alex had known since coming to live in his new home. He and Ginger took turns on his bicycle then played hide and seek and tig amongst the trees in the small copse at the end of the garden. By the time June called them in for their tea, they both had glowing cheeks and James no longer resembled the neat and tidy child who had been delivered to the door such a short time ago.

'Oh dear, what's his mother going to say when she sees the state of his trousers?' June fretted.

'If they're mucky they're healthy,' Mrs Dickinson told her as the two boys tucked into the small feast with gusto.

'Perhaps I shouldn't let them go out again,' June said as she looked towards the window. 'It's awfully cold out there and I don't want them to catch a cold.'

'Fiddlesticks! Good fresh air never hurt anyone,' the other woman beamed. 'They're well wrapped up, an' the way they're chasin' about they couldn't catch a cold if they was to try.'

It was then that Alex shocked them all when he suddenly turned to Jacob and asked, 'Ja . . . Father, do you think you could take us to Baggy Point after tea?'

Jacob flushed with pleasure. Up to now he had almost had to drag Alex out of the house kicking and screaming to get him to go anywhere with him, but here he was actually asking to go for a walk.

'Of course I will,' he agreed. 'But first let's get these candles lit, eh?'

As the candles were duly lit and they all sang 'Happy Birthday' to him, Alex's small face crumpled as he thought back to other birthdays that he had shared with his family. They hadn't been such grand affairs as this – in fact, his birthday cake had usually amounted to nothing more than a Swiss roll with a candle stuck in it, but right then he would have given his very soul to be sharing this one with them now.

Sensing that Alex wasn't enjoying it, Jacob looked vaguely annoyed and suggested, 'Why don't we get wrapped up for that walk then? We can have some cake when we get back.'

Only too happy to oblige, Alex led Ginger into the hall where they put their coats on and minutes later they were on their way.

As June watched them drive away from the window she frowned. Miss Verity had sidetracked her when she had picked Alex up from school the afternoon before and told her in no uncertain terms that Alex seemed to be miles behind all the other boys in his class.

Indignant, June had pointed out that this was his first week, but Miss Verity had folded her arms across her enormous breasts and shaken her head. 'Even so, most children starting school have some recognition of the alphabet and numbers. I suggest you spend some time with him getting him up to speed otherwise he'll lag even further behind,' she had informed her condescendingly, and with that she had turned and walked away with her nose in the air. June stifled the urge to call her back and tell her what a horrible woman she was. It was no wonder Alex appeared to have no liking for the woman. She was downright ignorant! Even so, this would give Jacob something else to get his teeth into. There was nothing June would have liked more than to take on the task of helping Alex with his letters and numbers, but knowing Jacob as she did, she doubted if he would allow that to happen. As soon as he learned what Miss Verity had said, he would want to do it himself, which Alex wouldn't like very much at all.

June Anderson had a grave suspicion that Alex was turning out to be a huge disappointment to her husband. She knew that he had looked forward to having a child in the house, but worried that his expectations of him were too much. He seemed to assume that Alex would forget all about the family he'd had before overnight – and even she, with her lack of parenting experience, knew that this wasn't going to happen. Jacob was just going to have to try to be a little more patient with him. Not that patience was one of his strong points. Sighing deeply, she started to take the dirty crockery into the kitchen where Mrs Dickinson was washing them up. She wouldn't say anything to Jacob until tomorrow, she decided. That way, Alex would get to enjoy the rest of his birthday at least.

Ginger had been born and brought up within the sound of the sea so the walk didn't hold quite the same fascination for him as it did for Alex. Even so he kept up a constant stream of cheerful chatter as they moved along and Jacob was impressed with the child's manners. If only Alex could have been more like him, he thought. But then there was plenty of time to whip him into shape. And whip him he would, if that's what it took. He would turn the child into a son to be proud of if it was the last thing he did.

When Baggy Point finally came into view, Alex smiled. He never tired of admiring the rugged cliffs and the seagulls that wheeled in the sky above them. Far below, the waves thundered on to the rocks and Alex watched the power of the sea in wonder. Should anyone ever slip from the cliff face or fall over the edge here, he knew they would never stand a chance of surviving and the fact fascinated him. Jacob had told him that during the summer months, the place was alive with mountain climbers and he was looking forward to seeing them brave the elements. He was also looking forward to seeing the surfers on Putsborough beach and walking Bruno there each day after school. But all that seemed a long way off right now and anyway, no doubt his mum would have been to fetch him by then.

Slightly cheered at the thought he glanced at Jacob who was showing a lot of attention to Ginger. He wondered how Ginger could be so happy-go-lucky all the time if his dad did the things to him that Jacob did to him most bath nights? Perhaps you got used to it after a time and the pain of it went away? Alex hoped so. Sometimes the throb in his private parts was almost unbearable. He was so lost in his own thoughts that it came as a shock to him when Ginger shook his arm.

'Here, you were miles away,' he grinned. 'Didn't you hear your father say it was time we were getting back? My dad will be picking me up soon, so we'd better get off.'

Alex fell into step with him, and shortly afterwards Ginger pointed to a field beyond a local farm. 'The gypsies park there each year,' he informed him. 'They always come for the potato picking.'

'Gypsies?' Alex's ears pricked up with interest. He had never seen any gypsies before. 'Do they stay for long?'

'Only until the potato-picking season is over.'

'Oh.' Alex turned his collar up. He was tired now and so the rest of the journey back to the car was made in silence.

June had steaming mugs of hot chocolate and slices of birthday cake ready for them, and the two boys tucked in as if they hadn't eaten for a month. The sea air and the long walk had given them both an appetite. Mrs Dickinson smiled her approval. Alex usually picked at his food like a bird so it was nice to see him enjoying it so much. Shortly afterwards, James's father arrived to collect him and once again Jacob answered the door, the epitome of charm and good manners.

'You really must bring your wife for tea one afternoon,' he gushed with a wide smile on his face.

'Thank you, Mr Anderson,' the man replied coolly as he took his son's hand. 'That would be very nice.' He actually had no intention of doing any such thing; he hadn't taken to the man at all, although Alex seemed like a nice enough little chap. 'Say thank you for having me, James.'

'Thank you for having me, sir,' the lad replied. 'Goodbye, Alex. I'll see you at school on Monday.' And with that he skipped away to his father's car as if he hadn't a care in the world. Alex found himself wishing that he could have gone with them. Ginger's father had a nice face, a kind sort of face somehow.

'Come along, Alex,' Jacob interrupted his thoughts. 'We shall have to think of getting you into the bath and ready for bed soon, birthday or not. I've no doubt you'll be tired tonight after the big day you've had.'

And suddenly all the joy had gone from the day as Alex thought of the nightmare that was before him again.

Mrs Dickinson, who was putting her coat on ready to go home, noticed the shuttered look that came into the child's eyes. Alex was a feisty little chap but it was more than obvious that he was afraid of Jacob. But why? she asked herself. The man was a bully, but she didn't think he was violent. It still hurt her to see that awful haunted look on the little boy's face though. Just what was it that was making him so unhappy? Sighing, she let herself out of the house into the bitterly cold late afternoon.

Alex spent the next hour in the kitchen rolling about the floor with Bruno. June was finishing the clearing up and she smiled indulgently at his antics – until Jacob entered the kitchen that was, and then both she and Alex instantly became solemn.

'Come along then. I have to be out in an hour, so let's get you bathed,' he addressed Alex.

Seeing the child's face fall, June quickly offered, 'I could bath him tonight if you're in a hurry, Jacob.'

'That won't be necessary.' Her husband's voice was ice cold. 'I don't shirk my parental duties, as you very well know. Come along, Alex.'

Alex slowly stood and followed Jacob to the door, his small shoulders stooped in defeat as June looked on helplessly. Just why did Jacob insist on bathing him every night? She supposed it was good that he took his role of parenting seriously, but surely it shouldn't be so regimental? Strict roles for her and others for him. Chewing on her lip, she gazed up at the ceiling.

'Right – in you get.'

Alex stepped past Jacob and into the steaming water, trying hard to keep his mind on his new bike. He knew all too well what was to come but perhaps if he concentrated on something else it wouldn't be so bad. No doubt Ginger would be enduring the same thing in his house right at this very moment, as his father bathed him. Jacob had told him that all fathers did the same thing, so it stood to reason that Ginger would be suffering too.

However, the torment had barely begun when Jacob said something that instantly had the whole of Alex's attention.

'I have another surprise for you but thought I'd wait until tonight to tell you about it,' he said, as his large hand settled on Alex's small shoulder.

As the boy looked at him questioningly, Jacob went on, 'Seeing as you're getting used to your new surname, I thought I'd let you know that your mother and I have decided to change your first name too. It won't be legal until the adoption is finalised, of course, but there's no reason why you shouldn't start to get used to it now. I've already informed the school that as from next Monday you will be known as Francis Anderson.'

'Francis! But that's a *cissy* name, a *girl's* name!' Alex objected as hot indignation flooded through him. 'Me name is Alex, why can't I just keep that?'

'You will keep that,' Jacob informed him calmly. 'Your full name will be Francis Alexander Anderson.'

Alex dared to glare at him resentfully as the man towered over him. This was almost more than he could bear. His mother had chosen his name, it was all he had left of her, and now they were going to take that away from him too. *Francis!* The name rolled round and round in his head as tears stung his eyes.

But there was something even worse in store for him, could he have known it. Jacob suddenly straightened and began to undo his trousers. 'Now that you're six and a big boy, I think it's time I taught you some of the other things that daddies and little boys do.'

Alex wanted to look away as Jacob's trousers slid down his hairy legs but his eyes seemed to be locked on the enormous bulge in the man's underpants.

'This is what yours will be like one day,' Jacob told him as Alex continued to stare in horrified fascination. 'Why don't you touch it?'

Alex's head snapped from side to side in terror but Jacob reached out and dragged his small hand towards him, and as Alex felt the heat of the man through the thin material the colour drained from his face. Jacob was holding his hand against it so tightly that it hurt but Alex bit down on his lip, determined not to cry out. Jacob began to move the child's hand, which had now clenched into a fist, up and down as weird noises issued from him. Alex didn't understand what was happening and began to cry; unable to hold the tears back any longer. And then suddenly Jacob gave a huge shudder and thrust Alex's hand away as he turned towards the window, and at last it was over. Alex sat quite still, afraid that it might all start up again, but presently, Jacob pulled up his trousers and as he hastily fastened them he snapped, 'Well, don't just sit there. Get out and get yourself dry. I have to be out soon.'

Alex was only too happy to oblige and shot from the bath like a bullet from a gun. He was trembling so much that he dropped the towel twice, but at last he had it wrapped around himself and was edging towards the door. Jacob didn't try to stop him, so Alex hared across the landing as if the hounds of hell were snapping at his heels, not daring to draw breath until his bedroom door was securely closed behind him.

June was in his room laying his pyjamas out on the bed and she turned to smile at him, but the smile froze on her face as she saw the state he was in. 'Why, whatever is the matter, dear?'

She made to move towards him but he shrank away from her, clutching the towel even more tightly about him. Suddenly realising what might be wrong, she held her hand out. 'Has Jacob told you that he . . . *we* want to change your name? Is that what's upset you?'

When Alex didn't answer she sighed and looked away, unable to bear the pain in his large soulful dark eyes.

'Francis is a very nice name,' she assured him. 'It was Jacob's grandfather's name. I'm sure you'll get used to it. In fact, I dare say in a few months' time you'll have forgotten you ever had another name.'

The sound of the front door closing made them both look towards it and now she moved away as she whispered, 'Get into your pyjamas, there's a good lad. I'll be back shortly when I've see Jac . . . your father off.'

Alex slung the wet towel aside the second she set foot out of the door and clambered into bed where he cowered beneath the covers. And finally the tears came; hot scalding tears that threatened to choke him. Where was his mum? Why didn't she come to save him? Why couldn't he have had the sort of mum that he sometimes saw meeting his classmates from school? Mums whose faces lit up when they caught sight of their children. Mums who kept their children safe. It was then a rage the like of which he had never known swept through him. He hated Jacob more than he had ever hated anyone in his short life – *but one day*, he promised himself, *I'll kill him!*

Chapter Eleven

It was almost one o'clock in the morning when June heard her husband's key in the lock, and she stiffened as she looked towards the door. She could faintly hear him walking about downstairs and then the sound of his tread, softened by the thick carpet on the stairs. The room was in darkness, save for the light of a watery moon that shone through the window, casting dancing shadows into the dark corners. She heard his step on the landing, pausing outside Francis's door, as she must now call him, then it moved on past their room and towards the smaller guest room at the far end of the corridor.

She turned over as tears pricked at the back of her eyes, wondering how everything could have gone so very wrong. She could still recall how she had felt the very first time she had set eyes on him. The much-adored and sheltered daughter of the local parson, she had never seen anyone quite as handsome as Jacob before, and he had swept her off her feet. On their wedding day as she walked down the aisle on the arm of her father, she clearly remembered thinking how very lucky she was, but the feeling hadn't lasted for long. Within months of their being married, Jacob had taken to going out and staying out with no explanation as to where he might be. Her first instinct had been to wonder if he had another woman, but somehow that didn't feel right. He had then started to help out with the Boy Scouts, spending numerous evenings and weekends away with them. June had tried desperately hard to be a good wife. Before their marriage she had been a little nervous about the sexual duties she would be expected to perform, as she had come to him a virgin. But on that score she soon realised she need have no worries. Jacob had little or no interest in sex, and it soon became she herself who would try to lure him into bed, for she desperately wanted a child. It was shortly after that, that he had begun to sleep in the spare room, using the excuse that he didn't like to disturb her when he came in late. And so the years crept by with no sign of a baby until she had begged him to go to the doctor's with her. 'There must be something wrong with one of us,' she had fretted, because even though they only slept together infrequently, and then only after her pleading, surely *something* should have happened by now?

Jacob had eventually agreed to tests, which he hated with a vengeance, but they had all come back clear, and there was no problem with her either, the doctor had assured them both. 'Perhaps you're trying too hard,' he had suggested. Huh! Fat chance of that, June had thought resentfully, but she had held her tongue and to outsiders they continued to appear the perfect couple. Jacob loved to be in the company of influential people and at his request June often held dinner-parties, at which he would laugh and joke and be the perfect host.

'They're such a lovely couple. It's a real shame they can't have a family,' the people in the village post office gossiped, overheard one day by June, whose cheeks burned with shame. It was then that she had suggested adoption – and was shocked when Jacob seemed keen on the idea. 'Only if we have a little boy though,' he had insisted. And so they had set the wheels in motion and now here was Alex, or Francis, as Jacob had insisted on renaming the child, and it wasn't turning out to be at all as June had hoped. She had prayed that a child would bring them closer – that they would become a real family who enjoyed spending time together – but now her dream seemed further away than ever.

Jacob monopolised the child at every opportunity, sometimes making her feel as if she wasn't there. Bath-times particularly had become a time to dread because Jacob insisted on bathing Francis himself, although the child obviously didn't enjoy it. Feeling utterly wretched, June Anderson burrowed down in the lonely double bed, and there she cried herself to sleep.

By Monday morning, Alex's eyes were red-rimmed with crying and he seemed nervy and on edge.

On the two previous evenings, he had been subjected to what he now termed as 'the bad things' during his bath, and his terror of Jacob had grown to such proportions that he had even considered running away. But where would he run to? And what would he do if his mother came for him while he wasn't there? And she would come . . . he was still sure of it.

'You would tell me if there was anything that was worrying you, wouldn't you, Francis?' June asked with concern as she drove him to school.

He stared ahead, his small lips set in a grim line. She must know what fathers did to little boys, so what would be the point of trying to tell her that he didn't like it?

Eventually she turned the car into the school gates and drew it to a halt at the steps leading up to the school doors.

'Have a good day, dear.'

Ignoring her, he slid out of his seat, and after slamming the car door resoundingly behind him, he entered the school without giving her so much as a backwards glance.

Ginger was waiting for him just inside the entrance and his freckled face broke into a wide grin at the sight of his friend. 'Hey, that was a great party,' he told him, but then the smile slid from his face as he saw Alex's tight expression. 'What's wrong?' he asked, as they fell into step.

'From now on, Jac . . . me father has informed me that I'm to be called Francis. He's spoken to Fatty Verity an' she's goin' to tell the whole school durin' assembly. They'll all be laughin' at me,' Alex mumbled miserably.

'Why are you going to be called Francis when your name is Alex?' Ginger asked eventually.

''Cos June an' Jac . . . I mean, Mother and Father, are goin' to adopt me, so that means they can decide on me name.'

'Why are they going to adopt you? Don't you have a real mum and dad?'

'I have a real mum,' Alex told him quietly as he struggled to hold back his tears. 'An' she'll be comin' to fetch me soon.'

'Oh, well, where is she now then?'

'A long way away . . . Nowhere,' Alex stated flatly.

'Well, she must be somewhere, and Francis isn't such a bad name,' Ginger said kindly. 'Especially if I shorten it to Franky. Would you like that better? I think Franky is a pretty good name.'

As Alex considered his words for a moment he sniffed loudly. 'That ain't half bad,' he admitted reluctantly, and from that moment on whenever he was out of the house, Franky it was.

Within six months Alex had reluctantly accepted his new name, although he still struggled to adjust to his new lifestyle. It did admittedly seem a little easier now that the summer was here and he got to spend time on the beach each day after school with June and Bruno. Putsborough beach had become his favourite. There he would watch the surfers effortlessly riding the waves on gaily-patterned surfboards, and dream of the day when he would be big enough to join them. At other times he and Bruno would fish for crabs in the crystal-clear rockpools that the sea had left behind, or he would build sandcastles with the bright red bucket and spade June had bought for him.

The sea and the white sandy beaches held a fascination for him and he never tired of romping in the waves with Bruno. The dog had now doubled in size and was a constant joy to the boy, who spent every minute he could with him. His fat puppy belly had disappeared now and he seemed to be all legs and ears that flew in all directions. Sadly, as Bruno grew, so did Jacob's hatred of him.

'The whole damn house stinks of dogs,' he would complain the second he set foot through the door after work each evening.

'I hardly see how it can, when Bruno is restricted to the kitchen,' June would point out patiently. Knowing how much Franky doted on the spaniel, she hated to think how he would react if Jacob forced them to get rid of him. She too called the child Franky now, as did Mrs Dickinson when Jacob was out of earshot. The only people who ever addressed him as Francis were Jacob, Miss Verity and Mr Miller, so the boy had come to accept it. He knew it wouldn't be for long anyway. When his mum came to fetch him home he could return to being Alex.

Despite his unhappiness, he had grown considerably during the time he had lived in Devon. The fresh air, which seemed to make him constantly hungry, and Mrs Dickinson's good home cooking had seen to that. Franky was a good head and shoulders above Ginger now – and every other boy in his class – and although he was still only six years old he could have easily been taken for seven or eight.

Strangely, the house too seemed to have taken on a completely different appearance in the summertime. The flowerbeds surrounding the rolling lawns had suddenly burst into glorious colour and were now full of every flower imaginable – hollyhocks, lupins and roses all married together along with brightly coloured daisies and azaleas. The walls of the house were hidden behind deep purple clematis and trailing wisterias that filled the night air with scent. Twice a week a retired gentleman from the village came to tend to the gardens, and Franky had taken to helping him on the odd occasions when he wasn't at school. At least, that's what he thought he was doing. Mr Golding might have told a different tale, had he been asked, but the child seemed so alone and sad that he was happy for him to potter about with him. Mr Golding was a Jewish gentleman who had settled in England after the war, and Franky loved to listen to the stories he told of his travels when he was young. His hair was snow-white and he sported a tiny white goatee beard that fascin-ated the boy.

Every couple of hours, the old chap would head off to the kitchen with Franky in tow, and Mrs Dickinson would serve them with ice-cold glasses of lemonade and cakes or scones fresh from the oven.

Franky was always amused to see the way Mrs Dickinson would blush and get all flustered whenever the old gentleman spoke to her. Mr Golding's wife was dead, as was her husband, and they seemed to enjoy each other's company. He had noticed that she always combed her hair and put a clean apron on whenever Mr Golding was coming, and wondered why – not that he dared to ask. Jacob was a great believer that children should be seen and not heard, and Franky now rarely spoke until he was spoken to unless it was to Bruno, who he whispered all his hopes and dreams to.

'One day soon,' the boy would promise him, 'me mam will come an' she'll take us both home.'

Bruno would wag his tail and stare back at him as if he understood every word Franky was saying. The problem was, Franky was finding it harder and harder to picture his family when he closed his eyes. He would think of Lauren, hugging the rag doll she insisted on taking everywhere with her, and Tasha, with her dull staring eyes, but their faces were blurry in his mind and it frightened him.

One evening, as he and June arrived home from the beach, they saw Jacob getting out of his car and just as it always did at the sight of him, Franky's heart sank into his shoes. His bath-time terrors continued, but he had become adept at putting them out of his mind until minutes before Jacob ordered him to the bathroom.

Even from the end of the drive they could see that Jacob was scowling, and June frowned. 'Oh dear,' she muttered beneath her breath. 'I wonder what's upset him now?'

Quickening their pace they moved on to join him. He was standing by the door with a face like thunder.

'Ah, here you are,' he addressed Francis abruptly. 'I'd like to speak to you inside. Right *now*, if you please.'

'But he's covered in sand,' June objected. 'Couldn't we just go round to the kitchen and get cleaned up first?'

'I said NOW!' Jacob thundered, and staring at Franky apprehensively, June nudged him in front of her. The second they set foot through the door, Bruno scampered off towards the kitchen with his tail between his legs. Franky found himself envying the dog and wished that he could do the same.

June brushed herself down as best she could before following her husband and the boy into the study.

'I had a call from Mr Miller today,' he informed them without preamble. 'It seems that you're getting to be quite a disruptive influence at school, Francis. What do you have to say for yourself, young man?'

Franky hung his head as he shuffled from foot to foot. Incensed, Jacob looked towards June and went on. 'It seems he was openly rude to his teacher when she told him off and—'

'Only 'cos she were tryin' to blame me for somethin' I didn't do,' Franky told him hotly. 'She reckoned it were me as—'

'How *dare* you interrupt me when I'm speaking,' Jacob bellowed. He was red in the face now and June clasped her hands together to stop them trembling.

'Haven't I managed to knock *any* manners into you yet?' Jacob ranted on. 'And while we're at it, your grammar is appalling, which is why I'm arranging elocution lessons for you. Do you deny that you were rude to Miss Verity?'

'No,' Franky answered in a small voice, 'but I'm tryin' to tell you, it were 'cos—'

'That is *quite* enough of your insolence.' Jacob looked ready to explode now and June was holding her breath. 'Get to your room right now. I shall be up to deal with you directly.'

As Franky shot away, June caught hold of his arm. 'Please go easily on him, Jacob,' she begged. 'Just remember he's only a little boy and—'

'Oh, *shut up*, woman,' Jacob said contemptuously. 'Haven't you ever heard the saying, "spare the rod and spoil the child"? My father gave me some rare good hidings when I was little and they didn't do me any harm. Francis has to learn that rudeness is unacceptable. Little as he is, he cannot learn this lesson too young. Now get out of my way.'

He pushed past her and as she watched him taking the stairs two at a time, she began to weep in fear. Seconds later, she heard Franky cry out and the tears fell faster. Sometimes she almost wished they had never taken the child, for when Jacob was in this mood she dreaded how far his punishment might go.

Much later that evening, when Jacob had left to go to a Scouts' meeting in the village hall, she prepared a tray and crept upstairs to Franky's room. She tapped on the bedroom door and when there was no answer she pushed it open and quietly entered the room. Franky was lying on his stomach, naked from the waist down, and her eyes were instantly drawn to his bare buttocks, where vicious red weals stood out in stark contrast to his milky-white skin.

Swallowing the sob that rose in her throat she kept her voice calm as she told him, 'I've brought you some tea, dear – ham sand-wiches and some of Mrs Dickinson's Victoria sponge cake. You like that, don't you?'

There was no answer, so placing the tray down she silently slipped from the room to return minutes later with a dish of warm water and some ointment. 'Now, I'm just going to bathe this,' she told him gently. 'Just try to be brave because it might sting a little, but then I'll put some cream on and it will soothe it.'

Franky made no protest although she felt him flinch as she gently bathed the wound with salt water and cottonwool. She then applied a generous amount of ointment before hurrying away to fetch his pyjama bottoms.

'Here, slip these on,' she told him, looking away as he turned over to do as he was told. When she turned back she was shocked to find him staring at her intently.

'I *HATE* HIM.' The venom in his voice shocked her and for a second she was speechless, but then she hastily told him, 'Oh, I'm sure you don't mean that, dear.'

'I do.' His face was twisted with hatred and a cold finger slid up her spine as he looked her straight in the eye and told her, 'One day, I'm goin' to kill him.'

'Oh, Franky . . .' She went to take him in her arms, but he pushed her away with a strength that astounded her, and his next words stabbed at her heart as he muttered, 'And I hate *you* too. I want my mum. My *real* mum, not you.'

Stumbling blindly, she left the room and once out on the landing, she sagged against the wall and sobbed as if her heart would break.

The letter from Mary Ingles arrived two days later. She would be visiting to see how the placement was going in a week's time. June sighed with resignation, wondering what Francis would tell her and if this might be the end of her first attempt at being a mother.

She informed Franky and Jacob of Mary's visit that evening over dinner, and for once when bath-time arrived, Jacob did nothing more than supervise as Franky washed himself.

'I'm sure you're going to tell your social worker how happy we all are, aren't you, Francis?' he told him as he loomed over the boy.

The child nodded as he glared up at him resentfully.

'Good. After all, we don't want to say anything to anyone that might stop you seeing your other mother again, do we?'

Franky's head wagged from side to side as the shutters came down over his glorious dark eyes, and all the time his hatred of Jacob grew.

'Well, I must say, you're certainly looking well . . . Francis.' Mary Ingles struggled over the child's new name. Of course, quite a few new parents chose to rename their adopted children but after all that Alex, as she had always known him, had gone through, she wondered if this change was such a good idea.

He seemed to be accepting it though, which she supposed was

a good sign, although he was very quiet. Quite unlike the child she had brought here at the end of last year.

Jacob's chest was puffed with pride as his hand rested on Francis's shoulder. 'He's doing really well,' he told her jovially. 'Getting to be quite a little scholar in fact, aren't you, son?'

Francis nodded in agreement as he lowered his head and Mary stared into her tea to stop Jacob seeing the frown that had settled across her face.

'I'm quite surprised to hear that,' she told him coolly. 'The school report I had said that Al . . . Francis was being somewhat disruptive.'

'Oh that.' Jacob waved his hand in the air dismissively. 'Nothing more than boyish pranks. You know what they can be like at this age. And boys will be boys. I should know – my Scouts can cause absolute mayhem when they've a mind to.'

From the corner of her eye, Mary saw June gulp and her worst fears were confirmed. She had intended to make this visit weeks ago but pressure at work, ongoing ill-health and one thing and another had prevented it. Now she wished that she had come sooner. Something wasn't right here. Every instinct she had was telling her so, yet what could she do about it?

Pulling herself together, she said brightly, 'Well, I'm really pleased to hear that you two are happy with how things are going, but I wonder if you would mind very much if I just had a few minutes alone with Francis, so that we could have a little chat? It always helps at this stage to get a feeling for how the child is coping with all the changes that are going on.'

She saw the look of uncertainty flash across Jacob's face and heard June's slight intake of breath, but then they had both composed themselves again as Jacob said cheerily, 'Of course you can. You'll be fine won't you, champ? Don't worry, Mother and I will only be in the kitchen.'

Was that a veiled threat? Mary wondered as the couple slipped from the room. Jacob left the door slightly ajar but Mary crossed to it and closed it before rejoining Francis.

'So, Francis.' She kept her voice light. 'Would you like to tell me how things are going from your point of view?'

Only silence answered her so she prompted, 'Do you like living by the sea? I believe Jacob and June take you on regular walks, don't they?'

Again the silence.

'And is it right what I'm hearing, that you have a dog now?'

At last, Franky nodded and his eyes were almost animated as he looked up to tell her, 'Yes, I do. His name is Bruno an' he's me best mate. Him an' Ginger, that is.'

'Ginger?'

'Yes, he goes to my school, an' sometimes June lets him come for tea.'

'I see, well, that's wonderful then.' The child's head went down again now as Mary studied him intently. He certainly looked well enough. He had filled out and grown taller and his skin was tanned, yet . . . She suddenly realised with a little jolt what it was that was concerning her. It was his eyes. They were guarded and she had the feeling that he was choosing his words carefully. June seemed ill at ease too. She was even jumpier than Mary remembered her being, but then, perhaps she was just terrified that Mary had come to tell them that she was taking Francis away.

'And what about your new name?' she probed gently. 'Are you quite happy with it?'

Franky shrugged as he scraped his toe along the carpet in front of him. He reminded her of a rabbit trapped in a snare that would make a bid for freedom at any second.

'You know, if there was anything worrying you, anything at all, you could talk to me about it.'

His chin drooped even further on to his chest as Mary bit her lip. Was this quiet child before her really the aggressive little imp she had come to know and love? He seemed much older than his six years. Some moments later she sighed heavily. It was more than obvious that Francis wanted to escape so she told him, 'If you're sure there's nothing you want to say, perhaps you could go and ask your mother and father to rejoin us?'

Sliding silently from the settee he hurried away to do as he was told, as alarm bells continued to clang in Mary's head. While he was gone, she looked around the room. It was still immaculately tidy, with nothing of the child's lying about at all. Gazing towards the powder-puff clouds that were moving across the gentian-blue sky outside the open window, she waited for June and Jacob to rejoin her. She would have no option but to say in her report that all seemed well. Courts were not known for wanting to hear of gut instincts.

Chapter Twelve

'That's all three adoptions legalised now then, is it?' Lorna enquired as she flicked her hair across her shoulder. This week it was a vibrant deep burgundy colour, which Mary was still getting used to. The week before it had been golden blond, but then you never knew what Lorna would do next, which was one of the things the older woman liked about her.

'Yes, Alex's – I mean, Francis's – adoption became legal on Friday. I don't think I shall ever get used to calling him that though.'

'It is pretty grotty, isn't it?' Lorna agreed. 'Though just the sort of thing you'd expect Jacob Anderson to come up with. Between you and me, I thought the man was an out-and-out snob.'

'That's as maybe, but that doesn't mean he might not turn out to be a wonderful father.'

'Who are you trying to convince, you or me?' Lorna asked with her head to the side. 'You can't pull the wool over my eyes, Mary. I know you didn't take to the bloke any more than I did.'

'Even so, it's done now and all we can do is hope that . . . er . . . Francis will settle there. Oh, and by the way, have you seen the time? Shouldn't you have been on that training course in Warwick today?'

'Oh, Christ, you're right!' Lorna snatched up her bag. 'I might just about make it if I put my foot down in old Mabel.'

'Never mind about putting your foot down, my girl. That old heap of a Mini you insist on driving around in is only held together

116

with rust, from what I can see of it. You just take your time, do you hear?'

'Yes, Boss,' Lorna shouted over her shoulder as she scooted out of the office.

Alone with her thoughts again, Mary chewed on her pencil as she stared sightlessly from the window. Lorna was right, she hadn't really taken to Jacob and yet there was nothing obvious that she could say against him. Francis was growing at the correct rate and looked well. It was just . . . she tried to pinpoint what was troubling her but could come up with nothing again except for the sad look in the child's eyes. That could well be down to the fact that he was still missing his birth mother. Francis was nearly three years older than the twins so it stood to reason that he could remember more of his past and would take longer to settle than the girls. Added to that was the fact that of all of them, Francis had always been the closest to his mother, especially since the arrival of the twins. She had seen first-hand on her numerous visits to the family, how the little boy would fly into a tantrum if Kay showed any attention to the girls. Mary had formed the opinion that this was caused by Kevin's total indifference to him. Kevin would never have won a 'father of the year' award even from his own little daughters, but he tended to ignore Francis completely because he wasn't his biological father. Mary had tried to address this with Kevin on more than one occasion but the man had just shrugged his shoulders.

Another major concern that Mary had was of how Francis refused to discuss his past at all. She had placed many children for adoption over the years and all of them, with no exception, at Francis's age had retained memories of their previous lives. Francis seemed to have completely shut out his beginnings, apart from his mother, who he was still convinced would come for him, and if anyone asked him where he had come from, he would always bleakly reply, 'Nowhere.' Mary found this fact unutterably sad. He had become 'The boy from nowhere'.

As her thoughts turned back to his siblings a little smile tweaked the corners of her mouth. Now there were two that she had no concerns whatsoever about. On her last visit to Tasha she had been pleasantly shocked to see the change that the little girl's presence had made to Beehive Cottage. It still reeked of olde worlde charm, but now you could see at a glance that a child lived there. Toys and books were scattered everywhere she looked and the child was talking now, albeit haltingly, thanks to her new parents' patience and devotion. The atmosphere in the cottage was cosy and the little girl was thriving. Gail and Joe had bought her a small pony that now grazed happily in the paddock at the back of the cottage, and Tasha spent every moment she could riding her, under the watchful eye of her parents who insisted that animals were therapeutic for her. Mary thought they might be right. Something was certainly bringing the child back from the awful place she had retired to following the last horrendous dive down the stairs.

And then there was Lauren, a real little bundle of mischief now, who seemed to have the whole of her new family wrapped firmly around her little finger. Penny and David were full of the latest addition to the family, and even Heather and Aiden were coming home from university as often as they could to spend time with their new little sister. Lauren had now taken to talking to an old man whom she addressed as Bert, who supposedly lived in the large sumptuously furnished lounge, as well as little Sarah, the playmate she had taken to when first going to live there. Mary had found this quite spooky. In fact, when during her visits, Lauren began to gabble cheerfully away to her new chums, Mary would feel the hairs on the back of her neck stand to attention. But still, whoever she was chatting to certainly wasn't having an adverse effect on the child, so Mary could only assume that there was more to this spirit thing than she had credited, being a disbeliever herself. Lauren now asked endless questions and was proving to be far brighter than her years. She was also showing a remarkable interest in music, and David was only too happy to encourage it.

Beyond the window, a bird was chirping merrily as Mary turned her attention back to the pile of reports waiting to be typed on her desk. It had been over a year now since the children had been placed with their new families, and soon it would be time to close the cases on all three children and leave them to their new lives. Since then, their mother Kay had been sentenced to twelve years in prison for the manslaughter of her partner. Mary supposed she had gotten off lightly under the circumstances, thanks to a psychiatrist who had pleaded her case, saying that the balance of her mind was unhinged due to the fact that she had just lost all three of her children. Twelve years still seemed like an awfully long time though, and what would the poor soul come out to when she had done her time? No home, no family, nothing. Mary sighed as she buried herself in her work and tried to forget her concerns about Francis.

As Franky stared out across the great expanse of sea he smiled. Up here on the top of Baggy Point was fast becoming his favourite place in the world. He was even willing to endure Jacob's company each Sunday afternoon for a drive out to see it. Jacob had begrudgingly allowed Franky to bring Bruno along for some time now and the dog was rolling on the grass, his legs waving delightedly in the air. During the time Franky had lived in Devon he had seen each changing season and he loved them all, for the rugged coastline seemed to find beauty in each one. The spring and summer offered a tumultuous show of wild flowers growing amongst the cracks and crevices on the cliff face that the rock climbers favoured during that time. In the bay, surfers with brightly coloured boards rode the waves, leaving Franky open-mouthed with admiration at their skill and bravery. Then came the autumn when the bright colours of the flowers were replaced by numerous shades of golds and tans. The wind would whistle through the grass, turning it into a neverending undulating carpet of greens, ranging from the brightest to the dullest of hues. And finally it was the winter, which was Franky's favourite time of all. The grass would stand to attention with hoar frost as far as the eye could see, and down below the sea would crash on to the rocks before surging away, only to return with renewed force, as if it was trying to force itself through the high rocky barrier that prevented it from spilling on to dry land.

It was late January and Franky was now seven years old, although anyone who saw him would have taken him for nine or ten at least. Tall and sturdy, Franky was a strikingly attractive child. His hair, which was almost black, was thick and glossy with a tendency to curl, and his eyes were a deep rich brown like the colour of warm treacle, heavily fringed with jet-black lashes that many a woman would have given her eye teeth for. Bath-time no longer held the terror that it once had for him. He was used to it now and had grown adept at shutting his mind off to what was happening.

Now as he rolled on the grass to stroke Bruno's stomach, Jacob commented, 'I think we should be starting back now, Francis. Your mother will want you bathed early tonight as we have friends coming to dinner.'

Franky bit back the comment that had almost escaped from him. Ginger had informed him the week before at school that seeing as he was seven now, he was being allowed to bath himself. Ever since then, Franky had been longing to ask if he too might be allowed to start seeing to his own ablutions, but commonsense told him that now wasn't the time to address it. Far better to wait and ask in front of June, he decided. She just might join forces with him against Jacob. His hatred of the man he was forced to call Father had now swelled to epic proportions. So much so that sometimes he could almost taste it and would have to force himself not to lash out at him. He still looked for his mother every single day, and never for a moment allowed himself to believe that she wouldn't eventually come for him.

Standing, he brushed the grass from the seat of his trousers as Jacob looked on disapprovingly, then calling Bruno to heel he set off down the slope that would lead them back to where the car was parked. They had just climbed the small drystone wall that skirted the car park when Jacob somehow stumbled and fell on to Franky, who went flying in the mud. Thinking that his beloved master was being attacked, Bruno hastily sprang to his defence and before Franky could stop him he sank his sharp teeth into Jacob's leg. Jacob howled as his hand dropped to his leg and Franky watched in horror as blood began to seep through the man's fingers.

'H–he didn't mean it. He thought you was g–goin' to hurt me,' he stuttered as he cuddled Bruno to him.

'The bloody mutt!' Jacob was red-faced with anger. 'That is it! I've just about had enough of that damn spaniel. There is no way in this world I am going to allow you to keep a vicious dog. First thing in the morning, when the vet opens, I'm taking him to have him put to sleep.'

'But he ain't vicious.' Franky was terrified of losing his best friend now. 'You just startled him an' he did it in defence.'

'Don't go making excuses for him. I've told you – he's going and that is final. Now come along. I shall have to drive straight to the hospital and get a tetanus jab now. There's no saying what diseases that mangy creature is carrying.'

'Bruno is clean as a whistle,' Franky stated indignantly as tears stung the back of his startling dark eyes, but his words were whipped away by the wind, unheard by Jacob who was striding ahead of him.

It was a sorry party indeed that arrived home some short time later. Jacob was in a towering rage by now and Franky looked as if the end of the world was nigh. June was standing at the kitchen table busily preparing the evening meal for their guests, and as they trooped in she stood straight and looked in bewilderment from one to the other.

'Whatever is the matter?' she asked.

'That blasted dog you insisted he should have has attacked me,' Jacob told her coldly as he strode to the sink for a damp cloth to place on his wound.

'Bruno attacked you?' June's voice was incredulous. 'But he wouldn't harm anyone.'

'He didn't attack him,' Franky chipped in, one arm protectively about Bruno. 'Father slipped an' fell on me an' Bruno were startled so he turned on him. He didn't mean to bite him.'

'Sit down and let me have a look at it,' June said shortly as she hurried away for the First Aid box. Minutes later, when the wound was clean, she sat back on her heels and declared, 'It isn't that bad, dear. It won't even need a stitch. I think with a little antiseptic cream and a plaster on, it should be as good as new in a couple of days.'

Jacob glared towards Franky and Bruno. 'Even so, I shall be taking him to the vet's first thing tomorrow to have him put to sleep.'

'Oh, Jacob! You can't possibly do that! Franky loves that dog.' It was rarely that June opposed her husband but now she stared at him silently threatening to do battle if need be. She knew how much the child doted on his pet and had no intention of allowing Jacob to go through with his threat.

The man seemed about to argue but then he clamped his mouth firmly shut for a few moments before muttering, 'I think it's time for a bath, don't you? We have visitors due to arrive in less than a couple of hours and at this rate we won't be ready for them, due to that stupid animal. Come along, Francis. We'll talk about this matter more in the morning.'

With a last soulful glance at June, Franky slowly followed the man upstairs. Soon the water was gurgling into the bath and Franky blurted out, 'Ginger's mum lets him bath himself now he's a big boy. Ain't it time I was bathin' meself too?' He had intended to make the request in front of June, but had had no opportunity after the unfortunate incident that had occurred on the way home. And now the words burst from him as if of their own volition.

For a moment he thought that Jacob hadn't heard him, but then he slowly straightened from the bath tub and turned to face the child, his eyes as cold as marble chips.

'Oh, so you think you're a big boy now, do you?'

Franky gulped nervously, feeling very vulnerable standing there naked as Jacob's eyes swept over him.

'*Get in!*' Jacob ordered in a voice that invited no argument, and stumbling in his haste to do as he was told, Franky lowered himself into the steaming water.

'Right, seeing as you think you're such a big chap now I think it's time to show you what big boys and fathers get up to, don't you?'

Franky was trembling with apprehension as Jacob slowly unbuttoned his flies and let his trousers slip to the floor. The familiar bulge that the boy had been forced to stroke more times than he cared to remember was visible through the material of his briefs but now he did something he had never done before as he slowly inched them down his legs and his bulging member pointed towards the child.

'Stroke it,' he ordered.

Franky's head wagged from side to side fearfully. 'I . . . I don't want to,' he whispered in a croak.

'Don't be so silly. You like me to stroke yours, don't you?' Jacob's voice was cajoling now as he closed in on the child and lifted his trembling hand to his private parts. Franky started as he felt the heat of the man. It was one thing to have to stroke him through his underwear, but this was something different entirely.

'There, now *that's* nice, isn't it?' Jacob sighed with pleasure as Franky's small hand curled around him. 'Now just rub up and down, up and down . . . Ah, that's it. Good lad.'

Franky was almost choking on his tears but too terrified to disobey as he did as the man asked and Jacob arched his back and thrust himself ever nearer to the child. And then suddenly the most awful thing happened as the man stiffened and liquid spurted from the end of what Franky had christened 'his willy'.

Dropping his hand away, Franky shuddered with disgust and then to his horror he leaned forward and deposited his undigested meal into the bathwater as he heaved his heart up.

'*Ugh!* You disgusting little creature.' Jacob leaned forward and dragged the child from the bath, dropping him in an undignified heap on the cold bathroom floor. He then flung a towel towards

123

him as he ground out, 'Get yourself cleaned up. Can't you do anything right?' He had pulled his trousers up by now and as Franky wrapped the towel about himself, Jacob shook his head. 'I really don't understand you, boy. Here I am trying to teach you about life and anyone would think I was torturing you. You'll be glad I taught you all about sex when you grow up. Now get yourself dressed and into bed. I don't want to hear another peep out of you tonight. Do you hear me?'

Franky nodded mutely. He had learned a long time ago that there was no point in arguing. Minutes later he snuck down between his cold sheets as tears poured from his eyes. How much longer would it be before his mum came to fetch him? Just wait till she did, he'd tell her all about how cruel Jacob was to him and she'd sort him out big time. His mind ranged back to Bruno and now the sobs increased. What if Jacob really did take him to the vet's in the morning? Life was only bearable because of his dog. It was then that an idea occurred to him and the tears stopped as if by magic. He would run away! Yes, that's what he would do. As soon as it was quiet tonight, after Jacob and June had gone to bed, he would creep down to the kitchen and take Bruno as far away from this place as he could get. Slightly heartened, he snuggled further down in the bed to wait as he plotted his escape.

Chapter Thirteen

Straining his ears in the darkness, Franky listened to Jacob and June saying good night to their dinner guests in the hallway. They were too far away for him to hear exactly what they were saying, but occasionally a snatch of laughter floated up the stairs to him, so he supposed that the evening had gone well. Hopefully they would soon retire to bed now and when all was quiet he would put his plan to run away into action. Outside, a bitterly cold wind was howling and a branch of the large oak tree outside his bedroom window tapped at the glass as if it were trying to get in. Franky's stomach was in a knot of excitement, coupled with fear. The excitement sprang from the fact that he might never have to see Jacob again; never have to endure the horrors he inflicted on him at bath-time. The fear was due to the fact that he had no idea at all where he and Bruno would be going. The world beyond his bedroom window was an enormous place and he didn't have an inkling which direction the home he had shared with his mum was in. Still, there would be time to worry about that once he had got himself and Bruno safely away from here, he reasoned. At least then Bruno would be safe from Jacob's threats, and when he did get home his mum would be waiting for him with her arms wide open and they could all live happily ever after.

He heard the front door close and the sound of a car driving away down the sloping drive, the tyres crunching on the iced surface of the gravel, then the ritual of Jacob going from room to room, turning off the lights and locking doors as he did each night.

No doubt the dirty crockery would be left for Mrs Dickinson to clear away the next morning. June's soft tread sounded on the landing and he squeezed his eyes tight shut in case she should peep in on him as she sometimes did. He heard the footsteps pause outside his bedroom door and held his breath, but then thankfully they continued and he heard her bedroom door click to softly behind her. Soon after he heard a second set of footsteps, muffled by the thick pile of the carpet on the stairs. Again they paused outside his bedroom door and now his heart thudded so loudly with sheer terror that he was afraid Jacob would hear it. But again they moved on and he heard the door further along the landing close. He wondered why Jacob and June chose to sleep in different rooms. His mother and Kevin had always slept together and Ginger had told him that his mother and father had an enormous bed, so why should June and Jacob sleep apart?

Not really caring one way or another, he rolled on to his back and, with his arms behind his head he listened to the sound of the house settling. Soon, he would put his plan into action, but first he would give Jacob and June time to go to sleep. It wouldn't do if they were to catch him trying to escape. He blinked and knuckled the sleep from his eyes, swallowing an enormous yawn. It had been a long day and now he was struggling to stay awake. In fact, he was tempted to curl up and go to sleep beneath the warm blankets, but knew that if he did, it might mean losing Bruno for ever and the thought of that was more than he could bear.

The time ticked on, each minute seeming like an hour to his young mind. There was nothing to be heard now but the sound of an owl hooting in the tree outside and the waves crashing on the beach in the distance. Hesitantly he dragged himself to the edge of the bed and listened, then certain that all was quiet he struggled into the clothes he had laid ready in the bottom of his wardrobe in the darkness. At the door he turned to glance briefly at the room he hoped he would never see again. It was deep in shadow, save for the pool of silver moonlight on the carpet beyond the window.

Inching the door open he glanced up and down the dark landing and only when he was sure that all was quiet did he tiptoe towards the staircase. During the time that he had lived there he had often crept down these very stairs to eavesdrop on June and Jacob in the hope that he would learn when his mother was coming for him. Each time he had been sadly disappointed but now that experience stood him in good stead. He knew every single stair that creaked and he avoided each one like the plague as he crept on with his heart in his mouth. The descent seemed to take for ever but at last he was in the kitchen and he let out a sigh of relief as Bruno padded out of his basket to greet him with his tail wagging furiously.

'Ssh,' Franky whispered, placing a warning finger to his lips. 'If you make a noise Jacob'll be down here faster than a shot from a gun an' then I won't be able to keep you safe.'

Bruno sat back on his haunches, staring up at his master from trusting eyes as Franky retrieved his shiny black Wellington boots and his warm duffel coat and woolly hat from the corner of the kitchen. Once he was muffled up he collected Bruno's lead then crept towards the kitchen door where he slowly turned the key in the lock. Every second he expected to feel Jacob's firm hand on his shoulder and he began to sweat despite the bitterly cold air that met him as he quietly opened the door. And then at last they were outside and he trod on the grass that bordered the drive, afraid to walk on the gravel in case Jacob might hear him.

Within minutes he was standing on the deserted road looking this way and that as he wondered which way to go. It was strange being out in the dark. Everywhere looked different and was strangely frightening. Even so, wild horses would not have dragged him back. To return might mean losing Bruno, so squaring his shoulders he set off resolutely, keeping a careful eye out for any cars that might pass. Thankfully, he saw only one on his way down into the village and he hopped behind a hedge dragging Bruno with him until it was safely past and its tail-lights had disappeared into the distance.

'That were a close call, weren't it, boy?' His eyes swept up and down the road as he stepped out again. He had no way of knowing what time it was but he correctly guessed that it must be very late, for most of the houses they passed were in darkness, their windows staring out into the night like great dark eyes.

'Which way do we go now?' he mumbled to himself when at last he came to the coastal path. He was shivering already and as he stood there he stamped his feet to keep them warm. A thin drizzle had begun to fall and the raindrops stung his cheeks. When a sudden gust of wind snatched his hat from his head his unruly mop of thick hair immediately began to whip about his head.

'Come on, let's go the way we know, eh?' he suggested to his friend, and with the dog keeping close to his heels they began the long walk to his favourite part of the cliffs. They hadn't even reached the top before Franky's eyes were starting from his head with terror and he was breathless and nervy. The familiar path looked nothing like it did in the daylight. There were any number of potholes just waiting to trip him up, and the wind howling through the leafless trees in his path could have been the souls of lost spirits wailing. Also, the rustlings and cries of night creatures, which sounded dangerously close, had him glancing about him in fear. What's more, he was terrified of falling from the edge of the cliff. It was difficult to see where he was going as the moon was hidden behind the banks of jet-black clouds that were scudding across the sky.

'We'll be all right,' he said aloud, more to convince himself than his companion, and they trudged cautiously on, growing colder and more miserable by the minute. He wished it was earlier in the year, when the gypsies had been camped there. They would have helped him, he was sure. On a few occasions he and Ginger had ventured near to their camp during the summer, and Franky had been entranced by it all. Huge dogs roamed freely about the brightly coloured vans, and large fires with cooking pots dangling over them sent lazy streams of smoke up into the cloudless blue sky. Children in ill-assorted clothes had shouted a greeting and Franky's young imagination had been fired as he wished with all his heart that he could join them on their travels. But it was no use wishing now; the gypsies would no doubt be cosy in their winter camps somewhere.

By now the drizzle had turned into a downpour and Franky could feel the rain spilling over the back of his coat collar and snaking down his back like icy fingers. When a farm came into view some short time later, he paused. He was soaked to the skin and his hands were blue with cold by now.

'How about we go an' kip in the barn?' he said to the dog. 'There ain't no way Jacob would think o' lookin' for us in there, an' then first thing in the mornin' we can be off again. We'll probably be miles away by the time they even realise we're missin'.'

Bruno looked up at him miserably before shaking himself vigorously. Seeing his pet's dejected expression, Franky climbed the farm gate as Bruno wriggled on his belly beneath it and cautiously approached the barn. Thankfully, the farmer had allowed the farm dog to sleep in the kitchen tonight and so they went on their way undetected. Once at the barn, Franky glanced over his shoulder before pushing the door open. It squeaked alarmingly but the sound of the wind masked the noise, and soon he and Bruno were out of the rain at least although it was still bitterly cold in there.

'Look, there are some bales o' hay over there. We could sleep on them.' Franky felt his way through the shadows to the corner of the barn where he collapsed into the straw, exhausted, as Bruno cowered against him, shivering. 'Snuggle up to me an' we'll soon get warm,' Franky whispered into the dog's ear as he wrapped his arms protectively about him. There was a grimy window above them through which a grey light was just managing to penetrate. The whole place smelled of cows and was damp and musty, but the way Franky saw it, at least they had some protection here from the storm raging outside. He determined to stay awake until first light when he would be on his way, but he was only a little boy and he'd had a very long day. Within minutes he was fast asleep with Bruno lying protectively at the side of him, his ears pricked as he nervously watched the rats dragging their fat tails through the thick dust on the floor around them.

The faraway sound of voices penetrated Franky's consciousness and he struggled to awake early the next morning, only to find a small crowd of people huddled around him.

Blinking rapidly, he stiffly pushed himself up on to his elbow and stared up straight into Jacob's face. The man's lips were set in a grim line but when he spoke his voice was reasonable.

'So, this is where you got to, eh?' He turned to smile disarmingly at a young Police Constable who was standing at his side. 'Kids, eh?' he said jokingly, then turning to Franky again he told him, 'You've had us in a right old quandary. Your mother is beside herself with worry. What made you run off like that?'

Sick with disappointment that he had been found so soon, Franky blinked to hold back his tears. 'Y-you said you was goin' to have Bruno put to sleep,' he muttered resentfully. He felt cold and wretched, and a dull headache was throbbing behind his eyes.

The officer looked at Jacob questioningly, and now Jacob took his elbow and drew him to one side where the two men had a muttered conversation. Franky strained to hear what they were saying but only the odd word reached him: '*vicious . . . unpredictable . . .*'

He saw the young officer raise his eyebrows as he listened to Jacob and look towards where Bruno was cowering against his young master. The dog certainly showed no signs of being vicious from what he could see of it, but then he supposed he would have to take the man's word for it.

Franky's attention was interrupted when the old farmer, who was looking down at him wringing his cap in his hands said quietly, 'It's a good job I spotted you there, lad. I recognised you from the times I've seen you walk past on a Sunday, and when I rang the police, your parents had just reported you missing, so I put two and two together. Lord knows what would have happened to you, had you wandered about and slept rough in this weather for long. It's no good for neither man nor beast, to be roaming about out there. The best thing you could do is go back home with your dad now and not try this stunt again.'

Franky glared at him as Jacob and the police officer now came to stand beside him again.

'Right then, young man,' the police officer said sternly. 'This time all's well that ends well, but things could have turned out very differently if you'd gone over the edge of the cliff in the dark. Had that happened, we would have had the coastguard out scouring the coast for a body. I suggest you get yourself off home with your father and behave yourself. We have better things to do with our time than spend it looking for runaways that go off for no good reason.'

Franky struggled to his feet. He felt achy and hot despite the chilly morning air that was blowing in through the open barn door.

The farmer, who was a kindly man, watched him go with a perplexed frown on his face. The poor little chap looked as if he had the weight of the world on his shoulders and there was something about his dad that he hadn't taken to. He seemed like a right smarmy sod, but still, it was nothing to do with him so he turned his attention to the chores that were waiting to be done as the uninvited visitors stepped out into the overcast morning.

Standing at the side of the police car in the farmyard, Jacob shook the officer's hand firmly. 'Thank you for your time,' he told him with a false smile fixed to his lips. 'I trust this will be the end of the matter?'

'Certainly from our side it will be,' the young officer replied. 'Just try and keep a tighter rein on our laddo here in future, eh?'

'Yes, Constable, of course, and I'm so sorry to have wasted your time. I assure you Francis won't be trying this trick again in a hurry, will you, Francis?'

Franky shuffled from foot to foot as he shook his head resentfully, and then the officer got into his car and drove away as Jacob took him by the hand and yanked him towards the farm gate.

The instant they were alone, Jacob's manner changed completely and Franky could feel him quivering with rage. 'Just what the *hell* did you think you were doing?' the big man ranted as he dragged Franky along behind him.

'I . . . I were scared what you'd do to Bruno,' Franky whispered through his tears. 'So I thought I'd take him somewhere safe where you couldn't hurt him.'

'Huh! Seems to me you care more for that damn mutt than you do for me and your mother,' Jacob told him grimly. 'And after all we've done for you as well! Private school, elocution lessons, though I'm beginning to think I'm throwing good money after bad there. You were nothing when you came to us, do you hear me? NOTHING! You came from the lowest of the low and a squalid council flat, and yet still you *continually* go against us and try to upset us.'

'Me mam *weren't* the lowest o' the low!' Franky shot back. 'Me mam were good an' kind, an' when she comes for me I'll tell her about the horrible things you do to me at bath-time.'

Jacob yanked him to a halt and shook him so roughly that the child thought his head was going to bounce off his shoulders. The man ground his teeth together before saying in an ominously low voice, 'If you tell *anyone* – and I mean *anyone* – about what you and I do, she will *never* come for you. I guarantee that. I shall tell people you made me do it, and who do you think they'll believe, eh?'

Franky's shoulders sagged as the truth of what the man was saying sank in. Jacob was right. No one would believe him; they would think it was all his fault.

Bruno was snapping at Jacob's heels in defence of Franky, and now Jacob raised his leg and kicked him so hard in the side that the animal yelped with pain and rolled a good two feet on the sodden frozen ground.

'You've hurt him now, you great bully!' Franky cried pluckily, desperately struggling to release his cold hand from Jacob's, but his strength was no match for the man's and he jerked him on his way to the car as Bruno rose and limped behind them with his head down and his tail between his legs.

The journey home seemed to take for ever. June was waiting at the door for them and she almost sobbed with relief when she saw Franky.

'Oh, thank God,' she cried as she ran down the steps to meet them. 'Are you all right?'

'Of course he's all right,' Jacob snapped furiously. 'It's me you should feel sorry for, having to go off on a wild-goose chase like that. It's time this young man was taught a lesson he won't forget. He's totally wilful and disobedient despite all our attempts to—'

'Not now, Jacob,' June uncharacteristically interrupted him as she laid her cool hand on Franky's forehead. 'He's burning up, yet shivering at the same time. I think we ought to phone for the doctor.'

'Huh! It's not a doctor he needs but a damn good hiding,' Jacob snorted.

Ignoring him, June took Franky's clammy hand and led him inside. The second they were through the door, Bruno slunk towards the kitchen where Mrs Dickinson, who had just arrived, immediately began to dry him with a warm towel. Like Franky, she was fond of the dog and was alarmed to see the swelling on his side.

'What's happened to you then?' she asked soothingly as the trembling animal leaned against her. 'Yer look like you've been in the wars rare an' proper. Never mind, yer home now an' we'll soon have yer bright as a button again.'

It was at that moment that June led Franky past the open door and she frowned as she saw the child's flushed cheeks and overly bright eyes.

'You'd best get the doctor out by the look o' him,' she remarked, but then a glare from Jacob silenced her as he followed his wife. She chewed her lip as Franky gazed at her imploringly.

Poor little poppet, she found herself thinking. Fancy havin' to get landed with a dad like that great oaf.

She had never been a lover of June's husband but lately her dislike had turned to hatred. From where she was standing he was little more than an overgrown bully, happy to pick on people smaller and more vulnerable than himself. But that wasn't the worst of it. Only the day before she had stood in the post office and overheard Gwen Bassett from the fishmongers and Cissie Lamb from the pub whispering animatedly with their heads together.

'So what's to do then?' she had interrupted blatantly, never being one to like being left out of a juicy bit of gossip.

Cissie had immediately included her in the conversation as she told her, 'Well, it's nothing really. Except Mary and Bob from the fish and chip shop have stopped their Darren from goin' to Scouts any more because o' him you work for.'

'Jacob?' Mrs Dickinson enquired. 'An' why's that then?'

'That's the thing . . . nobody seems to know, but Mary's keepin' him right away an' says fer as long as Jacob Anderson is Scoutmaster he'll not be goin' there again. Have you heard anythin'?'

'Not a dicky bird,' Mrs Dickinson answered truthfully. 'Fer as long as I've known the bloke he's always seemed right taken with the lads. In fact, that's half the trouble up there if you was to ask me. He spends more bloody time with his Scouts than he does with his missus.'

'It's funny when you come to think of it, that he ain't let that lad they've adopted join in the group, ain't it?'

Mrs Dickinson nodded thoughtfully. She had thought much the same but had never broached the subject to June, feeling it wasn't her place.

Now as she watched the sorry little procession troop up the stairs the conversation came to mind again. It was Bruno rubbing against her that brought her thoughts back to the present, and after stroking him gently she sighed before hurrying off to get him something to eat.

Once upstairs, it was June who led Franky to the bathroom, this time with no protest from Jacob, who had stamped off to his room at the end of the long hallway. She helped the boy undress before encouraging him into the water she had run for him. As he turned his back on her she was appalled to see the red marks on his backside still visible from Jacob's last chastising. Even so she kept up a constant chatter as she gently washed his hair and soothed him.

'I think the best thing we can do for you is get you tucked up all nice and warm in bed,' she told him. 'Then I'll go down and get Mrs Dickinson to warm up some of her chicken soup for you, eh?'

Franky sagged against the back of the bath, his eyes locked with hers. 'Will you make sure Bruno is all right an' all? What I mean is, you won't let Jacob take him to the vet's, will you?'

'No, I won't.' June's face set. So that was what this had been all about. The poor child must have been terrified that Jacob was going to carry out his threat and have Bruno put to sleep. So much so that he had actually resorted to running away to prevent it.

'Bruno will be staying right here with us,' she told him with a note of determination in her voice and for the first time since he had lived there, Franky felt himself warming to her a little.

'An' . . . an' now that I'm a big boy, can I start bathin' meself?' Franky felt that whilst June was on his side he might as well air all his troubles.

'But I thought you enjoyed the time you and your father spent together,' she remarked, not really believing a word of it. The closed look settled on his face again so she hastily told him, 'I shall certainly address it with him if you think you're big enough to manage on your own, but now let's get you out of the bath and into some nice warm pyjamas. There'll be time to worry about everything else when we've got that temperature of yours down.'

Franky allowed her to help him out of the bath and wrap him in a warm towel and in no time at all he was tucked into bed.

'That's better,' June commented approvingly as she gently wiped a lock of dark hair from his forehead. He looked very small and vulnerable lying there and she vowed to herself that from now on she would stand up to Jacob more on his behalf, whatever the consequences. 'Now you just lie there and relax while I go and see how Bruno is and get you something to eat.'

Franky settled back against his pillows contentedly. June had promised she would look out for Bruno and somehow he believed her. She might even be able to wangle it that he bathed alone from now on. Closing his eyes, he allowed himself to drift off to sleep and for the first time since he had lived there his dreams were happy ones. He could see his mother walking up the drive to collect him, and knew that soon he would be far away with her and Bruno, and he could forget all about the time he had spent here.

Chapter Fourteen

Later that day the sound of raised voices coming from Jacob's study below woke Franky. Glancing towards the window, he was surprised to see that the sky was darkening and he realised with a little shock that he must have slept for most of the day. His mouth felt dry and he ached in every limb, so after pulling himself to the edge of the bed he slipped off it and padded barefoot towards the door. As he cautiously crept down the stairs he saw that Mrs Dickinson's coat had gone from the coat rack in the hall and made towards the kitchen. Bruno instantly rose to greet him and as Franky stroked him, his mouth set in grim lines as he felt the swelling on the dog's side.

'Great bloody bully,' he muttered as he cuddled the dog to him. 'But don't worry, boy. June's gonna look out fer you now so things will be OK.'

It was at that instant that he heard the study door slam and the sound of footsteps heading towards the kitchen and he froze. Thankfully, it was June that appeared in the doorway some moments later and a look of surprise crossed her face as she saw Franky kneeling by the dog.

'How long have you been up?' she asked. Her eyes were red and Franky noticed that she was visibly shaking as he replied, 'Not long. I heard you two arguin' in the study so I came down to get a drink.'

'Right, and I dare say something to eat wouldn't go amiss either,' she said, ignoring his comment. 'You were fast asleep when I brought up a tray this morning so you must be ravenous.' In no time at all he was seated at the table with a big dish of chicken soup in front of him and two thick slices of Mrs Dickinson's delicious homemade bread.

June sighed with relief when she felt the boy's forehead and found that his temperature had dropped, then she busied herself about the kitchen as he cleared his plate in record time. Jacob had marched past the open doorway without a word and slammed the front door resoundingly behind him as he left the house.

'He's er . . . off to a Scouts' meeting,' June informed Franky when she felt his questioning eyes on her. 'And don't worry about Bruno any more. I've told your father quite clearly that he'll be staying, so that should be the end of that.'

As Franky let out an enormous sigh of relief and smiled, he looked totally transformed, and June determined there and then that in the future she would ensure he had more to smile about.

She kept him off school the next day, just to be on the safe side, but on Tuesday they set off on the school run as usual.

'I'm going into Barnstaple to do some shopping when I've dropped you off,' June informed him cheerfully. 'I can't remember when I last treated myself to a new outfit and while I'm there I'll get you some new school trousers too. I really don't know how you manage to go through the knees of them as you do.'

Franky smiled. Things were looking up. The night before, he had been allowed to go into the bath on his own and the lump on Bruno's side was going down, so everything was better than it ever had been at the minute.

'Have a good day,' June told him brightly as he clambered out of the car at the school gates, and for the first time he waved goodbye to her as she drove away, making her heart do a happy little somersault in her chest.

Back at the house, Mrs Dickinson tapped lightly at the study door. Jacob was working at home today as he sometimes did, and as it was approaching eleven o'clock she had no doubt he would be ready for his morning coffee.

'Come in,' a voice commanded, and balancing the tray on one hand she pushed the door open with the other.

'Put it there,' he told her abruptly, nodding towards the edge of the desk.

Hmm, she thought, it's a pity he don't practise the same manners as he knocks into his pupils.

Jacob was busily marking papers, so she said nothing until she got back to the door where she paused to ask, 'What time will yer be wantin' yer lunch?'

'What? Oh, er . . . don't worry about anything for me. I have to go out shortly and I'll get something while I'm out.'

'Have it yer own way,' she muttered, closing the door between them and she then disappeared upstairs to strip the sheets from the bed. It was as she was coming down again some short time later with her arms full of dirty linen that she heard the sound of the back door closing, which she found quite unusual. Jacob rarely ventured into the kitchen, let alone went out that way. Still, it was his house so she supposed it was up to him how he chose to come and go.

She was filling the twin tub washing machine with a pipe at the sink when she suddenly realised that Bruno wasn't in his basket.

'Lordie, I hope he ain't gone rampagin' about the house,' she said to herself. 'That would really get the boss's hackles up, if he were to find dog hairs about the place.' Quickly turning the tap off she hurried into the hallway where she called, 'Bruno, where are yer, boy? Get back here afore yer find yerself in any more bother.'

As she glanced towards the hall window she saw Jacob closing the back door of his car and she frowned, puzzled. In the kitchen she noticed that Bruno's lead was missing from the hook by the door, and a sinking feeling started up in the pit of her stomach. She then methodically searched the house from top to bottom, even venturing into Jacob's bedroom and his study, but there was no sign of the dog anywhere. Next she put her coat on and hurried out into the garden where she called his name until her voice was hoarse. Still there was no sign of him, so eventually she gave up her search and went back to the pile of laundry that was waiting for her, her mind troubled. It wasn't like the spaniel to go off, and it was strange that his lead was missing. But then Franky had probably forgotten to put his lead back in the right place and if Bruno had ventured out on his own he'd be back soon enough when he was hungry. Lifting a dirty sheet, she dunked it into the soapy water with long wooden tongs, and for the next couple of hours she was so busy that she had no time to think of anything but the job she was doing.

It was almost three o'clock by the time Mrs Dickinson had finished her household chores. All the beds were freshly made up with clean linen, even the spare bed that Jacob seemed to sleep in all the while now, which she found very strange. The way she saw it, a husband and wife should sleep together, but then she was an old-fashioned sort and was aware that times were changing. If truth were told, Miss June might be glad to escape Jacob's company at bedtime. She herself wouldn't have wanted to have him pawing over her. The house smelled of furniture polish and, gathering the dusters together, she looked round with satisfaction at the lounge, which was so clean it looked almost unlived in, just as Jacob liked it.

I'd better get a start made on the dinner, she thought to herself as she headed towards the doorway. In the hall she paused when she saw Jacob's car parked on the drive. She hadn't heard him come back, but then she had been so busy that she hadn't really had much time to notice anything. She hurried back to the kitchen and headed straight for the back door, hoping for a sign of Bruno, but once again she was sadly disappointed. As she prepared a joint of lamb for the oven she sighed. Young Franky would be home from school in no time and he'd be heartbroken if his pal wasn't back in his basket by then.

Half an hour later she heard Miss June's car pull on to the drive and, just as she had expected, Franky entered the kitchen within minutes and flung his school satchel on to the chair, asking, 'Where's Bruno?'

'I have no idea, love.' Mrs Dickinson's eyes darted about nervously. 'I noticed he were gone this mornin' an' I looked high an' low fer him. I even went out into the garden an' called him till me lungs were fit to burstin', but there weren't no sign o' him. I thought Jacob might have taken him out as his lead were missin', but he's been back fer some time an' Bruno weren't with him.'

'What do you mean, his lead was missing? It's there on the hook – look – where I always keep it.'

As the woman's eyes followed his she saw that he was right and she chewed on her lip in consternation. The lead had been missing; she would have staked her life on it, so how could it miraculously have reappeared? There had only been her and Jacob in the house all day. The same thought occurred to them both at once and Franky turned abruptly, almost colliding with June who was just entering the kitchen with a wide smile on her face and loaded down with shopping bags.

'Whoa there.' Dropping some bags she reached out to stop Franky. 'What's the rush? Is there a fire somewhere?'

Seeing the look on his face the smile instantly died, and turning towards Mrs Dickinson she kept a tight hold of Franky's arm as she asked, 'What's wrong?'

'It's Bruno. He's gone missin',' Mrs Dickinson replied tremulously. 'As I just told Franky, he were here when I came into work but then a while later I noticed him an' his lead were gone.'

'Did you leave the back door open?' June questioned her.

'What? On a day like this? You must be jokin'.' Mrs Dickinson glanced towards the window, spreading her hands. 'It's enough to freeze yer socks off out there. Why would I do a daft thing like that? An' even if I had, Bruno ain't never been one fer wanderin' off.'

'Then there must be some perfectly logical explanation for where he's gone. Dogs don't just disappear into thin air,' June stated matter-of-factly.

'It's *him*. He's done somethin' to Bruno. He said he would, an' he must have put the lead back when he got home,' Franky gabbled as panic gripped him.

'If by *him* you mean Jacob, then I'm sure you're wrong. And as for the lead, perhaps Mrs Dickinson was mistaken about it being missing.' June was still clinging to the child's arm as she tried to calm him. 'Jacob has been working at home all day. He hasn't been out, has he, Mrs Dickinson?'

'Well, as a matter o' fact, he *did* go out this mornin'. I ain't completely lost all me marbles yet, yer know?'

'An' is that when you noticed Bruno's lead were missin'?' Franky asked with a note of desperation in his voice.

Mrs Dickinson hesitated before answering. It had been then that she had noticed both Bruno and his lead were gone, but if she told them that now, the balloon was likely to go up big time, so what was she to do? Deciding that honestly was the best policy she nodded miserably and now tears sprang to Franky's eyes as he turned on June.

'See? It were him as took him. It must have been. There ain't been nobody else here if you've been shoppin' all day, has there?'

June's face set and pushing Franky gently towards Mrs Dickinson she said, 'Keep him in here with you while I go and have a word with Jacob, would you?'

The older woman nodded as she pressed Franky down on to the nearest hard-backed kitchen chair as June swept from the room like a ship in full sail. It was nice to see her being assertive for a change instead of bowing down to that husband of hers' commands all the while. And long may it continue, she thought as she hurried away to fetch Franky a glass of milk. If that arrogant bastard had harmed so much as a single hair of that dog's head she'd do for him herself, so help her.

The sound of heated voices came from the direction of Jacob's study and Franky and Mrs Dickinson exchanged a worried glance. Shortly afterwards, a door slammed shut and June marched back into the kitchen, her cheeks flushed and her eyes shining with temper.

'Jacob denies even setting eyes on Bruno today,' she told them. 'So I think the best thing we could do is get our warm clothes on and go out there and look for him.'

Minutes later, June was ready for the outdoors decked out in Wellington boots and an unbecoming waterproof coat that looked at least three sizes too big for her. Franky had never seen her dressed in anything other than her sedate twinsets and pearls before and under different circumstances might have found the sight highly amusing, but as it was, all he could think of was Bruno, so he took her hand and they set off together into the fast-darkening afternoon, leaving Mrs Dickinson to chew her nails and fret.

They took the local route up to the cliffs, constantly calling Bruno as they went, but the wind snatched their voices away, as did the angry waves crashing on the rocks far below. The lights in Puddlesea village twinkled in the gloom behind them, and Franky began to shiver with frustration and fear. Where could Bruno be?

Eventually, the lights of the village were far distant and June pulled Franky to a stop, as she tried to catch her breath.

'It's no good, we can't go any farther,' she informed him, having to shout to make herself heard above the howling wind. 'It's too dangerous to go on. The path narrows and one good gust of wind could have us over the edge of the cliff. Come on, dear, we'll start back.'

Franky opened his mouth to protest, but then seeing the sense in what she said he allowed her to turn him about. They picked their way precariously by the dim light of the torch that June had thought to bring with her, until at last the lights of Puddlesea shone once more through the darkness. They were down in the village heading for home when June suddenly stopped outside the veterinary surgery.

'Wait there – and *don't* move,' she told Franky as she stepped through the door and closed it firmly behind her. Stamping his feet to try and get warm, Franky gazed through the glass door to where

June was talking to the receptionist at the desk. The two women had a muttered conversation then he watched as the woman pulled a large book towards her and ran her finger down the page. She nodded before saying something to June and he saw June's hand fly to her mouth. She suddenly spun about and once she had joined him again he saw that her face was set in angry lines.

'What's wrong?' There was an icy finger running up and down his spine as a bad feeling settled about him like a cloak.

'N-nothing,' she stuttered. 'Come on, let's get home.'

Franky tramped along at the side of her, his short legs having to go like pistons to keep up with her. Something seemed to have given her renewed energy and she didn't slow her steps until they were safely inside the hallway of the house where she instructed him grimly, 'Get yourself off to the kitchen and don't come out until I tell you.' Then, flicking her wet hair out of her eyes, she stamped towards Jacob's study still in her wet boots leaving a trail of water and mud all along the hallway.

Franky slunk off dejectedly and the instant he entered the room, Mrs Dickinson asked, 'Well, did yer find him?'

As he shook his head, biting back tears, the woman's heart went out to him. It were a damn shame from where she were standing. The poor child hadn't known a happy moment since steppin' into this bloody place – apart from the times he'd spent with Bruno, from what she could see of it. She opened her mouth to speak but just then what sounded like a furious row erupted in the study and they both looked towards it.

Before she could stop him, Franky strode towards the door. 'Where are yer goin'?' Mrs Dickinson asked in a panic.

'I'm goin' to find out what's happened to my Bruno 'cos I reckon that's what they're arguin' about,' Franky shot over his shoulder.

'No, stay here,' she implored, but her words fell on deaf ears. Franky was already striding down the hallway.

Once outside the study he listened unashamedly to the dispute going on, on the other side of the door.

'So why don't you tell me exactly what you've done with Bruno?' This was from June.

'How many times do I have to say it? I have no idea whatsoever where the damn mutt has gone,' Jacob replied.

There was a silence then that seemed to stretch for ever until June said: 'I just happen to know differently, Jacob. I called into the vet's on my way home and Mrs Burrows the receptionist informed me that you took Bruno there earlier today. That's why his lead so miraculously disappeared and reappeared, isn't it? You brought his lead back with you and thought that Mrs Dickinson wouldn't notice that it had been missing, *didn't you?*'

Franky's hands clenched into fists and his eyes darkened to the colour of coal as he held his breath and waited for Jacob's reply, and then at last it came.

'So what if I did? The blasted dog was nothing but a nuisance and vicious into the bargain. I had no choice but to do what needed to be done. What if he'd attacked one of Francis's friends while he was here? What would we have done then, eh?'

'You know as well as I do that the poor beast was as soft as a lamb,' June told her husband in an ominously quiet voice. 'To do that . . . euthanasia . . . why, I can't believe that you'd sink so low.'

Euthanasia . . . the word rolled round and round in Franky's head. What did it mean and why was Bruno still at the vet's? Unable to bear to listen for a second longer and desperate for answers, Franky threw the door open and flew at Jacob, his small fists pummelling his stomach.

'*Where is he?*' he screamed as June hurried across to try and contain him. 'What's euthanasia an' why did you leave him at the vet's? He'll be frightened there. I want him home right now!'

Jacob's lip curled scornfully as he looked down on the boy, who June was struggling to hold at arm's length. 'That would be rather difficult,' he told him with a measure of satisfaction. 'Euthanasia is a lethal injection that puts dogs to sleep. Do you understand what I'm saying? Bruno is dead – and good riddance.

Perhaps now the damn pest is gone you'll concentrate more on your schoolwork.'

The colour drained from Franky's face as his hands suddenly dropped to his side and he stared at Jacob in disbelief. 'Y-you mean my Bruno won't be comin' home? You've *killed* him?'

'Oh, don't be so melodramatic,' Jacob said scathingly. 'At least now the place won't stink of dog the second we set foot through the door.'

He was silenced by the look on Franky's face. The child looked as if he had turned to stone but his eyes were black with a hatred that could almost be felt.

'I'll never forgive you for this,' he said, his voice barely a whisper. 'Bruno were me best friend in the whole world an' you've taken him away from me, but I'll pay you back 'cos I'm goin' to *kill* you, you just see if I don't.'

'Franky!' June was visibly shocked by the venom in the boy's voice and she tried to take him into her arms, but he pushed her away so violently that she almost toppled over.

'*Get off me!*' He lashed out with every ounce of strength he had, and had June not managed to lean back in time she had no doubt that the blow would have downed her.

'*I hate you! Do you hear me? I hate the pair o' you, an' soon you'll be sorry for what you've done.*' And with that he stumbled blindly from the room straight into the waiting arms of Mrs Dickinson who had come to stand in the hall and had heard every single word that had been said.

'Oh, lovie.' Her voice broke as she tried to gather Franky to her but he pushed her aside and fled up the stairs as tears gushed from his eyes.

She watched him go helplessly, knowing in that moment that nothing she could say would lessen his pain and hating Jacob almost as much as the child did. How could he have done such a wicked thing? Bruno had been a grand dog, a gentle soul who had wormed his way into her heart without her even realising it. She would miss him, but she knew her feeling of loss would be nothing compared to how Franky would feel. The boy had adored him and the two of them had been inseparable. It was then that the row in the study erupted again and she turned and hurried back to the kitchen with a sick feeling of foreboding in her stomach. What was it Franky had said? *I'm goin' to kill you*, that was it. And after seeing his face just now, she believed he might just be capable of carrying out his threat.

Chapter Fifteen

It was the evening following Bruno's death and Franky was still resolutely refusing to come out of his room. The storm of tears had subsided now and he simply stood for hour after hour by his bedroom window gazing out across the garden towards the sea.

As evening approached, Jacob strode into his room and told him harshly, 'It's time for your bath, Francis. Come along. I think we've had quite enough of this nonsense now.'

The look that the child turned on him was full of such sheer loathing that June, who was close behind her husband, blanched.

'I'm a big boy now. I can bath meself,' Franky told him shortly, with no effort at showing any respect.

Jacob opened his mouth to object, but thankfully June came to his defence. 'He's quite right, Jacob. If he needs any help he can shout for us.'

Jacob was used to being obeyed and his hands clenched into fists as he turned his wrath on his wife. 'Oh, I see. It's two against one now, is it?'

'Don't be so ridiculous.' She stood straight as she glared back at him. 'If he says he can manage on his own then I think we should let him. You accuse me of pampering him yet you insist on treating him as if he's a two year old.'

For a terrible moment she thought that Jacob was going to hit her as his eyes flashed fire, but then thankfully he turned on his heel and as he strode towards the bedroom door he threw across his shoulder, 'I shall be going out shortly. Expect me when you see me.'

Relief washed over her in waves. The way she was feeling at present he needn't come back at all if he didn't wish to. In fact, she secretly hoped that he wouldn't. The house felt strangely empty without Bruno to greet her each time she entered the kitchen and if she was feeling his loss she could only begin to imagine what Franky's emotions must be.

'How about I make you a tray up?' she asked kindly, now that they were alone.

Franky turned his back on her as he continued his vigil at the window. 'I ain't hungry!'

June sighed, feeling utterly helpless. 'All right then. I'll go and run your bath for you and perhaps you can have something a little later when you feel hungry?' she suggested hopefully.

Hovering by the door she waited for a reply and when none was forthcoming she eventually turned and trudged from the room with her chin on her chest.

Franky stirred in the darkness. He had no idea what time it was although he could see the moon riding high in a black velvet sky beyond his bedroom window. He had watched the darkness fall from that very window until sheer exhaustion had made him pad across to his bed where he had eventually fallen into a restless doze. Now he grimaced, his cheeks felt stiff where the tears had dried on them and his mouth was dry. But it wasn't that which had woken him, he was sure of it. It was something else. Some noise . . . Glancing about the shadowy room he started when his eyes settled on the outline of a large shape looming over him at the side of the bed. 'What the—' he began, but a strong hand clamped across his mouth, shutting off his words.

'Be quiet!'

Terror flooded through Franky's veins like iced water as he

recognised Jacob's voice. But what was he doing here? He knew that it must be very, very late because he had heard June retire to bed hours ago and Jacob had never entered his room at night before. Perhaps he's come into the wrong room by mistake in the dark, he comforted himself.

That notion was quashed within seconds when Jacob muttered, 'Move over. I want to get in with you.'

'*W-what?*'

'You heard! Now do as you're told else I'll make you wish you'd never been born.'

Franky felt the blankets lift from about him and then suddenly Jacob was lying so close that the child could feel his breath fanning his cheek. But that wasn't the worst of it: Jacob was completely naked and now Franky began to tremble.

'If you won't let me bath you any more we'll have to take our pleasure in here, won't we?' Jacob muttered. He pulled Franky's pyjama bottoms off with a single tug and his large hand fell on Jacob's small member. It was then that the strangest thing happened, for suddenly his small penis stood to attention as if it had a life of its own and Jacob groaned triumphantly.

'There! *Now* I believe you when you say you're a big boy,' Jacob muttered as his hand stroked relentlessly up and down. Franky was so terrified that he was rendered temporarily speechless. What was happening to him? Did he have some sort of disease that had affected him down below? While these frightening thoughts were running through his head he lay rigid but then as Jacob started to pant he began to struggle.

'I . . . I don't like it. Stop it,' he implored.

A low throaty chuckle sounded in his ear. 'Don't be silly. If you lie back you'll enjoy it,' Jacob assured him, then suddenly leaning on his elbows, he lowered his not inconsiderable weight on to the child and the air was pushed from Franky's lungs. He wanted to scream and opened his mouth to do just that, but nothing came out but a strangled gasp. And then Jacob began to rub himself up and down Franky's slight stomach and terror such as he had never known gripped the child as he fought him weakly.

'There, now isn't that nice?' Jacob gasped with pleasure. His member felt enormous and it was hot and throbbing. Franky had the awful feeling that he was going to vomit as he had last time. Tears gushed from his eyes. He felt as if he was choking and in his terror one word escaped his lips. '*Mum!*'

'Shut up, you little bastard, I'm nearly there now,' Jacob gasped.

Nearly there, what did he mean? And where was his mum? Why wasn't she there to save him from this terrible thing that was happening to him?

Jacob was moaning and pushing further into his stomach. The boy felt bruised and dirty although he had no idea what was happening to him. Then suddenly, Jacob stiffened and let out a long sigh as Franky felt hot liquid squirt on to his bare skin, causing him to shudder with revulsion.

Jacob rolled off him to lie panting at the side of him. Franky's stomach felt wet and sticky but he lay with his hands tight into his sides, too scared to feel what the wetness was. Was it blood? his mind screamed. Had Jacob injured him in some way?

The time seemed to stretch into eternity until Jacob's breathing had slowly regained a more regular rhythm and only then did he slide off the bed and begin to pull his trousers on.

'Me mam will get you for what you just did to me when she comes to fetch me,' Franky muttered with loathing.

Jacob chuckled; a wicked sound that made the hairs on the back of Franky's neck stand to attention.

'I hardly think there's much chance of that happening, seeing as she's in prison,' he told the child scathingly.

'What? What do you mean, she's in prison? She can't be . . . she told me she'd come an' get me.'

'And you've believed that all this time? Why, you must be even thicker than I thought you were.' Jacob was staring down at him now, his face dark and menacing in the light of the moon. 'If you must know, your mother stabbed your stepfather to death on the day she said goodbye to you, and if I'm any judge she'll be an old, old woman before she gets a chance to see anybody, let alone come and get you. It's about time you realised, June and I are your parents now. *No one* will be coming for you, so the sooner you accept that, the easier it will be for all of us. And another thing . . . what just happened – don't even think of telling anyone, will you? Children like you are *bad*, they make grown-ups do things they don't want to do. No one would believe you, even if you did tell them. And then there's the bogeyman. Have you heard about him? He comes out of the mirror in the dark to children who do bad things and upset their parents, and you wouldn't want that, would you? Now get to sleep and I'll see you tomorrow.'

Without another word he then left the room as Franky began to shake uncontrollably. His fear-filled eyes strayed to the deep shadows in the corner of the room and he hastily switched on the bedside lamp and nervously glanced at the mirror for a sign of the bogeyman. Finally sure that he was alone, he dared to look down at his stomach and the white glutinous mess that was spread across it. What was it? Grabbing the sheet he began to scrub himself and he didn't stop until his small stomach was swollen and red.

The next morning he cowered beneath the blankets until he heard the sound of Jacob's car drive away. He then crept from the bed and, lifting a cricket bat that was propped against his chair, he swung it with all his might at the mirror that took pride of place on the wall next to the window. It instantly splintered into a million pieces, showering the room with shards of glass that cut the back of his hands and settled in his curly mop of hair. Almost instantly, pounding footsteps sounded on the stairs and June and Mrs Dickinson appeared, their faces white and strained.

'Franky, whatever's happened?' June looked from the shattered mirror to the bat in the boy's hand in amazement.

'Never mind about that fer now.' Mrs Dickinson was already advancing on him. 'Let's get him into the bathroom quick an' get him cleaned up. There's blood everywhere.'

Once the wounds were cleaned the women were relieved to see that they were only superficial.

'Take him downstairs an' try to get him to eat somethin' now, Miss June, while I clear up the mess in his room,' Mrs Dickinson urged as she pushed Franky gently towards the bathroom door.

June obediently led him away and as the older woman watched them go she wondered who looked the worst of the two of them. June seemed to be living on her nerves just lately, even more so than was usual, if that was possible. Shaking her head, the house-keeper wondered where it was all going to end as she bustled away to clean the glass up.

Downstairs, June sat Franky at the table and after pouring him a glass of milk she asked softly, 'Are you still missing Bruno, dear?'

'Of course I am, but . . . well, there's somethin' else an' all.'

'Then tell me what it is.'

He chewed on his lip as he pushed visions of what Jacob had done to him the night before from his mind before asking tenta-tively, 'Is . . . is it true that me mam's in prison?'

June gulped with shock. She had somehow always known that he would find out one day, but why did it have to be now, when he was already grieving for Bruno? 'Yes, I'm afraid it is,' she answered eventually, holding back tears as she saw his small face crumple. 'But how did you find out?'

'Jacob told me last night.'

Anger replaced the shock as she pressed her joined hands into her waist to stop them trembling.

'Is that why you broke the mirror?' she asked.

Franky shook his head. 'No, that were to stop the bogeyman comin' out of it an' gettin' me in the night.'

'But Franky, there's no such thing as a bogeyman,' she assured him.

'Well, Jacob says there is,' he mumbled, though he consciously omitted to tell her the rest of what had gone on. The shame and humiliation of that and his fear of Jacob went too deep to ever confide in anyone.

He watched her draw herself up to her full height as the colour drained from her face like water down a plughole. Composing herself with what was obviously a great effort she managed to say, 'Then he was quite wrong to tell you such things and I shall speak to him as soon as he gets home from work. You shouldn't have to worry about things like that. Your room is a safe place. A good place to be.'

'Oh, no it ain't.'

Something about the look that flitted across the boy's face made her stomach muscles contract. There was something more going on here, something that he was choosing not to tell her – but what could it be? Forcing herself to appear calm she now told him, 'You sit there and finish your drink while I go and help Mrs Dickinson finish clearing up your room.'

She saw at a glance that he wasn't listening. His eyes were fixed on Bruno's empty basket and she made a mental note to put it in the garage as soon as Franky left the room. There was no point in rubbing salt into the wound.

The following day, before setting off for work, Jacob informed his wife, 'I've invited Henry and Marion to dinner tonight, dear. I hope that's all right?'

June groaned inwardly. She had endured more dinner-parties than she cared to remember with Henry Miller and his insipid little wife, and in her opinion, Jacob couldn't have chosen a worse time to invite guests to the house.

'Is there no way you could postpone it?' she asked timidly. 'I've rather got my hands full with seeing to Francis at the moment without having to organise a dinner-party.'

Jacob paused at the door to glower at her. 'That's the problem. You always pander to his moods. If it wasn't for the fact that Henry just so happens to be a close friend of mine, I think Francis would have been expelled by now. Henry has been more than understanding, having to manage the boy's disruptive behaviour, so I hardly feel it would be right to cancel at such short notice, do you? I'm sure Mrs Dickinson will stay later to help you prepare the meal, if you ask her.'

Knowing when she was beaten, June sighed and nodded and, satisfied, Jacob left.

When he arrived home late that afternoon, he eyed the dining room with satisfaction. It was laid with the best cutlery and candelabras as well as June's treasured Royal Doulton china. The kitchen was a hive of activity and the air was full of delicious smells. Mrs Dickinson was rolling pastry at the kitchen table as he entered the room. Ignoring her, Jacob turned his attention to his wife, who was just lifting a large joint of best roast beef from the oven.

'It seems that you have everything well under control, dear,' he commented with a smug smile.

She placed the joint on the edge of the table and wiped a stray lock of limp fair hair from her forehead. 'What time will they be. arriving?' she asked tiredly not looking forward to the evening ahead at all.

'Oh, I told them about seven-thirty,' Jacob answered. 'So that gives us time for a drink and a nice bath before they arrive.' He turned on his heel and left the room as Mrs Dickinson and June exchanged an exasperated glance.

The Millers arrived exactly on time. By then, June had hastily bathed and changed and now that everything was in order, Mrs Dickinson had finally set off for home, muttering beneath her breath as she went at the selfishness of the man. Did he have a swinging brick for a heart, she wondered, or was he merely blind? Surely he could see how upset that poor child was? She didn't know how Miss June managed to put up with him, she really didn't.

Jacob ushered Henry and Marion into the lounge and poured them a drink while June hurried away to fetch the starters, glad of an excuse to escape. She found Marion trying at the best of times, but tonight she just wasn't in the mood for inconsequential chitchat.

Luckily, Jacob was the perfect host and if June was somewhat quiet he managed to cover for her well throughout the meal, which their guests declared was delicious. They started with homemade chicken and asparagus soup, followed by a roast beef dinner with all the trimmings, and one of Mrs Dickinson's renowned treacle tarts to finish. As June rushed away to fetch the coffee and cheese and biscuits for anyone who wanted them she sighed with relief. Marion was never the most sparkling company but tonight she had complained incessantly throughout the meal of having a headache. June hoped rather uncharitably that her headache would get worse and that the guests might decide to leave early.

The men eventually retired to Jacob's study leaving the women in the lounge, and deciding that she should at least make an effort, June tried to strike up a conversation.

'So, are you busy at the moment, Marion?' she asked pleasantly.

Marion shook her head and June found herself thinking what an unlikely couple she and Henry made. He was thin to the point of being almost skeletal, whilst Marion was very overweight. She wore thick-lensed glasses and her straight mousy hair with its side parting and hair-grip was very unflattering. June had never seen her with so much as a scrap of make-up on in all the time she had known her, and tonight was no different. The only thing they had ever had in common was the fact that they were both childless, or at least they had been until June had adopted Franky; a fact that Marion was highly envious of.

'And how is the *dear* little chap?' she asked now as she sipped daintily at a glass of sherry.

'Oh, he's doing fine, thank you,' June told her, unwilling to let her know how bad things really were.

'Oh good, I'm so pleased to hear it, although Henry did say he was still having a few problems at school.'

June bristled. 'Well, there's bound to be a settling down period,' she snapped.

Realising that she had upset her, Marion stroked her forehead and moaned dramatically, 'Oh dear, I'm afraid this headache may be turning into a migraine. Would you be very offended if Henry and I were to leave a little early, dear?'

'Not at all,' June assured her, trying to hide her delight. 'I'll just pop into the study and tell him you're ready to go, shall I?'

'Yes, thank you,' Marion muttered with a martyred sigh.

June rose quickly and strode across the hallway then after tapping at the study door she opened it and began, 'Henry, Marion asked me to—' Her words died away as Jacob and Henry, who were standing close together by the window, sprang apart as if they had been scalded.

Quickly composing himself, Jacob gushed, 'I was . . . er . . . just telling Henry what a bad time we've been having with Francis, and he was comforting me.'

'Oh, I see,' June said, although she didn't, and began to hastily back out of the room again.

'Look, June, I don't know what you think you saw . . .' Jacob blustered but she silenced him when she told him coldly, 'Marion isn't feeling well and would like to leave now.'

'Er . . . yes, yes of course.' Henry made for the door, his cheeks burning as June stared at Jacob with all the contempt she felt for him shining in her eyes.

Once the Millers were gone, June retired to her room where she tossed and turned as the night shadows lengthened beyond the bedroom window. Again and again in her mind's eye she saw Henry and Jacob springing apart, and deep down, alarm bells began to ring until eventually she fell into a fitful doze.

The following night Franky lay in the darkness fighting to stay awake as he listened to the house settling around him. June and Jacob had retired to their separate rooms some time ago. The atmosphere in the house had been unbearable today and he had heard them rowing furiously, though he couldn't hear what it was about. And now there was only the sound of the distant waves and the night creatures beyond the window to be heard. Until, that was, he heard the door at the end of the landing open. He knew then that the nightmare was about to begin all over again.

It was the first Sunday without Bruno. The days before had passed quietly with Franky refusing to leave his room.

'We'll have to get him out of there soon,' June fretted as she dabbed at her lips with a white linen napkin. 'He hasn't eaten enough to keep a bird alive over the last few days. I've been taking trays up to him, and I know Mrs Dickinson has been trying to tempt him with tasty titbits, but everything we take up to him comes down untouched.'

Jacob glared at her over the shining expanse of the table that was set for dinner. The smell of roast pork was hanging on the air but even that had failed to tempt Franky out of his room. June had adamantly refused to speak to her husband since the night the Millers had been to dinner, unless it was about Franky, that was.

'He'll eat when he's hungry enough,' he told her carelessly as he helped himself to a large spoonful of applesauce. 'I can't see what all the fuss is about, to be honest. Bruno was only a *dog*, for Christ's sake. Anyone would think he'd lost his best friend.'

'Bruno *was* his best friend,' June answered resentfully as she pushed a dish of steaming cauliflower towards him.

He took a large portion before glancing at her plate, which was almost empty. 'Are you on hunger strike too then?'

She watched him studiously, wondering what she had ever seen in him. Where was the charmer who had swept her off her feet? The man who could turn her legs to jelly with just one glance? When he had first taken to sleeping in the spare room she had been heartbroken, but now each time she heard him pass their bedroom door she heaved a huge sigh of relief, for she knew she could never bear to have him lie next to her again. A silence settled between them until Jacob laid down his knife and fork and told her, 'I shall be taking Francis out for his walk shortly.'

She raised an eyebrow. 'I rather think you'll struggle to get him out of his room, let alone take a walk with you,' she commented caustically.

He rose from the table and left the room without a word as she sat there feeling as if her whole world was crashing about her ears.

It was something of a shock when she saw Franky dressed in his outdoor clothes shortly afterwards in the hallway.

'Oh, so you decided to go then,' she said unnecessarily as Jacob came to join them. 'I'm glad. The fresh air will do you good and hopefully put some colour back into your cheeks.'

Franky was unnaturally pale and his dark eyes seemed to be too large for his small pinched face. She resisted the urge to try and cuddle him, knowing of old that her attentions would be shunned. Instead she said quietly, 'Have a good time then.'

As Jacob steered the child unresisting towards the door, Franky suddenly paused to look her full in the face, and a terrible feeling of foreboding settled on her. Never in her entire life had she seen such a look of utter despair in anyone, and the feeling was so strong that once the door had closed behind them, June sank down on to the nearest chair and, burying her face in her hands, she wept unrestrainedly.

Once at the cliff walk, Franky pulled the hood of his coat up and gamely tried to keep up with Jacob's long strides, which was no mean feat as the rain was coming down in torrents and the ground was treacherously slippery underfoot once they got to the coastal path. More than once he stumbled and, by the time they drew abreast of the farm gates, the knees of Franky's jeans and his hands were thick with mud.

Jacob was in a rare good mood, keeping up a constant stream of chatter and pointing out things and places of interest, but Franky ignored him as his hatred simmered away inside like a great boil that was ready to burst at any minute. The coastal path was deserted and Franky was glad; it needed to be for what he planned to do. He just prayed that he would be physically strong enough to carry it through. Once they came to the rugged cliff face of Baggy Point,

Jacob paused as he always did to draw in great lungfuls of the bracing salty air.

'Look at it,' he said, as he spread his arms wide to encompass the stunning view. Far below him, the waves were crashing on to the rocks and above him, the gulls were swooping and diving as they foraged for food.

'What's that down there?' Franky pointed to the cliff face and, pleased that the child was speaking to him again, Jacob gingerly stepped closer to the edge to peer below him.

'What's what, Francis? I can't see anything.'

Franky's hands were clenching and unclenching as all the pain he had endured in his young life welled to the surface. He had been able to endure living here when he had thought that his mam would be coming for him, and whilst he had Bruno to confide in, but now that Jacob had told him where his mother was and Bruno was gone, all he could see was a lifetime of abuse stretching before him – and it was more than he could bear.

'Th-there – look.' His face was set in a hard mask as he inched closer to Jacob and then without warning he suddenly lunged forward and pushed the man in the small of his back with every ounce of strength he could muster.

Jacob's arms flew into the air as he struggled to keep his balance. The man was teetering on the very brink of the cliff, his feet slipping and sliding on the shiny grass beneath him. He briefly turned startled eyes to the boy but then suddenly soared off the edge as if he was a bird. He seemed to hover in the air for a moment before dropping like a stone, and Franky watched with grim satisfaction as he bounced off the cliff face again and again like a rag doll as his body plummeted towards the sea below. The waves sucked at him greedily and Franky saw him sink from sight. He then went and sat down on a protruding rock to wait. Someone would come looking for them eventually, and how sad they would be when he had to tell them that Jacob had slipped and fallen over the edge of the cliff.

Chapter Sixteen

It was dark by the time Franky saw torches slicing through the darkness towards him. He had no idea how long he had sat there, but it seemed like for ever. Although it was only late September, the night breeze from the sea was cutting and he was frozen through. Occasionally he had tentatively ventured to the edge of the cliff and peered down into the crashing waves, almost as if he were fearful that Jacob might somehow escape from his watery grave to climb back up and seek his revenge. Thankfully there was no sign of him; he had, in fact, been sucked beneath the waves and carried out to sea by hungry currents.

At one point Franky was so miserable that he'd actually thought of throwing himself over the edge and joining him. After all, he reasoned, what did he have left to live for? His mum was never going to come and fetch him now; he'd never see his sisters again and Bruno was gone, so what was the point of going on?

Commonsense took over. The person he hated most in all the world was Jacob and he was gone now, so perhaps things would get better. At least he would no longer have to fear the night-time. Never have to lie awake trembling with his ears straining into the darkness for the sound of Jacob's quiet footsteps on the landing. He shuddered as he thought of the despicable things the man had done to him, and vomit rose in his throat as he recalled the wet stickiness on his small stomach. Now as he watched the torches wavering towards him he steeled himself for what was ahead. Even at his young age he knew that what he'd done to Jacob was wrong and he must make out that it had been an accident. He would tell them that Jacob had simply slipped and gone over the edge of the cliff and there had been nothing he could do to help him.

By now he could hear people shouting his name. The sounds bounced and echoed eerily off the rock face as he sat with his eyes staring straight ahead.

'*FRANKY . . . FRANKY!*'

And then he saw June, and when she spotted him she began to sob with relief as she broke into a run and covered the distance between them.

'Franky, are you all right? And where's Jacob?'

She was kneeling in front of him, shaking his frozen hands up and down, but the words he'd practised were stuck in his throat as he stared sightlessly ahead. Now there was another man at the side of her and he too dropped to his knees as he told her softly, 'I think he's in shock, June. Let me take a look at him.'

June moved aside, her eyes never leaving Franky's face as the man waved his hand up and down in front of Franky's eyes before asking, 'Where's your dad, son?'

Franky recognised him as the doctor from the village and now his mouth began to work until eventually he stuttered, 'H–he slipped. There were nowt I could do.'

'All right, all right, take your time now. *Where* did he slip and where is he now?'

Franky nodded woodenly towards the edge of the cliff. 'He's down there. He fell . . .'

Some of the men who were now clustered around him instantly moved to the cliff edge as one of them shouted urgently, 'Bill, get down to the village and alert the coastguard. Tell him a man's gone over the edge of the cliff at Baggy Point. They'll need to get the lifeboat out.'

Franky noticed then that the doctor was still talking to him and he tried to drag his attention away from the crowd, who were peering down into the darkness as they sadly shook their heads.

'Franky, listen to me. Can you tell me how long it's been since Jacob fell?'

Franky shrugged as someone draped a heavy coat around his shoulders and then June was kneeling in front of him again and he had the feeling that she was looking right into his soul.

Her heart was racing and her mind was working overtime. And then suddenly the child calmly returned her stare – and in that instant she knew without a word being said that her worst suspicions were true. Franky was glad that Jacob was gone; it was there in his eyes. She thought of all the nights she had seen the boy shudder and the helpless look that would flare in his eyes as Jacob marched him off for his bath. The rumours she'd heard about certain parents refusing to allow their sons to attend the Scouts any more while Jacob was still Scoutmaster. The way Jacob and Henry had sprung apart in the study on the night that the Millers had come to supper. Jacob's aversion to sex . . . it all added up and now she could no longer deny what she had always suspected deep down. Jacob was a homosexual *and* a paedophile who had married her just as a smokescreen to appear respectable.

As if he could read her mind, Franky continued to stare back at her unflinchingly, and when the hint of a grin lifted the corners of his lips she recoiled from him with a startled gasp as she heard in her mind the threat he had once made. '*I'm goin' to kill you!*'

Jacob hadn't slipped at all. Franky had pushed him over the edge of the cliff in revenge for putting his beloved Bruno to sleep. She was sure of it, but what could she do? If she were to voice her suspicions, everyone would think she was mad – and at the end of the day did she really blame him?

Leaning towards him, she whispered, 'Did Jacob ever hurt you, Franky?'

He continued to stare back at her blankly, and again she felt sick. Surely Jacob wouldn't have sunk to touching the child . . . would he? And then there was a darkness rushing towards her and rather than fight it she gave herself up to it willingly because anything was better than the sense of total, ultimate betrayal she was feeling at that moment.

Later that night, June carried a cup of hot chocolate into the lounge and placed it on a small table at Franky's side. The police had recently left after questioning the child for what seemed like hours, but now they'd told June that it appeared that her husband's death had been nothing more than a tragic accident. They also told her solemnly that they would keep her informed of any news and assured her that the coastguards were still out looking for Jacob's body and would continue to do so until he was found.

When she finally closed the door on them she sighed with relief and headed off towards the kitchen where Mrs Dickinson was throwing together a hasty meal. She had come as soon as she'd heard what had happened. The village was alive with the gossip, and June was strangely glad of her company. She couldn't quite take in yet all that had happened, and kept expecting Jacob to walk through the door at any minute.

No one had eaten the meal, they'd barely picked at it, and now Mrs Dickinson had retired to bed after insisting that she wasn't going to leave Franky and June alone for tonight at least.

'Try and drink it,' June urged as she pushed a glass of milk towards Franky, but the child just continued to stare sightlessly ahead, ignoring her as if she wasn't even there.

Sighing heavily, she perched on the edge of the chair next to him and after a moment she said quietly, 'I think it's time you and I had a little talk, don't you, dear?'

When he turned his gaze on her she shrank away from the hatred she saw blazing in his eyes.

'There ain't nothin' to talk about,' he muttered resentfully, and June longed to leave it at that and hurry from the room, but somehow she knew that she couldn't. There had been too many secrets in this house and now it was time to bring them out into the open and clear the air.

'I rather think there is,' she said hesitantly. 'I want you to tell me the truth. Did Jacob, I mean, your father, ever—'

'He *weren't* my father!' Franky snapped. 'An' why are you so keen to know what went on all of a sudden? You didn't seem to much care every night when he dragged me off to the bathroom an' . . .' He stopped and suddenly gasped as he drew air into his lungs, but now June was eager to hear the rest, even if it proved to be something she really didn't want to know.

'Please,' she implored. 'Can't you tell me what's wrong?'

'What's *wrong*!' Franky bounced out of the chair and as he stood with his small fists clenched on his hips she had the feeling that she was being confronted by a man rather than a seven-year-old boy.

'All right then, if yer *really* want to know I'll tell yer what's wrong. Every night when he took me for a bath he . . .' Franky ran his tongue across his dry lips before continuing. 'He . . . did things to me – *bad* things, down here.' As his hand stabbed towards his private parts, June's hand flew to her mouth and she stifled a sob.

As Franky went doggedly on listing the atrocities he'd suffered at his adoptive father's hands, June's tears slid down her cheeks unchecked. But, she was forced to ask herself, hadn't the gut feeling that she'd chosen to ignore warned her that something was amiss? An old saying of her mother's suddenly sprang to mind: *Ignorance is bliss* – and now June realised just how true that was, because nothing could have prepared her for the words that were tripping out of Franky's mouth. It was like every mother's worst nightmare come true.

'I'm so sorry,' she managed to choke through her tears but it was as if a floodgate had opened up in the child, and now that he'd started to tell her of the terrible secrets he'd been forced to keep, he was keen for her to know it all.

'It got worse after you told him he weren't to bath me any more,' he said accusingly. 'He'd wait till he knew you were fast asleep an' then he'd come to my room an' he'd climb into bed with me, an' then . . .' He gulped deep in his throat and then the words were coming out in a torrent as all the pent-up hurt, humiliation and disappointment he had been forced to suffer in his young life spewed out of him. He remembered back to Mary, his social worker, who would gently question him each time a new bruise appeared on his body, and the warning looks his mother would flash him. Looks that said without words being spoken that if he told, he might never see her again. Well, the way he saw it, it was unlikely that he *would* ever see his mother again now if what Jacob had told him was true, so he had nothing to gain by keeping it all trapped inside any more. June was as much to blame anyway. Surely she must have guessed what was going on? But still she hadn't helped him, had she? So why should he spare her feelings now!

'He told me that all dads did things like that to their kids and that I mustn't tell anyone.' The words trembled on his tongue as he fought to hold back tears. He didn't want to give her the satisfaction of seeing how hurt he was. 'But Ginger never mentioned nothin' like that an' I reckon he would have if his dad had been doin' it to him too. An' then *he* went an' got rid of Bruno, so I . . . I had to stop him.'

'What do you mean?' June asked tremulously.

'He never fell over the edge o' the cliff . . . I *pushed* him.' Franky's chin jutted unrepentantly. 'An' I'd do it again,' he finished breathlessly. ''Cos I *hated* him. D'yer hear me? I *hated* him an' I hate *you* an' all.'

With that he barged past her and flew up the stairs as she stood there as if she had been turned to stone. Shame was stabbing at her like a knife as she thought of what the poor child had been forced to endure. She didn't blame him for feeling as he did. He was right; she could have stopped it if she hadn't shut her mind to what was going on. But it was too late now. Franky would never forgive her, she knew him well enough to realise that. And so the farce that she had been living was finally over, brought to a head by their own child. The news would spread round the village like wildfire and she would never be able to hold her head up again. And Franky . . . well, the way she saw it, he deserved better. The poor little mite had left one heartache behind only to find another when he came to live with Jacob and herself. He would never trust her again now.

Stumbling, she walked towards the kitchen and opened a drawer, then quietly she climbed the stairs and after entering the bathroom she clicked on the light and locked the door securely behind her. She turned on the bath taps before slowly peeling her clothes off and only then did her thoughts return to Jacob. Shouldn't she be feeling distraught at his death? Heartbroken at the thought of never seeing him again? After all, she had loved him, hadn't she? 'No,' a little voice in her head whispered. 'You stopped loving him a long time ago; you just didn't want to admit it to yourself.'

She switched off the taps and climbed slowly into the bath, letting the peace and quiet wash over her as she slid into the water. Then, after a few moments she lifted the wickedly sharp knife she had fetched from the kitchen drawer and raised her wrist. There had been so much pain, so much disappointment . . . but soon now it would be over. The blade slid across her skin and through her veins like a knife through butter, and she watched in fascination as the blood flowed into the water, changing the colour of it, before doing exactly the same to the second wrist. There was no pain, nothing but a deep feeling of relief as she lay back and closed her eyes. And her last thoughts were, I hope things will work out for Franky.

In his room, Franky stood at the window staring out at the blustery night. Big black clouds were scudding across the sky and the branches of the tree beyond the glass were bending in the wind as if they were involved in some macabre dance. The tears had stopped now and he felt strangely drained. But more than ever he knew that he had to get away from this place. If the police ever discovered that he had killed Jacob they might lock him up as they had his mother. He had no way of knowing he was too young to be imprisoned and no intention of staying around long enough to find out.

Heaving a small bag out of the bottom of the wardrobe he hastily stuffed some clothes into it, then crossing to the door he paused to listen. The landing light was on but the house was quiet so he supposed that June had gone to bed. On tiptoe he crept down the stairs, determined this time to make a better job of getting away than he had the last time. Once in the kitchen he dared to put on the light before pulling his coat and his Wellington boots on. He then quietly opened the fridge door and grabbed whatever food was the nearest. Two apples and a piece of apple pie were flung haphazardly on to the top of his clean clothes, followed by three slices of ham, which he snatched from a plate, and a banana. There was half a sliced loaf on the worktop and he rammed that in too and finally added an unopened pint bottle of milk. Happy now that he had enough food to keep him going for a while he snuck towards the kitchen door.

Once he had wrestled with the key he paused just once to glance at the place where Bruno had slept and a huge choking lump rose in his throat. Bruno had been his best friend, the only one that he could whisper all his fears to. Now there was no one. He had no one who cared and nowhere to go, but then anywhere was better than there, the way he saw it; so with a new resolve he slid out of the door, closing it softly behind him. Within minutes he was on the road and he stood uncertainly looking this way and that. Unlike the last time he had run away, he had no intention of heading for the coastal path, so he pulled his collar up and after hitching his bag higher on to his shoulder he set off in the direction of the village, keeping close to the hedges in case any cars should appear.

Some time later he left the lights of the village behind and started along a narrow winding lane. There was no light save for the moon, which now and again appeared from behind the scudding clouds, and he glanced nervously around. The trees that bordered the road were dipping towards him in the wind, and every now and again he started as some night creature shrieked from the surrounding copses. The true extent of his loneliness suddenly closed around him like a dense fog and he knuckled the tears from his eyes with his cold hand. Even so, he strode on resolutely.

When he suddenly saw lights in the distance he jumped across a ditch and hid behind a tree. Seconds later, car headlights sliced through the darkness and he crouched low until they had passed. He had no fear that it was someone looking for him because they had come from the opposite direction from which he had walked. Hopefully no one would even realise that he was missing until the morning, and by then he hoped to be long gone. Despite his desire to get far away and put a safe distance between himself and Puddlesea, by the time another hour had passed he was drooping with fatigue and fighting to keep his eyes open. The wind had chilled him to the bone and he shivered uncontrollably as he struggled to put one foot in front of the other. He was also surprisingly hungry now. More than once he had slipped in a pothole in the road and now his left ankle was paining him and he knew that he needed somewhere to rest. Preferably somewhere out of the biting wind.

Eventually a building loomed ahead and he slowed his steps as he came to the gates of what appeared to be a farmhouse. Everywhere was in darkness so he clambered over the double wooden gates and cautiously entered a large yard, keeping his eye out for dogs and on the bedroom windows for lights going on. Ahead he could just make out what appeared to be a large barn and he headed towards it, holding his breath as he went. The last time he had run away, he had sheltered in a barn and then been caught the very next morning. He had no intention of making the same mistake this time.

Thankfully the door was unlocked and he slid inside, sighing with relief to find himself out of the wind. The building smelled of cows and engine oil and hay, and he stood quietly, allowing his eyes to adjust to the deeper darkness. After a while he began to feel his way around the walls until he came to a loft ladder that stretched up into the gloom. Hitching his bag on to his back again he cautiously began to climb and soon he found himself in a large hayloft. Sighing with relief he dropped on to the hard wooden floor and undid his bag, then he had a hasty meal of dry bread, the slice of apple pie, and a large swig from the milk he had brought with him. Next he began to feel around for loose hay and soon he had made a pile that would serve as a bed. He sank on to it gratefully and lay staring up at the rafters as he thought back over the day's events. He still had no idea at all where he was going, but one thing he was sure of: nowhere could be as awful as the place he had just left, and eventually he would find his mum. He *had* to.

PART TWO

Chapter Seventeen

At first light, Franky's eyes snapped open and he lay disorientated in the gloom of the barn. His mouth felt itchy and dry from the hay he had slept on. But then, as he remembered back to the day before, he slowly relaxed and rummaged in his bag for food. Hastily he ate another two slices of dry bread with ham, leaving the last two slices for later, then he finished off his breakfast with a banana and a long swig from the milk bottle. Feeling slightly better he crept to the edge of the hay loft and, content that no one was about, he slipped down the ladder and into the yard, picking his way through the chickens that were scratching in the dirt as he headed for the gate. Once on the road again he let out a long sigh of relief. There was a nip in the air, but then he supposed it was to be expected in late September.

After a while he left the road and walked across some fields. He'd decided there was less chance of him being seen this way. Mid-morning the sun came out and he took off his coat and stopped to eat his last apple, very aware that all he had left to keep him going now were two slices of dry bread. He found a stream where the water bubbled over the rocks; it was crystal clear and so he stopped to drink and wash his face. A road ran along the side of the field he had found himself in, and seeing some signposts at a small cross-roads up ahead, he made towards it. He had no idea where he was going and at that moment in time he didn't much care, just so long as he didn't have to go back to that awful house again. There was an arrow on the signpost pointing towards Ilfracombe and, deciding that this was as good a place as any, he set off in that direction.

It was mid-afternoon when the town came into sight. Franky would have liked to walk into the centre and visit the sea-front but it was teeming with late holidaymakers and he was too afraid of being spotted. He had no doubt that June would have the police out looking for him by now, and as he had no intention of being found he decided it would be safer to keep away from areas where he might be recognised. It was quite warm by then and he was thirsty and hungry again so he ate the last two slices of bread, wishing now that he had brought more food with him. He had left the unfinished bottle of milk in the barn that morning and so he headed for the fields once more, hoping to find another brook where he could get a drink.

An hour later, his legs were getting tired and he was beginning to worry about where he might sleep when night came. He dropped despondently down in the shelter of a large oak tree and it was as he was sitting there that he heard the sound of children's laughter. Curious, he stood up and looked about, then realising that the sound was coming from the next field, he crept to the hedge and peeped over it. His mouth dropped open in amazement as he saw what appeared to be at first sight a large brightly painted van parked there. On closer inspection he realised that it was, in fact, a very old ambulance. There were curtains at the window and on the side of it in large letters was written JESUS LOVES YOU, surrounded by gaily painted flowers.

A young woman was sitting cross-legged in front of a fire over which hung a large soot-blackened pot. Her long fair hair reached way beyond her waist and it was tied back with a bright red ribbon. Her blouse was bright orange and she wore a flowered skirt that Franky guessed would reach past her ankles, should she stand up. The two children who were rolling on the grass not far from her were equally brightly clothed and Franky wondered if he had happened across a gypsy encampment. He looked around, but seeing no other vehicles, he quashed that idea almost immediately. The gypsies who stayed on Baggy Point had always come as a group, so who could these people be?

As he was standing there, he became aware of the delicious smell rising from the pot in front of the young woman and his stomach cramped with hunger, although he kept low so that he wouldn't be seen as he watched them. He also noticed a small Jack Russell dog that was looking towards him with interest. He ducked quickly, hoping that the dog wouldn't bark and draw attention to him.

'Echo, don't get Destiny too excited now,' he heard the young woman say to the two children rolling about on the grass. 'You know it will set her off coughing again.'

Destiny – Echo! Franky frowned. What sort of names were they? He'd certainly never heard them before, though they seemed to suit the two children somehow. He inched himself higher and dared to peep over the hedge again.

At that moment, a tall man with hair as long as the woman's emerged from the back of the strange vehicle, and after bending to plant a kiss on the woman's cheek he sat down and began to work on a part-finished wicker basket that was placed a short way from the fire. The dog loped over to him and began to lick his arm. Franky watched in fascination as the man's hands nimbly wove the wicker in and out. The woman meanwhile was adding chopped vegetables to the large cooking pot and Franky's mouth began to water. He stayed exactly where he was for another hour or so until eventually the woman disappeared into the back of the van and returned with a number of dishes, which she proceeded to fill with what looked like some sort of stew. The family assembled round the fire and Franky watched enviously as the woman now handed them all a spoon.

And then he visibly started as the tall man looked directly at the hedge he was hiding behind before saying, 'Would you care to come and join us?'

Colour flooded into his cheeks as he stumbled and landed solidly on his backside. By the time he had scrambled to his feet the man was looking over the hedge at him with a kind smile on his face and the dog at his heels was furiously wagging his tail.

'Come,' he said, holding out his hand. 'We don't have a feast but what we have we are more than happy to share with you.'

Franky snatched up his bag and hovered uncertainly, ready to break into a run. But then the smell of the food got the better of him and tentatively he squeezed through a gap in the hedge to stand staring up at the man nervously as he asked, 'How did you know I was there?'

The tall dark-haired man placed his great hand, which appeared as big as a shovel, on to Franky's trembling shoulder. 'I think it was the dog that gave the game away,' he grinned. Seeing the terror in the child's eyes, he told him kindly, 'You need not fear us. Now come and share our meal.'

Franky gulped as he approached the strange family. They were like no one he had ever seen before and yet they seemed friendly and he *was* ravenous.

He sat down between the boy and girl, who were staring at him curiously, and almost instantly the woman passed him a steaming bowl of food. 'It's rabbit,' she told him with a smile. 'Twig caught it earlier today.'

Franky was about to tuck in when the whole family suddenly bowed their heads and the man said solemnly, 'For what we are about to receive, may the Lord make us truly thankful.'

'Amen,' the family chanted in unison and now Franky grimaced as he looked down into his dish. He didn't much fancy the thought of eating a rabbit that had been hopping round in the fields only hours before. But then it did smell very appetising, so dipping his spoon into the stew he tried it and within minutes he had cleared his bowl.

'Fleur,' the man addressed the woman. 'I think our guest would like some more.'

Without a word she took the bowl and refilled it, and in no time at all Franky had cleared that too. Swiping the back of his hand across his mouth, Franky smiled tremulously as he passed the dish back to her.

'That were lovely, thank you,' he mumbled.

'You are most welcome, and now, would you like some fruit?' She produced a small wicker basket that contained some apples and plums, and after taking a large plum, Franky studied the children. The little girl, who the woman had referred to as Destiny, looked about two years old and Franky felt a sharp stab of pain as he thought of his twin sisters whom he had not seen since they had been about her age. She was small and delicate, and looked very like her mother with a mop of blond curly hair and huge sapphire-blue eyes. The boy, Echo, looked to be about four or five and resembled his father with long straight dark hair and golden-brown eyes. He was as sturdy as the little girl was delicate, and as they felt Franky's eyes on them, both children flashed him a warm smile.

He glanced away self-consciously, almost choking on the mouthful of plum he was eating. Once the meal was over he rose to leave but the man waved him back down again.

'Don't go rushing away,' he urged him. 'Unless you're in a hurry to get somewhere, that is?'

Franky shook his head. 'I ain't in no rush to get anywhere,' he muttered.

The man and woman exchanged a worried glance before the man went on, 'May I ask what your name is, son?'

Franky crossed his arms tightly about his chest. 'It's Franky.'

'Franky what?'

'Just Franky.'

'I see, and where do you come from?'

'Nowhere.'

'Oh, I see.'

An awkward silence settled between them until the children suddenly rose and scampered off to play again with the dog romping about them.

'What's the dog's name?' he dared to ask.

'He's just Dog, just as you are just Franky,' the man told him.

'Oh!' Franky was gazing at the old ambulance with open curiosity now and he suddenly blurted out, 'You lot gypsies, are you?'

The man called Twig threw back his head and laughed aloud. 'No, we're not gypsies, Franky. We're travellers.'

'Travellers? So where do you live then?'

Twig spread his arms. 'Wherever the fancy takes us. This is our home.' As he pointed towards the old ambulance, Franky frowned.

'What, you mean you live in that all the time?'

'We most certainly do, and we wouldn't have it any other way. Would you like to see inside?'

Franky got up like a shot and followed the man to the open back doors. When he peered inside he gasped with astonishment. It was like a small caravan inside, with a double mattress that was made up with a brightly-coloured patchwork quilt at the back end, and two small bunk beds to one side. Pretty little curtains hung at the window and there was a gaily-worked rag rug on the floor.

'Why, it's really cosy inside. Like a little caravan, ain't it? But why do you live like this?' He hoped he hadn't caused offence but he needn't have worried because Twig laughed again.

'I suppose both Fleur and I wanted to get out of the rat race,' he told him. 'We met at university and I instantly recognised her as my soulmate. Of course, our names weren't Twig and Fleur then and we came from very different backgrounds. Fleur's father was a very influential politician whereas I come from a council estate. Her family strongly disapproved of our relationship and in the end they told her in no uncertain terms that if she didn't finish with me they'd cut her off without a penny. And so we made the decision to leave, and this is the outcome – and I don't mind telling you, I don't regret what we did for an instant.' He flashed Fleur a smile as he said it and Franky noticed her blush prettily. No one had ever spoken to him like this before and he felt very grown up.

'So did you get married when you ran away then?'

Twig shook his head. 'No, we didn't. Fleur and I are kindred spirits. Children of the earth. We have no need of bits of paper to bind us.'

'But how do you live?' Franky asked with all the tactlessness of a child.

Twig nodded towards a pile of wicker baskets. 'I make those and take them into the market to sell them, and Fleur makes jewellery,' he explained. 'Then during certain times of the year we work on farms, potato picking, strawberry picking or helping with the harvesting. We trade our goods for eggs and milk from farms we pass on our travels, and Dog and I hunt for our meat and collect wild mushrooms and berries – but only for what we need to survive, of course. I believe that one should live and let live. I also do a bit of busking from time to time.'

'What's busking?'

'I have a guitar and sometimes I sit in a town and play and sing. People throw money into a hat. It all helps.'

Franky was totally in awe of the man and was sure he had never met anyone like him before.

'But now, tell me a little about you,' Twig said softly. 'How old are you, Franky?'

'I'm nearly eight,' Franky muttered, instantly on guard again.

'You surprise me, you're a big lad. I would have taken you for ten at least. Now I have no wish to pry, but are you in trouble? Won't your parents be worried about you?'

'I ain't in no trouble an' I ain't got no parents.' Franky dragged the toe of his shoe along the grass. 'At least, I never knew me dad an' me mam's in prison.'

Twig's face twisted with sympathy. 'In that case, how would you like to stay with us for a while until you decide what you want to do?'

Franky glared at him suspiciously. Why would this stranger be offering to help him? Was he planning to do the bad things that Jacob had done to him?

'Why are you bein' kind to me?' he asked before he could stop himself, and Twig stared off across the rolling fields as he shrugged.

'Because we are all brothers and sisters,' he told him gently. 'I believe in peace and love.'

'An' you wouldn't go tellin' the coppers where I am? I mean, I ain't in no trouble like I told you, but I just ran away from a bad place an' I ain't goin' back there. I'd rather *die*,' he said, and meant it with every fibre of his being.

Twig's great hand settled gently on his shoulder again as the man said, 'I sense great sorrow in you, child. But God is watching over you. He will give you peace of mind eventually.'

Franky seriously doubted it, but all the same he liked this family and seeing as he was just drifting aimlessly along, he supposed it would make sense to take the man up on his offer; for the time being at least, until he could find his mam.

'All right then, I'll stay for now,' he told him, as if he were bestowing some great honour on him. Twig pursed his lips to stop himself from laughing and so it was decided.

That night, which had turned surprisingly mild for the time of year, they all sat around the fire as Twig read extracts from the Bible and played his guitar for them. Earlier on, Fleur had taken the children down to wash in the stream that ran along the bottom of the field and now they were cuddled up to their parents as they listened intently to their father. Franky yawned as he looked longingly towards the small tent that Twig had erected for him to sleep in. There was no more room in the van, he'd explained, but Franky wondered if that was just an excuse to get him away from the rest of the family so that Twig could do the bad things to him as Jacob had.

Above them was a canopy of stars, twinkling in the black velvet sky, and when Twig stopped playing his guitar the only sounds to be heard were the night creatures and a lonely owl hooting in the copse behind them.

'This,' said Twig, as he put his guitar aside and looked around him, 'is what it's all about. Being at one with nature.'

Fleur smiled at him affectionately as she scooped a sleepy Destiny up into her arms. 'I think it's time I tucked these two in before they fall asleep on me,' she said, as she planted a gentle kiss on the child's springing blond curls. She headed for the van with Destiny in her arms and Echo close on her heels, and now Twig gave Franky his undivided attention.

'And what about you, son? Are you ready to hit the sack yet? You look all in.'

Franky bobbed his head, keeping a wary eye on the man all the time. The trauma of the last days had caught up with him now and his eyes were heavy, but even so he found it very hard to trust anyone. Admittedly, Twig seemed genuine enough, but then to the outside world so had Jacob and . . . he stopped his thoughts from going any further. There was nothing he could do to change the past. Instead he had to look to the future and avoid being taken back to Puddlesea. Somehow he had to get back to his hometown of Nuneaton and find out if what Jacob had said about his mother was true.

Twig took the elastic band from his ponytail and his long hair tumbled across his shoulders, concealing part of the garish shirt he was wearing as Dog scuttled on to a blanket in a basket beneath the van. 'Come on then, let's get you settled,' he said. 'I think I'm about ready to bed down myself. Shall I wake you in the morning? You could come and help me pick some mushrooms for breakfast if you like.'

Franky nodded as he stood up, clutching his bag close to his chest. Twig crossed to the tent and lifted the flap and Franky quickly scrambled in. Twig had collected some loose hay that was lying in the neighbouring field to serve as a mattress and he had put a thick blanket and a pillow in to keep Franky warm. Now he yawned and stretched his long arms above his head.

'You should be fine in there,' he assured him, 'but if you need us in the night, just give a rap on the door. Good night, Franky. God bless and sleep tight.'

The darkness was profound when the man dropped the flap of the tent back into place and for a while Franky sat, his heart beating a wild tattoo in his chest as he clutched his bag to him. Should Twig reappear he intended to be off like a shot, which was why he had no intentions of getting undressed. He waited for what seemed like an eternity, but there was nothing but the sound of the night breeze softly rustling through the trees, so eventually he lay down and pulled the blanket up to his chin – and then before he knew it he was fast asleep and he slept like a baby.

'Franky, wake up, sleepyhead. I'm off to collect some mushrooms for breakfast. Do you want to come along?'

Dragging himself up on to his elbow, Franky knuckled the sleep from his eyes as he stared blearily up at Twig who was framed in the doorway of the tent.

'What? Oh yes . . . just give me a minute,' he muttered as he struggled out of the blanket. He stepped from the tent to see a thick mist floating across the ground and shuddered. The grass was thick with dew and the birds in the surrounding trees were singing a chorus to welcome the new day. He hurried into the copse to do his toilet then quickly rejoined Twig, who was waiting for him.

An hour later they were back with not only a basket full of mushrooms but also a rabbit that Dog had chased into a rabbit hole.

Fleur, who had a bright fire blazing, soon had the mushrooms sizzling in the frying pan, and when Franky tasted them he was sure that he had never eaten anything so delicious in his whole life. After breakfast, Twig set off for market with a small barrow containing baskets of every shape and size, along with a number of pretty bead necklaces that Fleur had made.

'Have a good day. I'll see you all later,' he shouted cheerfully as he set off with a spring in his step. Franky slowly began to unwind as the peace of the place washed over him. Fleur carried a basketful of dirty washing down to the stream and after laundering the items, she hung them over the hedgerow to dry while she set off for the stream again to wash the breakfast things. Meantime, Franky entertained the children, playing ball with them and thoroughly enjoying himself. It was a long time since he had been allowed to be a child and he'd almost forgotten what it was like not to have to watch his P's and Q's all the while.

Twig came back just before lunchtime with an empty barrow and two large shopping bags of supplies.

'We'll eat like kings for the next couple of days.' He winked at Franky and the child felt himself smiling, really smiling, for the first time in a long, long while.

Chapter Eighteen

Franky would remember the next four weeks as being the happiest of his life. Fleur and Twig accepted him into their little family unit as if he belonged there, and although Franky was fearful for a time of the interrogation that was sure to come, it never did.

Each day, Twig would go off while Fleur stayed behind to entertain and care for the children. But it wasn't all play, as Franky soon discovered. Although neither of the children went to school or nursery, their parents were keen that they should be educated, so each day Fleur set aside between two to three hours to teach them basic maths and English. Even at the tender age of two, Destiny could already recognise the letters of the alphabet, and Echo could read fluently. They bathed in the stream where Fleur also got their water, which she boiled before they drank it, and the time passed pleasantly. On more than one occasion, Twig asked Franky if he would like to go into the market with him, but Franky always declined the offer. He was too afraid of being recognised and dragged back to live in Puddlesea, which held nothing but unhappy memories for him.

When Fleur wasn't doing household chores or teaching the children, she would sit for hours, patiently stringing brightly coloured beads into necklaces and bracelets, which Twig also took to the market to sell along with his wickerwork. They lived simply but adequately, and Franky soon learned that Fleur and Twig were not at all materialistic; they were perfectly happy with the way their life was and had no wish for it to be any different. The only luxuries that they afforded themselves from what Franky could see of it were the highly scented joss sticks they lit around the fireside each night and the sweet-scented cigarettes that Twig would roll for them.

He found himself looking forward to the readings from the Bible each evening before the haunting tunes that Twig would play to them on his guitar. The children would always be tired out by then and happy to snuggle down into the little bunk beds that their father had cleverly built for them in their travelling home. Franky had grown extremely close to Destiny, who had taken to following him about like a little puppy, and both Twig and Fleur were touched to see how gentle Franky was with her. They had enjoyed an Indian summer — long hot days when the children could run about bare-foot on the grass, or splodge in the edge of the stream — but in October, the weather suddenly changed and the days became colder, the nights even more so.

Slowly, the horror of the abuse Franky had suffered at Jacob's hands began to dim and he found he could smile again. The field they were living in seemed a world apart from the towns and villages along the Devon coastline, and Franky never grew tired of looking at the view. He would stare beyond the copse at the bottom of the field to the hazy distant hills beyond and wish that things could stay just as they were for ever, but deep down he had a feeling that they wouldn't. It was one night as they were sitting around the fire, huddled closer now because it had grown colder, that he plucked up the courage to ask, 'Will you be stayin' here for the winter?'

Twig shook his head. 'No, it will be time to move on soon. There are a number of festivals that we attend each year where we meet up with other people who live as we do.'

'Oh, an' where are they then?' Franky asked as he chewed on a chicken leg.

'Well, Stonehenge is the main gathering, but then there are any number of others. Appleby Fair is another one we don't like to miss.'

Franky felt sad as he thought of leaving the place he'd come to regard as a sanctuary. He was about to say something else, when

Destiny suddenly began to cough and Fleur and Twig were instantly distracted. The child had developed the cough some days ago and despite the herbs and plants that Fleur had boiled up and ground down into medicine for her it seemed to be getting worse.

'I think I'll get her into bed,' she told Twig, concern heavy in her voice. 'I'm beginning to think the medicine I'm giving her isn't strong enough.'

'It *will* work eventually,' Twig said irritably.

Franky frowned as he looked from one to the other. He had never heard them have a cross word before, but at the minute they were glaring at each other.

'Don't even *think* of asking to take her to a doctor again,' Twig told his partner uncharacteristically sharply. 'When we embarked on this life we agreed that we would be entirely self-sufficient, and that's how it's going to remain.'

'But she's getting worse, and she has a temperature now,' Fleur pointed out as she stood with the child clutched to her chest. 'You know she's always been prone to chest infections but I've always managed to get her better before. This time, nothing I try seems to be working.'

Twig's mouth set in a stubborn line and Fleur stormed off to the van as Franky chewed on his lip. Destiny had been really poorly all day, not even offering to follow him about, which was very unusual.

They listened to her clattering about as she tucked the children into their beds and when it eventually went quiet, Franky dared to ask, 'Why don't you want Destiny to see a doctor, Twig? Don't you care about her?'

'Of course I care,' Twig told him solemnly. 'But the medicines that doctors prescribe are manmade. Fleur and I agreed that we would go back to nature. I don't believe in pushing all these poisons into children. They do more harm than good. I don't believe in blood transfusions and suchlike either. Our Father never sends us more than we are able to bear and He will bring Destiny through this if that is what He wishes.'

Franky frowned. 'An' what if Our Father don't want her to get better?' he asked fearfully.

'Oh, for goodness' sake. I'm going to bed,' Twig replied crossly, and with a toss of his head he stood up and stamped away.

Left alone with his thoughts, Franky stared into the fire. He was suddenly terrified that something might happen to Destiny, and terrified of losing the lifestyle that he'd come to love. I wonder if they'll take me with them when they move on, he thought as he stared miserably into the dancing flames. They were flickering in the wind that had blown up, and pulling his coat collar tighter around his neck, Franky scuttled away to his tent. He lay shivering for a long time as he listened to Destiny's hacking cough, which he could hear even through the closed doors of the van, then turning over he huddled beneath his blanket and willed himself to sleep.

The next day, Fleur and Twig seemed to be on good terms again and Destiny looked slightly better though she was still very pale.

'Why don't we go into Ilfracombe and let the children have a bit of a romp on the beach?' Twig suggested over a breakfast of porridge.

Fleur considered his suggestion as she glanced at Destiny. 'Well, I suppose it wouldn't do any harm,' she admitted. 'What do you think, Franky? You haven't ventured out of the camp since you joined us.'

Franky swallowed the food in his mouth before nodding slowly. As Fleur had pointed out, it was Sunday, so there was every chance that the place would be quiet. Most of the holidaymakers had gone home now, and as there weren't any markets on it was highly unlikely that he'd run into anyone who might recognise him.

'All right,' he mumbled and so it was decided.

An hour later they set off with Echo skipping excitedly ahead of them. It was about a forty-minute walk into Ilfracombe, and not wanting to tire Destiny out, Fleur had tied a shawl about herself and carried the child in that. They made a colourful party in their garish clothes as they made their way through the lanes, and on the way Twig pointed out things of interest. He seemed to know the names of all the birds and plants they passed. At one point they took a short cut through a wooded area and Franky felt as if he had entered another world. A hushed world, where the sunlight struggled to squeeze its beams between the canopy of branches overhead, painting a golden picture on the floor beneath them. There was nothing to be heard except the sound of their footsteps crunching on the leaves underfoot, or the flurry of some unseen indignant animal crashing away through the undergrowth as it sensed the intruders' presence.

When they emerged on the other side, Ilfracombe was spread out before them and Franky thought he had never seen anything so beautiful. To one side of them whitewashed houses covered in ivy were nestling in the hills leading down to the Heritage Harbour and the quay where the boats that took sightseers on regular trips to Lundy Island were bobbing on the water. On the other side were the Victorian villas and terraces set amongst cobblestoned streets that spoke of another era, and stonewalled cottages, their stones bleached white by years of exposure to the sun and the salt sea air. As they all paused to admire the view, Twig once again surprised Franky with his knowledge.

'The coastal path over there stretches right from Hartland in the west to Lynmouth in the east,' he told them. 'And if you go in *that* direction,' he paused to point, 'you'll come to the mighty Hogback cliffs of Great Hangman. That way is Capstone Hill, and if you keep walking you'll come to Exmoor National Park. On a clear day you can see right across the water to the mountains in South Wales.'

'Yes, well, that was a lovely geography lesson, but can we get on now? Destiny is quite heavy,' Fleur complained.

'Sorry, love. Here, let me carry her for a while,' Twig offered, as he lifted the child from Fleur's arms. She instantly nestled her head into her father's shoulder and he became quiet as they continued and he felt the heat of her through his shirt. Fleur was right, the child did have a temperature, but hopefully a day on the beach would do her good.

When they eventually reached the beach, which was almost deserted, Franky and Echo instantly headed for the waves and began to splash about in them as Fleur and Twig sat down on the damp sand to watch them play.

'Franky is a nice child now he's coming out of his shell a bit, isn't he?' Fleur mused as she watched his antics.

Twig followed her eyes and nodded. 'Yes, he is, but you know, I think something very bad must have happened to him for him to keep to the camp as he does. He is getting a little more vocal with us now but I always feel that he's holding back . . . as if he doesn't completely trust us.'

'But that's hardly surprising if his mother's in jail and he doesn't know his father,' Fleur sensibly replied.

Twig nodded thoughtfully, his eyes still tight on the child in question. His hair had grown from the harsh short back and sides it had been when he had first joined them, and now it framed his head like a halo of jet-black curls. He was a stocky lad and Twig could see that he was going to grow into a very handsome young man.

'Do you think he'll want to come with us when we move on?' he asked, and now Fleur sighed heavily.

'I have no idea, though he doesn't seem to have anyone else, does he?'

They sat lost in thought as the sun rose higher in the sky and the boys rolled on the golden sand shouting with glee as Dog frolicked after them, his tail wagging in circles in his excitement. Once they tired of that they went crabbing in the rockpools left behind by the sea and then they collected shells, which Fleur told them she would make into necklaces. Eventually it was time to set off back to the camp and Fleur, who had cradled Destiny on her lap the whole time they had been there looked at her daughter with increasing concern. The child was flushed and she hadn't even attempted to play with the boys or leave her mother for a second.

Twig helped her to her feet and they set off with the boys running ahead of them.

'We'll sponge her down in cold water when we get back to the camp,' Twig said, sensing Fleur's fear. She looked at him scornfully for the first time since they had been together and he flinched. He knew that she was worried, but even so he had no intention of going back on his beliefs. They had made a pact to turn their back on conventional medicine long ago, and he was not going to renege on it now.

The rest of the journey was made in silence and immediately they got back to the camp, Twig went off to get a bowl of cold water from the stream while Fleur stripped Destiny out of her clothes and laid her on their bed. They then took it in turns to bathe the child with cold flannels but as the day slipped towards evening her temperature showed no signs of going down; in fact, if anything she seemed to get even hotter despite the chill that settled on the camp mid-afternoon.

Fleur left her briefly to fry up some bacon for their tea then she asked Franky to wash the dishes in the stream and returned to her daughter. All around the van were jam jars full of the wild flowers that Destiny had picked for her mother before she became ill, and now Franky felt sad as he looked at them. He hated to see the little girl looking so poorly and guessed correctly that despite her beliefs, Fleur would have taken her to a doctor if Twig had permitted it.

That night, Twig and the two boys said prayers for Destiny while her mother stayed in the van with her, constantly wiping her sweating brow and muttering soothing words to her. There was no guitar playing that evening. No one was in the mood for it and Franky took Echo into his tent with him, so that Fleur and Twig could give their daughter their undivided attention. Echo was subdued but dropped off to sleep almost immediately while Franky lay fretting about the little girl. Since the second he had set eyes on her she had reminded him of his sister, Natasha, and he hoped that she would soon get better.

★　★　★

The next morning, Destiny was even worse and now Fleur was panicking. She had stayed up all night watching over her daughter, and her eyes were heavy from lack of sleep. Destiny was deliriously hot now and didn't seem to recognise anyone.

'We have to do something, Twig!' Fleur cried desperately as she rocked the child to and fro in her arms.

'She's in God's hands – what will be will be,' Twig muttered defiantly, his mouth set in a grim line. He had already loaded the barrow with baskets to take into the market, but it was obvious that Fleur didn't want him to leave them.

'I could take 'em in an' sell 'em for you,' Frankie suggested before he had time to think about it. He had only left the camp once since joining them on the day they had visited the beach, and was terrified of going into the town in case he was recognised, but he hated to see his newfound friends so distressed, and reasoned that this was the least he could do for them.

'Are you sure you could manage?' Twig asked.

Gulping nervously, Franky said, 'Course I can, the barrow's as light as a feather.' He forced a smile to his lips.

'In that case, I'd better run through the prices with you, and tell you where to stand when you get there,' Twig told him, and for the next five minutes, Franky listened carefully as the man pointed out the different prices of the baskets.

'Right, now have you got that?' Twig asked when he'd finished, and Franky nodded as Twig took the handles of the makeshift barrow and began to drag it towards the lane for him. Franky smiled at Fleur then followed him. Once they came to the lane, Twig pointed downhill. 'Just keep to this lane and you'll come straight into the market. All right, son?'

'I'll be fine.'

'OK, off you go then. I'll see you later. And . . . thanks.'

Franky started to push the barrow, which was surprisingly light, and when he reached a bend in the lane he turned to wave but Twig had already disappeared back the way they had come. Shrugging,

191

Franky set off again. Forty minutes later, the marketplace came into sight and as Franky approached the corner where Twig had asked him to stand, he glanced nervously from left to right. There were brightly coloured stalls everywhere he looked, selling everything from material to fruit and veg. Stallholders were shouting to make themselves heard above the noise of the shoppers, and a delicious smell of fresh-caught fish and chips hung on the air.

Franky began to set the baskets out around the barrow and very soon people were approaching him to look at the goods.

By lunchtime, his pocket was bulging with the money he had taken and there were only two baskets left. Surprisingly, he'd quite enjoyed himself and now he was eager to get back to the camp to show Twig the money he had taken. An elderly lady approached to look at one of the wicker baskets he had left, and it was as he was serving her that he saw someone from the corner of his eye standing some distance away and watching him.

He took the old lady's money hastily, keeping his back to the woman who was still standing peering at him, then throwing the basket that was left into the barrow he set off at a trot towards the lane that would lead him back to the camp.

'Franky!'

The sound of someone shouting his name made his heart beat faster and now he literally ran the last few yards that would take him out of the marketplace. Hopefully, whoever it was would think they'd been mistaken and forget all about him. He didn't pause until he was on top of the hill overlooking Ilfracombe where he leaned on the handles of the barrow to catch his breath. Thankfully, no one seemed to be following him, so he proceeded at a more normal pace then. When the gap in the hedge that would lead him back to the camp came into sight he sighed with relief and clumsily dragged the barrow through the opening. He was still some yards away from the van when the sound of shouting reached his ears. He gaped in amazement as he realised that Twig and Fleur were in the middle of a blazing row.

Fleur was standing outside the van with Destiny cradled in her arms and Twig was standing in front of her with his hands on his hips as he blocked her way.

'You can stand there for as long as you like,' he heard her shout, 'but I'm telling you now, one way or another I'm getting her to the hospital!'

He saw Twig's shoulders sag in defeat as he stood aside and the next minute, Fleur was striding towards him with her brightly coloured skirts flapping about her ankles and her long blonde hair flying in the wind.

She barely acknowledged him, only to tell him, 'I'm getting Destiny to a hospital.'

He nodded numbly as he watched her stride purposefully away before pushing the barrow the short distance to the van. There was a look of such deep pain on Twig's face that Franky felt sorry for him.

'Why don't you go with her?' he suggested softly. 'I can stay here an' look after Echo.'

Twig stared at him as he wrestled with his conscience, and then he suddenly nodded and broke into a run as he rushed away to catch up with his family.

'Is Destiny gonna be all right, Franky?' Echo asked fearfully as he stared up at him from deep brown eyes.

Franky ruffled his hair and forced a smile to his face.

'She'll be fine,' he assured him. 'She'll be back in no time bright as a button again, you'll see.'

Echo adored Franky and never doubted his word for a minute as they settled down to wait for the family to return. As darkness fell, Franky collected some wood from the nearby copse and threw it on to the fire as they huddled around it. A thick fog had settled in the field and he felt strangely afraid and shut off from the world. Fleur and Twig had been gone for an awfully long time now and he was getting really worried, not that he showed it to Echo. He found some fruit in a basket and they ate it together before Franky suggested, 'Why don't you get tucked in, eh? By the time you wake up, your mam an' dad will be back.'

Echo obediently allowed Franky to tuck him into his bed and then after fetching his blanket from the tent, Franky wrapped it around him and settled down to wait. It was the sound of someone crying that woke him from an uneasy doze some time later and he peered into the fog, wondering how he had ever managed to drop off in the first place. The fire had almost died down now and he hastily threw some more wood on to it as he strained his eyes into the darkness. The sound of weeping was getting louder and then Fleur and Twig suddenly appeared like spectres from the mist.

Franky frowned as he saw that they were alone. 'Where's Destiny?' he asked, which only caused Fleur to burst into a fresh torrent of tears. They were standing at the side of him now and Franky would never forget the desolate expression on Fleur's face for as long as he lived.

'Destiny has gone to a better place,' Twig told him huskily as he kept his arm tight about Fleur.

'What do you mean – a better place? Have they moved her to another hospital?' the child asked innocently.

'No, Franky. The hospital couldn't help her – she'd developed pneumonia and there was nothing they could do. She has gone home to God. Destiny is an angel now.'

Franky stared at him uncomprehendingly, but then as the meaning of his words struck home, he wagged his head from side to side in angry denial. 'God can't have her,' he spat. 'Destiny belongs here with *us*. Go an' fetch her back *right now*! God can't have her!' Once again he was losing someone he had come to love, and it was almost more than he could bear. First it had been his mother and his sisters and Bruno, and now it was the dear little girl who had worked her way into his heart with her innocent smile and loving ways.

Twig stepped forward and enfolded Franky in his arms and as he felt the warmth of this kind man, who had been the nearest thing to a father he had ever known, Franky sobbed as if his heart would break.

★   ★   ★

The next few days were miserable. None of them seemed to have the heart to move or even speak, but eventually Twig pulled himself together enough to weave a tiny wicker coffin for Destiny's funeral that would take place the next day in the little church on the hill in Ilfracombe. He intended to deliver it to the chapel of rest where she was lying that very day and she would be buried overlooking the sea, which Twig felt she would have liked.

Franky had never been to a funeral before and the following day, his heart broke afresh as he watched Destiny's little coffin being lowered into the ground. At Twig's request it had been a very simple service. There were no elaborate wreaths, only late blooming wild flowers that Fleur had picked on the way to the church, and only themselves to mourn her.

Both Twig and Fleur were calm and dignified, but Franky and Echo, who wasn't really old enough to understand what was happening, wept openly.

When it was over they walked away from the grave and as Franky looked over his shoulder he shuddered as he saw two men with large spades approaching the grave. Soon, Destiny would be cut off from the sunshine she had loved for all time.

Chapter Nineteen

For a whole week they sat about the camp, each trapped in their
own unhappy thoughts. Twig still wove his baskets and Fleur still
made the pretty necklaces and bracelets that sold so well in the
marketplace, but neither of them seemed to have any heart in what
they were doing any more and the food supplies were running
dangerously low.

'I could take some o' these into the market for you,' Franky offered
one wet and dank day.

Twig looked up from the basket he was weaving and shrugged,
not much caring one way or another. The atmosphere between
himself and Fleur was strained, and Twig knew that she was blaming
him for not letting her get Destiny to the hospital sooner.

'We are getting a bit short on food supplies,' Franky pressed, 'an'
if I was to take some o' this stuff into market an' sell it I could get
some shoppin' on the way back.'

'I suppose he's right,' Fleur commented as she looked at Echo's
sad face. 'None of us have had a proper meal for days, and Echo's
going to get ill too if we keep on like this.'

Twig stood up resignedly and began to load his baskets into the
barrow without another word.

Once it was ready to go, Franky put his warm coat on and
uncharacteristically touched Twig's hand. 'We'll be all right,' he
told him solemnly, as if he were the adult and Twig the child.
Twig nodded absently; he had no idea how much his family had

come to mean to this child and was too locked into grief to respond.

Franky smiled at Fleur and Echo then began to drag the loaded barrow towards the gap in the hedge. He hoped that once he'd sold the wares and they'd all got some good food inside them that they'd feel better. Pausing at the opening, he looked back at them fondly. They were a good family and he knew that he owed them a lot. They were the first people who had accepted him just as he was – and he would never forget that.

The journey into the town was uneventful, and because of the overcast weather he saw immediately that there were nowhere near as many people about as there had been the last time he had come here. He thought briefly of the woman who had called his name but then pushed the thought away. The chances of her being there a second time were remote, and his need to provide some food for his new family was stronger than his fear of being found.

Even the stallholders didn't seem so cheerful today and they huddled underneath their awnings with glum faces as they waited for their customers. By lunchtime, Franky had only sold four baskets and a small amount of Fleur's jewellery, but he stood there doggedly, determined to sell at least enough to be able to do a modest food shop on the way home.

It was almost one o'clock when he glanced up to see a policeman standing talking to a woman who had her back to him some way away. He saw the policeman glance in his direction and suddenly feeling nervous he hastily began to cram the baskets back into the barrow. He had enough to get them at least a couple of good meals and he didn't want to risk hanging about any longer. He was so intent on what he was doing that he didn't see the policeman approaching and when the man suddenly grabbed his arm, Franky started. "'Ere, gerroff!' he shouted as he struggled to free his arm from the man's grasp.

'Now calm down, son. I only want to ask you a few questions,' the policeman said kindly as he clung on to the child. 'Come on now. Tell me your name, eh?'

Franky glared up at him sullenly and now the man said, 'Well, tell me where you live then. Are you from around here?'

'No, I ain't.' Franky was red in the face now as he fought to get away.

'Your name isn't Francis Anderson, by any chance, is it?' the man continued, but Franky had no chance to deny it as a woman stepped from behind him and the colour drained out of Franky's face.

'Aw, love. We've been worried sick about you,' she said, and he found himself looking up at Mrs Dickinson.

'Do I take it this *is* Francis then?' the policeman asked, addressing the woman now, and when she nodded he began to haul Franky through the marketplace.

'But me barrow,' Franky objected as he looked back at Twig's collection in distress.

'Don't get worrying about them,' the policeman advised. 'You won't be needing them any more. We need to get you somewhere safe.'

The woman who had once been Franky's ally was almost running to keep up with them, and there was a look of deep distress on her face.

'Where have you been? How have you been living?' she gabbled, but Franky ignored her as he continued to struggle to get free of the policeman's grasp.

When the police station came into sight, Franky brought his foot back and kicked the man on the shin with all his might but the officer's hold didn't weaken for a second and Franky began to panic. What were they going to do to him? And what would Twig think if he didn't go back to them? Tears of desperation started in his eyes now as the officer hauled him through the double doors and towards a desk.

'We've got a young runaway here. You'd better get hold of Social Services,' he informed the Desk Sergeant, never loosening his grip on the child for a second.

Mrs Dickinson, who was out of breath, reached out to him but

Franky slapped her hand away as he renewed his efforts to get free.

The Desk Sergeant eyed Franky warily as he nodded and reached for a phone book. Meanwhile the policeman dragged Franky kicking and screaming towards a door at the side of the desk as Mrs Dickinson followed.

Once inside a small room, the policeman released his hold on the child and stood in front of the door as Mrs Dickinson dropped breathlessly into a seat.

'Now then,' he said, 'I suggest while we wait for the social worker to arrive you tell us what you've been doing with yourself for the last few weeks and where you've been living.'

'I ain't been doin' *nothin'* and I ain't been livin' *nowhere,*' Franky replied grumpily as he dropped on to a chair and crossed his arms tightly about his chest. He would rather have died than get Twig and Fleur into any trouble, and now he stared down at the floor, avoiding the policeman's eyes.

'All right then, you haven't been living anywhere,' the policeman said good-naturedly. 'So who do those baskets you were selling belong to?'

'I found 'em,' Franky lied. It was clear that the man didn't believe him but Franky didn't much care. He didn't care about anything but getting back to the camp.

'I ain't goin' back to June,' he stated flatly, and he noticed Mrs Dickinson and the policeman exchange a worried glance. It was then that the woman hotched her chair a little closer to him and after gulping deeply she said quietly, 'You won't have to go back to June, Franky. She . . . er . . . died on the night that you ran away.'

'*She what?*' Franky stared at her incredulously. Surely it couldn't be true.

Mrs Dickinson hung her head as she thought back to the morning she had found June lying in a bath full of blood. It was an image that would be branded on her brain until the day she died, but she had no intention of telling Franky the gory details.

'I'm afraid it's true, dear. Both June and Jacob are gone now. The house is up for sale and there's no one living there any more.'

'So what'll happen to me then?' He supposed that he should feel sad, but all he felt was relief.

'That will be for the social worker to decide when she gets here,' the policeman told him.

'But why do I have to have another social worker? Why can't you just let me go?'

'Because you're still a child and you need someone to take care of you,' the policeman replied.

It was on the tip of the boy's tongue to tell them that he *had* someone to take care of him, but the fear of getting Twig and Fleur into trouble was still strong so he remained tight-lipped.

Seeing that he wasn't going to divulge anything the policeman asked him, 'Are you hungry, son?'

Franky opened his mouth to say no, he wasn't, but then his stomach gurgled and so he nodded resignedly. There was no point in cutting off his nose to spite his face.

'In that case I'll go and see what I can rustle up for you while Mrs Dickinson here keeps you company. And don't get thinking of trying to run away because I'll be just beyond that door.'

Franky scowled but remained silent as the man slipped out of the room. Once they were on their own, Mrs Dickinson surveyed him critically. His hair was curling on his collar now and he looked like a good wash wouldn't come amiss. His clothes looked as if they had never seen an iron too but in spite of all that he looked quite well.

'Where will I go now then?'

His question made her gulp. What could she tell him? She decided to be honest in the end and said simply, 'I dare say they'll put you into a foster-home till they decide what's going to happen.'

The look of horror that spread across his face made her wince.

'I don't *want* to go into a foster-home,' he told her indignantly. 'I want to go home to me mam.'

'I'm afraid that isn't possible, love.' June had told her about his mother being in prison so Mrs Dickinson knew that this wouldn't be an option.

'In that case I'm old enough to look after meself.'

She bowed her head. 'If I were twenty years younger, I'd take you in myself,' she told him. 'But the thing is, me and Mr Golding are going to be married and I can't see the department letting a pair of old codgers like us take you in.'

A silence settled between them until the policeman returned with a large plate piled high with sandwiches, a packet of crisps and a beaker full of milk.

'There you go,' he said cheerfully. 'That was the best I could do, but I dare say it will fill a hole.'

Both he and Mrs Dickinson then looked towards the window, and now that he wasn't being watched Franky attacked the food as if he hadn't eaten for a month, keeping a wary eye on his jailers all the time.

He had just finished the milk when there was a tap on the door and a woman entered the room. She was very thin and severe-looking, with steel-grey hair that was scraped back into a tight bun jammed full of hairpins. She nodded a greeting towards the policeman, then sitting herself down in front of Franky, she asked, 'And just where have you been for the last few weeks, young man? Are you aware that you've had almost the entire Devon police force out looking for you?'

Franky knew immediately that he was going to get scant sympathy from this quarter and he glared at her scathingly.

'Very well, it's obvious that you're not going to co-operate so I may as well just tell you what's going to happen next. I dare say that you know your adoptive mother is dead, so I've arranged for you to go into a temporary foster-home in Barnstaple while we consider your longterm future.'

A temporary foster-home? It sounded even worse than living with June, but then Franky remembered Jacob and decided that nothing could be as awful as what he had done to him. Suddenly his shoulders sagged. There was no point in arguing, and if he tried to run away they would only catch him. Perhaps he should go along with their suggestion and then run away and come back to Fleur and Twig as soon as he got the chance.

The woman now stood up and looking towards the policeman she said haughtily, 'Thank you, Officer. I think we've taken up quite enough of your time now so I'll get this young man over to Barnstaple.' She glanced at her wristwatch and tutted. 'It will be late already by the time I get home,' she said, and Franky suddenly felt as if he was a piece of baggage that she was keen to get rid of, which he supposed he probably was.

'Come along,' she told Franky brusquely. 'I have plans for this evening so I'd like to get this over with.' There was not an ounce of compassion in her voice and Franky hoped that she wouldn't be his social worker for long. He knew that he would never get along with her. But then he comforted himself, he wouldn't have to because the first chance he got he would slip away and rejoin Twig and Fleur.

Slightly comforted at the thought of being with them again, he rose from his seat and now Mrs Dickinson began to sniff into her handkerchief noisily as she fumbled in her bag with the other hand.

'Here you are, sweetheart.' She pressed some silver coins into his hand. 'Go carefully now an' look after yourself.'

Just for a second, Franky had to resist the urge to throw himself into her arms. Mrs Dickinson and Bruno had been the only ones to show him any kindness while he was living with the Andersons. But Bruno was gone now, and after today he would probably never see this kindly lady again.

'Thank you,' he muttered in a low voice, and with his head down he followed the social worker, who later informed him that he should call her Mrs Smythe, from the room.

They made the journey to Barnstaple in silence as Franky stared mutely from the car window. Mrs Smythe made no attempt at conversation and Franky was grateful for the fact. He kept wondering what Twig and Fleur would think when he didn't come home, and hoped that they wouldn't believe he'd run away with their takings from the goods he had sold. The money was resting against his leg in his trouser pocket and it seemed to be burning him. He knew how much they'd needed it and hated to think of them going hungry. He was so distressed that finally the tears he had so valiantly held back trembled on his lashes before spilling down his cheeks. Mrs Smythe looked at him critically.

'*Really*, boy – anyone would think I was taking you to prison,' she remarked unthinkingly, and the words made Franky sob all the harder.

It was dusk by the time they pulled up in front of a small terraced house in Barnstaple and Franky eyed it warily.

'This is where you'll be staying for now,' she informed him. 'Your carers' names are Mr and Mrs Hyde and I expect you to behave for them. If you don't, you'll have me to answer to. Now come along, let's go and get the paperwork out of the way and then perhaps I can get home.'

Franky climbed out of the car and stood next to her in front of a door that opened directly on to the pavement. He could hear noises coming from beyond it, but when a huge woman opened it some seconds later they stopped abruptly.

Franky blinked as he stared up at her. She was so enormous that she blocked out the light from the room behind her.

'Ah, you got here then,' she said unnecessarily, and when she stepped aside they moved past her into a small lounge that seemed to be bulging at the seams with children of all ages. They were all looking at Franky with interest and he felt himself blush.

''Ere, is that a boy or a girl?' the oldest of the boys quipped.

Franky glared back at him.

'This is Francis Anderson,' Mrs Smythe said and now the boy, who looked to be about twelve years old, put his hand across his mouth and sniggered mockingly.

'You could have fooled me, with that mop of hair,' he muttered sarcastically in the local accent.

Thankfully, the large woman intervened to shut him up. 'That'll be enough of your lip for now, Blake. At least let the lad get in before you start on him.' Jerking her head towards a door that led into an even smaller back room, she told her visitors, 'Come on, we'll go through there. It's quieter and this lot can watch the telly in peace then.'

Mrs Smythe inclined her head and followed the woman. Once inside the other room, Mrs Hyde closed the door firmly and pointing to a chair set against one wall, she told Franky, 'You sit there while we get this paperwork sorted out.'

There was no word of welcome and Franky found himself staring at her as she sat at a table with Mrs Smythe signing numerous forms that the social worker pushed across the table to her as if she didn't have a minute to spare.

'I think that's it then,' Mrs Smythe declared after a time as she collected the papers and transferred them back into an enormous black leather bag.

'I'm afraid Francis doesn't have any clothes apart from what he stands up in, but I'm sure you'll be able to sort him out with something that fits, Gillian. I shall be in touch within a few days to see how he's settling in, but meantime if you need anything at all don't hesitate to ring the office.'

The huge woman heaved herself out of her chair and followed Mrs Smythe back into the other room. Meantime, Franky looked around him and didn't much like what he saw. The house wasn't exactly dirty but it was certainly very untidy, with stacks of unironed clothes everywhere he looked. The curtains that framed the long narrow window set in one wall looked as if they had never been washed, and the carpet on the floor was grubby and of an indistinguishable colour.

The noise coming from the room he had just walked through was almost deafening now and he longed to be back in the camp with Twig and Fleur.

He heard the front door click and the woman who had admitted him appeared again, followed by the boy she'd addressed as Blake.

'Now then,' she said, as she looked him up and down appraisingly. 'You'll have to borrow a pair of Blake's pyjamas for tonight, till I can get to the shops to buy you some of your own. And a trip to the barber's wouldn't go amiss either, by the look of that mop.'

She turned to smile fondly at Blake, who Franky was soon to discover was her eldest son and the apple of her eye. 'You'll be one of seven kids while you're here,' she informed him next. 'So don't go expecting any special treatment. I've got my hands full, and that's a fact, so I expect good behaviour off the lot of you.'

She put her head to one side and hitched her gigantic breasts up as she said to Blake in a softer tone, 'Take him up and show him where he'll be sleeping, would you, love?'

'Yes, Mum.' Blake smiled sweetly and cocked his thumb towards a door that led to a steep staircase. Franky followed him without a word. They came to a long narrow landing and at the third door along, Blake told him, 'This is where you'll be sleeping with me and Duncan. Duncan's in care and all. He's Scottish and he's not a bad kid. He's seven – how old are you?'

'Nearly eight,' Franky muttered.

'*Eight?*' Blake looked astounded. 'You're a big bugger for your age then, aren't you? I'd have taken you for nine or ten at least. Big or not though, just remember I'm kingpin here and you'll be all right.'

He pushed him into a small bedroom into which three single beds covered in dull-coloured blankets were crammed, so close together that the only way of getting into them was from the bottom. There was not another stick of furniture in the room and Franky thought it smelled fusty and of smelly feet. He'd become used to sleeping on his hay mattress and wondered briefly what it would be like to sleep in a proper bed again.

'There're three bedrooms,' Blake told him. 'The four girls sleep in that one next to ours, and my mum and dad sleep in the last one along the landing.'

'The bathroom's along there,' he continued, vaguely waving his hand in the direction of the landing. 'I get to go in first in the morning, then it's up to you lot to fight over who goes next.'

Franky was fascinated by Blake's teeth: they protruded so far he was sure he had never seen anything like them apart from on a horse, but he stood mute as the older boy eyed him curiously before asking, 'Are you a gypsy?'

'No, I ain't,' Franky told him with a glare.

'Got any money on you, have you?'

When Franky's hand dropped protectively to the pocket of his jeans, Blake grinned triumphantly and pounced on him. Franky put up a valiant fight and protested loudly, but he was no match for the bigger lad and soon Blake laughed as he eyed the money in his hand.

'Give that back, it ain't yours!' Franky shouted as he watched Twig's money disappear into Blake's pocket.

The boy caught him by the scruff of the neck and shook him much as Dog had shaken the unsuspecting rabbits he had caught for their dinner. Then, with their noses almost touching he ground out, 'Just remember who the boss is here. What's yours is mine and what's mine's me own. And don't bother to go belly-aching to my mum either. She won't take any notice of you. I'm her blue-eyed boy.'

Franky clenched his fists with frustration. He had been hoping to run back to the camp and give Twig his hard-earned money, but now he would have to go back empty-handed.

'Go on, get yourself back downstairs, nipper.'

Franky stumbled as Blake pushed him viciously in the back, then squaring his shoulders he marched out of the room and back down the steep narrow staircase as fury pumped through him.

Gillian, his new foster-mum, was laying plates out on the table, and glancing up she told Blake, 'Your dad will be back from work soon and he's bringing us some chips for tea. Get the knives and forks out, would you, lovie?'

Meek as a lamb, Blake went off to do as he was told and now she turned her attention back to Franky and they eyed each other up and down. Franky's first impression of her was borne out as he returned her stare. She was the most enormous woman he had ever seen, bigger even than Miss Verity, with great rings of fat seeming to drop off every part of her. Even her arms hung in folds of flab. She had short dark brown hair that was cut in a style that did nothing to flatter her moon-shaped face, and her eyes were a cold watery grey that seemed to look straight through him. Feeling uncomfortable, Franky eventually shifted his gaze to glance around the room again. It was certainly nothing at all like the home he'd lived in with Jacob and June, which had been scrupulously clean to the point of being almost clinical.

At that moment the back door opened and a man entered, bringing with him the smell of chips that wafted from a large parcel he was carrying. He didn't even give Franky a second look as he told the woman, 'Here's your dinner then.'

'Thanks, love.' She took the parcel from him and began to hurl handfuls of greasy chips on to the plates and the next second the children poured out of the front room and snatched up a plate each before heading off back the way they'd come.

'They like to eat their dinner watching the telly,' she informed Franky. 'Here you go, help yourself. Oh, and by the way, this is my husband, Walter.'

Walter, who had stooped shoulders and thinning grey hair, looked at him briefly and grunted in acknowledgement before taking a plate and sitting down at the table. Franky found himself thinking of June; she would have had a fit if anyone had come to her dinner table without washing their hands, but it seemed that this behaviour was normal for this household. Even Fleur had insisted on them all washing their hands before a meal. Thoughts of the life and the people he'd just been dragged away from made tears sting the back of his eyes again, but determined not to be a crybaby he choked them back. Lifting the nearest plate, he trudged after the rest of the children who he found sitting cross-legged on the floor with their plates balanced precariously on their laps.

None of them paid him any attention as he tucked himself into a corner and miserably picked at the food in front of him, and as he sat there his resolution grew. He was not going to stay here for a second longer than was necessary. Somehow he *must* get back to Twig and Fleur.

At bedtime Gillian clapped her hands and the children instantly dispersed to their bedrooms. Franky discovered that the girls' room was even more cramped than the boys', with two lots of bunk beds squashed against the wall at either side of a single room. The girls' names were Milly, Josie, Cathy and Jodie. Jodie was Blake's younger sister and Franky soon found out that she and Blake always got preferential treatment.

He also discovered that chips and lumpy porridge seemed to be the staple diet of this household. By the time he had been there for a week he was still wearing the clothes he had arrived in and they were beginning to smell. He dared to mention it to Gillian one morning when she'd got the rest of the children off to their various schools, and she almost snapped his head off.

'Well, I haven't had time to get 'em washed or go shopping for you yet, have I?' she bawled in a voice loud enough to waken the dead. 'There's only so many hours in the day and I haven't got two pairs of hands, you know.'

Seeing as how she seemed to sit on her fat backside eating chocolate and watching TV for most of every day, Franky thought this was rather a dumb statement for her to make, but wisely kept his mouth shut and didn't answer back.

Walter didn't seem much more energetic, apart from the fact that he did turn out to work each day. Most evenings he'd return home with a parcel of chips in his hands and then after a quick change he'd be off to the pub and the children wouldn't see him again until the next evening.

Two days after Franky had arrived at the Hydes', Mrs Smythe

rang to say that she was doing her best to get him into a local school. The boy shuddered at the thought. His schooldays hadn't been happy experiences for him up to now, and he dreaded the thought of yet another one.

It was on the eighth night of being there that things came to a head for Franky. He had learned to keep out of Blake's way as much as he could, and while the others were all at school he spent most of his time sitting out in the tiny shared backyard dreaming of the day when he would escape back to Twig and Fleur again.

On this particular night he went to bed and turned his back on Duncan and Blake as usual. It was in the early hours of the morning when a sharp stab in his back brought him upright in the bed.

'What did you do *that* for?' he demanded, as he swiped the sleep from his eyes.

Blake, who was leaning on his elbow in the next bed, lashed out at him viciously. ''Cos you were crying in your sleep and keeping me awake, *that's* what for, you great bloody cissy. You were shouting for somebody called Fleur. What a name, I ask you! It's as bad as Francis.'

'It's *Franky*.' As the child glared back at him, Blake caught him by the neck and shook him fiercely.

'You are nothing but a gypsy ponce,' he growled. 'This place was much better before you arrived, looking down your stuck-up little nose at us all the time.'

'I do *not* look down my nose at you,' Franky growled back indignantly. 'An' don't think *I* like bein' here. It's as bad for me as it is for you, I can tell you. In fact, I can't *wait* to get away.'

'Well, why don't you just piss off then?' With that, Blake turned his back on him and disappeared under his blanket as Franky scowled into the darkness. He'd had enough, and there and then he resolved to escape that very night.

He lay for a long time until Blake's noisy snores resumed, then pulling himself to the end of the bed he slid soundlessly off it and padded the short distance across the room. After inching the door open he paused and when he was satisfied that Blake and Duncan were still fast asleep he tiptoed down the stairs. After quickly collecting his coat and shoes, he made for the back door, cursing softly when he found that it was locked and the key wasn't in it. The same thing happened at the front door, but he was determined to get away now, so pulling the curtains aside he heaved the window open, praying that no one would hear him. A quick glance across his shoulder to make sure that no one was there, and then he was scrabbling madly through the opening, almost landing on his head on the pavement outside in his haste to be away from the godforsaken place. He glanced fearfully up and down the road then took to his heels as if Old Nick himself were in pursuit. He was free again and had no intention of ever going back.

Chapter Twenty

On the day following Franky's escape from the Hydes' household at dead of night, Lorna Craine paused to admire some hand-knitted cardigans in the small window of a craft shop in Hockley Vale, on the North Yorks moors. She was on two weeks' holiday from work and was touring the country in her car, stopping for odd nights here and there in bed and breakfasts whenever the fancy took her. It was some years since she'd been there with Mary Ingles on the day they'd placed Natasha with the Salisburys. She had fallen in love with the place back then, which was one of the reasons she'd chosen to visit it again. She wondered briefly how Natasha was doing. Mary had relinquished the case following Natasha's adoption, and Lorna hoped that the child would have found a happy ending with her new mum and dad. The young woman was tempted to knock on their cottage door. It was only a stone's throw from here if she remembered rightly . . . but then she decided against it. It wouldn't have been a very professional thing to do and the Salisburys probably wouldn't want reminders of the past.

Mary had retired now, due to heart problems, and Lorna had taken over her casebook. Sadly, one of the first things on her agenda when she got back to work was to visit Alex, or Francis as he was now known. She'd heard the week before that his adoption placement had ended following the death of both his parents, and seeing as he was originally from the Nuneaton area she had agreed to take the case back on and look for somewhere else for him to live.

Meanwhile he was in temporary foster-care with a family in Barnstaple. She had received a call from a social worker called Mrs Smythe informing her of the child's circumstances and her heart had gone out to him, especially when she learned how his new parents had died. Apparently, his dad had slipped over a cliff and his mother had committed suicide the very same night. She shuddered to think of how it must have affected the poor child, to lose them both like that. And then he'd gone on the run, but she supposed that he'd been so distraught that he wouldn't have known what he was doing. Poor little mite, she'd make him a priority just as soon as she got back to work.

Her thoughts turned to Lauren, his sister, now happily living at Feathermill Lodge in Nuneaton. Now *there* was a success story, if ever she'd heard one. She'd been shopping in her lunch-hour in Nuneaton town centre only a couple of weeks before when Penny Daventry, with Lauren swinging from her hand, had come strolling through the marketplace and almost collided with her.

'Why it's Lorna, isn't it?' Penny had asked, after apologising for nearly bumping into her.

'Yes, it is. How are you?' Lorna had had no need to ask how Lauren was. She looked positively glowing and the picture of health. She'd grown quite considerably and had changed from the toddler Lorna remembered into a pretty young girl with long dark hair tied back in a ribbon and large grey eyes that seemed to twinkle with mischief. The child smiled up at her as she snuggled further into her mother's side.

'Oh, we're all really well, thank you,' Penny informed her. 'We're just off to get Lauren a new violin from the music shop in Abbey Street, aren't we, darling? She's doing ever so well – her music teacher says she has a natural gift. David and I have decided to let her attend a private school in Coventry that specialises in teaching children like Lauren who have a musical talent. We're very proud of her.'

'You must be,' Lorna beamed. 'I'm so pleased everything has turned out so well for you.'

'Adopting Lauren was the best thing we ever did,' Penny told her. 'I really can't remember a time without her now; she's our pride and joy.'

Long after the chance meeting, Lorna had felt uplifted. It was a well-known fact that, statistically, there were far more adoption breakdowns than fostering breakdowns, but that was one she wouldn't have to worry about, she was sure of it.

She was standing there lost in thought when a voice at her elbow said, 'Excuse me, but aren't you Lorna, the social worker who delivered my daughter to us with Mary Ingles some years ago?'

Lorna spun round to find herself face to face with Dr Joe Salisbury, as if thoughts of him and his family had conjured him up out of thin air.

'Why, I don't believe it!' She chuckled merrily. 'I was just standing here thinking about you and Natasha and wondering how you were all doing.'

'Natasha and I are fine, but I'm afraid Gail . . . well, she's been suffering with cancer. She's had all her chemotherapy and radiotherapy and now we just have to wait to see if it's worked.'

'Oh, Joe, I'm *so* sorry.' Lorna was horrified at his news. Gail, his wife, had been such a lively, vibrant person, and it was dreadful to think that she'd got this terrible illness at such a young age. Lorna guessed that Gail couldn't be that much older than she herself was.

'Why don't you come back and see them both?' Joe now offered. 'Tasha will be home from school for her lunch and I'm on my lunch-break too, before I start my afternoon visits.'

Lorna paused uncertainly. There was nothing she would have liked more than to see Natasha, but she didn't want to intrude.

'Please,' he added, seeing her hesitation. 'Gail isn't able to get out and about much at the moment, you know, for fear of catching infections, so she loves to have visitors and I'm sure you'll see a big difference in Tasha. You could perhaps have a bit of lunch with us, if you're not in a rush to get anywhere?'

He spoke of his family with such pride that Lorna found herself smiling as she nodded. 'All right then, if you're quite sure that Gail wouldn't mind. I'd love to see them both again, but I won't stay too long, I promise.'

They fell into step and threaded their way through the narrow cobblestoned streets that she remembered so well, and soon he pointed ahead. 'Here we are, home.' There was a measure of satisfaction in his voice as he approached the door of Beehive Cottage and placed his key in the lock.

'*Daddy!*' The second he set foot through the door a lovely blond-haired little girl hurtled towards him and threw herself into his arms, then seeing the visitor close behind him she blushed prettily as he chuckled.

'It's all right, sweetheart,' he assured her, as he fondly stroked her shining hair. 'This is Lorna. She knew you a long time ago before you came to live with me and Mummy, but I don't suppose you'll remember her now. I just bumped into her on my way home. Lorna is here on holiday so I thought it would be nice if she came to see you and Mummy. Do you think there'll be enough lunch for us all?'

Tasha flashed Lorna a charming smile before assuring him, 'Oh y-yes. Jessie cooked us a big c-cottage pie and left it in the oven for us.' She then turned her attention to Lorna and told her, 'Jessie is the l-lady who comes in to clean and cook for us since M-Mummy was ill, but I h-help too, don't I, Daddy?'

Lorna was struggling not to gape with amazement. Tasha had come on in leaps and bounds and now, apart from a slight speech impediment, no one would ever have guessed that she had once suffered brain damage at the hands of her natural mother.

'Mummy's in there,' Natasha now informed Joe solemnly and then she scampered away into the next room.

'Why, you've done wonders with her!' Laura exclaimed in a whisper. 'She's absolutely *beautiful*. Like a little doll. And she seems so bright.'

Natasha was still petite, whereas her twin Lauren was of a stockier build, and dark. No one would ever have guessed that they were twins.

'Oh, she's bright all right,' Joe answered proudly. 'And in more ways than one. She lightens our whole lives. I don't know how we would have got through these last dark months while Gail's been having her treatment without Tasha. I'm sure she's given her mummy the will to fight this damn disease. But do come on through. Gail will be thrilled to see you again.'

Lorna followed him into the next room where Gail was propped up on cushions on the settee with a pile of magazines at her side. There was a brightly coloured scarf wrapped turban-style around her head and her eyes looked sunken, but even so, when she saw Lorna she smiled and held her hand out in greeting.

'Why, what a wonderful surprise!' she gasped, recognising her instantly. 'What on earth are *you* doing in this neck of the woods?'

'Actually, I'm on holiday, just sort of drifting where the fancy takes me,' Lorna explained. 'I was in the High Street when I bumped into Joe and he invited me back. I hope you don't mind?'

'*Mind?* I'm absolutely delighted,' the young woman assured her sincerely. 'You don't have to rush away, do you? I get so bored when these two leave after lunch. It's always lovely to have another woman to chat to. Do say you'll stay and keep me company for a while.'

'If that's the case, I'd love to.' Lorna plonked herself down on the edge of the sofa and soon the two women were chatting away like old friends while Joe went off to get their lunch out of the oven.

The meal was a jovial affair. Gail joined them at the dining-room table and as she walked weakly towards it, Lorna was shocked to see how frail she was. She'd lost an enormous amount of weight and wasn't as far through as a stick insect. Even so, she kept up a cheerful chatter and when it was time for Natasha to go back to school and Joe back to his afternoon surgery before doing his house calls, she kissed them both soundly.

'I love you, Mummy,' Lorna heard Tasha whisper as she returned her mother's kiss, and then she took her father's hand and they left the cottage together. There was a great lump swelling in Lorna's throat and a warm feeling spreading through her. They were obviously a very close family and she hoped that Gail would recover, so that they could continue to be so.

Although Gail loudly protested, Lorna cleared the pots and washed up, as Jessie had gone home, before making them both a nice hot cup of tea and a biscuit. Then they settled down for a chat and before Lorna knew it, a couple of hours had flown by.

Gail told her of all the hard work Joe had put into Tasha, determined that she should grow up to lead a normal life. And his efforts had paid dividends. All the speech therapy, the endless patient hours he had spent each night teaching her to read and write had made her into the happy little girl that she was.

'Of course, I've tried too,' Gail assured her visitor. 'But I have to be honest and say that most of it is down to Joe. He absolutely adores her and she adores him back. They're almost inseparable.'

'I can see that.' Lorna chuckled. 'And I think you've both done a wonderful job. But look at the time – Tasha will be home from school again soon and I'm still parked here. I ought to get off and leave you in peace. I've rattled your ear off and you look tired.' As she spoke she reached for her coat and Gail smiled up at her.

'I can't tell you how lovely it's been to have a bit of company with someone who's near my own age,' Gail said. 'Do say that you'll keep in touch. You're not Tasha's social worker so there's no reason why we shouldn't be friends, is there?'

'None at all,' Lorna assured her as she buttoned her coat. 'And I'd love to keep in touch, although the next time I see you, I hope to find you well and truly on the mend.'

'Let's hope so,' Gail agreed, and then Lorna leaned down and kissed her on the cheek before slipping out into the chilly air. She was feeling happy. Both Tasha and Lauren were doing well. That just left Franky, as he was now known, to deal with – but at the end of the day two out of three wasn't bad.

Chapter Twenty-One

Franky had walked for some distance when he heard the sound of a lorry trundling along behind him. There was surprisingly little traffic on the road, but then he supposed it was to be expected, as it must be the early hours of the morning by now. His first instinct was to duck behind a hedge, but then changing his mind he boldly stepped out into the road and stuck his thumb out.

There was the sound of air hissing as the driver slammed on his brakes and the lorry slewed to a halt just yards away from him.

'Are you trying to get yourself killed?' an irate driver shouted as he hung out of his cab window.

'Sorry, I were wonderin' if yer might be able to give me a lift,' Franky called up to him.

The driver frowned when he saw a child standing down on the roadway. He only looked to be about nine or ten, so what the bloody hell was he doing out here all alone at this time of night?

'Where are you heading for?' he asked gruffly.

'Oh, anywhere near Ilfracombe would do,' Franky told him, gazing up at him hopefully.

The driver hesitated, then thumbing towards the passenger door of the cab he told him abruptly, 'Hop in then. I think I can manage that.'

Franky shot round to the door before the man could change his mind and clambered into the warm cab gratefully. It was bitterly cold outside and he was tired now.

The lorry pulled away, and when they had gone some way in silence, the driver asked, 'So what's a little 'un like you doing out at this time all by yourself?'

'Oh, I've been stayin' wi' me granny an' now I'm goin' home,' Franky lied glibly.

The driver didn't believe a word of it but he kept his eyes ahead as he now asked, 'And don't your folks mind you wandering the streets at night?'

'Oh, they don't know,' Franky gabbled. 'I wanted to be home by the time they got up in the mornin' to surprise 'em, so I left me granny a note an' set off. I'll be fine, honestly.'

'Mm,' the driver muttered, but he stayed silent then until Ilfracombe came into sight in the distance. 'And where would you like dropping off?' he enquired.

Franky had got his bearings now and pointing ahead, he told him, 'The end o' that lane there will be fine, thanks.'

'But there aren't any houses around here,' the man objected, not liking the thought of leaving the child all alone in the middle of nowhere.

'Oh, yes there is – our farm's set well back from the road. You just can't see it from here.'

The driver drew the lorry to a halt and when Franky had thanked him and begun to climb down from the cab he asked for one last time, 'Are you *sure* you're going to be all right, son?'

'Yes, thanks.' Franky smiled at him brightly, and once he'd slammed the cab door he stood and watched the lorry drive away until it disappeared around a bend in the lane leading down to Ilfracombe. His heart was thumping with excitement now as he thought of how thrilled Twig, Fleur and Echo would be to see him. He was sure they'd forgive him for the money that Blake had taken once he explained what had happened, and he could hardly wait to see them.

He set off across the fields in the direction of the camp, taking the short cut that Twig had shown him when he took him into the market. Thankfully the moon had risen, and although it was cold he could just about pick his way across the hillocky grass by its light. When he came to the lane that bordered the field he set off uphill and shortly afterwards came to the gap in the hedge that would lead to the camp. He was smiling broadly now as he tried to judge what their reaction would be when he hammered on the side of the brightly painted converted ambulance they lived in. Twig would probably slap him on the shoulder while Fleur burst into tears of joy and gave him a big hug. He'd probably have to wait to see Echo until the morning because he would most likely remain fast asleep, but then that wouldn't be so bad, he told himself. At least he would be home.

After squeezing through the hedge he set off at a run: just one more corner to go now and he would be back where he belonged. He reached the bend in seconds and burst into the field where he had spent so many hours with his friends – but then came to an abrupt halt. The field was empty. All that was left was the remains of the last fire, nothing more than ashes now. His friends had gone and he knew that the possibility of him ever finding them again was remote.

Misery washed through him as he realised the hopelessness of his position. He had nowhere to go, no one to turn to, and no doubt the police would soon find him again and he'd be shipped off to yet another foster-home. He walked to the place where his little tent had been pitched and looked down at the hay that had served as his mattress as tears slithered unheeded down his cheeks. Some of it had blown across the field and he could see that the grass was lighter beneath what was left where the sun hadn't shone upon it. Just a few more days and no one would ever know they had even been there.

Turning despondently, he set off for the gap in the hedge again. It hurt too much to stand there and think of what he had lost. It felt as if his whole life was made up of heartache and pain, and he wondered what he had done to deserve it. Perhaps Jacob had been right when he told him that he was bad. He knew that Stonehenge was the travellers' main meeting place and briefly considered trying to get there, but he had no idea which direction he should take or even if he would be welcome, should he find his way there.

Back on the deserted lane again he looked to left and right. He had no idea where to go or what to do – and then it came to him. If he was going to leave Ilfracombe for good, he would first go and say goodbye to Destiny. Twig and Fleur would have liked that. The spring in his step had gone now as he trooped wearily down to the town. There was no point in rushing. No one was waiting for him or missing him. The streets were deathly quiet, the windows of the houses unlit, staring out into the night like dark hungry eyes. He briefly thought of getting in touch with Ginger somehow, but abandoned the idea almost immediately. Once Ginger's parents found out that their son had seen him they would inform the police, who would catch him again.

He paused at the harbour quay to watch the boats bobbing gently up and down on the water for a while and wondered what it would be like to be swallowed by the waves. The moon was turning the sea to silver and everywhere was peaceful.

I could just jump in and then no one would ever find me and I'd never have to worry about anything again, he thought. But thinking it and having the courage to do it turned out to be two different things entirely.

After a while he set off with heavy tread up the hill towards the little church where Destiny was buried. He could remember the feel of her skinny little arms around his neck and the way she would squeal with delight when he'd piggy-backed her across the field. But she would never squeal with delight again. She was gone for ever, and although Twig had said she was with God now, Franky found himself doubting it. She was buried deep in the ground and could never return.

He reached the lychgate that led to the church and picked his way through the tombstones in the light of the moon. Some of them were very old and they leaned drunkenly towards him as if they were trying to reach out and touch him, but he didn't flinch. He had feared the things Jacob did to him far more than walking through a graveyard at night.

Destiny's grave looked pathetically small compared to the larger ones. The flowers that Fleur had laid on the mounded earth were wilted and drooping now, and all that marked the spot was a simple wooden cross that Twig had painstakingly carved with just her name on it.

'I'm goin' to have to go away now, Destiny, an' I probably won't be comin' back again,' Franky whispered into the night. 'But I just wanted yer to know that yer were the best little girl an' I'll never forget yer. I hope yer happy wherever you are. If you are with God I bet the angels will love yer like we did.'

He turned and walked back the way he had come with tears wet on his cheeks, and as he neared the church he paused. I wonder if the vicar's locked the door, he thought and, crossing to it, he tried it tentatively. It swung inwards and he gazed into the gloomy interior cautiously. Above the small altar at the opposite end the moon was shining through the stained-glass window, casting a rainbow of colours about the solid stone walls. Franky stepped inside, pulling the door to carefully behind him and then he stood gazing up at the figure of Christ, who seemed to be holding His hands out to him. The young boy walked down the aisle and now the figure was towering above him.

'I'm sorry I'm so bad,' he muttered. 'Perhaps Yer could make me into a better person, God? Then someone might love me an' not leave me all alone.'

He waited expectantly for some sign that the figure had heard him. Perhaps a voice from the darkness or a clap of thunder? Dust mites were dancing in the dim light like some tiny ethereal beings, but there was no sign. Eventually he turned away and headed for the front pew. The wooden seat was as hard as rocks but it was better than sleeping outside on the ground in the night chill. Franky lay down, tossing this way and that, and slowly his hurt turned to anger.

Why had Twig and Fleur gone off and left him like that? Surely they'd known how much they meant to him? They should have realised that he would never have left them willingly. He turned his eyes to the figure of Christ again and now his voice when he addressed Him echoed around the church and bounced off the walls.

'Nobody is ever goin' to hurt me again!' he vowed. 'From now on it'll be *me* doin' the hurtin' an' I'll never let meself care about anyone ever again. Do Yer hear me, God?'

Turning his back angrily on the sad-faced Saviour, he tried to get comfortable, and at last sheer exhaustion claimed him and he slept.

The sound of water woke him the next morning, and as he opened his eyes he saw the vicar filling the font from a large brass jug. The man obviously hadn't seen him when he entered the church, and when Franky sat up he visibly started.

'Oh, my dear child, you gave me quite a shock!' he exclaimed as one hand closed over his heart.

Franky stared back at him sullenly as the man put the jug down and crossed to stand near him. He was the same vicar who had conducted Destiny's funeral, but if the man recognised him he gave no sign of it.

He waited for Franky to speak and when the child didn't, he asked, 'How long is it since you've eaten?'

Franky shrugged.

'Then in that case why don't you come across to the vicarage with me. My wife will rustle something up for you in a jiffy, and I assure you she's an excellent cook.'

Not sure where his next meal was going to come from, Franky rose and began to walk the length of the aisle with him. There was no point in being silly. As they left the church they walked into a watery sun and Franky looked around. The grass was soaked in dew and everywhere looked clean and brand new, as if some great, unseen broom had cleansed the whole place during the night.

'It's this way,' the man pointed, and Franky fell into step with him as they skirted the church. The vicarage was directly behind it, nestled against the cliffside and surrounded by lawns and attractive flowerbeds.

They entered the building through a side door that led directly into a kitchen where a kindly-faced woman in a voluminous apron was scrubbing pans in the sink.

Like the vicar, she asked no questions but simply smiled at Franky as her husband told her, 'This young man sought sanctuary in the church last night and I wondered if you might be able to whip up some breakfast for him if it's no trouble?'

'It'll be no trouble at all, dear,' she assured him, as she hastily dried her hands on her apron and moved towards a fridge that looked as if it wouldn't be out of place in an antique shop.

'Now then,' she mused. 'How about some bacon and eggs? Would that suit you? I could do some sausages and beans too if you'd like?'

Franky nodded silently as he sat down at the table, and after taking the food from the fridge she placed a frying pan on the stove and dropped a large dab of lard in it. The vicar had left the room and now a silence settled as she expertly began to fry up Franky's break-fast. The meal that followed was the best he had tasted in a long while and he rubbed his stomach appreciatively as he mumbled, 'Thanks.'

'You're very welcome, dear. Now what would you like to drink? Tea, or perhaps a glass of milk?'

'I'll have tea, please.'

She obligingly filled the kettle at the sink and once she'd put it on the cooker to boil she began to prepare the tea pot and asked him, 'Do you live around these parts, dear?'

Here we go, thought Franky, but his reply was polite when he told her, 'I used to.'

'I see, and where do you live now?'

'Nowhere.' It was becoming his standard reply.

'But everyone has to live *somewhere*,' she said softly. 'Don't you have any parents?'

He shook his head, setting his dark curls dancing.

She wisely refrained from asking any more questions and made the tea without another word.

Franky had just lifted the delicate china cup to his lips when he heard the vicar speaking to someone in the hallway and instantly guessed who it was. The man had told the police of his whereabouts and they'd come to fetch him. He was proven right when the very same Constable who had dragged him off to the police station only the week before entered the room and respectfully took off his helmet as he nodded towards the vicar's wife, who was looking decidedly distressed.

'So we meet again, eh, Franky?'

Franky shrugged as he calmly continued to drink his tea. He wasn't going to try and run away this time. He had no one to run to any more. No doubt he'd find himself in some other foster-home before the day was out. He really hoped it wouldn't be the one he had just run away from.

'We had a phone call from Barnstaple police this morning saying that you'd gone missing again,' the officer informed him. 'Then when the vicar here kindly rang us and said he'd found a young boy sheltering in the church it didn't take too much adding up.'

As Franky looked at the vicar his eyes seemed to bore right through him and the clergyman tugged on his dog collar as if it was choking him. 'I'm sorry, Franky, but you're so young . . . I had to tell them about you. It was for your own good. I couldn't bear to think what might happen if you were left to roam the streets. Do please try to find it in your heart to forgive me.'

Franky concentrated on the drink in front of him. This time he would leave with the policeman when he was good and ready, and when he left Ilfracombe this time he vowed that he would never come back.

Just after lunchtime Franky was delivered to the next foster-home by the same po-faced social worker who had taken him to the Hydes'. Mrs Smythe had fully intended to take him straight back there, but Franky had kicked up such a fuss in the Social Services office that she had had to look for another place for him. This time she drove him into Woolacombe and pulled up outside a very nice semi-detached house in a street not far away from the sea-front.

'You'll be staying with Meg and Bill Vine this time,' she told him, her voice full of disapproval. 'And I just hope you have more respect for these people than you did for the last ones.' She was heartily sick of the boy already, and longing for the day when Lorna Craine would be back from holiday to take the case off her. This young man was proving to be far more trouble than he was worth, from what she could see of it.

When Franky stepped into his next home he couldn't fail but be impressed. Everywhere was neat and tidy, but it was also warm and homely.

'This is Meg Vine,' Mrs Smythe said as a slim lady with soft brown hair and dark eyes admitted them. 'And Meg, this is Francis.'

'Me name's Franky,' the boy said resentfully as his eyes swept around the room. There was a man sitting in a wheelchair at the side of a roaring coal fire and he smiled at him in welcome.

'Hello, son,' he said. 'Why don't you come and sit over here by me and get warm? It's turned nippy out there, hasn't it?'

'That's Bill, my husband,' Meg told Franky with a warm smile. 'Why don't you sit and have a chat to him while I go and get this damn paperwork done and out of the way. Why there has to be so much red tape I'll never know.' She sighed and disappeared off into the next room with Mrs Smythe as Franky perched uncomfortably on the edge of the settee.

'So what football team do you support then, son?' Bill asked him in a friendly manner.

'I don't,' Franky replied ungraciously.

'Right, so what sport *do* you like then?'

'I don't.'

Bill shook his head. 'Well, that's a shame. We'll have to see if we can't get you interested in something else. Though there's nothing

225

like a good game of football to get the old adrenalin going. I loved to play before this happened. Though I'd be a little long in the tooth to play now.' He slapped his legs in frustration. 'I miss it like mad, I don't mind telling you.'

Franky was curious despite himself. 'So what happened to your legs then?'

'Accident down the pit,' Bill told him regretfully. 'One of the prop shafts fell on me and this was the result. I can still walk for short distances and I can still get up the stairs to bed, though I have to sit on my backside and go up backwards. Still, I shouldn't complain, I don't suppose. There were some that didn't get out at all, but it's still hard to come to terms with when you've always been an active person. Meg and I have two sons, both married and left home now, and they both play football. I love to go along and watch them when they have a game on. Perhaps you'd like to keep me company sometime?'

Franky tried to look uninterested as he stared out of the window, but Bill was not going to be put off so easily. Changing the subject, he said, 'I hear you haven't got any clothes with you. Meg informs me that she's going to take you shopping for some this afternoon and you can choose some things you like. She'll love it – you know what women are like for shopping.'

Again no reply and finally getting the message, Bill lifted the newspaper he had been reading and turned his attention back to that. The child was as closed as a clam at present, but Bill and his wife had cared for enough children in their time to know that some of the youngsters needed a little space before they got to trust you. Well, that was fine, but he'd win him round in the end. He hadn't failed yet.

When Mrs Smythe left an hour later with a last threatening glare at Franky, Meg immediately took him upstairs to show him his room. It was a world away from the cramped conditions he'd been forced to sleep in back at the Hydes', but even so Franky showed no pleasure at all in it.

The room was medium-sized with a single bed along one wall and a mahogany chest of drawers and a wardrobe that had been polished until he could see his face in them. Underfoot there was a carpet that stretched from wall to wall in a bright blue colour, and lighter blue curtains hung at the tall window. Two fat pillows lay on top of a thick warm eiderdown and a small lamp stood on a bedside table. It was like a palace but Franky could find no pleasure in it. Like the other places he'd been forced to live in, it wasn't home and it never would be.

'So, do you like it then?' Meg asked expectantly.

Franky merely sniffed and picked at his fingernails.

'You're the only one staying with us at present,' Meg went on, determined to make him feel at ease. 'So we'll be able to spoil you a little. Anything you want, just ask, and within reason we'll get it for you. We're here for you, Franky, I want you to understand that. I know from what your social worker has told me that you've been through an awful lot, but things will get better for you now if you'll let them. Anyway, that's enough of me rabbiting on. Are you hungry yet?'

When Franky shook his head she nodded. 'Very well then. You put your feet up and have a rest for half an hour or so, and then we'll go shopping to buy you some new clothes. Then when we get home you can have a nice long soak in the bath, put some of your new things on and I'll get you a nice tea ready. How does that sound?'

A shrug was her only reply as she turned towards the door. 'Half an hour then,' she said softly, as she closed it behind her.

True to her word, Meg took Franky shopping that afternoon. Franky didn't really enjoy it. Clothes had never been high on the list of his priorities but he supposed it was kind of her; not that he cared much one way or another.

By the time they arrived home it was late afternoon and they were both loaded down with shopping bags.

'Good grief,' Bill chuckled. 'You must have bought enough to clothe an entire football team there.'

'Don't be so sarcastic,' Meg scolded. 'The poor child has nothing but what he's standing up in and we don't want him to go round looking like he doesn't belong to anyone, do we?'

'But I *don't* belong to anyone,' Franky muttered, disgruntled.

'Nonsense, you've got us now,' Meg told him hurriedly, her voice sad. 'I know you've had a rough time of it, Franky, what with your mum and dad dying as they did, but things will get better again now, you'll see. We'll always be here for you for as long as you need us.'

He stared back at her with his chin in the air. Who did she think she was anyway? She meant nothing to him and never would. He had absolutely no one now. Everyone he had ever cared about had hurt or abused him, or left him, but he wouldn't let it happen again. Oh no, from now on he wouldn't allow anyone to get close enough to cause him pain. The shutters were up and from now on they would stay that way.

That night he slept on a comfortable mattress in his own room for the first time in ages. He'd had a bath and wore fresh new pyjamas, but nothing could take away the pain of the loss of Twig and Fleur. The more he thought about it, the more he imagined they had betrayed and abandoned him, and it was a hurt that cut deep and would never truly heal.

Halfway through the night, Meg hurried along the landing, fastening the belt of her dressing-gown as she went. She had heard Franky crying out in his sleep, and when she flung his bedroom door open and saw him tossing about the bed in a tangle of blankets she hurried to his side and gently shook his arm as she clicked the lamp on.

'Franky, wake up, love,' she urged. 'You're having a bad dream, but don't worry. You're quite safe.'

His eyes snapped open, but for a moment he could see nothing for the tears that were blinding him.

'It's all right, lovie,' she soothed, as she perched at his side and attempted to take him in her arms.

He pushed her hands away as he screamed, 'Get away from me! Do yer hear? *Get away!*'

Meg stood up and backed away from the raw fury on his face. He looked like something demented.

'Calm down,' she urged, keeping her voice level. 'It was just a nightmare. I promise you things will be all right.'

'*Get out!*' He was sobbing now. He was back in his dream again, chasing after Fleur and Twig, but the faster he ran to catch up with them, the further away they seemed to get. Destiny was there too but now she had little wings sprouting from her back and she was flying above him and he couldn't reach her. Then there was his mother, but great iron bars divided them and he couldn't break them down. And Jacob . . . he was clawing his way up the cliff face covered in blood, intent on getting to him.

Realising that her presence was only making things worse, Meg quickly backed from the room to stand on the landing outside his door, chewing on her knuckles as she listened helplessly to his sobs.

In that moment she understood that she had taken on a very damaged child. The road ahead was not going to be easy, but she promised herself that she would give it her best shot. The poor little chap deserved that much at least.

Chapter Twenty-Two

'I've arranged for you to start at St Michael's School in Chapel Street next Monday,' Mrs Smythe informed Franky the following week. He crossed his arms and stared at the tablecloth hoping he wouldn't have to wear a soppy uniform like the one he'd been forced to wear when he'd lived with June and Jacob in Puddlesea. He hated his new social worker with a vengeance. She obviously had no time for him and she was so sour-faced that she reminded Franky of a bulldog sucking a wasp. Therefore her next words didn't trouble him at all.

'I shall be passing your case back to a social worker in Warwickshire after this visit,' she informed him.

'Why is that?' Meg asked.

'Because Francis originally came from there before his adoption with the Andersons,' Mrs Smythe told her imperiously.

'Oh, I see. Does that mean that he'll have to move back to the Midlands then?' The trace of regret in Meg's voice did nothing to touch Franky at all.

'Not necessarily. If you are prepared to keep Francis longterm and he's settled here, then his new social worker would travel to see him when necessary.'

'I see.' Meg hadn't considered a longterm placement before. Most of the children she'd cared for had been with her for only a number of weeks, but it was something to think about. She would have to discuss it with Bill and see how he felt about it, and Franky himself, of course. As she glanced at him now she had a funny feeling that he wouldn't be over the moon with the prospect of staying. Nothing seemed to please him, though both she and Bill had bent over backwards to try and make him feel at home during the short time he'd been with them. He'd spent most of his days closeted up in his room, only coming down for meals. The rest of the time he'd spent walking about Woolacombe, a fact that she was far from pleased with. He might be a big lad for his age, but as far as she was concerned, he was still far too young to be gallivanting off on his own all the time.

Bill had racked his brains to come up with suggestions that he'd thought might interest him. Perhaps he'd like to enrol in a local boys' club? How about joining a football team? Or perhaps he'd enjoy the local Scouts group? The last suggestion had gone down like a lead balloon. Bill had no way of knowing that Jacob had been heavily involved with the Scouts group in Puddlesea, and even a mention of Scouts now brought bad memories of the man who had abused Franky. Each suggestion had been met with a surly shake of the head, and Bill was fast running out of ideas.

'So, is there anything else you'd like to ask me, Francis?' Mrs Smythe now asked.

Franky shook his head and rose from the table, glad of the chance to escape. He didn't know why social workers had to keep coming and sticking their nose into his business all the time anyway.

'Very well then, you may leave now. And may I wish you all the best for the future. Just be a good boy and I'm sure things will work out for you.' Her remark was so shallow that Franky saw straight through it. He was under no illusion of what Mrs Smythe thought of him. She disliked him, but not half as much as he detested her.

As he slouched away and disappeared up the stairs, Mrs Smythe turned to Meg and asked, 'How has he been?'

Meg patted her short curly hair absently. 'It's difficult to tell, really. He doesn't say much but he's obviously a very troubled child. Sometimes I see this haunted look in his eyes, but when I try to get through to him he just pushes me away. And he has *dreadful* nightmares. He screams loud enough to waken the dead when he has a really bad one. And he's . . .' She paused and licked her lips. 'Well, the poor lad has started to wet the bed. I'm not complaining,' she assured Mrs Smythe hastily, 'but I know it embarrasses him. I found him trying to hide the sheets under his bed this morning, poor little soul. He looks so humiliated even though I always make light of it. How he thought I wouldn't find them I'll never know. I just feel . . . I don't know . . . that there's something he isn't telling us. Something that's troubling him.'

'I rather doubt that,' Mrs Smythe said pompously. 'I prefer to think that Francis is just a very spoiled, wilful child who wants everything his own way all the time. He had a *perfectly* respectable home with his adoptive parents. His father was a teacher and his mother was a gentlewoman. Sadly, some children just don't respond to anyone no matter *what* they do for them.'

'I'm afraid I have to disagree with you there,' Meg retorted. 'In my experience as a foster-carer, the children who present problems have usually had a lot to contend with.'

'Whatever.' Mrs Smythe waved her hand dismissively, obviously not much concerned about Franky one way or the other. She was just glad that some other social worker was about to take him off her hands and that she wouldn't have to see the little horror again.

When she left some minutes later, Meg sighed with relief. 'Do you know, Bill, I'm glad to see the back of her,' she confessed. 'It's clear that Franky doesn't like her, and between you and me I can't say that I blame him. That woman doesn't have one ounce of compassion in her whole body, and I can't think why she ever came into this sort of work. From what I can see of it, she doesn't even *like* children.'

Bill chuckled. Meg always amused him when she got on her high horse about something. She had a big heart and he knew that she always did her best for the children who stayed with them. But deep down he wondered if even she would ever get through to Franky. The lad appeared to have built a barrier between himself and anyone who tried to get close to him, from what he could see of it. He didn't tell his wife that, though. In fact, he hoped that she would prove him wrong. Only time would tell.

The following morning, Meg walked Franky to the gates of St Michael's School where she paused to straighten his tie. The playground was teeming with children and mothers and fathers who were dropping them off.

'Now, are you quite sure that you've got everything?' she asked for what he was sure was at least the hundredth time.

'Yes,' he sighed.

'Good. Well, off you go then. They'll be waiting for you in the reception and I'll be here to meet you after school. You have got your dinner money safe, haven't you?'

'Yes,' he sighed again, and turning about he walked away without a backwards glance.

He paused at the entrance doors to look back and there she was, waving away as if she might never see him again. Franky shook his head in disgust before trailing towards the desk to give his name.

He found that there were at least twice as many children in the classroom he was shown to than there had been in his previous school. But then that school had been private, of course. Jacob would never have allowed him to attend a state school; he'd been too much of a snob.

His teacher, Miss May, was young and colourful, and she reminded Franky a little of Fleur. The rest of the children watched him curiously as he was shown to his desk and he scowled at them as he took his seat. When it was time for the morning break he followed the others out into the playground and found a quiet corner where he stood observing them.

'What's your name then?'

He turned to find a boy with light brown hair watching him. He'd noticed him in the classroom when the boy had flashed him a friendly smile but he hadn't returned it.

'Franky,' he muttered, quickly looking away. Two or three other boys had sidled up to him by then and he felt himself flushing. Why couldn't they all just leave him alone?

'I'm Bobby,' the boy volunteered. 'Do you live round here?'

'In North Street,' Franky said ungraciously.

'Oh, well that isn't far from where I live,' the boy told him cheerfully in his North Devonian accent, so different from Franky's own way of speaking, which he had obstinately retained, despite the elocution lessons and living down there for the past several years. 'Do you ever come out to play? Me and my mates meet in the rec at the end of Down Street if you'd like to come and join us. In the summer we go down to the beach and have a go at surfing, but we're not very good at it yet.'

When Franky remained insultingly silent as he crossed his arms and stared off into the distance, a taller boy quipped, 'Ooh, perhaps the new kid thinks he's too good for the likes of us, eh?'

'Leave him alone,' Bobby said defensively. 'He's probably just a bit shy.'

'Stuck-up, more like,' the tall boy snapped in disgust.

Suddenly, Franky's fist flew out, catching him firmly on the chin, and the next instant there was a fully-fledged fight going on. A small crowd soon assembled and egged them on until a teacher suddenly appeared and shouted, 'Just *what* is going on here? Stop that, you two, this instant.' He took both boys by the scruff of the neck as the small crowd instantly dispersed.

'It was him.' The boy who had taunted Franky waved a trembling finger in his direction. 'He just set about me for no reason, sir.'

Franky glared at him as he swiped at the blood that was trickling from his nose but he remained obstinately silent.

'Is this true?' the teacher asked him.

Franky still remained quiet.

'Right, both of you get to the Headmaster's office immediately, and tell him I sent you,' the teacher ordered. 'We will *not* tolerate fighting in the playground. Is that clear?'

When he released his hold on them, Franky followed the other boy across the playground feeling very indignant. Why couldn't he have just left him alone? He'd been quite happy keeping himself to himself.

Glancing down at the knees of his new school trousers he stifled a groan. There was a big hole in one of them, so no doubt he'd get an ear-bashing from Meg too now when he got home. There was also a button missing off his shirt, which was spattered with blood from his nosebleed.

Once inside the school, the two boys sat on the chairs by the Headmaster's study studiously ignoring each other as they each thought of what might lie ahead of them. Eventually the door opened and a large man boomed, 'Get in here.'

They entered the room and stood with their heads bent as he stared at them sternly.

'So what have you two been up to then?' he demanded, although there was really no need to ask, looking at the state of them both.

'Mr Cookson sent us to you, sir,' Franky's tormentor told him in a small voice. 'We were fighting.'

'*Were* you now? Well, I think you know how I feel about fighting in my school, don't you, Reed?'

'Yes, sir,' Reed mumbled miserably, knowing what was ahead.

'And what's your name, young man?' The Headmaster now addressed Franky.

'Franky Anderson.'

'It's *sir* when you address me,' the man barked. 'Isn't this your first day here?'

'Yes . . . *sir*!' As Franky glared at him resentfully a faint hint of colour appeared in the man's cheeks and he straightened.

'Right, well, first day or not I think you need to learn that this sort of behaviour is not permissible in this school. And *you*, Reed, should know better.'

'Yes, sir.' All the bravado had gone now and Reed was visibly trembling.

Standing, the Headmaster loomed over them, before stabbing a finger at Reed. 'You will do an hour's detention every day after school for two weeks starting tomorrow,' he informed the trembling boy, and then turning his attention back to Franky, he snapped, 'And *you* will do the same, and also miss all your break-times as well for the said period. Do you both understand?'

Franky felt the injustice of it all course through him and gave Reed a filthy look.

'Now get out, the pair of you, and don't let me hear of anything like this ever happening again or I promise the punishment will be much worse next time.'

'Yes, sir,' the boys chorused as they inched towards the door. The Headmaster found himself grinning as he watched Franky stride indignantly away down the corridor. He was a plucky little chap, there was no doubt about it, although from the defiant look on his face he had an idea he was going to have problems with this one.

Reed was grudgingly envious of Franky now. He was painfully aware that he had been a crybaby compared to the new boy. But he'd get him. One way or another he would make him pay for the humiliation he had just caused him. It never occurred to him that he had been the instigator of the fight in the first place. All he could think of was revenge. Could Franky have known it, he had just made his first enemy at St Michael's.

When Meg saw Franky walking across the playground towards her at home time, her hand flew to her mouth in horror. He looked as if he'd been in a boxing ring with a heavyweight boxer. His shirt was flapping open and was covered in blood that had now dried to a dirty-brown colour, and there was a large tear in the knee of his new trousers. One of his hands was skinned and was pressed beneath his armpit and he looked so miserable that she feared he was going to burst into tears.

'What happened, love?' she asked as he drew level with her.

He walked on without answering as if she wasn't even there and she found herself almost running to try and keep up with him.

'Have you been in a fight?' she asked unnecessarily.

Franky nodded. 'Yes, an' I got detention fer it.'

'Oh!' Meg could think of nothing else to say. It certainly didn't seem that his first day had gone as she'd hoped it would for him. They completed the rest of the distance to the house in silence and once they entered the front room, Meg cast Bill a warning glance as she saw him staring at Franky.

Once Franky was safely out of earshot she told him in a hushed voice, 'He got into a fight and got detention.'

Bill raised his eyebrows as Meg shrugged her arms out of her coat.

'You'd better go and see if he's all right then,' he told her. She nodded and hurried towards the back room where she found Franky sitting with his sore hand spread open on the table. She winced as she looked at the skinned knuckles.

'I think we need to bathe that. It looks quite angry.'

When he didn't protest she went into the kitchen and returned some minutes later with a bowl of hot water and a tub of ointment.

'This is salt water,' she informed him as she gently guided his hand towards it. 'I'm afraid it's going to sting a bit but it will stop any infection getting in. When you've soaked it for a few minutes I'll put some of this ointment on and that should ease the pain.'

As she immersed his hand, Franky gasped but his expression didn't change at all and she thought how brave he was.

Ten minutes later the wound was dressed with a light bandage.

'There, does that feel better?' she asked sympathetically.

'It don't hurt,' Franky lied as he sidled away from the table.

She watched as he headed for the stairs door and once she had heard him clatter away up the stairs she sighed heavily and took the bowl back to the kitchen.

★　　★　　★

From that day on, Nathan Reed made Franky's life hell on earth every chance he got. Somehow he had found out that Franky was in care and every playtime and lunchtime he plagued him relentlessly.

'Didn't Mummy and Daddy *want* you then?' he would taunt. Franky took to hiding himself in the toilets at every opportunity, but Nathan soon discovered his hiding-place and he and his little gang would stand outside the locked door mocking him. 'Is poor little Franky frightened then?' he'd shout as his followers sniggered with delight.

Franky refused to let Nathan see how hurt he was. He knew that this would have only encouraged him to be worse. But why had Nathan chosen to pick on him? he wondered. All he had wanted to do was keep himself to himself.

Throughout this torture, Jamie Cox, the boy who had once tried to befriend him, would smile at him sympathetically every chance he got, but he was too afraid of Nathan and his gang to do more than that. It seemed that every child in the school was afraid of Nathan. Franky's nightmares got worse and Meg started to receive calls from the teachers at his school. He hadn't done his homework. He'd been rude to one of the teachers. He was unco-operative. He wasn't trying. On top of that his bed was wet almost every morning now. The list was endless and Meg began to despair despite her earlier resolve to stand by him. There was only so much she could do, and if Franky wasn't even prepared to come a step towards her, then his placement with them looked doomed to failure. As Bill sadly pointed out, there was no use in whipping herself. Some children had just gone through too much in too short a time, and they were beyond help. Meg began to think that perhaps he was right, although she wasn't ready to give up on Franky just yet.

One morning as she was walking him to school, much against his will, she told him, 'I shan't be able to fetch you home tonight, love. I have a dental appointment. Do you think you'll be all right finding your way back on your own?'

'Of course I will,' Franky answered with a sneer. He hated her taking him to school and meeting him out anyway. It just gave Nathan Reed another reason to ridicule him. 'Who's Mummy's little darling then?' he'd sneer. 'Aren't you big enough to find your way home on your own? Oh, but I forgot – she isn't your mum, is she? Your real mum doesn't want you, does she? That's why you're in care.' This was the cruellest taunt of all and Franky's hands would ball into fists of rage and despair. School had become a place to dread just as his bedroom had once been when he was living with Jacob. But for now, all he could do was grin and bear it.

At the school gates Meg reached out to him then dropped her hand. Franky hated human contact of any kind, as she'd soon discovered when he'd first come to live with them.

'Just be careful on your way home now. And come straight back, won't you? Bill will be waiting for you. Have a good day now.'

Huh! Franky thought. There was very little chance of that.

After school he fetched his coat from the cloakroom and set off. Nathan and his cronies were in the playground and as Franky passed them Nathan's eyes followed him to the gate. He grinned when he saw that Meg wasn't there to meet him. He still blamed Franky for the punishment he'd received on the day he'd met him, and at last he saw his chance of paying him back.

'Come on, lads. It's time we taught that cocky little sod from God knows where a lesson he won't forget.' His eyes were twinkling with malice as the boys followed him unquestioningly.

Franky had walked some way before he became aware of someone behind him. When he glanced across his shoulder to see Nathan and his troop, his heart started to thump wildly in his chest. Up ahead there was a row of shops and he knew that if he cut behind them and slipped into the alley that led to the back of Meg's house, he stood a chance of losing them. The downside of this idea was that if Nathan managed to catch up with him, there would be no one there to help him. Deciding to risk it, he broke into a run, but his school satchel hampered him; it was heavy with books and unfinished homework. Even so, he ran as fast as his legs would take him. The rear of the shops was strewn with empty boxes and litter that the shopkeepers had thrown out there and this further hampered his progress. His breath was coming in ragged gasps but there was the alley literally yards away now, and if he could only make it to there he would be safe.

When a hand closed on his shoulder and jerked him to a halt his heart sank, but when he turned to face Nathan there was no trace showing of the fear that was flooding through his veins.

'Why don't yer just leave me alone an' go an' pick on someone yer own size?' he spat with a bravery that he was far from feeling.

Nathan had been laughing, enjoying the chase, but now his face set. 'Still playing the cocky one, are we?' The gang was circling Franky now and he realised that there was no way out.

When Nathan's fist shot forward and connected with Franky's nose he saw stars and reeled backwards, bumping into one of Nathan's cronies.

'Here, that hurt,' he objected, and before Franky knew it they were all on him. In no time at all they had him on the ground, kicking and punching him as he rolled into a tight little ball and tried to protect his face. The pain was indescribable and now he couldn't stop the tears, which seemed to spur Nathan on all the more.

'Not feeling so bloody cocky now, are you?' Nathan gloated as his toe connected with Franky's ribcage.

Thankfully the back door of one of the shops opened then and a shop assistant who had been about to step outside for a sneaky cigarette saw what was happening.

'Here, what's going on?' she shouted indignantly. 'Get away from him, the lot of you. You bloody bullies. Clear off, I say, else I'll call the police.'

Nathan's gang dispersed this way and that as the woman hurried over to Franky, who was still on the ground crying pitiably.

'Oh love, are you all right?' she asked with concern as she helped him to his feet. His right eye was already swelling but his body had taken the worst of the beating. He felt tender and sore all over, but he straightened as best he could and after lifting his satchel he walked away from her without a word.

She shook her head as she watched him go, wondering what the world was coming to.

Bill almost had a fit when the boy walked in and he spotted the bruise spreading across his eye.

'Christ, what's happened now?' he asked.

'Oh, just a bit of a tiff with one o' the lads on the way home from school,' Franky told him airily, then walked on past him up to his room.

Once the door had closed behind him he threw himself on to the bed and sobbed as he thumped the pillows in his frustration. *Why* did things always have to happen to him? *Why* had his mum left him — and Twig and Fleur? It could only be for one reason. He was bad through and through, as Jacob had told him. He had no doubt that by tomorrow he would be black and blue all over, but thankfully the bruises, apart from the one on his face, could be hidden from Meg and Bill. He would suffer the pain in silence but one day soon — somehow — he would get his own back.

Chapter Twenty-Three

It was the first week in December when Franky came down the stairs one evening dressed for outdoors in the warm winter duffel coat that Meg had bought for him.

'Where are you off to?' she asked. 'It's gone six o'clock, Franky, and it's very dark and cold out there. I don't think you should be going out on your own.'

He stared at her as if he was daring her to try and stop him, and she sighed. 'All right then. But just have half an hour, eh?' She laid her knitting aside and glanced at Bill, who was looking as bewildered as she felt. Franky was a law unto himself and nothing they said or did seemed to get through to him. But then she consoled herself, it would soon be Christmas. It was always a happy affair in her house with her sons and their families visiting for Christmas dinner, and once Franky saw the bicycle she was planning on buying him, he was bound to soften towards them a little.

She waited until the door had closed behind him then returned to the jumper she was knitting for her little grandson for Christmas.

Once outside, Franky glanced up and down the street. The last few days at school had been hell, with Nathan Reed singling him out and making fun of him every chance he got. He'd tried to ignore and avoid the boy as much as he could, but it was getting harder, especially when he remembered the beating they'd given him. His ribs still ached and he sometimes wondered if they'd done him some permanent damage. Reed's taunts were getting to him now and he was greedy for revenge. Franky knew that Nathan and his cronies hung out in the recreation ground in Down Street out of school, and it was there that Franky was heading now. Perhaps Reed wouldn't be quite so brave and such a loudmouth if he could catch him on his own.

It took him ten minutes to walk there and sure enough, as he rounded the corner of Down Street, there was a small group of boys huddled over by the swings. They were laughing and giggling as Franky slipped behind one of the hedges that bordered the rec and hid in the shadows. Soon, he saw Reed right in the middle of his little gang of followers, cock-a-hoop, smirking. With a little bit of luck he'd swipe that smile right off his face tonight.

Franky stood there for what felt like an eternity, getting colder by the second, but at last the little group began to disperse. Some of them walked within an arm's breadth of where he was hiding, totally unaware that he was there. Soon there was only Nathan Reed and another boy left. They had a muttered conversation and then the boy went in one direction and Reed headed off across the park. Franky slunk out of the shadows and followed him as closely as he dared. Thankfully, once they were halfway across the rec, the light of the street-lamps no longer reached them and Franky was able to sneak closer as he pulled the hood of his duffel coat down low over his face. Reed was humming merrily to himself as Franky withdrew something from his pocket. It was very dark here and he could barely see the shape in front of him. When he was less than two steps away from his enemy he flicked a switch on the pocketknife in his hand and an evil-looking blade appeared as if by magic.

Reed suddenly paused and turned to ask nervously, 'Is anyone there?'

Franky was on him in a flash, and taken off-guard, the larger boy toppled to the ground. The blade glinted in the dim light as Franky slashed it towards the boy's face, grunting with pleasure when he heard a high-pitched squeal. He repeated his action, then flinging the knife as far away as he could into the bushes, he took to his heels, leaving the boy he detested squirming in agony on the cold sodden ground.

Once he arrived back at Meg's house he snuck in through the back door and hared away up the stairs where he locked himself in the bathroom. Just as he had thought, there was blood across the front of his coat and on his hands, so he hastily sponged it off with a flannel and ran some water into the bath. If she heard him, Meg would presume that he'd gone for an early bath, and his coat would be dry by morning if he hung it on the back of the bedroom door. Smiling smugly to himself, he settled back into the water as he remembered how Reed had squealed like a stuck pig when he attacked him. Now he would know what it felt like to be bullied. He chuckled as he stared into the steamy air. He was so glad that he'd happened on Bill's fishing box in the cupboard under the stairs one day when he'd gone in there to get his shoes out. It was in the box that he'd found the sharp penknife that Bill had used for gutting the fish he caught. Bill had told him that before his accident, fishing had been another of his hobbies. But since then Bill had been unable to fish, so the chances of him finding out that the knife had gone missing for some time to come were slight. The boy allowed himself to relax and let the hot water soothe his bruised and battered body.

During the assembly at school the next morning, the Headmaster addressed them all solemnly. 'Sadly, one of our pupils was attacked whilst he was on his way home crossing Down Street recreation ground last night,' he informed them. 'Nathan Reed is now in hospital with severe lacerations to his face, but worse than that, it seems that he may have been blinded in one eye. I am telling you all this to make you aware that it isn't safe to be going out on your own at the moment after dark, until the person who carried out this un-precedented attack is caught. The police are of course investigating the matter, but until further notice please take extra care.'

A hushed ripple spread through the gathered assembly as Franky battled to keep a smile from his face. It had turned out even better than he'd hoped. If Reed was blind in one eye, it served him right, as far as Franky was concerned. Perhaps in future he wouldn't be so keen to pick on kids smaller than himself.

As Christmas drew nearer, Meg transformed the whole of the downstairs rooms with Christmas decorations and fairy lights. Franky came home from school one day to find a large Christmas tree standing in the corner of the front room in an enormous bucket.

'I thought you might like to help me put all the baubles and lights on it tonight,' Meg suggested hopefully, but Franky shook his head. That was something that families did and these people weren't his family. He didn't have one any more.

'Then perhaps you could come with us when we go to collect some holly?' Bill said, determined to include the boy in the preparations.

Franky walked past him without bothering to answer. He knew what they were trying to do, but had no intention of getting close. Every time he got close to someone, something went wrong, so it was better to keep one's distance.

Things were slightly better at school. Nathan was still absent, and without him to rule them his little gang seemed to have disbanded, which was something at least.

Even so, Franky still hated every moment he spent there, and he began to play truant. He would walk to school with Meg each morning, then wait in the entrance to the school until he saw her set off for home before slipping quietly away. It was so easy he wondered why he hadn't thought of it before. Most times he would head for the beach and shelter in the sand dunes, staring thoughtfully out to sea. When he got hungry he would nip into the town and steal his lunch. Most of the fruit and veg shops had produce outside and he quickly became adept at strolling casually by, pocketing the odd apple or pear as he went. He would then arrive back at school in time for the afternoon bell to go and be waiting.

innocently by the gates when Meg arrived to collect him. He got away with it for nearly two weeks, but then one day as he saw her walking towards him, he noticed that she was looking far from pleased.

'Had a good day, have you?' she asked casually, as Franky fell into step beside her.

'Yeah, it were fine,' he replied cautiously, sensing that she wasn't her usual good-humoured self.

'Mm – and what lessons have you had today?'

'Oh, just the usual. English, maths and stuff.'

She looked him square in the eye. 'I know you're lying, Franky. The Headmaster rang me this morning and gave me a list of the days that you've been absent.'

Knowing that he was caught out, his expression became sullen. Why did she have to interfere anyway? The way he saw it, he shouldn't be forced to go to school if he didn't want to. He didn't admit to himself that the reason he had no friends was because he held everyone at arm's length.

'Why do you do it?' she asked with an exasperated sigh. 'You know that Bill and I care about you and we're going to stand by you, so *why* do you have to continually make everything so difficult? We want you to be part of the family, but you have to come a little way towards us at least.'

'I don't *want* to be part of your family,' Franky told her resentfully. 'You're *not* my family. I don't even know where my family is, except for my mum. I know she's in prison but when she comes out she'll come and fetch me – she promised!'

'Oh, Franky.' Meg's kind heart went out to him. There was so much pain bubbling away inside him, and until he could put that aside she knew that she stood no chance of getting through to him. She'd seen this too many times – children who were hurt and feeling betrayed testing the boundaries to see how far they could push her. And then when her patience finally snapped and the placement broke down, she and Bill became just another betrayal to add to their list. She didn't want this to happen to Franky. She sensed there was something deep-rooted that caused him to cry out and wet the bed during the night. Perhaps counselling would help? His new social worker was finally travelling from the Midlands to see them the next day, and she decided she'd mention it to her. Lorna Craine should have come weeks ago, but pressures at work had prevented her visit up to now. The way Meg saw it, anything was better than this state of affairs. She seemed to be banging her head against a solid brick wall.

Not daring to push his luck, Franky went to school the next day. As a punishment for playing truant he was made to stay in the classroom and write 100 lines during the breaks. *I must not play truant*, he wrote over and over again in untidy scrawls. Detentions didn't trouble him in the least; it meant he could sit in the warm rather than try to hide himself away in corners in the cold playground.

When Meg collected him that afternoon she seemed in a good mood. 'Your new social worker is at home waiting to meet you and she's ever so nice,' she told him. 'She was one of the ladies that took you to live with your other mum and dad. I wonder if you'll remember her?'

Franky didn't bother to answer her. What did he care who was waiting to see him? The only person he wanted to see was his mum, and he knew that there was little chance of that happening.

The sky had turned an eerie grey colour and it had gone bitterly cold. Choosing to ignore his silence, Meg commented cheerfully, 'I reckon it's going to snow. That would be nice, wouldn't it? If it snowed for Christmas, I mean. You break up from school next week for the holidays and I reckon there's an old sledge still in the shed. You could take it out and have some fun.'

Again, Franky blatantly ignored her, and knowing when she was beaten Meg finally fell silent.

When they entered the house a short while later they found

Lorna Craine chatting away to Bill in the front room. The lights on the Christmas tree were twinkling, and as she rose to greet Franky, Lorna beamed almost as brightly.

'Good grief!' she exclaimed. 'You've shot up since the last time I saw you, Franky! I think you're going to be a nuisance to the aeroplanes if you keep growing. How are you? You're certainly looking well.'

Franky grunted in reply as he focused on a point on the wall above her head. He hated it when he was the centre of attention.

Lorna had had a long talk with Meg and Bill before Meg had set off to fetch Franky from school, and now she could see first-hand what they had meant when they'd told her how unapproachable the child was. She supposed it was to be expected. Franky had gone through a lot in his short life and it was bound to have had an impact on him. First he'd been neglected and physically abused by his own mother. Then he'd been placed with new parents who had both died. And then his foster placement had broken down and he'd been shipped off yet again to Meg and Bill. It was no wonder that the child was introverted. He'd had a lot to come to terms with.

'So, are you looking forward to Christmas?' She was determined to stay upbeat. 'Meg tells me she has lots of surprises in store for you. Is there anything you'd especially like?'

'Yes. I'd like to go home to me mum an' me sisters,' Franky told her without blinking, and the adults in the room were temporarily dumbstruck.

It was Lorna who managed to compose herself first when she told him gently, 'I think you know that isn't possible, Franky. But what I can tell you is that both Natasha and Lauren are well and happy. Perhaps one day when you're all grown up, you'll be able to see each other again. In the meantime it's up to you to try and make the best of what you've got. I know Meg and Bill think very fondly of you and they're prepared to offer you a longterm home with them if that's what you want.'

His empty eyes saddened her. There was no spark of enthusiasm there for anything. It was as if Franky had locked himself away in a bubble that no one could penetrate.

'Can I go now?' he asked dully.

Lorna nodded. She could see that she was going to get nowhere with him. He left the room without a word and the second he'd gone, Meg said, 'I'm so sorry he was so rude. That's how Franky is all the time.'

'Has he ever displayed any inappropriate sexual behaviour?' Lorna asked musingly as some inner instinct rang her alarm bells.

'No, not that I've noticed.' Meg was horrified at the very idea. 'Have you picked up on anything like that, Bill?'

Her husband shook his head. 'Can't say that I have. He's just a surly little so-and-so.'

'Ah well, it's probably just me barking up the wrong tree,' Lorna told them quickly, not wishing to distress them further. She glanced at the clock and sighed regretfully as she told them, 'I really ought to get off now. It's obvious Franky isn't going to talk to me, so unless there's anything else you need to discuss, I think I'll be on my way. I have a long journey ahead of me.'

'Of course.' Meg hurried away to fetch her coat for her and soon after, Lorna went home, leaving the couple feeling even more depressed than they had been before her arrival.

Just as Meg had prophesied, the snow came the week before Christmas. She'd hoped it would lift Franky's spirits as her own children had loved the snow when they were little. But he showed no interest in it, even when Meg fetched her sons' old wooden sledge out of the shed for him – until her grandson, Stefan, arrived on the doorstep one day, that was. His mother and father were both at work, so Meg had offered to have him for the day as he was on holiday from school in the next town. Stefan was a year older than Franky and a sweet-natured boy who had a smile for everyone. Tall and slim, he had striking blue eyes and a shock of blond hair.

Within an hour of him arriving, he and his grandad were immersed in a game of Snakes and Ladders, and when Franky ventured downstairs he watched them closely, envying the easy relationship they had. Stefan flashed him a smile but then turned his attention back to the game. He was the first person who hadn't questioned Franky or tried to be over-friendly, and Franky found himself warming to him. When he asked if Franky would like a game the boy nodded self-consciously and for the next half an hour he enjoyed himself more than he had since he'd arrived there. At lunchtime, Meg fried them bacon, sausages and eggs, and for once there was a light-hearted atmosphere at the table. After lunch, Stefan suggested, 'Do you fancy taking the sledge out?'

Meg looked on, afraid to say a word in case she spoiled the moment. She had always thought that Franky was a good-looking lad but when he smiled he was extremely handsome.

'Yeah, if yer like,' Franky said shyly, and so both boys wrapped up warmly, and within minutes they were dragging the sledge behind them down the street.

'We could go to the sand dunes,' Stefan said thoughtfully. 'Some of them are quite high and we could take it in turns to sled down them.'

When Franky nodded his approval they continued on their way in a compatible silence. The afternoon that followed was the happiest Franky could remember spending in a long, long while. He pushed all his hurt and resentment aside and gave himself up to the pleasure of just being a little boy, happy doing what little boys do. Their giggles echoed along the beach and every now and again passers-by on the sea-front smiled at their antics.

As dusk approached, Stefan glanced at the sky regretfully. 'We'd better get back else Gran will have a search-party out looking for us.' He had to shout to make himself heard above the roar of the waves that were crashing on to the beach before skittering out to sea again, as if they were too afraid of staying on the sand for any length of time. The boys' faces were glowing and their hands were blue with cold but even so they were in fine high spirits as they set off for home. This time Franky glanced appreciatively at the windows they passed where Christmas trees decked out with glittering fairy lights shone out into the gloom, turning the snowy pavements into a magical carpet.

'Will you be comin' on Christmas Day?' Franky dared to ask, and when Stefan nodded he smiled. Suddenly it was something to look forward to. Perhaps things weren't so bad after all.

Chapter Twenty-Four

The whole house smelled of roast turkey and Christmas pudding that had been soaked for days in brandy when Franky got up on Christmas morning. Meg and Bill were waiting for him and Meg pointed excitedly towards a pile of gaily-wrapped presents.

'They're all for you. Go on, open them and see if you like them,' she urged, her eyes shining with excitement.

Franky slowly ripped open the nearest to hand to find a fine pair of leather gloves. He had only ever had mittens before and they made him feel very grown up. The second parcel revealed a cosy red and blue scarf, and so he went on until he had worked his way through them all. There were numerous other small gifts that had obviously been carefully chosen.

'Thanks,' he mumbled, his cheeks burning with embarrassment.

'Now come into the kitchen for your main present,' Meg told him. 'It was too big to bring through here but I'm sure you'll like it. Bill came with me especially to choose it.'

As Franky entered the small kitchen his eyes rested on a brand new bicycle propped up against the sink unit, and suddenly he was reminded of the one Jacob and June had given him for his birthday.

As he wondered briefly what might have become of it he shuddered involuntarily, and Meg's face dropped. 'D-don't you like it?' she asked falteringly.

'Yes . . . o' course I do,' Franky answered as he tried to plaster a smile on his face.

'Good. Perhaps you and Stefan might take it out for a trial run when he gets here — if the pavements are clear enough, that is.' The snow had stopped falling the day before and now everywhere was covered in slush that was dangerously slippy underfoot.

Meg started preparing the big Christmas dinner and Franky drifted back into the front room to watch TV until Stefan arrived.

By lunchtime the semi-detached house was bursting at the seams. Both of Meg's sons and their families had come bearing yet more brightly wrapped gifts, and there was a lot of laughter as they were exchanged.

Gordon and Gerald were both gentle-natured men and they slapped Franky on the back affectionately, keen to make him feel part of the family's festivities. Their wives, Tina and Evelyn, were equally keen to include him, but as always when he was made the centre of attention, Franky shrank back into his shell.

Seeing his discomfort, Stefan cocked his thumb towards the stairs door as he suggested tactfully, 'How about we go up to your room and have a game of Ludo? I've brought it with me — look — and I haven't had time to have a go with it yet.'

Franky smiled at him gratefully, glad of a chance to escape, and so for the rest of the morning the two boys entertained themselves quietly upstairs.

Dinner was a merry affair. They all pulled Christmas crackers and wore silly party hats and Franky ate so much he was sure he would burst. The meal started with homemade vegetable soup, followed by a turkey that was big enough to have fed an army. There were roast potatoes and four different vegetables to choose from, along with stuffing balls that melted in the mouth and thick creamy gravy. For dessert there was a choice of Christmas pudding or homemade sherry strawberry trifle dripping in thick fresh cream. Franky couldn't decide which one to choose so in the end Meg gave him a portion of each.

When the meal was over the women began to clear the table while the men retired to the front room to chat and let their dinner go down. The two boys sat crossed-legged at their feet as they idly listened to the men's chat. They were talking about the Lockerbie air disaster that had happened only days before.

'It's awful,' Bill sighed as he stuffed his pipe with tobacco. Meg wasn't too keen on him smoking it indoors but seeing as this was a special day she was prepared to turn a blind eye.

'All those lives lost and just before Christmas too. How must their loved ones be feeling? It doesn't bear thinking about.'

'It said on the news last night that all two hundred and fifty-nine passengers and crew died, as well as eleven people that were killed on the ground,' Gordon agreed sadly.

'Mm, it was a Pan American Jumbo jet that blew up in mid-air, wasn't it?' Gerald chipped in.

'Yes, it was.' Bill puffed on his pipe to get it alight. 'The wreckage crashed into Lockerbie below, and it's only a small market town, by all accounts. The poor people there must have wondered what the hell was happening. The locals they've interviewed said it looked as if a great fireball was hurtling towards them from the sky. The plane was on its way to New York when it happened.'

'Yes, and then at the beginning of December there was that train crash at Clapham Junction,' Gordon reminded them. 'Thirty-six dead and over a hundred people injured. All down to signal failure, apparently. It doesn't exactly encourage you to travel far, does it?'

Meg entered the room at that moment and clapped her hands impatiently as she told them sternly, 'Now come on, you lot. No more doom and gloom, eh? It is Christmas Day, after all. Let's just be thankful that our family is safe and sound and all together. Now who's for a glass of sherry?'

Franky's eyes suddenly grew dim with tears and he had to blink rapidly to force them back. '*Our family is safe and sound and all together.*' Meg's words rang in his ears and he was reminded that as nice as these people were, they weren't *his* family. He wondered what his mum and little sisters were doing, and if they ever thought of him. What sort of Christmas would his mum be having, locked away in prison? What would Lauren and Natasha be doing right now? They had been little more than babies the last time he had seen them, and he doubted if they would even remember him any more. He was ashamed to say that their faces were blurred in his own memory now and it was harder to picture them when he closed his eyes. But then, Lorna Craine had assured him when she visited that they were both happy, so that was something to be thankful for at least.

Suddenly the shine had gone from the day, and he chose a moment when no one was watching to slink away to his bedroom, where he curled up into a ball on his bed and cried helplessly as he felt his family's loss all over again.

Stefan found him there an hour later and looked at him with concern as Franky hastily swiped the tears from his cheeks with the sleeve of his jumper.

'I . . . er . . . got you a little present,' he said, holding a crudely wrapped package out to Franky.

With a look of surprise on his face, Franky took it from him and when he tore back the brown paper he found a small silver penknife. It instantly reminded him of the one he'd attacked Nathan Reed with, but he pushed the memory away.

'It's lovely.' He was deeply touched to think that Stefan had gone to any trouble on his behalf. He'd had lots of presents from Meg and Bill, but then they'd been expected. It was what adults did. But he'd never had anyone his own age buy him anything before.

'I didn't get you anything,' he said shyly.

'It's all right,' Stefan assured him with a bright smile. 'But mind how you use it, else Grandad will take it off you.'

Franky's heart was bursting with pure joy. He had a friend, a *real* friend at last. Jacob had told him that he would *never* have a friend because he was bad through and through, but perhaps he had been wrong?

He was desperate to show Stefan how grateful he was, and his mind was working overtime. What could he do to show the boy how much this meant to him? And then it came to him. To please Jacob he had to touch him . . . down there.

Without even thinking about it, he bounded off the bed and Stefan started as he rushed towards him. Franky's hand instantly fell to Stefan's private parts and he squeezed them gently through the boy's trousers as he asked him, 'Would you like me to be nice to you?'

Stefan sprang away from him as if he had been stung, and a look of horror crept across his face.

'*Get away from me!*' he shouted, as he held his hand out and backed towards the door. Seconds later, Meg burst into the room, trying to catch her breath as she looked from one to the other of them.

'Whatever's going on in here?' she demanded as Stefan threw himself into her arms. Tina and Gordon had come to stand behind her now and Franky felt himself shrivelling inside with shame. But what had he done that was so wrong? Stefan had been nice to him. He'd only been trying to be nice back.

Stefan was crying with shock now as he waved a frantic finger towards Franky. 'He . . . he touched me . . . down here.'

Shock rendered Meg temporarily speechless as her disbelieving eyes flew to Franky. And then all hell seemed to break loose when Tina snatched her son away from Meg and turned towards the door.

'You *filthy* little pervert!' she spat with contempt as she looked at Franky. 'Go and pick on your own kind. You'll not get a chance to touch my boy again because as God is my witness, we'll not set foot in here till you're long gone.'

'Aw Tina, please don't say that. You know how much I love that lad,' Meg implored her as Tina marched from the room. She made to follow her but Gordon held her back.

'Let her go, Mum,' he said stiffly. 'You must see that we can't risk Stefan being exposed to kids like him. I think she's right, we ought to go now.'

He turned away from his mother as she stood there sobbing

helplessly, and Franky hung his head in shame, still not knowing what he had done that was so wrong.

The sound of muted voices wafted up the stairs towards them, followed by the front door shutting, and it was only then that Meg seemed to come out of her trancelike state. She rounded on Franky furiously.

'Now see what you've done!' she screamed accusingly as she stabbed a trembling finger towards him. 'You've split me from my family. I'm telling you, this is the final straw. I've tried to be patient with you, God *knows* I have, but I'm at the end of my tether. As soon as the Social Services office opens after the holiday, I'm going to ask them to get you out of here.' With that she turned on her heel and slammed out of the room as Franky stood there shaking with shock.

If she wanted him out, that was fine. He'd never expected anyone to love him. But he certainly wasn't going to hang around to be carted off to yet another foster-home like a parcel. As soon as it was dark and Meg and Bill were asleep, he'd run away again. He was getting to be an expert at it now. It was a shame though, because despite promising himself that he wouldn't settle, he realised now that he'd got quite fond of living with Meg and Bill.

PART THREE

Chapter Twenty-Five

July 1994

'So how many times is this then, Franky?' Lorna sighed as she joined the surly-looking young man in a room at the police station in Norwich.

At fifteen years old, Franky towered head and shoulders above her. He was strikingly good-looking and could have been taken for eighteen at a glance. His thick black hair was still inclined to curl and now his body, which had always been sturdy, was heavily muscled. But it was his eyes that remained his most striking feature. A deep dark brown, they seemed to mirror his soul, and when he smiled, which was rarely, they lit up from within.

Now he stared past the police officer, who was standing to the side of the door with his arms crossed, to his social worker, and shrugged nonchalantly.

'Your foster-mum tells me you stole *another* car,' she said with exasperation as she sat down opposite him and folded her hands in her lap.

Another shrug. Reprimands and reproaches rolled off him like water off a duck's back.

'You have now had *eight* different foster-homes and you've managed to spoil things for yourself at every single one of them. You're only fifteen years old and you've been in court *three* times already. I hope you realise that if you'd been older you'd be in prison by now. Burglary, car theft, shoplifting – it's hardly a history to be proud of, is it? But you know, you could still turn yourself around. There's a whole world waiting for you out there and you could be anything you wanted to be, if you'd only set yourself to it.'

Franky strummed his fingers across his lips as he gazed about the room with a bored expression on his face. He'd heard it all before and as usual he wasn't going to listen. Lorna and the officer exchanged a glance as she took some paperwork out of her bag, and ignoring him now, she began to fill in the forms spread out in front of her.

Franky wasn't used to being ignored, and when he realised that he wasn't getting her full attention, he peeped at her out of the corner of his eye. She'd changed since she took over his case, no doubt due to the fact that she was now a married woman with a baby of her own. It had been she who had moved him from one home to another when his placements broke down. Sometimes it had been a relief to leave, other times he'd been forced to admit deep down that he couldn't blame the carers for getting rid of him. The last one had told him that he could have tried the patience of a saint, and he supposed that she'd been right. Not that what he'd done had been *that* bad. He'd only taken her husband's car from the drive and smashed it up. He'd learned how to hotwire cars months ago, and since then the world had been his oyster. There was no lock that he couldn't get into and he'd taken full advantage of the fact, stealing everything from Minis to BMWs. The fact that he usually ended up getting caught hadn't deterred him. He wasn't sixteen yet so the worst he could expect if he found himself in court was a slap on the wrist, and the thrill of driving a car of his choice was more than worth that. He'd sat by the sides of carers with martyred expressions in different courts waiting for his case to be heard, wondering what the hell they were so het up about. A car was only a car at the end of the day, wasn't it?

Now he wondered idly where Lorna was planning to place him next. He'd almost toured the country up to now. He had no fear whatsoever of moving on. One foster-home was much like another, but her next words had him sitting up straight in his seat.

'I'm afraid we've just about run out of foster-homes, or at least, ones that are prepared to take you.'

'Oh . . . so what does that mean?' He tried to keep the fear that had crept into him out of his voice.

'It means that you'll be going into a children's home.'

'A what?' He stared at her incredulously. He'd heard about what went on in some of those places and wasn't too keen on the idea at all.

'There are no other options,' she told him. 'I have tried to avoid this happening, but the more I think about it, the more I believe it may not be such a bad idea. You obviously don't want to be in a family unit, you've made that very clear, so perhaps this is the way to go? And don't look so worried, it's a home, not a prison, though I have a horrible feeling that might be the next step if you carry on as you are.'

His shoulders sagged as he tried to take in what she'd just told him. *A children's home!* Just the thought of it was enough to bring him out in goosebumps. But then, he wondered, could it be any worse than some of the foster-homes he'd lived in? He dared not allow himself to think that he'd been treated as he deserved. It was always someone else's fault as far as Franky was concerned. He had a chip on his shoulder that was as big as a house brick, and the older he got the bigger it grew, along with the pain inside him and the constant need to find his family again. He briefly thought of trying to run back to Nuneaton, but then asked himself what would be the point? As far as he knew, his mother was still in prison and his sisters could be anywhere by now. They might not even remember that they had a brother.

'So what's this place like then?' he asked, seeing no way out of the predicament.

'It has mainly teenagers like yourself staying there and I'm assured the staff are very good. But I have to warn you; you have to earn your privileges there. It won't be quite as easygoing as the foster-homes you've stayed in. If you step out of line you'll be punished.

It's as simple as that. They have their own in-house tutors too, so you won't be able to bunk off school either, as you've been able to in the past, which I can only think is a good thing.'

Franky's lips curled back in disgust. The place sounded horrible and he couldn't see himself remaining there for two minutes. *If* they managed to get him there, that was.

As if she could read his mind, Lorna leaned across the table and wagged a finger at him. 'I'm afraid you have no choice in the matter,' she told him matter-of-factly. 'And if you show the slightest inclination of trying to run away from me or if you refuse to go, I shall ask an officer from here to accompany us.'

The breath went out of Franky like air from a balloon. 'An' just where is this hellhole?' he asked glumly.

'It's on the outskirts of South London. And it *isn't* a hellhole, I assure you. We've had children in there in the past that have done really well for themselves. It's all up to you now. You can make this as hard or as easy as you like. So . . . what do you say?'

'There ain't much point me sayin' anythin', is there? You've got me over a barrel. I ain't got no choice in the matter.'

Lorna shrugged. The way she saw it, the sooner they got this over with now, the better for both of them.

'Are you ready then?'

'What about me stuff? It's still at the Bennets',' Franky said, hoping to delay the inevitable.

'No, it isn't. It's all packed in the back of my car,' Lorna assured him.

Just for a second he glanced towards the window, but then commonsense took over. If he did a runner they'd catch him in no time. They always had in the past. Rising slowly from the table, he followed her from the room and out to her car without another word.

It was mid-afternoon when Lorna steered her car through the gates of the children's home. It had been a long drive. They were both hungry by now and Lorna had briefly considered stopping somewhere for lunch, but then had quickly decided against it. Knowing Franky as she did, she had no doubt at all that he'd run away given half a chance, and she didn't want to give him that chance.

The boy had remained stubbornly quiet for most of the journey, his arms crossed as he slouched down in the seat with a sullen expression on his face, but now he inched himself up and peered ahead. To one side of the enormous wrought-iron gates was a large sign which read WOODSIDE CHILDREN'S HOME. They drove down a long tree-lined entrance, and in the distance they could just make out the home. It certainly didn't look very welcoming, Franky thought. There was a small woodland to one side of it, which he supposed had given it its name. It was a large imposing Victorian building built of red brick, which still managed to look gloomy despite the bright July sunshine that was shining down on it. An overgrown tangle of ivy sprawled across its frontage; its tendrils seemed to be fighting to get through the numerous windows that blinked dully in the light.

Steps led up to impressive oak double doors that had stood the test of time. On either side of the entrance were countless sash-cord windows from which the dirty green paint was peeling, making the building look at variance with the beautifully kept grounds that surrounded it.

As Franky climbed out of the car and collected his luggage, which consisted of three large plastic carrier bags full of clothes, the smell of new-mown grass assailed his nostrils. He stared up at the bleak façade of the house. It looked . . . he struggled to think of a word that might describe it and then it came to him. *Unloved*. That's what it looked like – unloved – like himself.

They entered the enormous hallway side by side, their eyes instantly drawn towards a huge marble staircase. It rose from the centre of the hall on to a galleried landing that ran along either side of it. No doubt at one time it would have been a glorious feature, but now it was chipped and neglected, worn away in parts by the many pairs of feet that must have tripped up and down it. The oak panels on the walls had been painted a drab cream colour and the tiles on the floor were dull. Franky felt his heart sink. He certainly couldn't see himself staying there for long, and that was a fact. The whole place was depressing and unnaturally quiet, considering it was a children's home. He'd expected to see young people everywhere but there wasn't one in sight.

They were standing there uncertainly when a woman who reminded Franky of a ferret appeared from one of the numerous doorways leading off from the hallway. She was tall and thin to the point of looking anorexic and she had the most enormous hooked nose he had ever seen. It seemed to cover half her face and sat strangely above her thin straight lips.

'Ah, you must be Franky Anderson – we've been expecting you,' she said as she approached them, and Franky was surprised to hear that her voice was almost musical. It was totally at variance with her looks and was soft and strangely comforting.

'I'm Miss Hough, the house mother,' she introduced herself.

There were certainly no surprises there. Franky wouldn't have expected her to be a Mrs with a face like hers. She and Lorna shook hands and then Lorna put her hand in the small of Franky's back and gently nudged him forward.

Miss Hough's small-heeled court shoes made a tap-tapping sound on the tiles as they followed her along a dingy corridor until she paused to usher them into an equally dingy office. It seemed that every wall was painted in the same drab cream, and the dark green curtains that hung at the long window did nothing to lift the air of depression that seemed to hang in the air.

'Now then,' she addressed Franky. 'You will be staying in the Cedar wing. Each wing is named after a tree, as you'll discover. There are four in all, the Cedar wing, Oak, Willow and Yew wing. You will share a dormitory with three other boys who are all of a similar age to yourself. After dinner this evening I shall get someone to show you around and you'll be given a timetable so that you know where you should be at all times. Monday to Friday you will get up at six-thirty in the morning and join the other boys in the showers before breakfast, then after breakfast there will be lessons until lunchtime. After lunch you will go back to lessons again and after four o'clock you will be allocated certain chores to do until dinner. After dinner is your free time. There are certain activities you may do if you feel so inclined, such as table tennis, or you may prefer to watch television in the day room or visit the library, which is in Willow wing. Lights out are at nine o'clock on week-days but—'

'*Nine o'clock!*' Franky gasped in horror. 'I ain't a baby, yer know.'

'No, you aren't,' Miss Hough answered patiently. 'But you have to remember you are just one of many here, Franky. We have to have strict routines for the place to function smoothly. It wouldn't be right if we allowed everyone to do as they pleased.'

Franky flashed an imploring glance at Lorna who avoided his eyes. This place was beginning to sound more like a prison than a home and already Franky knew that he was going to hate it.

Miss Hough coughed slightly and addressed Lorna saying, 'Now, Mrs Drewry, unless there's anything you'd like to ask, I think you can leave Franky with us now. I'm aware you have a fair distance to travel and I've no doubt you'd like to be on your way.'

'Yes, yes, I would. Thank you.' Lorna rose hastily and lifted her bag before turning to Franky. 'Good luck,' she said awkwardly, suddenly hating to leave him there. For all the brash front he put on for the world, Lorna had always been able to see through it to the vulnerable boy beneath the surface, and although she knew it was totally unprofessional of her, she had a huge soft spot for him. 'Just do as you're told and you'll be fine.'

Franky glared at her as he crossed his arms across his chest and slouched in his chair. It was all very well for her to say that. She was going home to her family while he had to stay here in this dump.

Lorna left the room with Miss Hough who reappeared moments

later to tell him, 'Bring your bags, dear. I'll get someone to show you to your room.'

Franky slithered out of his chair with a resentful expression on his face and snatched up his pathetically few possessions. He was feeling very sorry for himself, even though he knew that he had brought this situation about himself. There had been so many chances for him to settle with the families he had been placed with, but always he had put up a barrier that none of them could penetrate. The way he saw it, that was the safest thing to do then no one could hurt him.

Once out in the corridor he saw a young woman striding towards them with a bright smile on her face.

'This is Ella, she's one of the social workers who work here,' Miss Hough introduced her, then addressing the woman she asked her, 'Would you take Franky up to his room? I'm sure he can entertain himself until dinner's ready while he puts his things away.'

'Of course.' Ella smiled at Franky as she cocked her thumb towards the sweeping staircase. 'Follow me,' she invited, and he set off after her.

At the top of the stairs she led him along a seemingly endless corridor. It was dark and gloomy despite the sunshine that was struggling to find its way through the windows, and Franky's spirits sank lower with every step he took.

'Here we are,' she said at last, as she stopped to fling open a door. 'This will be your room.'

He stepped past her into a long narrow room, which contained four beds all lined up against one wall. Standing between each one was a tall shabby wardrobe and a small chest of drawers. There was a chair beneath the window and more tired green curtains framed the windows.

'This will be your bed,' she told him, pausing at the one that was nearest to the door. Franky dropped his bag on to it and glanced around. It was surprisingly tidy considering four boys shared it, and as if reading his thoughts she laughed – a light tinkling laugh that sounded strangely out of place in the gloomy surroundings.

'You'll soon get used to it,' she assured him. 'As long as you stick to the rules you'll be just fine. Miss Hough inspects the rooms each morning and expects them to be tidy. If they're not, you'll be in for a roasting, so be warned. She doesn't suffer disobedience easily, though I have to say her bark is worse than her bite, as you'll discover in time.'

Glancing at her watch she then made for the door before saying apologetically, 'I shall have to get off now. I'm helping out in the dining room this evening. The boys you'll be sharing with will be up to the room after lessons and then you can all get acquainted. Don't be nervous of Pickle, though he can come across as being a bit daunting.'

'Pickle?' Franky raised a curious eyebrow as she paused to tell him, 'Pickle's real name is Tyrone Hannam but he likes to be called Pickle though I have no idea why. He tends to rule the roost amongst the boys here, but if you stand up to him and don't let him boss you about he'll leave you alone . . . eventually.'

She smiled one last time and slipped from the room as Franky sank down on to the edge of his bed. The mattress was hard and lumpy, but then he supposed he'd slept on worse in his time.

Pickle . . . he rolled the name around in his mind. It was a strange title but then he'd soon show this would-be bully that he wasn't going to boss *him* around. Over the last couple of years, Franky had become accustomed to being the boss in whatever household he'd been staying in, until the people decided they'd had enough of his wild behaviour and kicked him out, that was. Ah well, he shrugged before tipping his scant belongings out on to the bed. He was already fifteen and if he could only stay here until he was sixteen in six months' time it wasn't so bad. He would be beholden to no one then.

He began to toss the small amount of underwear he possessed into the scratched and battered chest of drawers at the side of the bed, then flung the rest of his clothes into an untidy heap in the bottom of the wardrobe. For better or worse he was here now and he decided he'd better make the best of it. He lay on the bed with his arms folded behind his head to await the arrival of his room-mates and stared up at the ceiling above, which was criss-crossed with cracks. Eventually he fell into a doze and dreamed that he was back with Twig and Fleur. Destiny and Echo were there too and even though he was fast asleep, the sight of the lovely little girl he had been so fond of caused tears to squeeze from the corners of his shut eyes and slide down and soak into the coarse white pillowslip that he was lying on.

In his dream it was a beautiful summer evening and the only sounds to be heard were the haunting tunes that Twig was strum-ming on his guitar and the night creatures that were creeping around in the copse beside their camp. His stomach was full and he was more content than he had ever been. Then suddenly his mother was there and he was a small child again; she was gazing at him tenderly as she told him, '*I'll come for you . . .*'

But she hadn't come, although he had looked for her every single day since their parting . . . and now the tears flowed faster.

Chapter Twenty-Six

'Ooh, what've we 'ere then – eh, lads? Seems we've got a poofy crybaby amongst us.'

Franky was in that strange place between sleeping and waking as the words penetrated his brain. He was with his mother and was reluctant to leave her, but though he struggled to hold on to her she was slowly slipping away . . . and as his eyes blinked open he found himself staring into a face that was hovering over him.

'Who're you?' he demanded as he struggled up on to one elbow.

'I'm Pickle,' a tall boy informed him as he straightened to stare down at him with a sneer on his face. Franky saw now that there were two other boys standing close behind him and rightly guessed that these must be his roommates. He swung his legs over the edge of the bed and self-consciously swiped the tears from his damp cheeks as he surveyed the other boys.

Pickle was enormous, head and shoulders above Franky, who had always considered himself to be tall. He was muscular too, with an unruly mop of brown hair that stood out from his head in springing curls. His eyes were a cold grey colour and as they stared at Franky now he saw the threat in them. He looked past the boy to the two standing behind him and they instantly introduced themselves.

'I'm Laurence, but yer can call me Lilo,' a small stockily built boy told him. He wore glasses and had the worst case of acne Franky had ever seen. His hair was mousy and cut into a short back and sides, and he looked like a mini-professor.

'An' I'm Connor,' the second boy piped up. His hair was blond and he had striking blue eyes. He was slightly built and Franky found himself thinking what a pretty girl he would have made.

'An' *you* are?'

Franky glanced back at Pickle who was standing hands on hips regarding him with a threatening glint in his eye.

'Franky Anderson.' Franky returned the stare coldly. This chap might think he was cock o' the walk here, but he had no intentions of letting him push *him* around. Better to start off as he meant to go on.

'Franky, eh? An' where are you from? Up north, is it?'

'Nowhere,' Franky retorted boldly.

'Oh, another cocky little bastard, eh? Well, we know how to sort his type out, don't we, lads?'

The two heads nodded in unison as Pickle sauntered over to the window and pushed it open. He then withdrew a crumpled packet from his trouser pocket and extracted a cigarette, which he lit and inhaled on deeply before turning his attention back to Franky. He blew the smoke out before saying ominously, 'There's a few things yer need to get yer head round if yer to stay in here with us. The first being – *I'm* the boss around here. *Get it?*'

Franky stared back at him insolently as the taller boy again took a long drag of his cigarette. The other two were watching him intently and Franky realised in that moment that they were afraid of Pickle, no doubt because of his gigantic size and bullying nature.

'The second thing yer need to know is that if yer do as yer told, I can get yer most anythin' yer want. Fer a price, o' course; *these* fer a start.' He waved his cigarette in the air and fixed his gaze on Franky, but still he remained obstinately quiet.

Pickle felt a grudging admiration for him. Most boys quaked in their shoes when he told them his rules but Franky appeared totally fearless.

A silence settled on the room, broken eventually by Lilo, who told Franky, 'Pickle can get you *anything*.' The words came out on a rush of air and Franky stared at him with contempt shining in his eyes. These two might be prepared to hero-worship Pickle, but he certainly wasn't.

'As it so happens I don't need anythin', an' if I do, I'm quite capable o' gettin' it for meself,' he ground out.

Pickle flicked his cigarette butt out of the open window before advancing on Franky menacingly as the two smaller boys backed away.

'Seems to me you need to be taken down a peg or two, smart-arse,' he spat, and the next second Franky had leaped off the bed and was squaring up to him.

'Try it then,' he taunted him. 'You don't scare me, mate! You know the old sayin', the bigger they are, the harder they fall, so come on . . .'

He lifted his fists as the other two boys hurriedly backed into a corner, but the situation was saved from going any further when the door suddenly opened and a middle-aged man appeared.

Taking in what was happening at a glance, he frowned at Pickle. 'At it again, are you, Hannam?' His face expressed his displeasure. 'Can't you even let the lad settle in before you start throwing your weight about?' Without waiting for an answer he jerked his thumb towards the door. 'Come along, there are jobs you can be doing downstairs to make yourself useful while this lot get ready for dinner.'

Just for an instant, Franky thought the boy was going to disobey him. He was taller than the man, but then he left the room without a word as the man winked at Franky in a friendly fashion before pulling the door shut behind them.

'That was Mr Wicks,' Lilo informed him. 'He's one of the social workers here an' he ain't a bad sort if you keep yer nose clean.'

'So how many are there in this home?' Franky asked.

Lilo frowned as he concentrated on the question before answering, 'No more than forty, I shouldn't think. It ain't a very big home as these sort o' places go.'

'Are there any girls here?'

Lilo laughed as he shook his head. 'Nah, not one, worst luck. It ain't a children's home as such. It's more for kids who . . . well, who've gone off the rails a bit. Like a bad boys' home if yer know what I mean.'

Franky silently cursed Lorna for not telling him. Not that it really mattered. He wasn't going to be here for long, if he had anything to do with it.

'So why are you here?' he asked curiously. Lilo didn't seem like the type who would say boo to a goose.

'I got in with a bad crowd from near where I lived an' we stole a car an' got caught,' he admitted regretfully. 'Me dad is a copper an' he went off his rocker an' refused to have me in the house any longer so I ended up in this place.'

'An' what about you?' Franky addressed Connor, who had said not a word up to now.

The boy giggled, a girlish sound. 'I'm here 'cos I did naughty things to me little brothers,' he said without a shred of remorse.

Franky stared at him uncomprehendingly but then as the meaning of the boy's words sank in, he flushed. 'What, you mean you . . .'

The boy nodded. 'I like boys,' he told him with his chin defiantly in the air. 'I can't be doin' with girls. All them fiddly bits, ugh! In here, I'm classed as Pickles's girlfriend.'

'You . . . you're a *queer*?'

Connor nodded, his blue eyes amused. 'I prefer to say gay,' he said quietly. 'But my mum an' dad didn't see it that way.'

'Oh! So does that mean Pickle is that way inclined an' all?'

Connor nodded solemnly. 'A lot of the boys in here are. You shouldn't have no trouble findin' yerself a boyfriend if that's what turns you on.'

'It don't,' Franky stated flatly, but his mind was working overtime. How did he know which way he was inclined? He'd had nothing to do with girls at all. Nothing to do with anyone sexually, if it came to that, since his encounters with Jacob. Sex was a dirty word, as far as he was concerned. Something that was forced upon you, certainly not something that you would do for pleasure. He knew that he was a good-looking lad and over the last couple of years he'd had more than a few very pretty girls set their caps at him, but he'd walked away from each one without a qualm. He wasn't interested and could never see a time when he would be. Still, he supposed it was each to his own. So long as Connor and Pickle left him alone they could do what they liked. He just wanted a quiet life until he could get out of here. By then he'd be old enough to set off in search of his mother, and no one would chase after him any more and force him into places where he didn't want to be. After all, she would be out of prison by now, surely?

The sky outside had darkened and the air had become humid. Franky glanced towards the window as he tugged at the neck of his T-shirt. There was going to a thunderstorm by the look of it and he suddenly longed to be outside, to feel the cool air on his skin and stand in the rain. However, there was no time for that now.

'Do yer want us to show you the way to the dining room?' Connor offered, his voice friendly.

Franky's stomach grumbled as he remembered that he'd eaten little that day.

'Please,' he muttered, stepping back as Connor made to place his hand on his arm.

'It's all right,' the boy chuckled. 'I won't pounce on you.'

Franky flushed and turned towards the door, the other two boys following him closely. The landing outside was alive with sounds now, and boys of all shapes and sizes were streaming out of the dormitories and down the once-grand staircase. Some of them glanced towards him curiously as he dropped behind the other two, trying to make himself as inconspicuous as possible. The dining room was as dismal as the rest of the rooms he'd entered – the same drab walls and faded curtains with no ornament or picture anywhere to relieve the tedium.

Around the high ceilings were plaster covings that must once have been beautiful, but were now painted the same dull colour as the walls, causing them to almost disappear into the depressing surroundings. The same fate had befallen the carved dado rails, and Franky had to stifle a grin as he imagined a crazed decorator splashing paint everywhere. It wouldn't have mattered a jot if he had missed his target; every wall and ceiling looked exactly the same.

Two long tables stretched from one end of the room to the other, and on either side of them chairs were spaced at regular intervals. At the end of the room, boys were queuing and three women who were standing behind a counter were slapping food on to their plates without even giving the boys a cursory glance. The food looked fairly unappetising but seeing as he was hungry, Franky was prepared to eat anything.

'Come on, else all the best stuff will be gone,' Connor encouraged him.

Soon Franky had a plate full of food, which consisted of cabbage that had been boiled almost to death, some potatoes that he assumed should have been mashed but which remained solid and lumpy, and a sorry-looking slice of meat. A woman further along the row added a spoonful of carrots and a dollop of lukewarm gravy. He had no idea what sort of meat it was, but it looked so tough that he was sure it could have been used to sole shoes. He followed Connor and Lilo to the far end of the nearest table and shortly after, Pickles joined them and slapped his plate down on the table.

'Welcome to the Ritz,' he said sarcastically as he grabbed up his knife and fork and attacked the food in front of him. Claps of thunder were sounding overhead now and a sudden flash of lightning briefly illuminated the room. Franky looked down at the food in front of him with dismay but then stoically followed the other boys' examples and tucked in. The dessert was almost as unpalatable as the main course. The apple pie had been kept warm for so long that the pastry was rock hard and almost bent Franky's spoon, and the custard was so runny it slopped over the side of the dish to form pale yellow pools on the bare surface of the wooden table. Even so, he ate every last little bit and felt slightly better with his stomach full. The boys then took their dirty dishes and placed them neatly into piles on the tables that the women had served them from before drifting from the room in little groups. Outside it had started to rain and it lashed at the windows.

'Well, that puts paid to our stroll fer this evenin' then,' Lilo muttered regretfully.

'We'll go round to the bike sheds,' Pickle told him, determined not to miss the chance of his after-dinner cigarette. Franky tagged along after them. He had nothing better to do and anyway, he didn't know his way about yet so supposed that he might as well follow them.

They took him through the back entrance, pausing at the doors that led out into the grounds as the rain hurled itself at them with a vengeance. The wind had picked up too and the trees in the woodland that ran along one side of the house were bowing and dancing as it whistled through their branches.

'C'mon – let's make a run fer it!' Pickle yelled above the howl of the wind and they all bent their heads and followed him, splashing through the fast-forming puddles as they went. Thankfully, Franky discovered that the bike sheds were no more than a few yards away from the back of the house, but even so by the time they arrived there they were all soaked to the skin and their hair was plastered to their heads.

'Phew, this is some storm.' Pickle shook himself like a dog, sending droplets of water flying everywhere. He then took his cigarettes from his pocket and, after eyeing Franky for a moment, tentatively offered him one. Before Franky's arrival, Pickle had expected another boy he could bully and boss about, but the way the boy had stood up to him in their room earlier on had warned him that Franky wasn't someone to be trifled with, even if he wasn't quite as big as himself.

Franky took a cigarette and lit it with a lighter he had in his pocket as he stared at Pickle from hooded eyes. The rain was bouncing off the tin roof of the bike shed and it had gone bitterly cold now.

'Thanks.' He took a long drag, his eyes never leaving Pickle's face as they weighed each other up.

Connor and Lilo glanced at each other, sensing the silent battle that was taking place, each wondering if Pickle had finally met his match. He had been top dog in the home for a long time now, and they knew that he wouldn't welcome competition even if he was due to go out into the world shortly.

'So,' it was Franky who eventually broke the silence, 'when are you due to leave here?'

'In two weeks' time when I'm sixteen.' Pickle dropped his cigarette butt and ground it out with the heel of his shoe.

Franky stifled a sigh of relief. If he could just get through the next two weeks he had an idea that the atmosphere wouldn't be so tense about this place. He suddenly smiled and held his hand out, much to Pickle's amazement, and his whole countenance was transformed. Pickle felt a stirring in his groin as he realised that Franky was in actual fact a very attractive young man. He had known long ago where his sexual preferences lay. His father had abused him as a young child and in a strange way he had come to enjoy it and now felt more at home with men than he did with women.

'Let's try an' be mates, eh?' he suggested as he took the proffered hand and shook it firmly, and so it was agreed.

That night, Franky lay awake staring up at the ceiling as the snores of the other occupants of the room echoed off the walls. Loneliness settled around him like a blanket and it took a great effort to hold back his tears. Loneliness had been his constant companion over the years but somehow he felt that there was nowhere else to go now. No one in the whole world who cared. He wondered what his mother and his little sisters would be doing and then grinned ruefully. His sisters wouldn't be so little now. In fact, he could pass them in the street now and not recognise them any more. They would be growing up as he was. He wondered how Natasha was and if Lauren still had the little rag doll called Polly that she had cherished back at home. And still he clung to the hope that one day they would all be reunited. It was the only thing that kept him going. There had been so many times over the years when he had wanted to just run back to his home town and try to find them all, but he never had. Perhaps deep down he was afraid that they wouldn't be there.

Turning his head, he looked at Pickle who was lying flat on his back with his huge feet sticking out of the end of the bed. He looked ridiculously vulnerable in this position despite his size, and Franky felt an unexpected rush of sympathy for him, possibly because in the boy's brash front he recognised the inner loneliness that bubbled away beneath the surface in himself. During the evening the other three boys had told him a little of their history and the reasons that had led to them being incarcerated in this godforsaken place. It had not been easy to hear, but Franky had remained stubbornly tight-lipped about his own circumstances. The pain of his past went too deep to share with anyone, especially boys he had only just met.

In his mind he relived the places he had stayed in over the long years since he had been torn away from his family. There had been some good kind people who had been willing to give him a chance; willing to welcome him into their families and their hearts, but Franky had stubbornly shut them out. They weren't his family. His family was somewhere waiting for him, and one day they would all be together again – they had to be. An image of his mother floated once more in front of his eyes and now the tears slid down his cheeks. It was safe to cry in the dark when no one could see him, but never in the day when his tears might be taken as a sign of weakness. He was old enough now to know that his mother had not been the best mum in the world. But even so, she had been there for him. He thought of the numerous hospital visits and the injuries he and his sisters had sustained during their time with her. If only she had . . .

He sharply stopped his thoughts from going any further. There was no point; he had made her a solemn promise and he would never break it. But one day . . . one day the truth would come out and all would be right with the world again. On this comforting thought he snuggled into the lumpy mattress and as dawn was streaking the sky with a canvas of vivid colours, he finally slept.

Chapter Twenty-Seven

'All right then, you lot. Rise and shine!'

Franky started awake as sunlight flooded into the room to see a small man whipping back the curtains. He was middle-aged, short and flabby with wild greying hair that stood out from his head like straggling snakes' tails. A pair of thick-lensed glasses perched on the end of a bulbous nose, revealing lifeless eyes.

He glanced around the room, his eyes resting momentarily on Franky, then certain that all the boys were awake, he shambled towards the door. 'Get yourselves into the showers and don't be late for breakfast,' he told them as he left the room, closing the door none too quietly behind him.

'Who was that?' Franky asked.

Lilo threw himself off the edge of the bed. 'That was Creepin' Cannon,' he informed him. 'An' you'd best keep out of his way if yer can. He quite likes the new lads.'

'What do you mean?'

'I mean he ain't averse to a bit of a grope, the dirty old bastard. But then it's hardly surprisin', is it? He ain't never goin' to get a woman, lookin' like that. That's probably why he lives in. He's one of the house masters.'

'Oh!' Franky felt his stomach sink as he thought back to Jacob, but then he was hastily scrambling out of bed to follow the others to the shower block and for now he had no more time to think on what Lilo had told him.

The shower block was as rundown as the rest of the home. It consisted of long rows of open showers, where boys vied to be next in line. Franky felt slightly embarrassed as he eventually took his place at the side of Pickle and washed himself down with the coarse soap that was provided. There was no privacy whatsoever, though the other boys were so used to it now that they seemed oblivious to the fact. At almost six foot in his stockinged feet, Franky was easily the tallest boy there, apart from Pickle, and he felt curious eyes on him as he quickly wrapped himself in a scratchy towel that was so worn, its original colour was un-distinguishable.

They then trooped back to their room where they dressed quickly before heading once more for the dining room.

Breakfast consisted of lumpy porridge that seemed reluctant to part with the spoon, and bacon so hard that it shot off his plate as Franky tried to cut it. His lip curled with distaste as he tackled it, but even so he ate every bit, supposing that anything was better than nothing. He'd had many days while living rough between his numerous foster placements when he didn't know where his next meal might come from, and so now he never refused food no matter how unpalatable it was.

As soon as breakfast was over, Mr Cannon bore down on him like an avenging angel to tell him, 'You're in maths this morning, Anderson. Follow me and I'll show you where the classroom is.'

Franky spent a miserable morning struggling with the lesson. Because of his numerous absences from school he was way behind every boy in the class and he could see them sniggering at him behind their hands as the teacher asked him questions that he was unable to answer.

When lunchtime arrived he breathed a sigh of relief and hurried outside to the bike sheds where he found Pickle and the rest of his roommates waiting for him.

'How did it go?' Pickle asked as he offered Franky a cigarette.

Franky took it and dragged on it gratefully. 'Bloody awful,' he said resentfully. 'I can't see why they have to make us go into lessons like a bunch o' bloody kids anyway.'

When the boys laughed, Franky felt himself warming to them. The way he saw it, they had something in common. They were all separated from their families for one reason or another and probably hurting beneath the surface just as much as he was, unlike many of the children of the numerous carers he had stayed with who had demanded preferential treatment from their parents and made him feel like an outsider.

'It won't be for long,' Pickle consoled him. 'You'll be booted out of here when you're sixteen, just as I'm gonna be in less than two weeks' time.'

'Where will you go?' Franky asked as he stared at him through a haze of cigarette smoke.

'They'll probably stick me in some grotty flat somewhere an' find me a dead-end job to do.' Pickle blew out a smoke ring. 'Not that I intend on stayin' in either fer long. I shall head for the West End. There's a fortune to be made there if you play your cards right.'

'Doin' what?'

Pickle rolled his eyes. 'What do you think? Jonno, a lad who left here not long ago, was makin' a mint from the queens that hang around the public bogs in London. They call it cottaging.'

Franky frowned as the meaning of Pickle's words sank in. He stared at him incredulously. 'What, yer mean they *sell* themselves?'

Pickle nodded knowingly. 'They certainly do, and to my way of thinking it's easier money than slogging your guts out all day in some job yer hate. I ain't too proud to sell me arse. Jonno is living in the lap of luxury now, with some queer that befriended him and thinks the sun shines out of his arse, an' if he can do it, then so can I.'

Franky fell silent as he absorbed what Pickle had told him. He doubted that he could do it; the memories of what Jacob had put him through were still too fresh in his mind. He only had to close his eyes all these years on and he could still feel the touch of Jacob's hands crawling all over him as clearly as he had when it had happened.

He was about to say something more when they suddenly noticed Mr Cannon striding towards them. They all hastily dropped their cigarette ends and ground them underfoot as the short man came abreast of them.

'Come along,' he barked. 'Let's have you all into the dining room.'

They turned to do as they were told, and as Franky made to follow them the man put his hand on his arm and held him back until the others, who were glancing sympathetically over their shoulders at him, were out of earshot.

'So how are you settling in then, Anderson?' His tongue flicked out to lick his slack wet lips and Franky's stomach plummeted into his shoes. He could have downed the man with one thump, but knew that this would be an unwise thing to do so soon after arriving there.

'I'm fine, thanks,' he muttered as he slowly prised the man's fingers from his arms.

'Good, good.' The man was staring at him with open admiration as he looked him up and down, then suddenly he leaned towards him and whispered, 'Come and find me after lessons this afternoon, son. All the boys have chores to do before dinner and I'll wangle it so that you get to work in the garden. It's so much nicer than kitchen chores, peeling potatoes and such. All the lads want gardening duties but I always fix it so that only the *nice* boys get that job. In fact, I can fix lots of things round here if the boys are *nice* to me.'

As he cast Franky a lascivious smile, the boy felt colour flood into his cheeks. He took a hasty step back and almost tripped before fleeing in the direction of the dining room. Even here, it seemed, he was not going to be safe from the Jacobs of the world, and he wondered what it was about him that seemed to attract that sort of man like a magnet?

When he left the classroom late that afternoon following an English lesson that seemed to go on for ever, he found Mr Cannon waiting for him with an expectant smile on his face. 'Ah, here you are!' he exclaimed as if he were greeting a longlost friend. 'Follow me and I'll show you the way to the kitchen gardens. We grow most of our own fruit and vegetables here.'

Franky looked round helplessly, hoping for a sight of his room-mates but they were nowhere to be seen, so with a resigned sigh he followed the man through the building and out through the French doors adjacent to the enormous kitchen.

He was pleasantly surprised when he saw the place. It was walled and so quiet that he might have been in the middle of the countryside instead of in a children's home on the outskirts of London.

Roses grew up the walls in a profusion of colour and their scent hung on the air. The garden was laid out in neat beds in which grew all manner of vegetables in straight regimental lines. But it wasn't these that Mr Cannon pointed to but an overgrown plot in a far corner.

'I thought you might dig that over for me,' he said. 'I know you won't get it all done this afternoon but you may as well make a start. I think the head gardener wants it prepared so he can plant some late potatoes. You'll find the spades and everything you need in that shed over there.'

'Fair enough.' Franky started towards the shed without a murmur, glad of a chance to escape. When he emerged from the shed moments later, there was no sign of the man and he let out a huge sigh of relief as he set to on the job that had been allotted to him. There was something strangely therapeutic about being alone as he worked with the sun on his back and nothing but the sounds of the birds in the trees to be heard, so it was a shock when Mr Cannon re-appeared some time later to tell him, 'That's enough for tonight, lad. You've made a really good start on it.'

The time had flown by and as Franky looked at what he had achieved he felt a little thrill of satisfaction. The muscles in his arms and his back ached but he was feeling relaxed and almost happy.

'You can come back and do some more tomorrow,' the small man told him as if he was bestowing some great honour, 'but you'd better wash your hands and come and get your dinner now.'

Franky returned the spade to the shed under Mr Cannon's watchful eye and then sidled past him and shot off to the washroom. As long as he could avoid that old lech, perhaps things wouldn't be so bad here after all.

After dinner, Pickle introduced Franky to the delights of the common room where the boys were allowed to relax before bedtime. There was a television set in one corner and a huge shelf heaving under the weight of books of various titles. A table tennis table took up one corner of the room and as Franky entered, curious eyes watched his progress across the room. It was rare for a new boy to be accepted by Pickle so soon, so he escaped the taunts that he would normally have had to endure. No one willingly upset Pickle; they knew better.

The next day followed much the same pattern but Franky could cope with the lessons now and found himself looking forward to working in the garden. Mr Cannon was waiting for him when he arrived fresh from the classroom, but Franky inched by him and collected his spade without acknowledging him.

On the third day, the skies overhead were leaden and grey and the earth was muddy from the downpour they had had earlier in the day.

'You could leave it for today if you like,' Mr Cannon offered when Franky arrived after classes.

The boy shook his head. 'Nah, it'll be fine,' he assured him. 'I ain't scared of a bit o' mud an' rain.' And so he collected his tools and started work, eyeing the ground he had turned over with a measure of satisfaction. One more day after today should do it, he reckoned, and hoped that Mr Cannon would then find him some other job to do out there.

He had barely set to when the heavens opened yet again and within minutes he was soaked to the skin and knee-deep in slimy mud. He carried on, enjoying the peace and tranquillity of the place regardless of the atrocious weather.

'Oh dear,' Mr Cannon commented when he came to fetch him some time later. 'I think you'd better go and have a quick shower before dinner. You can't go in like that.'

Franky looked down at himself and nodded in agreement. The man was right but if he hurried up he'd still make it to the dining room in time for his meal. The work had given him an appetite and his stomach was growling with hunger.

He hurried off to his room and collected a clean outfit. The staff had laundered the meagre selection of clothes he had brought with him. They weren't anything to get excited about, just jeans and T-shirts, plus another pair of trainers and some underwear, but Franky had never been a follower of fashion and had never set any store on how he dressed.

Now he headed off to the shower block with the dry outfit slung across his arm, leaving puddles of water in his wake. It was deserted, as he'd expected it to be. All the other boys and the staff were no doubt already in the dining room. It was pleasant to have the place to himself for a change and he stood beneath the slow stream of lukewarm water, letting it wash over him. He had been there for no more than a few minutes when he suddenly had the sensation of being watched and his head jerked to look behind him. Mr Cannon was standing only feet away from him, his tongue flicking in and out across his slimy lips and his eyes lit with some inner light as he looked Franky up and down appreciatively. His hand was un-consciously stroking the bulge that was evident in his trousers and Franky fought panic as he realised what a predicament he was in. He could scream for all he was worth but at the moment there was no one upstairs to hear him. Stepping hastily out of the shower he snatched up a towel and wrapped it around him as he inched towards his clothes.

'What do you want?' he asked, never taking his eyes off the man's slavering lips.

Mr Cannon chuckled, a dry evil sound that turned Franky's blood to water.

'Now what do *you* think?' His voice was husky and loaded with lust. 'It's time to pay me back for how kind I've been to you, Franky. Not every lad that comes here gets the privilege of working in the gardens, you know.'

'*Piss off!*' The words erupted from Franky's mouth before he could stop them. 'Just get out an' leave me alone, can't you?' He was pulling his T-shirt on over his still-damp body, and it was whilst he was struggling with it that Mr Cannon stepped forward and snatched the towel from about his waist in one easy movement, exposing Franky's private parts.

'Beautiful,' he sighed with ecstasy. 'You are truly beautiful, Franky. I think you could have it very cushy here if you're prepared to be nice to me.'

Franky pushed him away with all his might and shrank back against the cold tiled wall, hopping from foot to foot as he tried to drag his jeans on. Mr Cannon advanced on him again and now his hand fell to Franky's penis and to the boy's horror it began to grow in front of his eyes as the man began to fondle it.

'Leave me alone . . . *please.*' Suddenly he was a little boy again and panic took over as Jacob's face swam in front of Mr Cannon's. The bad things were starting to happen all over again and he knew that somehow he had to stop it. He just *had* to. The man had him pinned up against the wall now and Franky could feel his warm breath fanning his chest as the man's breathing became more erratic.

'Gerroff. *Gerroff me!*' Franky was pushing him blindly away, but the more he pushed, the tighter the man's grip was on him, and worst of all he could feel himself responding. Shame and humiliation flooded through him, along with a feeling of total panic. And it was then that he lashed out and caught the man squarely under the chin with his fist. Mr Cannon's head snapped back on his shoulders and he staggered away as Franky's fist shot out again, this time landing with a sickening thud on his nose. Blood immediately spurted from it and he moaned as his hand rose to his face. But he wasn't Mr Cannon any more. He was *Jacob* – and suddenly all the hurt and anger that Franky had buried deep inside for so many years bubbled to the surface as he advanced on him again, lashing out with his fists and cursing him loudly with every foul name he could think of.

'You fuckin' *sick* perverted *bastard*!' He was sobbing now, his breath coming in harsh rasping sobs. 'You were supposed to be the dad I'd never had. You were supposed to keep me safe but instead you *abused* me.'

Again and again his fists connected with the man's face until Mr Cannon slid to his knees, too weak to try and fend him off any more.

'S-stop,' he implored, as the blood ran down his face and puddled on the floor beneath him. Now Franky brought his foot up and kicked the despicable creature in the ribs as hard as he could. The man went down like a ninepin but still Franky frenziedly continued to beat him until the pleas subsided to gurgling choking noises.

A sharp voice brought him back to his senses and he straightened with a jolt to find Pickle standing in the doorway, gazing down at Mr Cannon with a look of horror on his face.

'What the fuck have you done?' he gasped as Franky breathlessly rested against the wall. The man on the floor was ominously quiet now, and as Pickle approached and stared down at him, he sucked in his breath.

'Jesus, man, I think you've *killed* him,' he whispered.

Suddenly Jacob's face disappeared and Franky found himself looking at the inert figure of Mr Cannon.

He was paralysed with fear but after a moment Pickle took control of the situation. 'You have to get away, mate,' he advised him. 'They'll lock you up an' throw away the fuckin' key if they catch you after this.'

'B-but where will I go?'

Pickle could see that Franky was in shock and he scratched his head as his mind raced ahead.

'I'm gonna get yer away,' he told him after a second. 'I'd have been out o' here soon anyway, so I may as well leave now. You certainly ain't in no state to try an' get away on yer own. But we'll have to go now. Someone could come in at any minute, an' if they do, you've bleedin' had it, mate. Make no bones about it.'

He shook Franky roughly. The boy was shivering as if he had the ague and his eyes were wild and staring.

'Come on.' Helping Franky on with his clothes, he yanked him towards the door then peeped up and down the deserted corridor. 'It's clear so let's go while we can, and just think yerself lucky I popped up to get a packet of fags out of our room. Now just try and look normal. If anyone sees us, they'll just think we're popping outside fer a smoke before dinner. Do yer think yer can do that?'

Franky nodded numbly as they set off along the landing. His knees were knocking and his heart was beating so loudly that he was sure, should they bump into anyone, they would hear it.

Once down the hallway, a social worker who had just come on duty for the night-shift passed them by without giving them a second glance as Pickle led the way to the back entrance.

'It's best to go out this way,' he whispered, keeping his eyes straight ahead. 'If they see us headin' fer the front door they might smell somethin' fishy an' then we'll be done for.'

The door was in sight now and then they were through it, and now Pickle's attitude changed as he grabbed Franky's elbow and marched him briskly round to the side of the house.

'The woods over there.' He cocked his head towards them. 'There's a short cut through there that'll lead us to the main road. Do yer think yer can make a run fer it?'

Again Franky nodded and then he was running like the wind as he tried to match Pickle's lengthy strides. Once under the shelter of the trees they paused to get their breath back before Pickle told him, 'Right, it's this way. Try an' keep up.'

Franky followed like an automaton as the full horror of what he'd done to Creepin' Cannon struck home. He'd *killed* a man. But then, he reasoned, he wasn't the first, was he? He'd killed Jacob too, but hadn't both men deserved what they'd got for violating him? There was no answer to his question, only sharp branches that tore at his hands and clothes and the wind whistling past his face as he raced after Pickle. Whether they'd deserved it or not, it was too late to undo what was done now and he had to get away. Yet another chapter of his life was about to close – and who knew what lay in store for him next?

Chapter Twenty-Eight

'Why, Joe, how lovely to hear from you.' Lorna Drewry's voice held genuine pleasure as she heard Joe Salisbury's voice on the line. Over the years she had kept in touch with Gail and Joe in a purely non-professional way, and they had all become good friends. The couple had even come to stay with her and her husband, Jason, recently when they'd had their baby daughter, Jade, christened. But now she detected that something was wrong and she frowned. Joe didn't sound his usual bubbly self, nor was it like him to phone her at work.

'Is everything all right? There's nothing wrong with Tasha, is there?' she asked with a trace of fear in her voice.

There was silence for a moment until he said quietly, 'Tasha is fine, Lorna. It's Gail.'

'Gail? Why, what's wrong?'

'It's the cancer – it's come back.'

Lorna gulped. Gail had fought valiantly against the illness and had seemed to make a full recovery, staying in remission for all these years, but now Joe was telling her it was back, and Lorna felt as if someone had thumped her in her guts.

'Oh,' she managed to say when she had pulled herself together. 'Is it bad?'

'Very bad, I'm afraid.'

Her heart went out to him; he, Gail and Tasha were such a close-knit family that it didn't seem fair at all. But then, when did cancer ever seem fair? she asked herself. It wrecked lives, not just of those who were suffering from it, but of whole family units.

'Is there anything that can be done?' she asked, dreading the answer, and when it came it was just as awful as she'd feared it would be.

'No, nothing.' His voice was bleak and without hope. 'She collapsed with pains in her side two days ago and they rushed her into hospital thinking it was appendicitis, but when they opened her up they found she was full of it. It's spread everywhere, so they stitched her up, sent her home and told her to enjoy whatever time she has left.'

Lorna was speechless. What could she say to such terrible news? The silence stretched between them until Joe eventually said brokenly, 'I just thought you should know. You've been so good to us and Gail thinks the world of you.'

'How long?' she asked.

'Huh! How long is a piece of string? I've asked my friend in Harley Street to have a look at her and give us a second opinion, of course, but I think deep down I know there's not much more they can do. They've offered her chemotherapy again, but she's not sure if she wants to go all through that again. It will only be delaying the inevitable.'

Lorna swiped a tear from her cheek. 'Tell her I'll be there as soon as I can,' she said softly. 'And Joe . . . thanks for letting me know.' She replaced the phone in its cradle and sat staring off into space for a long time as she wondered at the injustices of life.

Earlier in the morning she'd had a call from a very irate social worker at Woodside Children's Home who had informed her that Franky had done a disappearing act after beating one of the house masters almost senseless in the showers. The man was in hospital, in a bad way by all accounts, with broken ribs and cuts and bruises all over him. And now this on top. It certainly hadn't started out to be the best day she had ever had.

★　★　★

On the following Saturday morning Lorna drew her car to a halt outside Beehive Cottage, wondering if it had been such a good idea to come here, after all. What was she supposed to say to Gail anyway? *'Oh, hi Gail, I'm so sorry to hear that you're dying.'* She shook herself mentally. Gail was her friend and somehow she would help her to get through this. Jade was safe at home with her husband and it was only going to be a flying visit, so she determined to make it as positive as possible. The last thing this family needed was for her to go in weeping and wailing like a banshee. Fixing a bright smile to her face, she clambered out of the car and headed for the door.

Tasha admitted her with a loving hug and once again, Lorna was shocked when she saw her. She was growing into a beautiful young woman who totally adored her parents, particularly Joe, whom she shadowed like a faithful little puppy dog. Her fair hair hung right down her back in shining waves now and she was petite and slender, so petite in fact, that Joe often teased her that she was going to be a model. She certainly had the figure and the looks for it, although she was still a little slow, which showed when she talked, although she could hold an intelligent conversation with the best of them.

'Hello, darling,' Lorna greeted her, returning her hug. 'I swear you've shot up another inch since I last saw you.'

Tasha giggled and ushered her towards the back room where Joe was in the process of making a large pot of tea. 'Now that's what I call good timing,' he teased, for all the world as if this was just a normal social visit. 'But then I know what you social workers are like. I swear you can smell a brew from a mile off. It's no wonder you never have any time to get any work done.'

'You cheeky devil,' Lorna cuffed his ear gently then asked, 'Where's Gail?'

'She's in the sitting room, taking it easy. Go through to her and I'll fetch this in as soon as it's ready.'

She found Gail sitting on the sofa under a blanket and propped up against a mountain of pillows looking remarkably pretty and chirpy. She smiled and held her hands out to her guest as she scolded,

'Lorna, it's lovely to see you. Joe told me he'd rung you but you shouldn't have come all this way.'

'Why shouldn't I come and see you if I've a mind to?' Lorna demanded lightly. 'You're my friend, aren't you?'

'I sincerely hope so.' Gail looked towards Tasha and keeping her voice cheery she asked her, 'Would you mind popping up to my room and getting me another hankie, sweetheart?'

Tasha nodded obligingly and hurried away, and now that they were alone, Lorna took her hand and asked softly, 'How are you feeling, love?'

'Oh, a bit sore from the stitches, but other than that I feel fine.'

Lorna suddenly bowed her head, afraid that the tears that had sprung to her eyes might spill over, and strangely it was Gail who comforted her.

'Listen, I'm not ready to go *anywhere* just yet,' she told her, shaking her hand gently up and down. 'I've decided to take the doctors up on their offer of another dose of chemo and they've said that if I'm prepared to have that, I could have between three and five years left. Tasha will be left school by then and more able to look after herself. So . . . the long and the short of it is I'm going to fight this bloody thing all over again. You just see if I don't. I want to see my daughter grow up.' She said it with such determination that Lorna's admiration of the woman grew even more.

'Do you know, I rather think you will.' She squeezed Gail's hand.

'Lorna,' Gail's face became solemn, 'I shall never be able to thank you and Mary enough for bringing Tasha to us. I can't remember what it was like without her now.'

'Well, she certainly loves you, that's for sure. She seemed to settle with you from day one, but tell me, does she never mention her mother or Alex or Lauren?'

'Never.' Gail shook her head. 'It's almost as if she's forgotten the life she had before she came to us. But why do you ask?'

'Kay Slater is due to be released from prison next month,' Lorna told her gently, and Gail visibly paled.

'You don't think she'll come looking for Tasha, do you?' she whispered fearfully.

Lorna smiled reassuringly. 'I shouldn't think so for a minute,' she said. 'I just thought I ought to tell you, that's all.'

Gail nodded and then they quickly turned the conversation to happier things as Tasha ran back into the room with a wide smile on her face.

The day passed pleasantly and quickly, with the two women having little chance to speak much on their own, but all the same, Lorna was glad she'd taken the trouble to come. Somehow she knew that Joe and Tasha would survive when anything did happen to Gail, just so long as they still had each other. They were a family now and had been for a long, long time.

Now she just had to wait for the police to find Tasha's errant brother again, and this time it was proving to be easier said than done. He'd been missing for three days now without a trace. Still, he'd been missing before for far longer than that, and she had no doubt that he would turn up eventually like a bad penny. Franky Anderson always did.

Chapter Twenty-Nine

The woman on the pavement gripped the carrier bag she was holding and gazed fearfully up and down the street as the heavy metal doors clanged shut behind her.

Her heart was pounding and she felt sure that everyone who passed was looking at her. But then she asked herself, why should they? Kay Slater no longer resembled the brassy peroxide blonde who had been incarcerated in the prison all those years before. Now she looked like a prematurely aged, frail woman. During the years she had spent at Her Majesty's pleasure she had rubbed shoulders with villains and murderers. She had fought off lesbians and thieves who would steal off their own granny, and had learned the hard way that the safest way to survive was to keep her head down and keep herself to herself.

And now it was over, but instead of feeling relief she was battling the urge to throw herself against the prison doors and beg them to take her back in. The world seemed so much larger than she remembered it. Larger and noisier, and panic began to make her tremble. Her probation officer had found her a flat to live in and had assured her that she would help her to find a job. She supposed it was a start. Now she had to get to the station and from there she would be able to get a train back to Nuneaton. Not that there was anything there for her any more. She knew that her children had all gone to adoptive families long ago. Even so, it was her only option. Where else was there to go? She had no one in the world. During the first years in prison she had dreamed of being released so that she could track her children down and fetch them home, but that dream had died some long time ago. Too much water had gone under the bridge since then and she doubted if the children would even remember her now. They would be all grown up.

As she thought of Alex, tears began to trickle down her cheeks. She had loved all her children but if forced to, she would have had to admit that he held a special place in her heart. She had promised him that she would come to fetch him on the day they had parted, and she wondered how he had coped with the fact that she never had. Of course, it was far too late for that now, but even so she was determined to try and find out where the children had all gone. At least then she would be able to sleep knowing that they were safe.

Gripping the handles of the carrier bag that contained all she owned, she set off with a new energy. The sooner she got back to her home town, the sooner she could start to try and find the whereabouts of her children.

'So where are we gonna go?' Franky was trying hard to keep the panic from his voice as he followed Pickle along the busy pavement.

'I seem to remember Jonno sayin' that he was livin' somewhere in South Kensington, so I reckon we'll head there. We're bound to bump into him sooner or later if we hang about fer long enough, an' then he'll be able to help us.' All the while he was speaking, Pickle was scanning the congested roads for the sight of a police car that might already be looking for them.

Franky meanwhile was watching him curiously out of the corner of his eye. Suddenly he asked, 'Why are you doin' this for me?'

Pickle's broad shoulders shrugged. 'I dunno really. Let's just say I ain't got a lot to lose. I'd have been out of that dump before yer could bat yer bloody eyelids anyway. An' if I ain't very much mistaken, yer could do with a friend right now.'

A friend. Franky looked straight ahead as he thought on what

Pickle had said. He'd never had a friend before. Not a *real* friend his own age, at any rate, unless he included Ginger, and that had been a long, long time ago. Ginger would be all grown up now, just as he was, and Franky wondered if he ever gave him a thought.

He was totally lost but as Pickle seemed to know where he was going he fell silent and followed him closely. They'd gone a mile or so when Pickle asked, 'Got any money on yer?'

Franky fumbled in his pocket and withdrew a handful of change; as Pickle eyed it, he snorted with disgust. 'That ain't goin' to get us very far, is it? It's a bleedin' good job I've got a few quid on me. At least we'll be able to get on a bus and have some grub tonight.'

'That's somethin', I suppose,' Franky agreed. 'But where are we gonna sleep?'

'We'll worry about that later,' Pickle shot back. 'Fer now I just want to get us as far away from the home as we can. Otherwise the coppers will pick us up and then I think you'll find you won't have to worry about where you'll be sleepin' fer a long time.'

Franky shuddered and glanced anxiously over his shoulder, expecting a hand to close across it at any moment. He felt no remorse for the beating he'd given the house master. The way he saw it, the perverted old bastard had deserved all he got and he was only surprised that someone hadn't done it sooner. They came to a huge crossroads with a bus station, and after studying the signs for a while, Pickle pointed off into the distance.

'We can get a bus over there up to Westminster – see? Then we can find our way to South Ken from there,' he told Franky and they moved on. As they waited at the bus station, the day's events began to catch up with Franky and he felt exhausted.

'Can't we stop for a drink?' he pleaded as he stopped to slip his trainer off and rub his sore ankle. 'I bet it takes ages to get to London from here.'

Pickle paused and sighed. 'I dare say we can afford to do that,' he told him, then he pointed. 'Look, there's a café over there. We'll grab ourselves a drink an' then a bit later on we'll get a bag of chips between us. But keep yer head down. We don't want to be spotted.'

They entered the small café and as Pickle headed off towards the counter, Franky dropped gratefully on to one of the hard-backed wooden chairs placed around a shabby-looking table. The place smelled of grease and stewed tea but he was so tired that he felt as if he were in heaven.

Minutes later, Pickle returned and slapped a cracked mug unceremoniously in front of him.

'Here, get that down yer,' he ordered. 'You'll feel better when you've had a drink.'

Franky eyed it with distaste. There was what appeared to be a film of grease on the weak-looking liquid and when he sipped it he discovered that it was only lukewarm. Even so he dumped three heaped spoonfuls of sugar into it, stirred it vigorously and within seconds he had drained the cup.

'Cor, that hit the spot,' Pickle commented as he swiped his hand across the back of his mouth. 'Are yer ready fer the off again?'

Franky nodded and within minutes they were back outside on the bus and heading for London. It was evening by the time they reached the Embankment of the River Thames, and Franky's eyes were out on stalks as he took in sights he had only ever seen before in books and on the telly, like Big Ben and the House of Parliament.

Large river cruisers were sailing along full of tourists whose cameras were flashing, and there seemed to be people teeming about everywhere he looked. 'Westminster Abbey is just up there,' Pickle said. Seeing the look of awe on Franky's face, he grinned before asking, 'Ain't yer never been to The Smoke before?'

Franky shook his head.

'Well, when we've found somewhere to sleep an' we're settled, I'll take yer sightseeing,' Pickle offered, then he looked up and down the road. 'If I remember rightly, Kensington is that way. Must be a good couple of miles. We'll go up to Trafalgar Square and head off that way.'

Franky set off after him again, being jostled this way and that by the people that were thronging the pavements of Whitehall. Pickle was suddenly brought to an abrupt halt when he barged straight into one particular giant of a man. The man had a large camera slung across his shoulder and was wearing a brightly coloured short-sleeved shirt that would have looked more in place on a beach in Hawaii than in the centre of London. The picture was completed by knobbly hairy knees that stuck out from a pair of long shorts and a wide-brimmed stetson hat.

'Sorry,' Pickle said pleasantly as he reached out to steady the chap.

'S'alright, buddy.' The accent immediately told Franky that the chap was an American as he slapped Pickle good-naturedly on the shoulder. 'No harm done. Y'have a good night now, y'hear?'

The boys hurried on, and once they had put some distance between the man and themselves, Pickle drew Franky to a halt beneath one of the lions in Trafalgar Square and waved a wallet in his face.

'Looks like we won't be sleepin' rough tonight after all,' he joked as Franky's mouth gaped open.

'Where did you get that?' he gasped.

'From that fat American I just bumped into, of course,' Pickle said. 'Yer didn't really think it were an accident, did yer, yer bleedin' thickhead. I did it so I could get close enough to pick his pocket.'

After quickly opening the wallet he cursed softly. 'Ah, bugger it! There's only about thirty quid in here all told. I thought it would be *loaded*. Still, never mind. At least we can get a few decent meals out of it. I don't know about you, but me stomach's beginning to think me throat's cut.'

He took Franky's elbow and they walked for some distance until they eventually found a McDonald's.

'Wait here,' Pickle commanded. 'I shan't be a tick.'

True to his word he was back in no time with two brown paper bags. They smelled so delicious that Franky's mouth began to water.

'Here yer go.' Pickle passed one of them to Franky before joining him on the kerb as they tucked into their feast. Woodside Children's Home suddenly seemed a million miles away, and as Franky ravenously ate his burger and chips, his spirits began to lift a little. After all, he thought, this is the beginning of a new life. There was no way the social workers would bother to look for him this time. They'd probably just write him off at his age, and he and Pickle were bound to find work here. There was sure to be any number of jobs they could do in the city.

As a picture of Mr Cannon lying on the floor of the shower room, battered and bloodied, flashed in front of his eyes, he shuddered. The Social Services might not bother to look for him but the police certainly would, especially if the man was dead as Pickle had feared. But he mustn't think of that now. The next thing they needed to do was find somewhere to sleep for the night. They finished their meal then wended their way haphazardly towards Kensington via Hyde Park.

Franky was yawning now and felt as if his feet were on fire, so eventually they sank down on to a bench.

'I don't reckon there's much chance of finding Jonno tonight now,' Pickle said regretfully. 'Let's go and kip down under them trees over there, eh? It's a fine night so we shouldn't get too cold, an' we're sure to find him tomorrow,' he said optimistically.

Franky tailed him without argument. Sleeping rough held no fears for him, he had done it numerous times before, and as Pickle had pointed out – the weather was fine, which was something at least.

Soon they were lying side by side on the grass staring up into the branches of the tree above them. Franky was feeling pleasantly tired and the background noise of the heavy traffic beyond the fence was like a lullaby. In no time at all he was fast asleep and he stayed that way without stirring until the early hours of the next morning.

Chapter Thirty

'Fuckin' hell, I've got a crick in me neck.' Pickle groaned as he stirred on the grass and rolled over the next morning.

Franky started awake and blinked in the early-morning sunshine that was filtering through the branches of the tree. His mouth was dry and he too felt stiff and uncomfortable.

Pickle felt in his pocket and flicked a cigarette across to Franky as he lit one for himself. 'I reckon we ought to get some breakfast down us then go and look for Jonno.'

Franky nodded in agreement as he took a long drag of his cigarette. His stomach was grumbling and he felt dirty, though there was little chance of them finding anywhere to wash. Pickle stood up and urinated against the tree, then doing his zip up he told Franky, 'Well, come on then. Sittin' there ain't gonna get us nowhere, is it, mate?'

Franky stumbled to his feet and followed Pickle across the park, and once they'd reached the Albert Memorial, Pickle steered them in the direction of a small side street.

'The eatin' places will be cheaper there,' he informed Franky. 'On the main road it would cost more than I found in the wallet I lifted to even walk through the fuckin' door, that's if they'd even let us in.'

Franky could well believe it. The townhouses and apartment blocks they had passed looked classy and expensive and he gazed at them curiously, wondering who could ever afford to live in them.

Pickle seemed to know his way about, a fact that Franky was grateful for as he was hopelessly lost.

Soon they came to a small café and Pickle headed inside, taking his ill-gotten gains from his pocket as he approached the counter. Franky found a seat away from the window, just in case a policeman should happen by, and in no time at all they were both tucking into plates piled high with greasy overcooked sausages and bacon that was dripping in fat. They were so hungry that they set to without a thought and had cleared their plates within minutes.

'Phew, that's better.' Pickle leaned back in his seat and sighed with satisfaction as he rubbed his full stomach and burped. 'What say we go an' have a good wash in the toilet here before we go off huntin' fer Jonno again, eh? I can smell me own sweat an' I don't half pong, but here we are without so much as a toothbrush between us.'

They passed the café owner who had a cigarette dangling from the corner of his mouth, and Franky noticed that his hands looked as if they hadn't seen soap and water for a month. It didn't concern him; he had more pressing things to worry about than hygiene at that moment in time, like somewhere to live for a start.

Ten minutes later they strolled out on to the pavement feeling slightly more human and Pickle once again led the way back towards Kensington High Street and the area all around Church Street. Pickle couldn't remember anything about his mate Jonno's address, except that it was swanky. They spent the day traipsing round the area, but as night once more approached they had still not had so much as a glimpse of Pickle's friend. Franky was getting despondent and about to give up when suddenly Pickle shouted, 'Hey, Jonno! Over here, mate!'

A young man on the other side of the street paused to look across at them, and when he saw Pickle his face lit up in a grin and he diced with death as he threaded his way through the fast-moving traffic.

'What the hell are you doing here?' he asked as he drew level with them and began to pump Pickle's hand up and down, whilst giving Franky the once-over.

'We did a runner from the home an' were hopin' that you might know somewhere we could kip,' Pickle told him.

Franky eyed the boy curiously. He was dressed in designer gear and was very good-looking in a smarmy sort of way. His legs were clad in jeans so tight-fitting that he looked as if he had been poured into them, and he was wearing a shocking pink T-shirt that looked extremely expensive. His hair was golden blond; Franky suspected the colour was not entirely natural but had to admit that it suited him. His eyes were a striking shade of blue and after a moment Franky decided that he was too pretty to be a boy. He was very effeminate – even the way he stood put Franky in mind of a girl.

'Well, now then, let me think . . .' The boy tapped his chin before grinning. 'I know where you could kip down for the time being, just so long as you aren't too fussy. Hugo, that's my bloke, keeps some of his kids in a flat in Kings Cross. It ain't posh, so be warned, but it would be better than being on the streets and I've no doubt he'd set you on with work and all. Especially *him*.' As his eyes lingered on Franky, his face broke into a smile again. 'His sort, the David Essex lookalikes, always go down well with the punters.'

'What do yer mean, the punters?' Franky asked warily.

'Hugo is a pimp,' Jonno told him without a qualm. 'He's got a string of prostitutes working for him. Both sexes, mind. Hugo ain't fussy just so long as they bring the cash in. The rent boys earn as much, sometimes more than the toms.'

'Yer mean . . . yer want me to be a *rent boy*?' Franky's eyes were almost popping out of his head. 'Is that what *you* are?'

Jonno laughed good-naturedly. 'No, not exactly – at least only for Hugo. He's my chap. You know, he keeps me exclusively to himself and I live with him in his pad over there.' He gestured at a trendy modern block of flats. 'I tell you, it's like something out of a magazine. He's got every mod con available and I live in the lap of luxury, just so long as I pander to his every whim. He is a lot older than me, of course. But what I say is, enjoy it while you can. Hugo likes 'em young, so I suppose when I get a bit older he'll be looking round for a replacement, so I'm making hay while the sun shines. I'll worry about what I'm going to do and where I'm going to go when the time comes. For now, Hugo treats me like a prince and I'm loving every minute of it.'

Franky gulped. He didn't like the sound of this at all and suddenly had visions of Jacob and Creepin' Cannon manhandling him. But then what other options did he have, unless he was prepared to pound the streets trying to find a job – and that could bring its own problems. He already knew from what Pickle had told him that jobs hereabouts were like gold dust to find. Still, at least there was somewhere to stay on the horizon, so he decided he'd go along with what Jonno was proposing for now. Once he had somewhere to put his head down, he'd worry about the rest.

'Right, you two wait here and I'll go and see what Hugo has to say,' Jonno told them affably. 'I shan't be a tick.' With that he scooted off and Franky and Pickle watched him once again cross the road and disappear into a large glass-fronted foyer slightly down the road on the other side. Franky eyed the building enviously. It looked classy and he guessed that you would have to be very rich to live there. A doorman in livery was at the door, checking everyone who went in, but the boys saw that he let Jonno pass him without a word.

'That was a bit of luck, my spotting him like that, weren't it?' Pickle looked inordinately pleased with himself as he ran his fingers through his hair and tried to make himself look presentable. Franky scowled, not much liking the outcome of the meeting but seeing no alternative for now.

Minutes later, Jonno reappeared with a great bear of a man at his side. Franky gulped as they crossed the road and walked towards them. He tried to gauge how old the man might be. He guessed that he was somewhere in his forties and although at some point he might have been handsome, he now looked ravaged.

'So, lads. I hear you're in a spot of bother and need a job and somewhere to stay.' As the man's eyes swept over them, they lingered on Franky and he felt his cheeks grow hot.

Franky was already approaching six foot tall but this man towered over him and appeared to be almost as wide as he was tall, though he seemed to be made of solid muscle rather than fat. There was an ugly scar that ran from the corner of his right eye down to his chin, and when he smiled his face looked vaguely deformed. His eyes were a deep brown, appearing to be almost black, and his hair, which had obviously once been very dark, was thinning. The light cream suit he was wearing was immaculate, and beneath it was a dark brown silk shirt open at the neck revealing at least three heavy gold chains that nestled into the hair on his chest. His hands were also covered in gold rings studded with diamonds that winked as the sun caught them, and the whiff of expensive aftershave hit Franky as the man extended his great spade of a hand and shook his.

'So where are you both from then?' he asked now and Pickle immediately answered, 'We did a runner from the home where I met Jonno. Franky had a bit of a run in with a teacher called Creepin' Cannon. He were a bit too hands-on for Franky's taste, if yer know what I mean, an' we left him lyin' on the shower-room floor.'

'I see.' The man frowned. 'Was he dead?'

Pickle shrugged his shoulders. 'We never stopped long enough to find out, to be honest. We just fuckin' legged it.'

'Well, it's not a bad thing to be able to defend yourself,' Hugo responded with no sympathy at all for the man that Franky had pasted. 'If you're going to work for me, you need to be able to look out for yourselves. Some of the punters can cut up rough when you least expect it. But don't worry about that for now. Let's go and see if we can't get you settled in somewhere, eh?'

As Pickle looked at him admiringly, Franky knew then that he would have swapped places with Jonno like a shot if he'd had the opportunity. The man led them along the pavement and back across the road into an underground car park beneath the penthouse where he lived. He paused in front of a brand new black BMW and Pickle sighed with envy as he stared at it. The smell of new leather assailed their nostrils as he and Pickle piled into the back seat while Jonno took the seat at the side of Hugo in the front.

'I've got a couple of flats in Kings Cross where some of my youngsters stay,' Hugo informed them, as he steered the car expertly out into the heavy traffic. Franky closed his eyes, convinced that something was about to crash into them at any minute. There seemed to be cars, buses and taxis coming at them from every direction but Hugo didn't appear to be at all phased by the fact. The car purred along and eventually Franky dared to open his eyes again to find Hugo watching him with amusement in the driver's mirror. 'This your first trip to the big city then is it, son?'

Franky nodded numbly.

'And where are you originally from?'

Franky shrugged. 'Nowhere really. I've just bodged about from here to there for almost as long as I can remember.'

'Fair enough. Ask no questions an' you'll be told no lies, eh?' The man shrugged his enormous shoulders and Franky saw the muscles ripple beneath his smart suit jacket. This Hugo was a man to be reckoned with, and certainly not someone you would try to mess about.

The rest of the journey was made in silence until eventually Hugo drew the car to a halt on a grubby back street. It seemed a world away from the apartment where he lived, but then Franky was wise enough to know that beggars couldn't be choosers and was just grateful for the fact that he and Pickle wouldn't have to spend another night sleeping in the park.

'This is it.' Hugo heaved his great frame out of the car and nodded towards some steps that led up to a first-floor flat. 'It's not the Ritz, I'll grant you, but it's better than sleeping rough.'

The boys followed him up the steps, and when he opened the door to the flat the sickly-sweet scent of cannabis wafted out to meet them. Franky found himself in a small lounge that seemed to be crammed with young people of both sexes. Two boys, who looked to be not much older than himself, were reclining on grubby bean-bags beneath the dingy window, and in a far corner a young Asian girl with a gaunt face and sunken eyes was nursing a tiny baby who was sucking furiously at her small breast. She didn't bat an eyelid when they walked in, although Franky quickly looked away. Another girl was sitting at a table that was leaning drunkenly to one side, painting her toenails a bright purple, and as Franky caught her eyes he saw the hopelessness reflected in them.

'Right you lot, this is Franky and Pickle,' Hugo addressed them. 'They'll be staying here for a while.'

'But we've only got two bedrooms an' there's already the two lads in one an' us three in the other,' the girl at the table objected. She clamped her mouth shut instantly when Hugo looked towards her with a baleful glare.

'Then you'll just have to make do, won't you?' Hugo waved his heavily ringed hand towards a settee of indeterminate colour, sending rainbows of colour shooting around the nicotine-stained walls. 'That makes into a bed if I remember rightly, so these two can sleep on there for now. Have you any objections?'

Hearing the menace in his voice the girl shook her head quickly and now Hugo was all charm again. 'Good, that's sorted then. Make sure you get the newcomers something to eat and I'll be round in a couple of days when they've settled in. All right, lads?'

'Yes, sir, thanks,' Pickle gushed as the man headed back towards the door – and then he was gone and Franky had time to look more closely at his surroundings. Hugo certainly hadn't been joking when he told them that it wasn't the Ritz. The Pits would have been a more apt description. The carpet was sticking to the soles of his feet and the heavy smell of drugs was making him feel nauseous.

'I'm Pickle an' this is Franky,' his friend introduced them, and the boy nearest to them dragged himself off the beanbag and advanced on them with his hand held out. 'I'm Gav, mate. An' that there is Boy.'

When Franky raised a quizzical eyebrow the boy took a deep toke on his spliff. 'Yer can be anyone yer want to be while yer here,' he explained. 'It's a case of the least said the better. That one there paintin' her nails is Madison an' that's Zara. The baby is called Sunny an' she is sunny by nature, an' all. We all take turns in lookin' after her when Zara is out.'

The occupants of the room all nodded towards Franky and Pickle in a friendly manner and suddenly Franky had the feeling that despite the grotty surroundings it wouldn't be so hard living here after all. They seemed a nice group.

'Have you eaten?' Gav now asked.

Pickle shook his head. 'Not since this mornin', an' I'm famished to be honest,' he admitted.

'In that case help yerselves to anythin' yer can find in there.' Gav pointed towards a small kitchenette. 'Hugo supplies us with plenty of money for food so don't get goin' hungry. I ain't got time to cook you anythin' 'cos I should be gettin' ready for work now.'

'Work?' Franky asked and Gav chuckled.

'Yeah, *work*. Yer don't think Hugo provides us with this place to live in an' the food we eat fer nothin', do yer? He's our pimp. We all hand over seventy-five per cent o' the money we take off the punters, an' he provides us with anythin' else we need.'

As Franky glanced down he noticed the needle pricks on Gav's arm but wisely said nothing, and now the young man strode off towards a door that obviously led to the bedroom he shared with Boy.

Once he was gone Madison rose from the table and headed towards the adjoining door with a friendly grin. Franky saw that she wasn't as old as he'd first taken her for; in fact, he judged that she was little older than himself.

'I ought to be getting ready too or I'll lose my pitch,' she told them apologetically. 'The toms round here will scratch your eyes out if you try to encroach on their territory,' she explained, and then she too disappeared.

Franky now looked towards the young man they called Boy, but saw at a glance that he was well out of it. He was leaning back against the wall on his beanbag shrouded in smoke and with a dreamy look in his eye.

'Don't mind him,' Zara told them. 'He works for Hugo as a debt collector. Most of the places round here pay Hugo to see that they don't get any trouble and Boy collects the money for him, amongst other things. He sells drugs for him too. Trouble is, he's getting a bit too fond of sampling the merchandise. Hugo will be kicking his arse if he doesn't get a grip on himself soon. It's no use trying to tell him though. Boy thinks he's invincible.'

Franky saw that Boy was quite large, muscled and tall, which probably explained why Hugo used him as a rent collector. He looked powerful and Franky decided that he wouldn't like to get on the wrong side of him. He turned his attention back to Zara. She was very well-spoken and he saw immediately that she was quite beautiful. Or at least, she could have been if she hadn't looked so drawn and ill. Her dark eyes were huge in her small face, and her jet-black hair hung down her back like a sleek velvet curtain. Pickle had disappeared off into the small kitchenette and Franky could hear him rummaging about in his search for food, so he dared to venture a little closer to the girl, and as he stared down at the small baby in her arms he commented, 'She's lovely.'

Her face momentarily lit up as she smiled at the compliment and he saw the love in her eyes for the baby, who was now gurgling contentedly. 'Yes, she is, isn't she?' Pride was evident in her voice. 'She's just about the best thing that's ever happened to me,' she told him gravely. 'I can't imagine being without her now, although I admit I was appalled when I first discovered I was pregnant.'

'Wouldn't the father stand by you?' Franky probed gently, thinking how different she seemed to the other occupants of the flat.

She lowered her head in shame before replying softly. 'I'm a prostitute, Franky. I don't even know who her father is.'

'Oh, I see . . . I'm sorry,' Franky mumbled, wishing he could have bitten his tongue off. What business of his was it anyway? He'd had no right to ask such a personal question. Particularly of someone he had only just met.

'It's quite all right,' she assured him, seeing his embarrassment, and now a silence settled between them, broken eventually by Pickle, who poked his head out of the kitchen to inform Franky, 'I've got some toast on the go. Do yer want some?'

Franky flashed Zara a brief smile and hurried away to join his friend, glad of an excuse to escape from the tense atmosphere he had created with his loose tongue.

When they had eaten their fill of toast and jam and a couple of leftover cold sausages, they filed back into the small living room to find it empty. Boy had managed to drag himself off to bed and Zara had joined Madison in the girls' room.

'It ain't a bad gaff, is it?' Pickle looked around as if they'd landed in a four-star hotel. 'I reckon we've dropped on our feet here. And what about that Hugo, eh? Lucky old Jonno to land a bloke like him. I wouldn't mind wakin' up next to him every day, I don't mind tellin' yer.'

Franky shuddered at the thought but managed to swallow the hasty retort that sprang to his lips. The chap had given them somewhere to stay, after all, and he should be grateful for that at least. It was what Hugo would want in return that was weighing heavily on his mind. There was no need to brood on that for now though. Hugo had said that he wouldn't be calling on them for a few days, so for now he'd just try to relax and get to know his flatmates. Franky's life was about to change yet again and he knew from past experiences that the next episode could be as good or as bad as he made it.

Chapter Thirty-One

They had been living in the flat for almost a week and as yet there had been no sign of Hugo, a fact that had lulled Franky into a false sense of security. During the time he had stayed there his cold heart had slowly started to thaw as he grew to know his flatmates. Each of them was running away from something just as he had all his life, and for the first time in many years he felt as if he belonged. They were all hurting and unloved, and Franky could recognise the loneliness in each of them that never really went away.

Zara had confided to him one evening when they were in alone that her real name was Jasdeep and that she was a Sikh. She came from a very wealthy family in Sussex who were deeply religious and attended their Temple regularly. She had run away from them when her father had informed her that she would be going into an arranged marriage. The man he had in mind for her was thirty years older than her and Zara had found him repulsive; she rebelled against her parents to the point that they were keeping her a virtual prisoner until she agreed to comply with their wishes. Feeling that there was no other option open to her, she had crept out of the house late one night and headed for London, hoping that she would find the streets there paved with gold. Like so many other young people before her, she had soon found out the truth and had spent the first week sleeping on the Embankment in a cardboard box. Then she had met Hugo and he had brought her here and she had worked for him ever since.

'It was hard at first,' she admitted to Franky, 'but as time goes on you sort of get used to this way of life and accept it. It was a blow when I found out I was pregnant a year after I arrived here, but in fairness to Hugo, he stood by me. I'm in big demand and he gave me time off to have the baby before I went back to work.'

Franky had felt his anger build. Of course Hugo would have stood by her! Zara earned him a lot of money, from what she had told him. Even so, he hadn't forced her into an abortion as many of the other pimps would have done, so that was something to his credit.

Then there was Madison. Franky had soon discovered that no one here went by their real name, but if she had another one she hadn't told him what it was as yet. She had escaped from the clutches of an abusive bullying father and at just sixteen she was very street-wise with no regrets about leaving home. She was like two totally different people. By day she would bill and coo over Sunny and look remarkably young with her hair tied up into a ponytail and no make-up on at all. But when she emerged from her bedroom each night before going on the streets, she appeared much older and Franky was sure he could have scraped her slap off with a trowel. She would backcomb her hair until it almost stood on end, and with her short skirts and skimpy tops she looked exactly what she was — a street girl, or tom as they were known hereabouts. Franky liked her nonetheless.

Boy was the quiet one of the group and very close-lipped about his past, although Franky had passed him coming out of the bath-room one day without his shirt on and had been appalled to see the scars all across his back. No doubt he would have a sad tale to tell too when the time was right.

Gav was the joker of the bunch, always ready with a smile and his last penny should any of them need it. He had left home after confessing to his father, who was a vicar, that he was gay. His father had been unable to accept the fact and had pilloried him, so rather than cause him any embarrassment, Gav had run away from home, vowing never to return. Of all of them he was the most content with his lot and happy to do what he was doing.

It was a bright sunny day, and the door and all the windows to the small overcrowded flat were flung open to let in what little breeze there was. As Franky had soon found out, during the day the place was sweltering, but come evening it could turn as cold as a fridge within minutes. He was sitting rocking Sunny on his lap when a shadow suddenly fell across the open doorway and there he was, twice as large as Franky remembered him and twice as ugly. Hugo.

'Ah, I see the little 'un has got you under her spell and all then?' He crossed the room and chucked the baby under the chin as he grinned in a friendly fashion. Only a few days before, Hugo had read in the newspaper about the beating that Franky had given to Mr Cannon back at the home. The man had not been seriously injured as it happened, although Franky was clearly of the opinion that he had killed him. Hugo was not about to enlighten him otherwise. Far better for the boy to live in fear of having his collar felt. He would be more likely to comply with his wishes then.

Pickle had gone to the shop to buy some cigarettes with the money he had stolen from his latest pickpocket escapade that morning, and Franky wished he would hurry back. He felt ill at ease with Hugo on his own. Zara and Madison had gone off to the laundrette with the dirty washing and Boy was out rent collecting, which left Franky literally holding the baby. Not that he minded. She was a lovely little girl with coffee and cream skin and huge brown eyes that could have charmed the ducks off the water.

'Er . . . Pickle's just popped out to the shop but he should be back any minute,' Franky told him for want of something to say.

Hugo settled himself on the sofa that doubled as the boys' bed.

'There's no rush. I can wait.' Hugo began to examine his perfectly manicured nails as Franky gulped to hide his nerves. He was silently cursing himself; he should have known that it was too good to last. He had been sleeping in this man's flat and eating his food, and now he had turned up to claim his pound of flesh. Franky couldn't blame him. After all, he couldn't be expected to take in waifs and strays off the street without expecting something in return. It was *what* he might be expecting that troubled Franky. It was then that Pickle appeared in the doorway, and when he saw Hugo his face broke into a grin. He looked genuinely pleased to see him, and Franky knew then without a shadow of a doubt that he had a serious crush on the man.

Extending his hand he shook Hugo's warmly, hanging on to it for a fraction longer than was necessary.

'You've settled in then?' Hugo asked.

Pickle beamed at him. 'We certainly have. Thanks. It's good here.'

'I'm pleased to hear it. But now let's get down to business, eh? Do you feel ready to start work?'

Pickle nodded without hesitation. 'Whenever yer like, boss.'

'In that case I think you should both go out with Gav tonight. He can show you the ropes.' As his gaze flickered over Franky the boy felt his stomach sink. So this was it then. The moment he had dreaded.

'I call round at least once a week.' Hugo flicked an imaginary fleck of dust from his immaculately pressed trousers. 'I expect you each to hand over threequarters of what you earn and I'll continue to keep you housed and fed. What I *don't* want is you trying to pull the wool over my eyes. I know roughly what each of you can drag in each night, and if I find out that you've been trying to fiddle me . . . Well, let's just say I won't be quite so nice then.'

'Understood, boss.' Pickle's face was serious now. Hugo was not someone to upset, as others had found to their cost in the past.

'In that case, I may as well get off. I'm taking Jonno to a show in the West End this evening and I've got a bit of business to do before then.' Hugo was all smiles again now as he stood and headed towards the door. 'Gav will tell you what rates to charge, et cetera,' he informed them, and Franky and Pickle nodded solemnly as he slipped through the door and took the steps leading down to the street two at a time, with an agility that would have done credit to a man half his size.

'This is it then.' Pickle looked quite pleased with the fact that they had now got to start earning their keep. His smile slipped as he saw the expression on Franky's face. His mate looked as if he'd just been handed a date with the Grim Reaper. 'What's up?' he asked. 'You won't be doin' anythin' you ain't fuckin' done before.'

The silence from Franky told him otherwise and now his jaw dropped. 'Fuck's sake! You're a *virgin*, ain't yer?'

Deeply ashamed of the fact, Franky nodded miserably. Up until now he had avoided any sexual encounter like the plague. But even worse was the fact that he had never had any sexual urges towards either sex, which he knew was strange for a boy of his age. It was as if something inside had shut down, closing him off from having feelings for anyone. The abuse he had suffered as a child had acted like a barrier, and now he was afraid that no one would ever be able to break it down. Perhaps he was destined to be alone for always? To never know what it was like to truly love someone or have someone love him in return.

The thought made him shudder as Pickle sank down beside him. 'Ain't yer never had a girlfriend or a boyfriend?' he queried incredulously.

Hot colour flamed in Franky's cheeks and Pickle scratched his head, bemused. He had known from a very early age which sex he was attracted to, but Franky was totally naïve, which would make what they were about to do all the harder for him.

'Well, all yer can do is follow what me an' Gav do, then grit yer teeth an' bear it,' he told him matter-of-factly. 'Hugo won't let yer stay here fer nothin'.'

'I know.' Franky wiped the sweat from his forehead and after laying Sunny, who was now fast asleep, in her crib, he crept away to the bathroom like a wounded cat.

★   ★   ★

After the heat of the day the night had turned chilly and as the three boys got off the 73 bus and strode towards Soho, Gav kept up a running commentary.

'You'll catch most of yer punters as they're chucking 'em out of the clubs,' he told them. 'Usually, they'll be pissed out of their heads an' be happy with a quickie in a back alley. But remember, it's always money up front – an' don't ever get goin' off with anyone yer don't like the look of. Go with yer gut instinct. Some of the bastards can cut up rough when they've done the deed an' refuse to pay yer. Oh, an' insist they wear a condom if yer can. HIV is rife round here an' definitely somethin' to avoid.'

'How much do we charge?' Pickle asked.

'As much as yer think they can afford,' Gav advised. 'You'll soon get the hang of sussin' 'em out. If they're dressed posh yer stick the price up, but whatever they look like yer don't do it fer less than thirty quid. A straightforward suck-off no less than twenty. Got it?'

Both boys nodded and they proceeded on their way. Soon they were in the dingy back streets, the lap-dancing clubs and the strip joints they passed shedding their flashing gaudy lights on to the litter-strewn pavements. Some other young men and women had already beaten them to it and eyed the trio as they passed, gauging how much competition they would be. Gav spoke to some of them and they acknowledged him with a nod of their heads and a wary glance at his companions.

'Right then, you Franky, go an' stand outside the door o' that club over there, an' you, Pickle, go to that one farther down. When the punters come out just smile an' be friendly, an' if they're interested they'll proposition yer. Watch out fer the Old Bill though. Every now an' then they stick their noses in, an' if you make a wrong move towards 'em they'll have yer in the back o' the fuckin' Black Marias quicker than yer can say Jack Robinson. Hugo will have to come an' bail yer out then, an' let me tell yer, he will *not* be amused so be on yer guard.'

Content that he had told them as much as they needed to know, he now ambled off and positioned himself with half a dozen other young hopefuls outside a club doorway and promptly forgot all about them.

Franky and Pickle took up their positions and as Franky lit a joint with shaking fingers he drew on it deeply to calm his nerves. The bouncers on the doors eyed them warily, content to let them go about their business unless they encroached too near to their territory.

The time seemed to pass interminably slowly but eventually the club clients began to pour out of the open double doors. Two or three men eyed up the girls that were posing sassily for them and promptly led them away, while others walked amongst the boys, looking them up and down as if they were cattle.

An elderly man with a bald head and glasses paused in front of Franky and flashed him a smile. He only came up to Franky's shoulder and the boy's stomach churned with revulsion as his eyes dropped to the man's little pot belly, but he managed to keep his false smile firmly in place.

'You're new here, aren't you, son?' The man was extremely well-spoken and sounded friendly.

'Yeah, I am.'

'Mm. Done this before, have you?'

Franky thought quickly before nodding. 'Yeah, an' I ain't cheap, but I can guarantee yer won't be disappointed.'

'In that case you'd better follow me.' The man licked his fat lips with anticipation as he took Franky firmly by the elbow and began to lead him along the pavement. Franky's eyes moved this way and that for a sign of Pickle or Gav but they were nowhere to be seen, which probably meant they had gone off with punters too.

Eventually they turned a corner and the man gestured towards a block of public toilets up ahead.

'In there will do. How much do you charge?' he asked, trying hard to keep the excitement from his voice. Franky might have told him he was streetwise but the man could spot a virgin from a mile off and knew he was in for a good time.

'Er . . .' Franky looked at the man's expensive suit and his pure silk tie, trying to remember what Gav had told him before muttering, 'Sixty quid . . . up front.'

The man raised an eyebrow. 'You're not cheap, are you? Let's just hope you turn out to be worth it, eh?'

He delved into his pocket and pressed three crisp twenty-pound notes into Franky's hand before pushing him into the toilet block. Once inside, Franky tried to swallow the feeling of panic that was overwhelming him. What was he doing here anyway, with some twisted little pervert who was about to make his worst nightmare come true? But it was too late to think about it now; he had taken the man's money, it was burning a hole in his pocket, so he allowed him to shove him into one of the cubicles and lock the door behind them. The stale smell of urine made him gag and at such close proximity the smell of the man's aftershave was making it even worse. He could see the man's eyes glittering with lust behind the thick-lensed glasses, and now he became like a different creature as his fat arms snaked about Franky's waist and he pulled the boy to him.

'How about a little kiss then?' His breath was coming in quick gasps as Franky swiftly turned his head. The man had been eating garlic and his breath stank.

'I . . . I don't do kissin',' he whimpered.

A soft chuckle came to him from the gloom as the man's hands continued to roam over him. They were on his flies now and he could feel his zip being undone.

'A bit shy, are we?' he panted. 'Well, never mind.' He was sliding Franky's jeans down now and Franky felt acute humiliation as the man then fumbled with his own trousers before guiding Franky's hand to his flaccid member. 'Come on,' he urged. 'Play with it a bit, eh?' He sighed with pleasure as Franky obliged. The way he saw it, there was no going back now. He stifled a shudder as he felt the despicable punter's member start to swell. His breath was coming faster and faster, and then suddenly he swung Franky round with surprising strength and told him, 'Lean over the bowl. That's it. Ah, my God but you're *so* beautiful.'

Franky found himself staring down into a filthy toilet and suddenly the tears he had tried to hold back slid down his cheeks and dripped into the stinking water below. The man was feverishly stroking the cheeks of his backside and then suddenly he became still and Franky cried out as he felt him thrust into him. The pain was unbearable, worse than any he had ever known, as the man pummelled away, oblivious to everything now but his own release. Franky was sure he was going to be ripped in two but thankfully the man was so excited that he came within minutes and withdrew to lean heavily against the cubicle walls that were covered in graffiti, with no thought for the expensive suit he was wearing.

Franky swiped at his wet face with one hand while trying to pull his jeans up with the other. The sounds of a couple doing exactly what they had just done came loudly from the adjoining cubicle and Franky knew in that moment that his humiliation was complete. He had hit rock bottom and from now on this would be his life. It was a daunting thought.

PART FOUR

Chapter Thirty-Two

December 1997

'How is she?' Lorna stepped past Joe into Beehive Cottage and dumped her bag on the ground. When Joe had phoned her the evening before to tell her that Gail was fading fast, wild horses could not have kept her away.

The poor soul had lived for eight happy and healthy years after the recurrence and treatment all that time ago. She always laid her recovery at Natasha's door, saying she just couldn't leave her, but the remission was over, the cancer was back, all-consuming, and this time there would be no reprieve. They all knew that the fight was almost over.

Joe looked a shadow of the man he had been, drawn and gaunt, but now he hugged Lorna and tried to put a brave face on before helping her off with her coat and telling her, 'Oh, you know – up and down. She's asleep for most of the time now.'

'Wouldn't she be better in a hospice?' Lorna asked softly.

He shook his head. 'Gail made Tasha and me promise that we wouldn't let her die there. She wanted to be at home with us, and that's the least I could do for her. Tasha has been absolutely marvellous. In fact, I don't know how she's coped, bless her. She's run herself ragged looking after her mum, and been much stronger than me.'

Lorna could see that Joe was on the verge of breaking down, but pulling himself together with an enormous effort, he fixed a faltering smile on his face before telling her, 'Come on through to the kitchen.

Tasha is doing some lunch and I'm sure you must be hungry after your journey. Then I'll take you up to see Gail.'

'I don't know about hungry but I could kill for a cup of tea,' Gail told him with a brightness that she was far from feeling as she followed him through the cosy lounge.

Tasha was checking the joint of pork in the oven when they entered the kitchen and Lorna was shocked to see how she had changed in the time since she had last seen her.

'Why, my love . . . you've grown up!' she laughed as she drew the girl into her arms and hugged her. Tasha returned her smile, revealing straight white teeth. She was now sixteen years old and stunningly pretty. She was still not overly tall and barely reached to Lorna's shoulders, but she was slim and dainty and there was an ethereal quality about her. Since leaving school earlier in the year she had devoted herself to caring for her mother and father, and now the bond between the two of them as she looked across at him was obviously stronger than ever.

'Come and sit down, Dad,' she told him softly as if she was the adult and he was the child. Her speech was still a little slow and halting, but it suited her. 'You look whacked. Why don't you go and lie down for a while and I'll entertain Lorna until Mum wakes up again.'

'I most *certainly* will not,' he argued. 'It's nice to have company. I'll catch a few hours later on when Lorna has gone. That's if you're going, of course,' he said, apologetically turning to Lorna. 'You know you're more than welcome to stay.'

'I'd love to, but I'm afraid I have to get back,' she answered quickly. 'I just wanted to come before . . .' She felt herself flush but Joe broke the uncomfortable moment by saying, 'Then I insist you at least share our lunch. The nurse will be in about two o'clock and then you and Gail can have some time together, but she does tend to drop off in the middle of a conversation, so be warned. She's on a very high dose of morphine now, so don't be offended if she does, will you?'

'As if!' Lorna was fighting the urge to cry. Joe and Tasha were being so brave when inside, their hearts must be breaking. She doubted if she could have been so brave, had she been in their position.

Tasha was setting the table now and in her manner seemed much older than her years, but then Lorna supposed she'd had to grow up quickly with her mother being so ill for so long.

'Come on,' the girl told them. 'Sit yourselves down. The meal is ready to serve now.'

Lorna watched her expertly carve the meat and soon they were seated with steaming vegetables and crisp roast potatoes in snow-white china dishes laid out along the middle of the table in front of them.

Lorna tried valiantly to do justice to the meal but the food seemed to lodge in her throat. Joe and Tasha fared little better and eventually the girl cleared the almost untouched dishes away.

'Right, I'll just go up and check on Her Ladyship then,' Joe said as he rose from the table.

Tasha was preparing a plate of lunch for her mother though she had little hope of her eating it. Gail hardly ate enough to keep a bird alive lately but Tasha still religiously cooked for her every single day.

Lorna rose too and asked, 'Would you mind if I came up with you?'

'Not at all. After all, that was the whole purpose of you coming, wasn't it?' Joe held his hand out to her and she squeezed it affectionately before following him from the room.

On the landing he paused with his hand on the door of the bedroom he shared with Gail, and the smile slipped from his face as he turned to tell her tentatively, 'Lorna, I think I ought to warn you . . . She might have changed since you last saw her.'

Lorna swallowed deeply. The urge was on her to break down and cry again at the unfairness of it all, but as he opened the door she steeled herself, determined to be as brave as he was.

The bedroom curtains were open, and Lorna saw the row of

beehives in the garden that had so enchanted her on her very first visit here all those years ago with Mary Ingles. Mary had passed away suddenly the year before, following a massive heart attack. And now, Lorna thought sadly, she was about to lose someone else who had become dear to her. It just went to show how life moved on.

She then forced herself to look towards the bed and the sight that she saw made the breath catch in her throat. Gail was gone, and in her place was a poor fragile wreck who seemed to be struggling to take each shuddering breath.

Her frail hands were laid on the top of the crisp white sheet that covered her, and her once luxuriant hair now stood up around her head in wispy grey clumps. Lorna approached the bed cautiously as Joe stood aside, and suddenly Gail's blue-lined eyelids blinked open and her poor face was transformed as it lit up in a radiant smile.

'L . . . orna, it's so good to see you.'

Lorna took the thin hand and now the tears she had tried so hard to hold back came in a great gushing torrent that threatened to choke her. Joe slipped quietly from the room, leaving the two friends to say their last goodbye as Gail gently stroked Lorna's hand.

'Please don't cry,' she urged softly. 'I've had a good innings and I've been *so* lucky. I've known more happiness in my lifetime than most women of double my age ever do, so I'm not complaining.'

'But it's . . . it's so unfair,' Lorna gulped.

Gail smiled sadly. 'I can't fight it any more. And I don't have to now. When I was first diagnosed I was terrified about how Joe and Tasha would cope, but she's sixteen now and they're so close. They have something very special between them – always have had, looking back. They'll get along fine without me, now that's she's older. They adore each other.'

Lorna sniffed into her handkerchief. Gail weakly patted the bed at the side of her. 'Come and talk to me,' she urged her friend. 'And in the years ahead I want you to remember . . . some things were meant to be. Tasha came to us for a reason – she will be a comfort to Joe when I'm gone.'

Lorna and Gail talked softly together until eventually the nurse arrived. The afternoon was drawing on by then and Lorna knew that she should be setting off for home and her own family, so she bent to kiss her friend goodbye, aware that it would be for the very last time.

'Thank you,' Gail whispered, 'for bringing Tasha to us.'

Blinded by tears, Lorna staggered from the room and once out on the landing she tried to compose herself before rejoining Tasha and Joe downstairs.

In the car on the way home she was consumed with sadness. What seemed like a lifetime ago now she had helped to place three children with three very different families. Franky, or Alex as he had been known then, had never really settled with anyone, and since he had done a runner from Woodside Children's Home where she had placed him over two years ago, she had seen neither hide nor hair of him, and very much doubted that she ever would now, despite all the police's attempts to find him. He would be eighteen years old. Poor lad, he had never got over the loss of his mother and twin sisters, but she hoped that wherever he was, he was all right.

And now Tasha was about to have her heart broken too. Poor lamb. Joe and Gail had worked tirelessly to make her into the lovely young woman she was today. No one would ever have believed she could turn out as she had all those years ago, so it just went to prove what the power of love could do.

And finally there was Lauren. With Penny and David Daventry's support she had turned into a very talented musician. In fact, her parents were hoping she would get a place at the Royal Academy of Music in London after her A-levels; it seemed clear that Lauren had a great career ahead of her.

The call from Joe came three days later to tell her that Gail had passed away peacefully in her sleep in her own bed, with himself and Tasha at her side, holding her hands just as she had wished.

Chapter Thirty-Three

It was Christmas Eve and the flat looked quite festive. Zara and Madison had bought a small tree that was now standing in the corner decked out with cheap baubles and fairy lights. Sunny, who was now a stocky two-year-old toddler, clapped her chubby hands with delight every time she saw it, and they all seemed to spend most of their time trying to keep her away from it.

Franky was the first up on this particular day and he sighed with exasperation as he looked towards Boy who had not gone to bed yet again. He was lying on the beanbag at the other side of the room. It was getting to be a regular occurrence. Boy seemed to be on a self-destruct mission and was using more drugs lately than he was selling, a fact that was irking Hugo greatly. He had also fallen behind with his rent collecting, and Franky was worried now that soon Hugo would give him a short sharp shock. He didn't suffer fools gladly and from what he could see of it, Boy was heading for trouble. Big trouble. They had all tried to warn him, but Boy seemed to be sinking into a deep depression that none of them could shake him out of, even Sunny, whom he adored.

'Come on, mate. Let's be havin' you,' Franky said, as he yawned and filled the kettle at the sink. Silence, but then Franky wasn't overly worried as yet. Some days, waking Boy was like trying to wake the dead, and he was sure he would have slept the clock round if they'd left him to it.

He mashed the tea and as he prepared two mugs he smiled as he saw the presents that were peeping out from behind the settee. There was one for each of his flatmates and at least half a dozen for Sunny. He could hardly wait to see her face when she opened them.

After pouring the tea he padded across to Boy with a steaming mug in his hand and gently nudged him with his foot. 'Come on now. You're due out early today with Hugo. Get this down you an' get yerself ready else the boss will have yer guts for garters if you ain't shipshape an' Bristol fashion when he gets here. *Boy* . . . do you hear me?'

He plonked the tea down on the scratched coffee-table and leaned down to shake Boy, then gasped with dismay when the lad fell life-lessly to one side. Panic gripped him as he looked towards the silver paper that was screwed up on the floor at Boy's feet. He'd been snorting lines of cocaine again, but how many had he had? Surely he couldn't have overdosed? Hugo had warned him how powerful the new batch they had had in was.

At that moment Zara emerged from her bedroom tying the belt on her faded dressing-gown, and when she saw Franky leaning over Boy she asked, 'What's wrong? You look like you've seen a ghost.'

'It's Boy.' Franky nodded down at him. 'I can't get him to wake up.'

She instantly bent down and shook Boy's arm fiercely before grasping his wrist and looking for a pulse. 'I can't feel anything,' she said, staring up at Franky fearfully. 'Should I call an ambulance?'

'No, don't do that,' he snapped as his mind went into overdrive. 'Phone Hugo an' tell him to get his arse over here as quick as he knows how.'

Pickle, who had been sound asleep until then, suddenly yawned and stretched, and as he saw Zara running for the phone he asked, 'What the fuck's goin' on here then?'

When Franky told him, he leaped out of bed, and when Hugo arrived half an hour later with Jonno close behind him, he found all three of them sitting by Boy with frightened eyes.

Quickly following Zara's example, he felt for a pulse, then rested his hand on Boy's heart before shaking his head.

'He's gone,' he said flatly, and a startled silence settled on the room, broken only by Zara's gentle sobs.

'Wh . . . what we gonna do now?' Franky eventually asked.

'We're going to get rid of him, of course. We can't fucking leave him here, can we?' Hugo barked, rattled.

'*Get rid* of him?'

Hugo glared at Franky, then started to pace up and down the confined space of the room as he tried to think. Suddenly it came to him and he paused to tell them, 'We'll have to keep him here till it's dark tonight, then when it's quiet we'll chuck him into the Thames.'

Franky was horrified. Even a dog deserved a better send-off than that, to his way of thinking.

'Don't look at me like that,' Hugo threatened. 'What other choice do we have? No one ever knew where he came from or who he really was, so he can't be traced back here. When they fish him out they'll just think he's one of many runaways that end up in the river.'

Franky bowed his head, but then it snapped up again when Hugo told him, 'This might mean a career change for you if you play your cards right.'

'What do you mean?'

'I mean this dickhead hasn't been doing his job right for some time now, and you have never made any secret of the fact that you aren't exactly enamoured of the way you've been earning your living. So what do you say? I need someone I can rely on to collect my debts, and I think you might be ready to take it on now.'

Franky felt his spirits soar. What Hugo had just said was an understatement, although he had learned long ago to switch off when he was with a punter. Had learned to resist the temptation to smash his fist into their ugly faces and pound them to a pulp as they abused his body. He was young and handsome and always in great demand, but he hated every second of what he was forced to do.

Seeing his reaction, Hugo visibly relaxed. 'Keep him here till tonight and I'll get some of my men to come and pick him up when it's dark,' he instructed them all.

Franky's mouth set in a grim line as Hugo turned and strode away, with Jonno following closely behind. His eyes then returned to Boy and he felt unfamiliar tears prick sharply at the back of his eyes. Poor sod. His life was over and he had never even really lived. He had never confided whatever demon was chasing him, but at least his suffering was over now. The soft sobs of the girls brought his thoughts back to the present and now he took charge.

'Help me get him wrapped in a sheet or something,' he said with authority. 'An' then we'll put him in the boys' room out o' the way until they come for him.'

'But it don't seem right, to just get rid of him that way,' Madison whimpered. 'He must have *someone* somewhere who cared about him. Shouldn't they be told about what's happened?'

'An' just how the bleedin' hell are we supposed to do that when we have no idea where they are?' Franky retorted hotly. He didn't like what was happening any more than she did, but what alternative was there? What Hugo had suggested actually made sense.

Zara hurried away to return minutes later with a white sheet folded across her arm. She held it out to Franky, 'You do it,' she told him nervously. She had witnessed a lot of things in her short life, but she had never handled a corpse before, particularly someone she had been close to.

Franky took the sheet without a word, trying hard to hide his own distress. The girls were upset enough as it was, so someone had to stay strong. But the thought of what was about to happen to Boy was sobering. He would be disposed of like a dead dog, and Franky knew now that the same fate would await any one of them, should something happen to them. They were nothing. Nonentities, as far as Hugo was concerned. Still, if what the man had said was true, at least some good would come of this for himself. There would be no more standing outside seedy clubs or toilets, waiting for punters. He was about to go up in the world; become.

one of Hugo's right-hand men. And that, he knew, was a big step up. Hugo was feared and respected in this world he lived in, and anyone connected with him immediately commanded the same respect. Wrapping the sheet about Boy, and with the girls each holding one of Boy's legs, Franky lifted him under the arms and they dragged him into the bedroom where they dumped him on to his bed.

As they re-entered the lounge, closing the bedroom door hastily behind them, Franky's eyes strayed to the Christmas tree. Strangely, he had been looking forward to this Christmas for the first time in many years. The people he shared the flat with had become like a family to him – the first since he had been snatched away from his real family so many years ago. He still thought of his mother and sisters, and had even considered going back to the Midlands to find them, but he had been just four years old when he left them, and had no idea where to begin. He was also afraid that the police might still be looking for him for the beating he had given Mr Cannon. He could remember that he had lived in Nuneaton, but beyond that his mind was a blank. He couldn't even remember where the flat he had lived in was. His twin sisters could be anywhere now, and he wouldn't have a snowball's chance in hell of recognising them even if he were to bump into them on the street. He supposed he should put the past behind him, but it had proved to be easier said than done. He had realised that his mother would be out of prison now, and his hopes of her coming to find him had finally died. But would she have returned to her roots or started a new life somewhere else? She certainly hadn't gone out of her way to find him, and that fact had cut deep.

He knew that what he saw as her betrayal of him had shaped his life. She had promised him that she would come and fetch him, but she never had, and now he had closed his heart against anyone. He would admit to being fond of his flatmates – after all, each of them had been let down in some way or another as he had, so he could relate to them – but the feelings he had for them did not go beyond fondness. Love was an alien word to Franky Anderson, and he sometimes wondered if he would recognise what love was if it were to come up and slap him in the face. These days, he was nothing more than a rent boy, used and abused by any man who had the cash to pay for sex with him. In the early days he would have to force himself not to vomit with revulsion after every encounter with a punter, but that feeling had passed to be replaced by a dull acceptance of his situation. He had already managed to amass some considerable savings even after giving Hugo 75 per cent of what he earned. After all, what did he have to spend money on? His accommodation and food were paid for, plus any drugs he might care to sample, and apart from the odd treat for Sunny he stashed his cash away. Now things might be about to change, but first he would have to watch Boy being carted away like so much rubbish.

He forced himself to put the kettle on again. The girls looked as though a good strong brew might help them and somehow they had to get through the day, knowing that Boy's body was lying only feet away in the very next room.

It was gone midnight when Franky heard footsteps on the stairs leading up to the flat. The girls had been sent to bed for an early night as they were allowed three days off for Christmas. Franky glanced at Pickle who was smoking a joint as if his very life depended upon it. It was the first of many he had lit that night and Franky knew he must be as high as a kite.

He moved to the door and admitted two of Hugo's men who gave no other greeting except to ask, 'Where is he?'

Franky cocked his head towards the bedroom door. Now that the time had come for Boy to be disposed of, it didn't feel right somehow, not that he could do a thing about it. Hugo was the boss, and what he said went.

Both men were heavily muscled. One of them was quite attract-ive and looked as if he had stepped out of the pages of a fashion magazine, but the other was badly scarred on his face and looked a mean character, as most of Hugo's men were. They had to be to do the job they did.

Franky prayed that the girls would stay inside their own room until this was over and Boy was gone. He knew that they weren't asleep. He had heard them whispering and crying. Thankfully their door remained firmly shut as the two men came back into the lounge dragging Boy's body between them.

'You can come with us,' one of them instructed him. 'You can act as look-out while we get shut of him.'

Pickle had visibly paled, terrified that he would be asked to go along too, but Franky merely nodded and followed them outside, watching as they dragged Boy's form down the litter-strewn steps as if it were no more than a carcass of meat.

The ugly one nodded towards the deserted street and hissed, 'Get yer arse out there an' tell us if the coast is clear.'

Franky slipped past them and after looking up and down, he nodded. They then slid past him and deposited the body in the boot of a shiny Jaguar. They got into the front while Franky clambered into the back seat with his heart in his mouth. If they were to be caught, this was going to take some explaining away, for sure.

His thoughts were so disturbed that it was almost a shock when the car drew to a halt on a bridge over a dark stretch of the river. It was relatively quiet here, although the sounds of traffic could still be heard in the distance.

'Right, you get out an' keep yer eyes an' ears peeled,' the handsome one of the pair ordered him.

Franky did as he was told, intermittently gazing down at the dark water that was flowing along far beneath him. It looked almost black and he shuddered. The men were hoisting Boy's body out of the boot and then they were at Franky's side, steadying themselves in readiness.

'Here we go then,' one of them grunted and suddenly Boy, who had come clear of the sheet that had served as his shroud, was hurtling down towards the water.

There was a loud plop and then he was floating away from them, his arms and legs flailing in the current as if he were waving for help. It hit Franky then. The poor bastard was gone as if he had never existed, and one day the very same thing could happen to him. Like Boy, he had no one to care. No one to come looking for him or to wonder where he might be. He was totally alone in the world. And never more so than at that very minute.

Chapter Thirty-Four

June 2001

Lorna shifted the toddler on her lap to a more comfortable position as she smiled down the phone. At the age of thirty-eight she was the mother of two children, Jade, now seven, and her little brother Joshua, and had decided some time ago to give up her job as a social worker – at least until the youngest got to school. She adored her children, and much as she had enjoyed her job she had no wish to miss a second of them growing up. She had seen too many parents have to do that in her profession.

'So when will you be coming?' she asked Joe, who was on the other end of the line.

'Hopefully we'll be there by the end of the month,' he told her with an edge of excitement in his voice. 'Dr Cawthorne has already taken me on as a partner in the practice and I've sold the cottage, so it's just a matter of upping sticks now. I'm hoping to sign for the house I've bought down there next week.'

'And how is Tasha feeling about the move?' Lorna asked.

'Absolutely fine,' he assured her. 'Between you and me, I think she's looking forward to it. Dr Cawthorne has already offered her a part-time job on the reception desk, and I think a brand new start is just what she needs.'

Lorna secretly agreed with him. It had been four years since Gail had passed away and she had the strangest feeling that neither of them would ever completely move on in the home they had all shared. There were too many memories there for them. Not that Tasha hadn't coped admirably with the death of her adoptive mother. She had, and had taken on the role of the woman of the house with no trouble at all. The fact that they would be moving to Nuneaton was a bonus. In fact, it had been Lorna herself who had suggested it when she heard that a local doctor was retiring. The remaining GP was looking for a new partner in the practice and when Joe had come to meet him and look at the surgery, the two men had got on like a house on fire.

Tasha was now twenty years old and stunningly pretty. She always put Lorna in mind of a china doll when she saw her, yet since the death of her mother she had displayed remarkable strength. But then as Lorna had discovered long ago, it was usually the ones who you expected to fold in a crisis that came up trumps. Initially, Lorna had been concerned about the fact that Tasha would be coming back to her roots, but then when she'd had time to think about it, she saw that it really couldn't be a problem. When Gail and Joe had adopted her, she had been just two years old and her name had been Natasha Slater. She was now a young woman and her surname was Salisbury. Who could ever make the connection? And even if they did, and Tasha and Lauren were to meet up again, would it be such a bad thing? They were still twin sisters by birth, after all.

As far as Lorna knew, Kay Slater had disappeared off the face of the earth after being released from prison. It was doubtful if anyone would ever know what had become of her. So why shouldn't Joe and Tasha come and settle here, and have a fresh start? In truth, she herself could hardly wait to have them nearer at hand.

'Well, I for one am looking forward to having you both here,' she told him with sincerity. 'In fact, as soon as you get the keys to the house, Jason and I will go in and start to get it ready for you.'

'Now *there's* an offer I won't refuse,' Joe chuckled. 'But anyway, I just thought I'd give you an update on how things are going. I shall have to go now else I'll be late for afternoon surgery – and I don't want to leave with a bad mark against my name, do I? Bye, love.'

'Bye, Joe.' Lorna placed the phone down and cuddled her infant son as she whispered in his ear, 'You aren't half going to be spoiled when Aunt Tasha and Uncle Joe get here, Joshy.' She then went about her daily business with a spring in her step.

Four weeks later, Joe locked the door of Beehive Cottage for the very last time. The delivery van with the furniture they wanted to take with them had gone before them and now all he had left to do was drop off the keys of the cottage to the local estate agent.

Seeing the sadness etched on his face, Tasha gave him a hug. 'Come on, Dad,' she whispered softly. 'It's time to move on now.'

He nodded, turning to her and returning her embrace. He didn't know what he would have done without his daughter in the time since he had lost his wife, though he did sometimes worry that she didn't act as other young women her age did. To the best of his knowledge she had never even had a boyfriend, though it hadn't been for the lack of asking from the local lads. With her looks and nature she could have had any one of them she wanted, but she had never shown any interest, preferring to stay at home with him. She had held him when he cried and pandered to his every whim, even more so than Gail had done when she had been alive. Of course, he was fully aware that things might change when they started their new life. But he hoped that they wouldn't because he selfishly couldn't imagine his life without her now.

She took his hand gently in her own and they both gazed at the little leaded windows sparkling in the sunlight for one last time before walking away hand-in-hand.

The journey to Nuneaton was uneventful and they made it in good time. Tasha had no memories of ever having lived there and so she gazed at the town curiously as they passed through it. It looked a nice enough place and she had a feeling that they would be happy there. Joe had bought a modest four-bedroomed house on the Poplar Tree Farm estate. The house had only been built round about twenty odd years or so ago, and seemed very modern compared to the cottage they had just left behind, but Tasha liked it immediately. It will be much easier to keep clean, she found herself thinking with a woman's logic.

On the front path they passed the removal men who were busy carrying their furniture inside.

'You can put that sideboard there, please,' Tasha told one of them, instantly taking control.

When she went to inspect the garden, the fellow winked at his mate and grinned. 'Tasty bit o' stuff, ain't she?'

Unknown to him, Tasha had heard every word he said, and she blushed as she followed Joe through the back door.

'So what do you think?' Joe asked when the men had finally gone and they had completed their tour of inspection.

'I think it's lovely, Dad.' Tasha smiled at him.

It was some hours later before they had unpacked everything they would immediately need for the night, and Joe collapsed on to the sofa, exhausted.

'Phew, I never realised we had so much stuff,' he groaned.

Tasha handed him a mug of tea and sank down beside him. 'You know, our furniture is very nice,' she said, 'but I think something a little more modern might be more suited to this place.'

Joe frowned. He supposed she was right. The dark wood dresser and sideboard had looked fine in the cottage, but they did seem a little heavy for this house. He suddenly found himself remembering the day he and Gail had bought them, shortly before their marriage, and his eyes grew misty. They had been at an antique auction, and she had been determined to have them from the moment she set eyes on them, to the point that Joe knew he had ended up paying probably far more than they were worth.

'I know you're right but I don't think I can bring myself to part with some of them just yet,' he admitted.

Leaning over, she kissed him gently on the cheek. 'That's fine, Dad,' she whispered, feeling his pain. 'In your own good time.

You'll know when the time is right, and then we'll go shopping for something more suitable.'

He nodded in agreement and they lapsed into a compatible silence as they sipped at their tea.

Joe started at his new surgery the following Monday, and from the second he set foot through the door he knew that he was going to like it there. Dr Cawthorne, his partner, was a charming person, as was Mrs Bell the receptionist, who would share the reception duties with Tasha.

Dr Cawthorne's previous partner, Dr Kashir, had retired the month before and the GP was grateful for someone to take half the workload off his shoulders again. There was also a nurse, Teresa Bend, who tended the patients who needed home visits, and she made Tasha and Joe feel instantly at home. The only other person who worked there was Mrs Dixon, the cleaner, who came in each morning and evening after surgery to ensure that the building was kept spic and span. She appeared to prefer to keep herself to herself, not that this worried Joe in the slightest. He was too busy studying the list of patients' files that had been allocated to him.

Teresa Bend was a remarkably pretty, outgoing person in her late thirties, recently divorced, and from the moment Dr Joe Salisbury stepped through the door, Dr Cawthorne was amused to see the twinkle in her eye. If he was any judge, a romance could develop there in time. From his point of view, it would be no bad thing. Joe was awfully young to be condemned to spend the rest of his life on his own. He could certainly do a lot worse than Teresa, who was loved unreservedly by all the patients. Nothing was ever too much trouble for her, and Dr Cawthorne thought she and Joe would be perfect together. Not that he had any intentions of sticking his oar in, of course. He was a great believer that what would be, would be – and was happy to stand back and let nature take its course.

*   *   *

Lorna had already visited Joe and Tasha in their new home and had been a great help in hanging curtains and helping Tasha about the house. They had also been to her home for supper, where Tasha had billed and cooed over Jade and Joshua. All in all, Lorna was delighted to have them there, especially as the only concern she'd had about them living in Nuneaton was now out of the way. She had briefly wondered what might happen if Tasha and Lauren were to find each other again. After all, Lauren had lived in Nuneaton all her life. But the chances of that happening were remote now as she had heard that Lauren had flown the nest and was now living away at university in London. Of course, there was always the possibility that the girls might bump into one another on one of Lauren's visits home, but, as Lorna had asked herself before, would that be so terrible? Not really. It might even be a very good thing. Like Dr Cawthorne, she decided to let this matter happen as fate and nature intended.

Joe was pleased with his consulting room. It wasn't overly large but contained everything he needed to do his job efficiently, and was remarkably clean and tidy due to Mrs Dixon's efforts. All in all, he was sure now that he and Tasha had done the right thing by making a fresh start away from Hockley Vale, and if there was a lump in his throat as he thought back to the little cottage where he had shared such love with Gail, the first patient Miss Bell sent in to him certainly didn't notice it.

Chapter Thirty-Five

'So collect that first and then get back to me, eh?' Hugo told Franky as he passed him a slip of paper. 'Will you need a couple of the lads to come with you?'

Shaking his head, Franky stuck the paper into his jacket pocket. The man he had been asked to visit had owed Hugo money for some time, and despite being threatened on numerous occasions, the debt was still outstanding. So now it was pay-back time – or else. Hugo lived on his reputation of not being a man to trifle with, and if he was seen to be making exceptions or going soft, he knew it could have grave consequences. The rest of the people who dealt with him might get to hear of it, and then he'd be in big trouble because they'd all no doubt try the same trick.

It was a situation Franky had been called on to deal with several times over the last couple of years – and he had done just that without a qualm.

He was now twenty-two years old and a stunningly attractive man who caused heads to turn wherever he went. Not that it bothered him. It was a well-known fact that Franky Steel's heart was as cold as ice. Franky had changed his surname shortly after moving into the flat in London. He hoped that a new one would make it more difficult for the police to find him, and also because Anderson was Jacob's name it held only poisoned memories for him. *No one* got through to Franky Steel, which was why Hugo set such store by him. If requested, he would go and break people's legs or do whatever had to be done without blinking and nobody messed with him. Word was out that it was better not to.

Franky now dressed in designer clothes, not that fashion held any more allure for him than it ever had, but because as Hugo's right-hand man it was expected of him. He was earning more money than he had ever dreamed of, although he still lived in the same overcrowded flat in Kings Cross. Somehow this option seemed better than living on his own, although he could have now afforded to live anywhere he liked within reason. His flatmates had changed over the years. He now shared a bedroom with Jonno. Hugo had soon grown tired of him, and now Jonno had been demoted to a rent boy, just as Franky had once been, destined to haunt the clubs and public toilets to earn a living.

Madison had had the good fortune to hook a wealthy punter the year before. He was old enough to be her father, but had offered to make an honest woman of her and give her the sort of lifestyle she had only ever dreamed of. She had snatched at the chance with both hands and was now living in a beautiful house in Campden Hill Road, in the Borough of Kensington and Chelsea, not far from Hugo's apartment. Sometimes she would cruise by Franky in her shiny new convertible BMW with her hair blowing in the wind and wave at him gaily, and the sight never failed to make him smile. Madison had had a hard life and he was pleased for her.

Pickle was doing a three-year stretch at Her Majesty's pleasure after being caught pickpocketing, and so now only Gav, Zara and Sunny remained of the original people he had first lived with.

Zara was probably the closest thing to a friend Franky had, and he would have done anything for her. He had guessed long ago that her feelings for him went beyond friendship, but something deep inside him always held back. Franky was afraid that he didn't have the capacity to truly love anyone, and felt that Zara needed someone who would love her back as she deserved to be loved. And so his life went on from one day to another, and as the years drifted by he feared that he was destined to a life of loneliness, and knew that it was his fault but was unable to do anything about it. It was as if there was something inside him that stopped him from caring. Some wall that he had built up that no one could penetrate – and which even he himself could not knock down. To care might bring yet more hurt, and Franky had had enough of that to last a whole lifetime.

He took the glass-fronted lift from Hugo's penthouse to the ground floor, and once outside he paused to raise his face to the sun that was shining brightly down on London. It was a beautiful day and he was tempted to take a stroll along the Serpentine, to feel the cool breeze that came off the water on his skin. But he thought better of it. Best go and get this job out of the way first, and then he had the rest of the day to do as he pleased.

Taking his car keys from his pocket he climbed into his new toy. It was the latest top-of-the-range Mercedes and he had fallen in love with its smooth sleek lines the second he set eyes on it on the forecourt. As he settled into the driver's seat the smell of leather assailed his nostrils and he sighed with pleasure. He looked down at his cream linen suit. It had cost an arm and a leg, and he hoped he wouldn't get blood on it.

Franky knew central London like the back of his hand now, and he easily found the address Hugo had given him. Parking outside, regardless of the double yellow lines, he took a baseball bat from the boot, then entered the restaurant where waiters in smart black jackets were laying gleaming cutlery on to crisp white tablecloths in readiness for the night ahead. They all stood up respectfully as he entered.

'Where's the boss?'

The Maître d' glanced nervously down at the baseball bat that Franky was gripping. 'He's in the office, Mr Steel . . . sir.'

Franky passed him without another word. The sooner he got this over with, the better. Will Weatherall, the restaurant-owner, had been selling drugs for Hugo for years, but lately he had been slow to forward the readies, and word had it that the restaurent was losing trade. Hugo was tired of waiting now. The man had had enough chances and it was time he had a wake-up call to remind him who he was dealing with.

When Franky barged into the office without knocking, Will's eyes dropped to the bat he was carrying and he flinched.

'All right then, Franky lad?' He forced himself to sound cheerful as he rose from the desk, but sweat stood out in beads on his forehead. 'Got time for a swift one, have you?' He was standing next to a cabinet, fumbling inside for the whisky and the glasses he kept in there, as Franky tapped the bat menacingly in the palm of his hand.

'I ain't come for a drink, Will.' His voice was cold. 'Hugo sent me. It's time to pay up or else.'

Will turned and held his hands out beseechingly as panic swamped him. 'Tell him I'll have it for him by the end of the week, eh?' he begged.

Franky shook his head. 'Sorry, Will. No can do this time, I'm afraid.'

Will began to babble. 'I'll tell you what then, give me an hour. That ain't too much to ask, is it?'

As Franky silently began to advance on him he swung about and headed for a picture that hung on one wall. Grasping the frame, he swung it aside revealing a wall safe as he told Franky over his shoulder, 'If I give you this now, I'm going to lose the restaurant. Trade has been falling off and—'

'Cut the cackle, Will. It won't wash this time. Just fuckin' cough up, eh?'

Franky eyed Will Weatherall with contempt. He was a small man with a big mouth and a leaning towards the finer things in life. Everyone who was acquainted with him knew that he had a serious gambling problem, which was partly what had led to him owing so much money to Hugo.

He was only fifty-eight years old but fast living and too much wine and food had aged him so he looked at least a decade older. He was like a little barrel and Franky was sure that if he were to knock him over, he would roll all around London. His face was heavily lined and the greying moustache perched on his upper lip reminded Franky of a slug. Word had it that he had been married five times and Franky wondered how any woman could ever have found him remotely attractive, let alone marry him. But then, Will wasn't scared to flash his cash when he had it, so Franky supposed that was the attraction. The women definitely hadn't married him for his charm or good looks, that was for sure.

As Will looked into the younger man's hard eyes he seemed to deflate like a balloon. Slowly, he reached into his trouser pocket and withdrew a small key, with which he unlocked the safe, sighing heavily. Under Franky's watchful eye he then proceeded to count out a huge pile of notes.

'Check that,' he said resignedly. 'I think you'll find it's all there.'

Franky took up the wad and after licking his finger he quickly counted it before rolling it into a bundle and stuffing it into his jacket pocket. He then lifted the bat and advanced on Will.

'Here, what are you doing?' Will backed away with his hands held up to protect his face as the first blow rained down on him.

'Just givin' you somethin' to remind you not to be late wi' Hugo's payment next time.'

Franky was aware of waiters walking by the glass door that led into the office but not one of them intervened. They simply hurried by with their heads bent. They knew better than to interfere with Franky Steel.

Five minutes later, Franky stopped his hammering and paused to allow his breathing to steady before crossing to a mirror and smoothing his hair in the glass. Will was barely conscious and was whimpering as he lay curled into a bloodied foetal position on the floor.

Franky then turned and left the room, the door swinging open behind him. The staff would give him time to get away before calling for an ambulance, he was sure.

★   ★   ★

That evening, after delivering the money to Hugo, Franky went for a stroll in Regents Park. He liked to watch the families there. The fathers racing around after their youngsters while the mothers fed the ducks with the smaller children at the pretty pond near the Rose Garden. And yet it also made him sad, the realisation that he might never experience any of these things. He didn't even know if he was capable of sex, or what gender he was attracted to, and was beginning to wonder if he was some sort of freak. He had allowed men to use his body for money, but at twenty-two years old he had never had a girlfriend or even kissed one, if it came to that, and surely that couldn't be natural.

Sinking on to a bench, he let his mind drift back over time to when he had stayed briefly with Twig and Fleur and their children in the field in Devon. He still looked upon that brief interlude as the happiest time of his life, and hoped that wherever they were, they were happy. He was so lost in thought that he stretched his legs out without thinking and a young woman who happened to be walking by fell headlong across them to land in an undignified heap on the path.

'Oh, Christ. I'm so sorry!' Franky leaped up and helped the girl to her feet.

She brushed down her long flowered skirt and bent to retrieve the violin case she had been carrying, opening it to check that the instrument was intact. 'It's all right. There's no harm done,' she told him, as she grinned up into his dark eyes. And it was then that the strangest thing happened, for a million butterflies suddenly seemed to flutter to life in his stomach as he stared into her laughing grey eyes. On closer inspection, he realised that she wasn't the most beautiful girl he had ever seen. She was well-built – 'curvy' was the word that sprang to mind – and her thick dark hair had just escaped being classed as wild, but there was a vivacity about her that seemed to light up the whole area around her.

'I . . . I really don't know what to say. I'm not usually that clumsy,' Franky muttered as he felt colour pour into his cheeks.

'I've told you, it really doesn't matter,' she assured him. 'I've got enough fat on my bones to pad me from a fall. More's the pity, I might add. I can't think why I'm not all sylph-like but then we can't all be perfect.'

'Oh, but you *are*.' Franky clamped his mouth shut, more confused by the minute. Whatever had made him say that? 'W-what I meant was—'

'Now *don't* go and spoil it. No one has ever told me I'm perfect before,' she giggled.

He was aware that she was teasing him and surprised that the fact didn't offend him. 'Look, let me carry that for you,' he offered. 'You must be shook up, after that fall.' Without waiting for her answer he snatched her violin case from her.

'Do you . . . er . . . live round here?' he asked for want of something to say, suddenly feeling as if the cat had got his tongue.

She pointed towards Marylebone Road. 'I'm studying at the Royal Academy of Music actually and staying in a students' house near there.'

He was impressed; she must be gifted as well as beautiful. They wandered on until eventually they came to the edge of the park where she stopped, and holding her hand out, she told him, 'I can carry that from here, thanks.'

Franky was thinking of a way to delay her leaving, but coming up with no ideas he reluctantly handed the case over, saying, 'Well, there you go – and once again, I'm so sorry.'

'Don't be. I told you, it would take more than a little trip like that to hurt me. Goodbye.'

She took the case and he watched helplessly as she crossed the busy road, cursing himself silently. Why hadn't he asked her what her name was, or if he could see her again? He watched until she had disappeared into the crowd then turned and hailed a taxi. Suddenly he just wanted to get back to the sanctuary of the flat, such as it was, and try to put his thoughts into some sort of order.

★   ★   ★

For no reason that he could explain, Franky walked up to Regents Park every night for the rest of that week, but although he sat on the same bench each evening he didn't get so much as a glimpse of the girl he had met there and who had made such an impact on him.

He had almost given up hope of ever seeing her again when, one evening as he approached the bench, he saw someone sitting there with their head buried in a book. It was the girl.

'Hi there,' she greeted him when he came to stand in front of her. It was as if it was the most natural thing in the world to see him there, and she spoke as if they had known each other for years.

She hotched along the bench and after placing her book down, she patted the seat at the side of her.

He hesitantly sat down, painfully aware of her closeness.

'Had a good week, have you?' she asked, and again when he looked at her that strange butterfly feeling in the pit of his stomach was back, but even worse this time.

'So-so, how about you?'

'Great, actually. I got to play a solo with a well-known orchestra yesterday, and it was wonderful. What do you do for a living?'

If anyone else had asked him that question he would have taken offence at their nosiness, but because it came from her he answered, 'Oh, you know – a bit of this and a bit of that.'

Whatever it was he did, she had the idea he must be well-off from the clothes he was wearing. They certainly hadn't come from a charity shop, that was for sure. And those eyes of his . . . She was sure she could have drowned in them and hadn't stopped thinking about him since their last meeting.

They began to chat – everything from music to politics – as the world passed them by, and he started to relax. She was so easy to talk to, it would have been hard not to. The early evening began to give way to night, and when she suddenly shuddered he took his jacket off and draped it around her shoulders.

'I'm sorry,' he told her sincerely. 'I've so enjoyed talking to you that I lost track of time. You must be cold. Would you like to come for something to eat to warm you up a bit? My treat, of course.' He could hardly believe that he had asked her, and held his breath as he waited for her reply, hoping that she wouldn't presume he was too forward.

She hesitated for just a fraction of a second, and then flashing him the smile that could turn his legs to jelly she told him, 'I'd love to. But nowhere too expensive, mind. We students have to watch our pennies and I insist on paying my way.'

'You'll do no such thing,' Franky told her indignantly. '*I* issued the invitation and *I* want to pay.'

'Very well then,' she said coyly. 'But next time it's *my* turn.'

Next time, next time, next time . . . the words reverberated in Franky's head. She wanted to see him again. He had no idea why the fact caused him so much pleasure, he only knew that it did and for now that was enough.

He took her to a swanky restaurant in the West End and the meal probably cost more than most families would spend on shopping for a whole week, but Franky didn't care. He was enjoying himself, a fact that came as a shock as he had thought he had forgotten how to. They drank two whole bottles of wine between them, and by the time they left the restaurant they were both in fine high spirits.

'Would you like to go to a club or something?' he asked hopefully but she shook her head.

'There's nothing I'd like more,' she told him, 'but I have an early music lesson tomorrow so I'd better get back.'

'Then may I get you a taxi?'

'Actually, it would be quite nice if we were to walk,' she told him, suddenly looking shy, and he felt as if his heart was going to burst with joy.

They fell into step along Baker Street, heading for Marylebone and her student hostel, and when she gently slipped her hand into his, it felt as if it belonged there . . . and in that moment Franky knew that he had finally discovered what it was to be in love. He knew very little about her, apart from the fact that she came from the Midlands and her name was Lou, but that was enough. He loved her and he wanted to shout it from the rooftops, though he was far too embarrassed to tell her that, of course.

She in turn could feel fire shooting up her arm from his touch, and as she peeped at him she knew that she would never love anyone as much as she loved this young man beside her. She had found her soulmate – and intended to cling on to him for dear life.

Chapter Thirty-Six

'Franky, did you hear me or what? I swear to God, your head's up in the clouds half the time nowadays,' Zara said in exasperation.

'What? Oh, sorry. I was thinking.' When he looked at her from his big dark eyes, Zara's stomach flipped. She loved him so much, but of course she would never compromise him by telling him how she felt. She knew that he could have had any girl he wanted with his smouldering dark looks, and the fact that he had never even dated one to the best of her knowledge was a constant worry to her. What if he was gay? He would never look at her then. But then she doubted it. She had seen how miserable he had used to be during the time when he had first come to live in the flat and had been a rent boy. It would be nice to know what had suddenly put the smile on his face though. He'd been really chirpy for the last few weeks now.

'What were you saying?'

Franky's voice made her jump. 'I was saying, I wondered if you'd look after Sunny for me this evening. Everyone else is going to be out and I don't want to leave her on her own, but I should go out to work or else Hugo . . . Well, I don't need to tell you what he's like if we don't bring our whack in.'

Franky thought quickly. He had arranged to see Lou tonight, and the thought of standing her up was unthinkable. Jonno had been missing for the last three days now, off on a jaunt with some new sugar daddy he had met. Gav had already gone to work and so what was he supposed to do? It suddenly came to him. Lou would be out of her classes by now, and as soon as Zara left he would ring and ask her to come to the flat. He was sure she wouldn't mind, and Sunny would be in bed by then so they'd get to have some private time together. He was like a cat on hot bricks as Zara bathed Sunny and got herself ready for work, and when she finally left the flat after tucking her child into bed he sighed with relief and hastily rang Lou's mobile. She answered on the second ring and he hastily explained what had happened. She was aware of his flatmates and touched that he was kind enough to offer to babysit for one of them.

'The flat isn't up to much, mind,' he warned her, looking round at the drab surroundings and wondering what she would think of it. Perhaps it was time to get his own place, after all? But then, how would Zara manage with Sunny? She had come to rely on him and he was fond enough of them both not to want to let her down.

'I won't be coming to see the flat, I'll be coming to see you,' she assured him, and after giving her the address he put his phone away and had a mad clean-up.

By the time she arrived the place was relatively tidy. He had even managed to prepare them a meal of sorts from food he had found in the fridge, and as he let her in, his heart swelled as it always did at the sight of her.

She was huddled in a warm coat to keep out the late September chill, and when she planted a gentle kiss on his lips, her own felt cold.

'Come over and sit by the gas fire.' He took her coat and steered her towards a chair.

She chuckled. 'I've never seen you being all domestic before. I think it suits you.'

He flushed as he hung her coat up and hurried away to the small kitchen to check on her dinner.

It wasn't much, just a readymade cottage pie and some frozen.

peas, but they enjoyed it and were soon snuggled up together on the settee.

'Mm, this is nice,' she sighed as she rested her head on his shoulder contentedly. During the last few weeks they had rarely been alone, always dining in public places or going off to see some show or another. Franky had never gone beyond kissing and cuddling her, which was one of the things she loved about him. He wasn't intent on just getting her into bed as most of the boys she had been out with were. The day before, he had taken her on the London Eye. It had been launched the year before and they had both been mesmerised by the panoramic view from the top of it. They had been on a cruise on a riverboat on the River Thames and visited both Tate art galleries and Madame Tussaud's. They had fed the pigeons in Trafalgar Square and watched the changing of the guard at Buckingham Palace but now at last they were alone and it felt right.

It was Lou who planted the first tender kiss on his lips and he returned the kiss ardently as his hands tentatively began to travel across her body. And then suddenly he jerked away from her and she looked at him, appalled.

'What is it? Have I upset you?' she whispered fearfully.

Franky bowed his head in shame. 'No, no, of course you haven't. It's just that . . .' he gulped deep in his throat. 'It's just that I haven't . . . you know.'

'You're still a virgin?' There was an edge of incredulity in her voice. How could this wonderful good-looking man still be a virgin? He must have had women *throwing* themselves at his feet. She herself had only had two very brief fumbling relationships with young men from the college during her time in London, but at least she had some knowledge of sex.

And then as she looked at his bowed head it suddenly didn't matter. Franky had told her very little about himself, and sometimes when she had talked about her own happy childhood she had seen a look of deep pain flit across his face. She guessed that he must have had a very unhappy childhood, but she would be the one to take the pain away, she was determined of it, and now she gently took his hand and guided it to her blouse to rest on her breast.

It was like an electric shock and he stared at her as he felt her nipple grow hard beneath his touch. He could feel himself hardening and it was like a miracle taking place, for he had believed that he would never encounter feelings the like of which were coursing through him now.

'Which is your bedroom?' she asked, and when he cocked his head over his shoulder she took his hand and led him towards it. Once inside she slowly peeled off her clothes and he gazed at her in awe. She was truly beautiful, with full hips and long legs. Her waist was small and her breasts heavy, and as he watched her in fascination he saw her erect nipples swell.

She then proceeded to undress him and when his trousers slid to the floor she fondled his stiffened member, almost driving him wild with desire. He pushed her on to the bed and sucked at her nipples greedily, making her moan and arch her back with pleasure. Then his hands played across her stomach to her most private place and he felt the wetness of her.

She pulled him on top of her and when she opened her legs and he entered her they made love frenziedly. It was over within minutes and they lay at peace, content to be wrapped in each other's arms. Within no time at all, Franky felt himself hardening again as he stroked her satin-soft skin, and this time their lovemaking was slow and tender.

Franky felt like a king. He knew now without a doubt that he had found the woman he wanted to spend the rest of his life with. They would get married and have children, children who would never know the heartache and abandonment that he had been subjected to. He would buy them a house and get a real job, and they would live happily ever after just as they did in storybooks.

'I *love* you,' he whispered into the gloom, and they were words he had been sure he would never hear himself say.

'I love you too,' she whispered back, and his happiness was complete. At last he had someone of his very own to love.

When Zara came in later that night she dropped her bag wearily on to the settee and frowned. There was a woman's coat tossed over the back of it but it certainly wasn't hers.

'Franky,' she called softly, not wishing to disturb Sunny. There was no reply so she crossed to his bedroom door and tapped on it.

'Franky, are you there?' she whispered. Again no reply so she cautiously inched the door open and peeped inside. The sight that met her eyes made her hastily close it again, and then she staggered across to the settee and dropped down on to it as she bit on her knuckles to stop herself from crying. He had been lying on the bed fast asleep with a young woman cuddled up to him, and they had looked so right together that her heart was broken as all her dreams came crashing down around her. She had always believed that one day Franky would return her feelings for him, but now she knew that it had only been a pipe dream. She also realised why he had been acting so happy just lately. He had finally met someone he could care for – and that someone wasn't her.

Suddenly she saw her life stretching before her. A life spent standing on street corners letting anyone with money use her body just so that she could live and support her child. In her dreams Franky had taken her away from all that, but she knew now that it was never going to happen, and lowering her head she sobbed as her heart broke afresh.

As December approached, Lou began to grow excited about the prospect of going home for the holidays. She waved a letter at Franky one afternoon when he met her out of the Academy and told him, 'Mum and Dad want you to come home for Christmas with me so that they can meet you. Oh, please say that you'll come! They're so longing to meet you. And you'll love them – I know you will.'

Franky frowned. He felt as if he was caught between the devil and the deep blue sea. One part of him couldn't bear the thought of being without Lou for two whole weeks. The other part of him wondered what her parents would think of him. What would they say if they ever got to learn of his past, or knew how he earned a living? *But then why should they?* a little voice whispered in his head. *They can only ever know what you choose to tell them, and if it means losing Lou you know that you would lie through your teeth if need be.*

'Let me have a think about it,' he told her. 'I'd hate to think that I was imposing.'

She playfully slapped at his arm. 'You idiot, how can you be imposing? You're their future son-in-law, so they're bound to want to meet you.' She suddenly looked stricken as she whispered, 'You *are* going to marry me, aren't you?'

'O' course I am, when the time is right.' Franky pulled her into his arms and kissed her soundly. 'I'm just worried what they'll think o' me, that's all. I ain't been brought up all posh like you have.'

'Huh! That won't bother Mum and Dad,' Lou assured him. 'They'll judge you on the person you are, and not where you came from or what you sound like. Anyway, *I* think everything about you is just perfect.'

As he gazed into her eyes he could hardly believe his luck. To think that a girl like her would ever look at a bloke like him. It was unbelievable, and yet it was true, and he knew that he was the luckiest chap alive.

'Oh, all right then, you've twisted me arm,' he told her, and she hooted with joy. 'But come on now, I've managed to get two tickets for that show you wanted to see an' they've cost me an arm an' a leg an' if we don't get a shufty on we'll miss the beginnin'.'

She linked her arm through his, aware that every woman they passed was staring at her enviously as they hurried on their way. It was going to be a wonderful Christmas, she was sure of it now.

When Franky arrived home later that evening he found Zara curled up on the settee and was shocked to see that she was crying.

'Why — what's up, love?' he asked, instantly concerned.

'Oh, it's nothing,' she assured him as she wiped her cheeks on the sleeve of her dressing-gown. 'It was just a sad film on telly made me cry, that's all.'

He stared at the blank screen in confusion as she rushed on, 'It . . . er . . . just finished. I just turned it off.'

'Oh right. Well, do yer fancy a cuppa? I'm just goin' to make one before I hit the sack.'

'No, thanks. I reckon I'll get off to bed now. Good night, Franky.'

He watched her race towards her bedroom and scratched his head in bewilderment. Until recently, Zara had always waited up for him and they'd shared a last cup of tea before bed. But lately she seemed to be avoiding him and couldn't look him in the eye. She was looking peaky and all. Franky shrugged as he filled the kettle at the sink. Women could be strange creatures at times, there was no doubt about it.

That weekend, as a special surprise, Franky collected Lou from the Academy, and after he had put her weekend bag in the boot they set off down the Westway and on towards the countryside.

'Where are we going?' she asked.

'You'll see.'

Realising that he wasn't going to tell, Lou grinned and settled back in her seat. It didn't really matter where he took her; she was content just to be with him.

When they drove into North Devon some hours later, Lou beamed.

'I know it's not exactly the right time of year for a trip to the seaside but I thought it would make a change from the hustle and bustle of London,' Franky told her. For no reason that he could explain, he had felt the urge to bring her back to the place where he had shared the happy interlude in his life with Twig and Fleur — not that he would ever tell her about them. They belonged to his past, and the least said about that the better, as far as he was concerned.

They booked into a small hotel overlooking the harbour and after wrapping up warmly they then took the coastal path to Baggy Point. It was just as he remembered it. So much so that he could almost see Jacob standing on the edge of the cliff before he had pushed him. He shuddered and Lou placed her arm about him.

'Are you cold?' she asked with concern.

'No, not really. It was just someone walking over my grave,' he told her.

She took his hand, and as they turned about and headed back to the hotel, Franky knew that he would never go to that place again. It was as they were nearing the hotel, arm in arm, that a middle-aged man with a young boy at his side, who was walking towards them, paused. He was smartly dressed in a suit and he stared at Franky intently. No, it can't be, he told himself, but then the child tugged on his hand. 'Come on, Dad. I'm cold,' he complained. The man smiled down at him then shrugged and moved on.

The next day Franky took her to the field where he had lived with Twig and Fleur, Destiny and Echo. That too looked just as he remembered it, but now he could smile when he thought of them. He had a life to look forward to with Lou now. He had laid his demons to rest, and when they finally set off for home on Sunday evening, his heart was full of hopes for the future.

Chapter Thirty-Seven

'Ready, steady, go!' As Tasha took her hands from Joe's eyes she watched his reaction to the new furniture and was not disappointed.

'Why, you were absolutely right!' he gasped. 'This does look so much better than the dark stuff in here. It's like a completely different room.'

She had been pleasantly surprised the week before when, out of the blue, her father had informed her that he had someone from an antique shop coming to look at the furniture they had brought with them from Beehive Cottage. She had been even more pleased when he then gave her permission to go out and order all new. It had been delivered that afternoon, and even though she said so herself, the new look was a big success.

'I'm glad you like it,' she told him, as she rubbed her hand across the surface of the honey pine dining-table. 'And now you can sit yourself down 'cos dinner's ready and we have to christen the new table, don't we?'

As she bustled away to the kitchen, he chuckled. Tasha had held him together since Gail's death and he couldn't envisage life without her, although he was painfully aware that one day he would have to. She was a beautiful young woman, and no doubt some day soon some handsome young stud would whip her away from right under his nose and she would fly the nest.

His face creased into a frown as he thought of Teresa, the nurse at the surgery. She was a lovely woman and had gone out of her way to make him feel welcome. The problem was, she had now asked him to supper at her home four times and he had refused her invitation each time. He wondered how long it would be before she took offence at his rejections, and whether it would change their working relationship. Joe had been a happily married man for many years and the death of his wife had hit him hard, but lately he'd found that he could think of Gail and smile, and he knew that he was moving on. Teresa had given him very clear signals that she was available – in a very subtle way, of course. The trouble was, he found that he couldn't look at her in that way, despite the fact that she was a very attractive woman. He wondered why, for he was still a relatively young man and had urges as any other. Teresa would be a good catch for anyone, so why, he wondered, did he not take her up on her offer?

His thoughts were saved from going any further when Tasha breezed back into the room holding a large tureen that was emitting delicious odours.

'I've done you your favourite – beef casserole – and it should be nice and tender because I've left it in the oven on a really low heat all afternoon,' she told him.

As he helped himself she poured them both a large glass of wine and Joe had to resist the urge to tell her that she shouldn't be drinking. He still thought of her as his little girl, and yet when he looked at her these days, he saw a very pretty young woman. Now he came to think of it, Tasha seemed to have come out of her shell since moving to Nuneaton. She had even been to the pictures a couple of times with a young woman who had befriended her in the street where they lived, and she was suddenly taking an interest in make-up and perfume. He sighed. Tasha was growing up and there was nothing he could do about it.

They finished the bottle of wine between them and after the meal Joe tackled a pile of paperwork while Tasha cleared away before settling down to watch the television. At nine-thirty she told him, 'I'm going up now. Night Dad.'

'Good night, love.'

After she had gone to bed he found it hard to concentrate, so eventually he put his paperwork away and headed for the bathroom where he took a long hot bath. The wine had relaxed him and after a soak he felt as good as new again. Wrapping a towel around his waist, he made for his bedroom and once inside he let it slip to the floor before heading towards the bed.

As he lay there, his thoughts turned once more to Teresa. It felt wrong to be thinking of another woman – but would Gail have wanted him to spend the rest of his life alone? He had a strong suspicion that she would have thoroughly approved of Teresa, could she have met her.

Turning over restlessly, he buried himself in the pillow and tried to lose himself in sleep.

Joe left for the surgery extra early the next morning in order to tackle the paperwork he had failed to do the night before. The cleaner was still there, busily swinging a mop around the waiting room.

'Morning, Mrs Dixon,' he greeted her. It was the first time he had taken much notice of her, but now he saw that she was nowhere near as old as he had first thought. It was just the way she dressed and wore her hair, and the tired look on her face that made her appear older. He doubted that she was much more than forty years old, and wondered what it was about her that made him feel sorry for her. Apparently she lived alone, but no one seemed to know why or whether she had any family. Mrs Dixon never talked about her private life. She rarely talked at all, if it came to that, but then Joe supposed it was her prerogative. Sitting down at the reception desk, he turned his attention to the files in front of him, and it was a shock when Mrs Dixon suddenly asked him, 'How old is your daughter?'

'My daughter? Er . . . Natasha is twenty. Why do you ask?'

'Oh, just curious, that's all.'

She went back to what she was doing without another word and after a moment, Joe did the same, but he found it hard to concentrate. He was deeply troubled. Natasha had originated from Nuneaton. What if someone here were to recognise her? He scolded himself mentally. The chances of that happening were remote. Natasha had left Nuneaton as a very tiny girl and returned as a young woman with a new name and a new identity. In the years in between he had come to look upon her as his own flesh and blood, and he knew deep down that he was probably just being over-protective. He had considered all these possibilities before coming here and decided that it was worth the risk in order for them both to start a new life. At the end of the day, there was nothing he could do now. What would be, would be.

It was late that evening when he finally got home and he was tired. Tasha had a meal ready for him and she smiled at him as she took it from the oven where it was keeping warm and carried it to the table. Normally Joe was starving when he came home from work, but tonight she saw that her father was nervy and on edge.

'Is something wrong?' she asked.

'No, nothing at all. I'm just a bit tired, that's all,' he assured her.

'Well, come and eat this then while it's hot,' she urged, and then avoiding his eye she said, 'My friend Becky – you know, the one I've been to the pictures with a couple of times – well, she has a brother called Ben and he's asked me if I'd like to go out with him one evening. Would you mind very much if I went? He's very nice.'

'N . . . no, of course I wouldn't,' Joe almost choked. 'It's only right that you should be making friends at your age and getting out and about a bit.'

Tasha grinned. 'I was thinking perhaps on the night I go out you could take Teresa up on her dinner invite,' she suggested coyly.

Joe felt his cheeks flame. 'I'm not so sure about that,' he muttered, feeling decidedly uncomfortable.

Solemn now, Tasha gently pressed his hand. 'You know, Dad, Teresa is a lovely person and Mum's been gone a long time now. I think perhaps we should both start to move on.'

Joe bowed his head and chose not to reply.

Lorna called in to see them later that week and the instant she set foot in the house she sensed an atmosphere. Tasha looked pale and Joe was very quiet, which was unusual. Gail had always used to tease him that he could talk the hind legs off a donkey.

'Is everything all right here?' she asked, as Tasha hurried away to put the kettle on.

'Everything's fine,' Joe told her, but she was not convinced and wondered if the two of them had had a row. She dismissed that idea almost immediately. In all the years she had known them, they had never had a cross word.

'I've left my poor hubby babysitting,' she told him, hoping to lighten things. 'I don't mind telling you, those kids of mine are a pair of holy terrors, especially Joshua, the youngest. I wouldn't be without them though. It's just nice being able to escape for a while. But that's enough about me, how are you settling in here and at work? Dr Cawthorne thinks you're the best thing since sliced bread, from what I can make of it, and I believe you have your own little fan club going too, headed by Nurse Teresa.' There was a mischievous twinkle in her eye, but it brought no response from Joe.

Leaning towards him, she said quietly, 'You can't grieve for ever you know, Joe. Gail was one of the nicest people I've ever met and we'll never forget her, but you still have your life before you. You're too young to condemn yourself to a life of chastity and Gail wouldn't have wanted that for you. You and Tasha were the most important people in her life and she wanted you both to be happy.'

To her horror he suddenly put his head into his hands and began to sob. She hadn't meant to upset him but she obviously had. Instantly contrite, she placed her arm around his shoulders. 'I'm *so* sorry, Joe,' she whispered, 'I didn't mean to be unfeeling. Do you want to talk about it?'

He glanced towards the kitchen door to make sure that they couldn't be overheard, and she had the feeling that he was about to confide something to her . . . but then he suddenly clamped his mouth shut and shook his head.

'No thanks, Lorna, I'm fine really. I'm just being silly and feeling sorry for myself, that's all.'

Lorna struggled to keep the conversation going for the rest of her visit but it was hard going and she was relieved when she could make an exit. 'I shall have to be going to see what the holy terrors are up to,' she told them. 'But how about you both come for supper on Saturday evening?'

'I'll . . . er . . . let you know if we can make it,' Joe told her, and she knew then that something was wrong. He had never refused an invite before and Tasha had barely said more than two words during the whole of the time she'd been there.

As she drove home she felt sad. Joe and Tasha were such lovely people. She hoped that there wasn't any trouble between them. But then how could there be? Tasha never went anywhere as far as she knew, only to her part-time job at the surgery, and she and Joe had always been inseparable.

It was none of her business at the end of the day, but Lorna hoped that they would soon sort out whatever it was. She didn't like to see them both looking so miserable.

Chapter Thirty-Eight

'Zara, are you sure you're all right? You've been very quiet just lately.'

As Zara looked up into Franky's face her heart twisted in pain. She had never seen him so happy, but she wished it could have been her that had made him look like that. She had met Lou on several occasions now and wished that she could hate her. The trouble was, Lou was so nice. There was nothing about her to hate.

'I'm fine,' she answered, watching Sunny, who was playing on the floor with some brightly-coloured building bricks that Franky had bought her the week before. 'When are you planning on going to Lou's for Christmas?' It was now only two weeks away and she was dreading him going. The flat would seem so empty without him.

'We'll be leaving on Saturday,' he informed her as he shrugged his broad shoulders into a smart black overcoat. 'I've got a few jobs to sort out for Hugo and then we'll be off, though I don't mind admittin' I ain't lookin' forward to it.'

'Why not?'

He shrugged. 'I'm worried they won't think I'm good enough for her,' he mumbled.

Zara snorted with disgust. 'Huh! How could they think that? You're good enough for *anybody*. In fact, Lou is lucky to have you, you're . . .' Her words trailed away and his heart ached for her.

Poor Zara. She was a lovely girl and he had grown very fond of her over the time they had shared the flat together. The only reason she had been reduced to doing what she did for a living was to escape her past, just as he had tried to. But he knew now, even after meeting Lou, which was the best thing that had ever happened to him, that you could never truly get away from it. The pain was still there, deep down like an abscess that was waiting to be lanced. It was funny, but he had never really looked at Zara as a woman until he had met Lou, but now he had a sneaky feeling that if Lou hadn't come on the scene when she had, they might have got together as a couple eventually. And he knew that he could have done a lot worse than Zara. She was big-hearted and warm, as well as being extremely attractive – not that she could ever hold a candle to Lou, of course. He hoped that some day she would find a man who would treat her with the respect she deserved. A man who would be able to look past the life she had been forced to lead to the person she really was. But that wasn't his concern now. He had an appointment. A very special appointment, and if he didn't get a move on he would be late for it.

He squeezed Zara's arm gently before hurrying towards the door, then racing down the steps he hailed a taxi and sped towards Bond Street.

Within fifteen minutes he was standing at the counter of a very high-class jewellery shop and the owner handed him a small leather box, saying, 'It's been altered to the correct size, Mr Steel. I do hope you will be happy with it.'

Franky snapped the lid open, and as three perfectly matched diamonds on a slim gold band twinkled in the light, he beamed. 'It's perfect,' he told the man. 'Now, let me pay you.' He left the shop minutes later with his wallet considerably lighter but with a broad smile on his face. He intended to ask Lou to marry him on Christmas Day and could hardly wait to see the look on her face when he presented her with the ring. They had been strolling along Bond Street the week before when they had spotted it in the jeweller's shop window, and she had sighed dreamily. 'Isn't that just the *most* beautiful ring you've ever seen?' she had said.

'Then let's go in and get it,' Franky had said.

Lou had stared at him in horror. 'Are you *joking*?' she'd gasped. 'Have you seen the price of it? Why, I'd be afraid to wear it. If, and I say *if*, you do ever buy me a ring, I promise to choose one much cheaper than that.'

'We'll see,' he'd told her with a grin, but the very next day he had slipped back to the shop and ordered it, and now it was nestling in his coat pocket and he could hardly wait to give it to her. He had even known what size she was, as she had given him one of her rings to wear on his little finger. Humming merrily, he hurried on to see what Hugo had lined up for him. He knew that his time working for the man was coming to a close now, although he hadn't told Hugo yet, of course. He had enough money in the bank to make a brand new start somewhere with Lou when she was ready, and that was exactly what he intended to do. Move right away from London, get a proper job and make sure that his children, when they came along, would never feel unloved or abandoned as he had.

For the first time in his life, his future was looking bright.

On Saturday afternoon, Franky drew the car to a halt outside the student house of the Royal Academy and Lou came tripping towards him with a broad smile on her face and her arms loaded with gaily wrapped Christmas presents. She was looking radiant in a faux fur cream coat and knee-high boots, and Franky's heart swelled with love at the sight of her.

'Good grief!' he exclaimed as he clambered out of the car to open the boot. 'You look as if you've got enough presents there to go round the whole of Nuneaton.'

'This is only half of them,' she told him. 'Come on, help me get the rest out of the foyer, and my case has got to come too.'

By the time they had finished loading everything into the boot it was wedged full. Franky had felt a little uneasy when he originally learned that she came from Nuneaton. It was, after all, his hometown – although he hadn't told Lou that. As far as he was concerned, the less she knew about his past the better. All she really knew about him was that he had spent most of his life in care.

As they drove along the motorway her excitement at the prospect of seeing her parents grew. 'Sadly, you won't get to meet my brother and sister,' she told him. 'They've both moved away from home now. Heather married a chap in the Army and lives in Germany, and Aiden is backpacking around Australia between jobs. Still, at least you'll get to meet Mum and Dad and I know they're going to love you just as much as I do. You'll probably have a few encounters with the resident ghosts as well, but don't worry, they're all friendly. They've lived at Feathermill longer than we have.'

Franky was very sceptical when it came to the subject of ghosts, but he wisely hadn't voiced his thoughts on the subject. As they cruised along the M1 Lou kept up a cheerful stream of chatter and Franky felt his mood lift. She was so easy to be with that he felt as if he had known her for ever and couldn't envisage his life without her now.

By the time they turned on to the M6, Lou was in a high state of excitement. 'We shouldn't be long now,' she told him chirpily.

As they approached the A444 that would take them into her hometown she told him, 'Turn there and then I'll direct you the quickest way.'

They drove into Nuneaton and Franky glanced about curiously. It had been so long since he had been there and there had been so many alterations to the place that nowhere looked familiar. After driving through the town she directed him straight up Tuttle Hill and then they took a right turn; she pointed ahead, barely able to conceal her excitement. 'That's Feathermill Lane there on your right – look, just ahead. Turn down there.'

He did as he was told and soon they were driving along the lane that led to the house, and as it came into sight his eyes almost popped out of his head. It was enormous, surrounded by elegant gardens that were landscaped to perfection.

'Blimey, I didn't realise it were goin' to be *this* posh,' he gulped, feeling like a fish out of water.

'Now don't be like that,' Lou chided him. 'Just be yourself and they'll love you.'

He pulled up at the back entrance in the large gravelled court-yard and Lou immediately spilled out of the car as the back door opened and two people stepped outside with broad smiles on their faces. Lou flew towards them and a lot of giggling and hugging went on as Franky shrank behind the steering-wheel, wondering if this had been such a good idea, after all.

As if she'd just remembered him, Lou left her parents and gestured frantically to Franky. He climbed out of the car and as he walked towards them, Penny smiled in welcome. He was certainly a hand-some chap, there was no doubt about that, she thought. He shook David's hand and was then caught in a bear hug by Penny, who told him, 'Now come on in. I want you to feel at home here, Franky. We're so pleased to meet you after all Lou has been telling us about you.'

He followed them into the spacious kitchen and soon they were all sitting round the table as Lou told them of all that she had been doing. 'I'll be playing with international artists soon,' she sighed. 'Can you even begin to imagine how wonderful that will be? All the music students are given a chance to do it.'

Penny and David smiled at her indulgently. She had a brilliant career ahead of her and she was obviously enjoying her life, which was all they had ever wanted for her. And she was certainly taken with this young man. That was more than plain from the way she looked at him. Perhaps things between the two of them were a little more serious than they had thought, judging by the way Lou's face lit up every time she so much as looked at him.

Penny decided she didn't have any objections. This Franky did seem a little quiet, but then she was ready to forgive him for that. She and David were strangers to him and she had no doubt that once he got to know them, he would open up a little. No one could be quiet around Lou for long. She had such a bubbly personality that everyone loved her. Penny gazed at the two young lovebirds.

They reminded her of herself and David when they had met, all those years ago. She could only pray that they would be as happy as she and David had been. One thing was for sure – it looked as if they were in for a very good Christmas.

When Penny showed Franky up to his room some time later, Lou grinned at him on the landing. They had been sleeping together every chance they got for months, but for the sake of propriety she would abide by her parents' rules and while they were at Feathermill they would sleep apart, not that she could promise she wouldn't be sneaking along the corridor to him.

His room took his breath away, and as he gazed from the window to the lake beyond, he knew that he would have to work very hard indeed to keep Lou in the lifestyle she had been brought up in. He liked her parents immensely. They had made him feel at home, and he wondered if he was finally going to have the sort of Christmas he had always dreamed of. It was certainly looking that way.

During the first week in Nuneaton, in between her music practice, Lou took Franky on sightseeing trips of the area – and never once did he mention that this was his hometown. He could have been anywhere. Not a single place looked familiar, not that he had expected it to. It had been a long, long time since he had been there, but even so he found himself studying the faces of women he passed who looked even vaguely like his mother. Had she returned here after being released from prison? he wondered. He had no idea how to go about finding out. He had long since given up hope of being reunited with her, but it would have been nice to know what had become of her. Not that she figured highly in the great scheme of things any more. He had Lou now, and she was all he needed.

Chapter Thirty-Nine

Lorna was curled up on the settee one evening the week before Christmas reading a book when the doorbell rang. She frowned. It was gone nine o'clock and she hadn't been expecting anyone. Jason had gone out to the golf club to have a pre-Christmas drink with his friends and the children were fast asleep in bed so she'd been hoping for a quiet evening. Even so she heaved herself out of her seat and, tightening the belt on her dressing-gown, she hurried to answer it. She was mildly surprised to find Joe standing on the doorstep, but flashed him a smile and ushered him past her into the cosy lounge.

As she saw him looking at the toys that were strewn about the place she felt vaguely embarrassed. Tasha always kept their home as neat as a new pin and she wished now that she'd taken the trouble to tidy up instead of having a nice long soak in the bath.

'Do excuse the place,' she said, as she bent to pick up a teddy bear that her youngest had flung on to the easy chair. 'I'm afraid I've been rather idle today. It's been so hectic this week what with shopping for presents and food for Christmas that I thought I'd go on strike just for tonight.'

'It looks fine . . . sort of homely,' Joe assured her as he sank on to the chair she had just cleared, then glancing about, he asked nervously, 'Are we alone?'

She nodded. 'We certainly are. Hubby's gone off for a drink with his mates and the kids are fast asleep in bed, thank God. They're so excited I swear they'll burst before Christmas Day. But what's wrong? You look troubled, and if I'm to be honest, I haven't thought you've been yourself for some weeks. Aren't you happy here, Joe?'

She watched the different expressions flitting across his face, and moving to the sideboard now she took out a bottle of whisky. 'I was going to offer you a cup of tea, but sod it. It is nearly Christmas, isn't it? Let's have a drop of the hard stuff, eh?'

She shot off to the kitchen and came back with two glasses, then after pouring them both a small one, mindful of the fact that Joe was driving, she sat down in the chair opposite him. 'Right then.' She was smiling at him encouragingly. 'What say you spill the beans? There's obviously something troubling you.'

He took a hasty gulp from his glass, choking as the amber liquid burned its way down into his stomach. Lorna had been the only one he could think of that he could really talk to, but now that he was here it was proving to be more difficult than he'd anticipated.

She waited patiently, giving him time to compose himself, and eventually he told her falteringly, 'I'm afraid I have a problem concerning Tasha.'

'*Tasha?*' Lorna was amazed. The girl was an angel, and as far as she knew, had never caused him a moment's worry in her entire life. 'What's she done?' she asked.

He gulped at his drink again, before saying cautiously, 'It's not what she's *done* exactly.'

'Then what is it?' Lorna was intrigued now and determined to drag the truth out of him even if she had to chain him up and keep him there all night.

'The thing is . . . she's started to see a young man who lives in the same street as us and she seems very taken with him. I don't quite know what to do about it.'

'Is that all?' Lorna chuckled as she let out a sigh of relief. 'But surely you knew that she would start dating one day, Joe? She's a beautiful young woman, and I'm only surprised she hasn't met someone before now. I think she would have, if she hadn't been so intent on looking after you and her mum.'

'B . . . but what will I do if she leaves me?' he asked, looking totally bereft.

'You'll wave her off with your blessing,' Lorna replied wisely. 'Sometimes the only way to keep a person is to let them go. And you know there's no reason for you to be alone. I'm sure there are loads of women out there who would love to spend time with you, given half a chance. One in particular springs to mind straight away.'

Joe blushed. 'Do you mean Teresa?'

'Yes, I do actually. She's a lovely person, Joe.'

He shrugged. 'I know she is, but . . . well, I suppose I just feel that I'd be betraying Gail if I got into another relationship.'

'So just sit back and let things progress in their own time,' Lorna suggested, and Joe nodded, feeling slightly better.

'I suppose you're right,' he replied. 'I've always been like a mother hen where Tasha was concerned. But I ought to be getting back now. She'll think I've abandoned her.'

'You do that,' she smiled as he drained his glass. 'And try and keep your chin up.'

He let himself out, and as she watched him go, Lorna marvelled at the complexities of life. Joe was obviously terrified of losing Tasha, but children grew up and that was a fact of life – something that no one could change. It was going to happen to her and Jason one day, when their two left home.

The following morning when Tasha got to work, she was surprised to find Mrs Dixon still there. She had usually gone by the time Tasha arrived, but she smiled at the woman as she hung up her coat and took her position behind the reception desk. Her first job would be to look in the appointment book and then get the patients' files out so that they would be ready to go in with them to the doctor's. She was busily doing just that when she became aware of Mrs Dixon looking at her closely across the desk.

'I wanted yer to have this fer Christmas.' Before Tasha could protest, the woman self-consciously slid a small package across the counter to her. Tasha was so embarrassed that for a moment she didn't know what to say.

'W-why, th-thank you,' she eventually managed to say. Her stammer always came back worse than ever when she was upset or nervous about anything, and lately it had been as bad as ever.

The woman was watching her face so closely that she felt herself flush, and then suddenly Mrs Dixon reached across the counter and patted Tasha's hand. 'You turned into a beautiful girl, love . . . I'm glad,' she told her. With that she turned and walked away, leaving the girl to stare after her open-mouthed.

'H-have a good day,' Tasha called after her, and when the woman turned at the door to smile at her, Tasha was shocked to see that there were tears running down her face.

She stared down in confusion at the small package in her hand. Why would the woman have bought her a gift? Admittedly, Tasha had always gone out of her way to speak to her, but as far as Tasha knew, Mrs Dixon hadn't bought any other members of staff a gift.

Just then the phone rang and, hastily pushing the parcel under the desk, Tasha quickly returned to her duties.

An hour later, Franky drew his car to a halt outside the butcher's on Abbey Green. Penny had asked him to call in and fetch some meat she had ordered, and he'd gladly obliged as Lou was shut away in the music room, religiously doing her practising.

Over the road, a woman stopped in her tracks, her hand covering her mouth. It was her son; she would have recognised Alex anywhere, even after all these years. He had the same coal-black wavy hair, the same striking deep brown eyes. Her little boy had grown into a man, but facially he had not changed all that much at all. But what was he doing back in Nuneaton? She had been led to believe that he had been adopted by a couple living at the coast. Well, it didn't matter now. All that mattered was that she was seeing him and he had grown into a son that any mother would be proud of. She watched him disappear into the butcher's and then as her heart steadied, she crossed the road and stood not far away from the door.

She longed to approach him, but how could she? How could he ever forgive her for letting him down? And she had no doubt at all that he would resent her for not fulfilling her promise to fetch him home. She was sure that he wouldn't recognise her after all these years. Time had not been kind to her, but she wasn't complaining. She had got what she had deserved. Prison had been nothing compared to the loss of her children, and she would continue to pay the penalty for being a bad mother for the rest of her life. But if she could only get near enough to really look at him closely, just once more . . .

The woman positioned herself so that she could see him through the shop window. The female assistants behind the counter had open admiration shining in their eyes and she felt her heart swell with pride. This was *her* son, the one she had thought she would never see again. All too soon he was served and she saw him striding towards the door again as she stepped back around the corner of the shop. She wouldn't speak to him; it wouldn't be fair. He had a new life to live that didn't include her, and she had no intention of causing him yet more heartache.

He was halfway across the pavement when he suddenly paused as if he could somehow sense her presence, and then he turned slowly and looked directly into her face . . . and her heart did a somersault as she saw the confusion in his eyes. He found himself staring at what appeared at first glance to be a middle-aged woman. Her shoulders were stooped and her hair was prematurely grey, but there was something about her . . . *something* . . . And then as he suddenly realised who she was, the parcel of meat slid from his hands to land with a loud plop on the cold pavement as he stared at her incredulously.

'*Mum?* Is it you?'

She was crying so hard that she could barely see him now.

Years and years of hopeless pent-up tears were finally flowing out of her and she felt as if she was choking. They took a tentative step towards each other and she saw that he was crying too now, and then he had covered the distance between them in two long strides.

They stared at one another for long moments, then Franky suggested, 'There's a café over there. Shall we go and get a cup of tea or something?'

She nodded numbly, afraid that she would wake up at any moment and find this had all been a dream.

Now that the initial shock of seeing her was over, a million emotions were coursing through him, bubbling away inside him, and right at that moment he wasn't sure how he felt.

'Shh,' she soothed, as she saw his lips quivering when mother and son were finally seated in the small steamy café with cups of tea in front of them. 'It's all right, Alex.'

'I'm not Alex any more. My name is Franky now,' he told her flatly, and she recoiled in shock.

He seemed to gather himself before going on, 'Why did you tell me that you would come for me? You promised you would, and *every single night* I looked out of my bedroom window for you. I waited and waited . . . for years, I waited, but you never came.'

She bowed her head in shame.

'And why didn't you look for us when you got out of prison?' he demanded, and there was a note of anger in his voice now.

'It wouldn't have been fair,' she told him quietly, as shame washed over her. 'Look at me, Franky. I'm just a wreck. Mary Ingles told me that all three of you had been adopted and that you were all doing well. I wouldn't have stood a chance if I'd tried to get you back. The courts would never have returned you to a mother who'd done a prison sentence for murder. And besides, it wouldn't have been fair to you. You were all settled by then and I didn't want to hurt you any more than I already had. But it didn't stop me thinking of you every single day, when I opened my eyes and last thing at night before I went to sleep.'

Franky gazed at her resentfully. Oh, what he could have told her. 'Settled', she had said. *Huh!* He could have informed her differently, but suddenly he realised that there wouldn't be any point. They had all suffered through one lie told so many years ago, and nothing could turn the clock back now. For her to know what he had really gone through could only bring her more pain, and from where he was standing it looked like she had suffered enough.

'I . . . I know where one of your sisters is,' she told him tentatively, and his eyes snapped wide as he stared back at her.

'Natasha is working in the doctor's surgery in Manor Court Road. She was adopted by a couple who lived in Hockley Vale, a small place in Yorkshire, but her adoptive mum died some time ago and she came here with her father, who is one of the doctors at the surgery. She's a lovely girl.'

'Does she know who you are?' he asked, and Kay shook her head.

'No, I didn't think it would be right to remind her of her past. She was so young when she went away, I doubt she would even remember her former life now.'

'And what about Lauren?'

'I have no idea where she is,' Kay said sadly. 'I can only hope she's well and happy.'

Franky took a deep, shuddering breath. In just one day he had found his mother and now knew where to find one of his sisters. It was almost too much to take in.

But first and foremost in his mind was the question he was longing to ask. Their family had been torn apart by one enormous lie; a lie he had been forced to keep to himself, with truly devastating consequences.

'Why did you lie to the police about what was happening to us all?' he asked. 'Why didn't you tell them the truth − *that it was Kevin injuring us and not you?*' Even saying the words out loud gave him so much distress that he felt he might faint.

Kay bowed her head and said in a voice he could barely hear, 'I intended to do just that, I truly did. On the day they took you away,

I went back to the flat, planning to tell Kevin that I couldn't bear it. That he would have to leave because I was going to tell the authorities the truth and get you all back. He had made me make you promise never to tell it was him that was injuring you all, and I knew a little boy shouldn't be forced to keep bad secrets like that. But when I saw him, something inside me just snapped.' She paused to mop her eyes. 'I suddenly saw him for what he really was and I . . . I stabbed him. And I knew then that I had really burned my bridges. I had lost any chance of ever getting any of you back because I would be going to prison for murder – and I did.'

Franky gazed at her unspeaking.

'I'm sorry, son. Everything went wrong and I know I can never put it right, but you look wonderful. Where are you living?' she asked shakily.

'I live in London but I'm courting a girl from Nuneaton and I'm here to spend Christmas with her family.'

'Then I'm pleased for you. You look as if you've done well for yourself.'

As he saw the pride in her eyes as she stared fondly over at him, Franky cringed. *Done well for himself.* What would she think if he told her what he *really* was? That he had murdered his adoptive father and worked as a rent boy in London. That he had once blinded a boy without a second's thought. That he now worked for a well-known thug who paid him to maim and hurt people who owed him money. It wasn't much to be proud of, and as he stood there he suddenly felt ashamed and wished that he'd tried harder.

'I work at the doctor's surgery as a cleaner,' his mother now explained. 'My probation officer got me the job there when I first came out of prison. She helped me to find a little flat on Abbey Green as well. But I use the name Dixon now. If I'd come out as Kay Slater the people hereabouts would have run me out of town, thinking it was me that had abused you all.'

'And you have no idea at all where Lauren is or what became of her?'

She shook her head. 'No. Mary would never tell me where any of you were. She wasn't allowed to. I found you and Natasha purely by chance. I can only pray that one day I'll find Lauren again too now.'

'Oh, Mum.' His voice was loaded with despair. All this heartache and so many lives ruined – just to protect one worthless individual. Kay raised her hand and tentatively stroked his cheek, relishing the feel and the sight of her big, handsome son.

'So what do we do now?' he asked, terrified at the feelings that were coursing through him. He knew that he should be feeling pleased at being reunited with her, but all he felt was anger, resentment and a profound bitterness towards her. Her foolish infatuation, putting that psychotic bastard Kevin Darley's well-being before their own had destroyed their little family and condemned him to years of unhappiness.

'We don't do anything.' Her eyes were sad. She knew without a shadow of a doubt that there would be no grand reunion now. This was as good as it was going to get. She could see it in the fury simmering in his eyes. But at least she had seen him, and that was something she could cling on to, in the lonely years ahead. 'I want you to go back to the life you've made for yourself and put the past behind you now. It's enough for me to know that you're all right. And Alex . . . don't be sad. Be happy and make a good life for yourself. Goodbye, son.'

She stood up and walked from the café, and something inside told him that he should be chasing after her, but he was rooted to the spot. He watched until she turned a corner and disappeared from sight, then slowly he too left the café and made his way back to the car, retrieving the parcel of meat he had dropped on the way. Once inside, he lowered his head over the steering-wheel and there he did something that he rarely did. He cried for all the lost dreams. But still, he told himself, he could put the past to rest now and move on, particularly as he now knew where one of his long-lost sisters worked. As soon as Christmas was over he would go and introduce himself before beginning his new life with Lou. It would be wonderful to see Natasha, if only once more.

The thought cheered him, and after drying his eyes and blowing his nose, he started the car and headed slowly back towards Feathermill Lodge and his new family.

Chapter Forty

In the surgery, Joe was just tidying his desk before setting off for home to begin the Christmas holidays when he heard the main front door open. The rest of the staff had left over half an hour ago, keen to get home to their families to begin Christmas, and he had promised to lock up and make sure that everywhere was secure before leaving. He heard someone walk across the waiting room, and then there was a tap at the door. It was Lorna.

'Hello, Joe.' Without waiting for an invitation she took a seat and looked him in the eyes. 'I've been thinking about the other night and wondered how you were feeling?'

'Better,' he admitted with a rueful grin. 'In fact, I've finally accepted Teresa's dinner invitation and I'm going to have a meal with her tomorrow.'

She beamed with delight. 'Well, good for you. Somehow you two look right together. Does Tasha know about it?'

'She does actually, and she's all in favour of it. It just so happens that she has a date with her young man too. She seems quite smitten with this Ben, and now that I've met him I have to admit that he seems like a thoroughly good lad.'

'Then that's wonderful. What's more, I think Gail would approve. She loved you and Tasha with all her heart and would want you both to be happy. So there; I've told you what I think. The rest is up to you now.'

She stood up and now he too rose, and holding his hand out, he grasped hers across the desk. 'We will still remain friends, won't we?' he asked.

'Always,' she assured him, and then said slowly, 'During my career as a social worker, Joe, I've seen many things. Things that could break your heart. Children physically, sexually and mentally abused by their own parents. Incest, rape – I've seen it all. But with you and Tasha it's different. You loved that little girl from the moment you set eyes on her, and you and Gail made her into the lovely young woman she is today. From what you've told me, Tasha is keen to grow up now, and that's all down to having the confidence you and Gail instilled in her. I just hope you'll both be really happy from now on, so go and have your dinner date with Teresa and have a wonderful Christmas, and I'll see you both in the New Year.'

He watched her quietly let herself out and then he sat at his desk and thought on her words for a long, long time before finally turning off the lights and heading for home.

Tasha was getting ready for her date when he walked in; she held her wrist out to show him a pretty silver charm bracelet.

'Look, Mrs Dixon the cleaner gave it to me,' she told him.

'Really?' He was faintly surprised. The woman barely spoke to anyone, let alone gave out presents, so he wondered what she had found so special in Tasha. Not that it wasn't a lovely thought, of course. He could have no way of knowing that the bracelet had once belonged to Tasha's grandmother.

He watched her walk into the kitchen to fetch his dinner before blurting out, 'Look, pet, I know I've been a bit of a pain lately, but it was only because I was worried about you. But I want you to know that I really like your young man. In fact, I thought it might be nice if you invited him to come and join us for Christmas dinner, if his family don't mind. I thought it would be nice to invite Teresa too. What do you think?'

She looked at him for long moments before crossing to him and laying her head on his shoulder, and as his arm closed around her he knew that they were going to be all right.

It was mid-morning on Christmas Eve and the town was heaving with people as Lorna struggled with all her last-minute Christmas shopping. She had left her husband Jason looking after the children and would be glad to get home now. She had decided to take the bus into town as she knew that parking places would be like gold dust, and she had certainly been right there. Now her feet were aching and her arms felt about to drop off with the weight of the bags she was carrying.

Once she was home she still had a few cards to hand-deliver, including one to Penny and David at Feathermill Lodge. She had done the same thing each year since they had adopted Lauren, and wondered if the girl would be home from college for Christmas. She would be surprised if she wasn't, because Lauren had never yet missed a Christmas with her family. She sometimes asked herself if she should tell Lauren that her sister was now living back in Nuneaton, but as yet she hadn't been able to reach a decision. It was a very delicate situation and she had decided to say nothing until she had sussed out how Penny and David felt about it. The way she saw it, they should make the decision on whether or not the girls should be reunited.

It was as she was standing at the bus stop, stamping her feet to try and keep warm, that a shiny Mercedes passed her and she got a glimpse of a handsome dark-haired young man at the wheel. She watched the car until it turned a bend in the road, a puzzled frown on her face. What was it about him that she had recognised? Shrugging, she went back to stamping her feet and forgot all about him as she listed in her mind all the big and small things she still had to do that day.

Chapter Forty-One

In Feathermill Lodge, Lou eyed Franky with concern. He had been very quiet and preoccupied since going to the butcher's for her mother, although she couldn't for the life of her think why.

'Is everything all right, sweetheart?' she asked tenderly.

'What? Oh, yes, yes, everything's fine, love. I was off with the fairies, that's all.'

She planted a kiss on his forehead then hurried away to answer the doorbell. Minutes later, he heard her exclaim with delight as she admitted someone into the hallway, and peeping around the door, his heart stopped in shock. It was Lorna, his old social worker. He hadn't seen her since the day she had delivered him to the children's home all those years ago – but he would have recognised her anywhere. What could she be doing here? Panic gripped him. He had to get out of here before she saw him, but then he heard them moving towards the door and knew he was trapped.

Hurrying to the window, he pretended to be staring out across the rolling lawns to the lake.

'I'm sorry to call so late,' he heard Lorna say. 'I've been run off my feet all day. But it's great to see you, love. Your mum and dad are so proud of you. They tell me you have a wonderful musical career ahead of you.'

Lou blushed prettily. 'Well, I'm not so sure about that,' she said modestly, and it was then that Penny walked into the room.

'Why, Lorna, what a lovely surprise,' she gushed as she kissed the younger woman. 'How are the children – and will you stay for tea? I'm just getting it ready.'

'In answer to your first question, the children are fine, growing like weeds.' Lorna grinned. 'And in answer to your second question I'd love to stay but I daren't. I've still got a million and one things to do. Jason will be tearing his hair out – the kids are so hyper I wonder if they'll make it through to the morning. I just popped in to drop your Christmas card off.'

'Oh well, perhaps you could all come for tea in the New Year,' Penny suggested. 'But before you go, you must meet Lou's young man. He's here to spend Christmas with us.'

Franky wished the ground could just open up and swallow him, but realising that he had no option, he slowly turned from the window and held his hand out.

'Lorna, this Franky Steel. Franky, this is Lorna, a friend of ours.'

Lorna struggled to stop the shock that was coursing through her from showing on her face as she shook Franky's hand. It was years since she had seen him but she knew without a shadow of a doubt who he was. Franky's dark good looks and smouldering brown eyes could not easily be forgotten.

'H . . . how do you do, Franky.'

'Very well, thank you.' He held her gaze as if he was daring her to say something, and suddenly Lorna knew that she must get out of there while she tried to sort things out in her mind.

'Well, it was very nice to meet you,' she said hastily, 'but now you'll have to excuse me. As I said, I have loads to do and I really ought to be getting home.'

'Of course.' Franky watched Penny escort her back to the door with his heart in his boots. At least she hadn't said anything. For now.

'Franky, whatever is wrong with you?' Lou asked. 'You look as if you've seen a ghost. Have you? There are enough of them here at the Lodge, after all.'

'To tell the truth, I've got a bit of a headache,' he told her, while smiling at her joke. 'Would you mind very much if I went up to my room to lie down for a while?'

'Of course not.' Taking his hand, she went with him to the bottom of the stairs, where she kissed him tenderly. 'Go on,' she urged. 'You go and get some rest and I'll give you a shout when tea is ready.'

He put his foot on the first step then pausing, he asked her solemnly, 'Have I told you lately how very much I love you?'

'Only about ten times today, but you can tell me again if you like,' she teased, and turning about she tripped merrily away as Franky slowly climbed the stairs.

Lou was helping her mother into her coat later that evening as David looked on with amusement.

'Now you will remember to put the mince pies out on the table ready for the morning, won't you?' Penny fussed.

Lou grinned. As far back as she could remember, they had always had mince pies for breakfast on Christmas morning, and Penny was determined that this year would be no different. She and David had agreed to go out with friends for a meal but already she was regretting it and wishing that she had stayed in with Lou and her lovely boyfriend. It didn't feel right to be leaving them alone on Christmas Eve somehow. Added to this was the fact that she had had a bad feeling inside her all day, and she couldn't shift it. A feeling of foreboding as if something dreadful was about to happen.

'*Yes*, Mum, I'll put them out,' Lou promised.

David winked at Franky behind his wife's back. Franky was still reeling from the shock of seeing his mother and Lorna, but was looking forward to having some time alone with Lou now. Not that he didn't enjoy Penny and David's company. He already felt like part of the family and was looking forward to spending Christmas Day with them. The whole place resembled a Christmas grotto and Penny had fed him so well that he felt he would burst if she forced so much as another crumb down him.

As the door closed behind her parents, Lou grinned. 'Phew, peace at last, eh?'

Franky held his arms out to her and she went into them, and as he held her close he knew that he could never love anyone as he loved her. They put the pies out together then she took him by the hand and led him to her bedroom and he went unprotesting.

He had never been in Lou's bedroom before and he didn't see much of it now because the room was in darkness. As she undressed he slipped the small box containing her engagement ring on to her dressing-table. She would find it first thing in the morning, and hopefully it would be a good start to Christmas Day for her. Then he was undressing and for the next hour, the ring, his meeting with his mother and Lorna and everything else faded into insignificance as he made love to the only person in the world who mattered to him.

They lay together for some time when they had finished making love, then Lou slipped from the bed and put her dressing-gown on, telling him sternly, 'Now you stay *right* there, do you hear me? I'm going to make us a nice tray of tea before we go to bed. Or at least before *you* go to your own bed.' She snapped the bedside light on and he saw the twinkle in her eye as she left the room. He lay back against the pillows with a grin on his face, feeling that he really belonged and was loved for the very first time. He and Lou were going to be happy together, he just knew it. There was a whole life waiting to be lived stretching out before them, and the future looked rosy. If Lorna chose to tell the family about his past he would simply have to come clean and share some of it with them.

His eyes strayed around the room. It was just as he had imagined it would be. There were music posters Blu-Tacked to the walls and cuddly toys everywhere he looked, as well as a selection of make-up on the dressing-table. All in all, a real girly room. And it was then that his eyes came to rest on a chair standing in the bay window. There was a rag doll sitting on it. It was old and tattered, but something about it struck a chord deep inside him, although he couldn't for the life of him think what it was.

Climbing out of bed, he crossed naked to the chair and lifted the doll up, turning it this way and that as he tried to think what it was about it that was so familiar. And then suddenly he knew and the air seemed to leave his lungs as he gasped for breath. *One blue eye and one brown eye.* Lauren's rag doll Polly had been exactly the same, and he had never seen another one like it – so where could Lou have got it from?

When she clattered back into the room some minutes later with a loaded tray, she found him sitting on the edge of the bed with the doll grasped in his hands.

'Ah, so you've met Polly then,' she grinned.

'Y-yes, I have – but where did you get her from? She's very unusual.'

Lou shrugged as she placed the tray on the bedside table and started to spoon sugar into two mugs. 'I don't really remember,' she admitted. 'I've had her for as long as I can remember. Since before I came to live here, I believe.'

'Before you came to live here?'

'Yes. Mum and Dad adopted me when I was just two years old. I should have mentioned it before, I suppose, but to be honest I never think about it. Why do you ask?'

Franky had the most awful feeling that the new life he had planned for them both was about to come crashing round his ears, but he had to know it all and so he asked, 'Is Lou your *real* name?'

She chuckled. 'No, not at all. Dad used to call me Lulu when I was little, then when I got a bit older it was shortened to Lou, but my real name is Lauren.'

As he gripped the edge of the bed the floor rushed up to meet him and now there was a huge lump forming in his throat as he dropped the doll on to the carpet, got up and staggered towards the door. He had to get away from her – and quickly – or he would break down.

'Franky! Where are you going?' she asked in bewilderment. 'I've got you a cup of tea here.'

'I . . . er . . . just need a little time on my own,' he gabbled. 'I think I'm just a bit overwhelmed with everythin'. I ain't never been part of a real family before, see. But Lou – I love you more than anythin' else in the whole world . . . Always remember that.'

'But won't you jus—' Her voice was cut off with the slamming of the door. She slowly placed the mug back on the tray and wondered whatever could be the matter.

It was then that she spotted the small box on her dressing-table. Curious, she went to take a closer look at it. She snapped open the lid, and as she looked down at the glittering diamond ring inside, tears started to her eyes. It was the ring she had admired in London. Franky must have gone back to the shop and bought it for her.

Lifting it from its velvet cushion, she slipped it on to her finger. It fitted perfectly, and she turned it this way and that as she admired it. The diamonds snatched at the light and sent rainbows of colours spiralling around the room, and Tasha thought it was the most beautiful ring she had ever seen. But not half as wonderful as the man who had given it to her. She thought of the gold St Christopher medal and chain she would give him tomorrow, and hoped that he would be half as thrilled with it as she was with his gift, although it wasn't the value of the ring that she would treasure, it was what it meant. This would tie her to Franky for all time. They would grow old together and she could think of no better fate. She thought of rushing across the landing to thank him for it, but then decided against it. He'd obviously expected her to find it on Christmas morning so she would wait until tomorrow, when she could show it off to the family over breakfast. She knew that they would be pleased for her. Both her mum and dad had obviously taken to Franky, and it would be another occasion to celebrate as well as it being Christmas Day.

She briefly wondered why he had dashed off as he had, but he'd said he needed some time to himself, so she felt she should respect that. Now that she came to think of it, she realised that she knew very little of Franky's past. It was something they had never really talked about. But then he hadn't known that she had been adopted until tonight. Still, it was no big deal. They had all the time in the world to really get to know each other from now on. Settling against the pillows on her bed she again admired her ring as a warm glow enveloped her.

Once Franky reached his room, he crossed to the dressing-table and leaned heavily on it as hot tears poured from his eyes. He should have known that this was too good to last. Happy endings weren't meant for the likes of him. No wonder Lorna had called earlier. It all made sense now. Lou was his *sister*, for God's sake! They could never come together now, and the knowledge was tearing him apart. She was the first thing in his life that had made any sense; the first person who had ever really meant anything to him, and now he would lose her too. But how was he going to tell her that they must stop seeing each other? *That they were brother and sister?* It would break her heart and he would gladly have died rather than do that.

He was still naked, and the scent of her was still on him. He had just made love to his own sister and the thought tore him apart. What was he going to do?

He knew that he could just go on with their relationship and not say anything – that was, if Lorna kept quiet. No one need ever be any the wiser, but even *he* had some decency in him, and he knew that Lou deserved better than that. He could return to the flat in London, but then that would be no solution. Lou knew where he lived and she would come looking for him. He could return to the flat and collect Zara and Sunny and just head off and make a new life for them all somewhere far away. Zara had made no secret of the fact that she loved him, and he knew that she would welcome him with open arms and go to the ends of the earth with him if he asked her to. But then that would be unfair to *her*. She could

393

only ever come a poor second in his eyes to Lou, and Zara deserved better than that too.

And then it came to him! There was only one solution to this problem, and he must take it, for this would cause the least heartache to the woman he loved. It would be the one truly good thing in his life he had ever done. He was inordinately proud of Lou and the sparkling career that was predicted for her, and nothing must be allowed to spoil that.

Crossing to his wardrobe, he took out some clothes. The ones he had been wearing were still thrown about in Lou's room and he knew that he couldn't face her again. It would be just too hard.

Tugging on a pair of jeans and a sweatshirt he then shoved his feet into a pair of trainers. He looked around the room for one last time. This beautiful place would have become his second home if he had married Lou, and he knew that they would have been happy here. He would have been happy living in a shed with her, if it came to that, but now he knew that it was not meant to be.

Slipping silently from his room, he paused on the landing outside her bedroom door, trying to picture what she would say when she found her ring in the morning. He hoped it would comfort her in the time ahead.

He then crept through the house like a thief in the night. At the bottom of the stairs he paused to stroke Belle and Harry as they ran to greet him, then after ushering them back to their baskets in the kitchen, he let himself out into the courtyard, where his sleek Mercedes glistened beneath its covering of frost.

Now he understood why Lorna had looked so shocked earlier that evening. It hadn't simply been because she knew of his past. She had also realised that he was Lou's brother. No wonder she had made such a hasty exit! If he stayed around, everything would come out – and Lou would be heartbroken, and also tainted, somehow. There might even be a scandal, if the truth got out. He couldn't risk that. Lou meant everything to him, and he was determined to save her feelings at all costs.

After walking around to the front of the lodge he glanced up towards Lou's bedroom window. The curtains were tightly drawn but the light was shining through them, so he supposed that she was still awake. He could imagine her lying in bed with a happy smile on her face and it broke his heart.

As he turned, he looked at the lawns rolling down to the lake and beyond to the perimeter of the grounds, where the River Anker was slowly flowing along, glistening in the cold moonlight. His trainers crunched on the thick hoar frost and he shivered as he moved on towards the water. When he came to the banks of the lake he blinked away his tears. The water looked black and uninviting, and a thick mist was floating across it, but he knew what he had to do. All his life he had been bad, just as Jacob had told him. Meeting Lou had shown him that there was good in the world, and that he could change. But that hope and the wonderful future he had envisaged for them was gone now.

Glancing once more towards Lou's bedroom window, he took a deep breath and steeled himself before slowly walking into the lake. The freezing water took his breath away and he gasped as it soaked into his clothes. He hesitated. What he was about to do was so final. Surely there must be some other way?

And then he saw her face in his mind's eye when she discovered that she had fallen in love with her own brother – had even committed incest with him – and he knew that he was doing the right thing; the only one good thing that he could do to protect her.

He steadfastly moved on until the water was lapping around his shoulders. He could feel the reeds beneath him wrapping themselves around his legs, and already he was beginning to lose the sensation in his hands and feet. And then he took a deep breath and pushed himself forward . . . and now he was out of his depth as the water closed over his head and he slowly sank. Within seconds his lungs felt as if they would burst. He had never been so cold in his life and he began to panic.

A series of images began to flash before him: he was a little boy again and Kevin was beating him as his mother Kay tried to drag him away. And then he was in the bungalow in Harry Street and his mother was leaving him. He was kicking and screaming, and Kay was promising that she would come for him, as Mary held him tightly. He was in the bath with Jacob's hands doing despicable things to him, and he was crying for his mother. Now he was in the field with Fleur and Twig. Twig was strumming on his guitar and Echo and Destiny were chasing around the campfire laughing hilariously, with Dog in hot pursuit. The images speeded up: he was with Mrs Smythe, being shunted from one foster placement to another as she glared at him with contempt. Lorna was there now, leaving him at the children's home, and then he was in the shower room with Mr Cannon. He could feel the man's blood on his hands. Zara and Sunny were there too, playing Snakes and Ladders in the homely sitting room of the flat with Boy before his overdose . . . and now Franky was reaching out to take his earnings from Hugo — blood money for all the terrible things he had done.

As the water claimed him, Franky began to struggle but his arms and legs would no longer do what he told them. And then suddenly a picture of Lou floated in front of his eyes and a feeling of warmth enveloped him. He stopped fighting and began to relax as the peace he had always yearned for finally entered his soul. There was a bright light ahead of him now and he floated towards it, and in seconds he knew no more.

The house was in darkness when Penny and David arrived home and David looked slightly disappointed.

'I was hoping to have a nightcap with young Franky before I went up,' he said regretfully.

Penny poked him playfully in the ribs. 'I think you've had quite enough for one night,' she told him, as she pushed him towards the stairs. 'Go on, get yourself off to bed. I'll lock up and join you in a minute.'

David did as he was told and alone again, Penny frowned as she stood in the hallway. There was something not right; she knew it, and the feeling was stronger than ever now. Even the resident ghosts had seemed to be agitated today. Sarah, the child ghost, was there now standing in the hallway looking at her solemnly as if she was trying to tell her something. In all the years that Penny had lived in Feathermill she had never known the little girl to venture off the landing.

Sighing heavily, Penny went from room to room, turning off the lights and checking that the doors were locked. Whatever it was that was wrong she would know about it soon enough, but right now she was exhausted, although she doubted that she would get much sleep that night.

On Christmas morning, Lou awoke bright and early. She stretched lazily and yawned, and then as her eyes settled on the glittering ring on her finger she smiled. It was going to be the best Christmas ever, she just knew it. Throwing back the covers, she snatched up her dressing-gown and after slipping her feet into her slippers she ran across the landing to Franky's room without even bothering to brush her hair. She wanted to spend a few minutes alone with him before they went together to tell her parents the good news and show off her beautiful ring.

She tapped at his door but there was no reply so she tapped again, louder this time.

'*Franky*. Franky — wake up. It's Christmas Day!' Still no reply, so she inched the door open, swallowing her disappointment when she saw that the room was empty.

Damn it, she thought. He probably got up early and didn't want to disturb me. He must have gone downstairs to have an early morning cup of tea with Mum and Dad. That was just one of the things she loved about Franky — he was so kind and thoughtful.

Tightening the belt of her dressing-gown, she made for the stairs and in no time at all was down in the kitchen, her shining eyes looking round for a sign of her new fiancé.

Penny was at the stove stirring a large saucepan full of porridge and David was unlocking the back door to let the dogs out for their run.

'Morning, love, and Merry Christmas,' her mother greeted her.

'Merry Christmas, Mum – and Dad.' Lou gave them both a hug, before asking, 'Have you seen Franky this morning, Mum?'

Penny turned the stove off. 'No, I haven't. I thought he was still in bed.'

'Just hark at the dogs,' David grumbled. 'They're barking their heads off.' He stood watching them haring towards the lake from the kitchen window as Lou crossed to join him.

'I bet it's Franky they're barking at.' Lou smiled up at him. 'He must have got up early and gone out for a walk.'

'Brrr, rather him than me.' David shuddered at the very thought of it. 'You'd have to have the constitution of an ox to venture out in this.'

The dogs were on the banks of the lake now, yapping furiously at something in the water.

David opened the door. '*Get back here, you two!*' he shouted, but the dogs ignored him. 'That's funny.' He frowned. Both dogs were very well trained and they usually obeyed his commands instantly.

'Harry, Belle! Get back *here* this minute!' He tried again.

Still the dogs ignored him and now he was beginning to get annoyed. They were making enough noise to waken the dead – not that they had any close neighbours to worry about, thankfully.

'Oh, just leave them, love, and come and have this tea,' Penny urged him. 'They'll come back soon enough.'

The three of them sat down at the table but Lou felt uneasy and her eyes kept straying to the door.

'I'll wait until Franky comes back before I serve the porridge. He shouldn't be long, should he?' Penny said, as she poured them all a cup of tea.

After a while David stood up and sighed. 'It's no good, I shall have to put my boots and my coat on and go and fetch them in,' he grumbled. 'All that barking is getting on my nerves.'

The women watched him as he bustled away, only to return moments later looking as if he was wrapped up for a trip to Antarctica. They exchanged a grin as he let himself out of the back door into the bitterly cold morning and Penny poured them a fresh cup.

When David reappeared some short time later, clutching the dogs' collars, one in each hand, they saw that he was ghastly pale.

'What's wrong, love?' Penny asked, and after shoving the dogs in the direction of their baskets, he beckoned her into the hallway.

Lou's heart was thumping. Why was her father behaving that way? And why were the dogs so subdued? They had slunk away with their tails between their legs and were gazing at her from soulful brown eyes.

'Lou . . .'

Her eyes snapped back to her mother who was standing in the kitchen doorway again.

'Your father is phoning for an ambulance . . . I'm afraid there's been a terrible accident.'

'An accident? What do you mean?' And then a cold hand closed around her heart, and before her mother could stop her, she was running towards the doorway and through it, leaving it flapping open as she fled towards the lake with her dressing-gown flying out behind her.

'I'm so sorry, love.' Penny squeezed Lou's hand, wishing that she could take the heartache from her poor girl's eyes. 'What's happened is absolutely tragic. Franky must have gone out for a walk last night before going to bed and slipped on the frost on the banks of the lake; the police think that can be the only explanation. There were certainly no signs of foul play.'

The ambulance had just left with Franky's cold body lying in the back of it, and Lou was still reeling from shock. She would never forget the sight of Franky floating in the water face down for as long as she lived, and she couldn't believe that she would never see him again. Today was the day they should have become engaged. They should be opening their presents by the Christmas tree right now – but instead, Franky was heading towards the morgue. It was just too much to take in. He had looked so peaceful lying on the stretcher, as if he was just asleep and might waken at any second and smile at her with his wonderful dark eyes. But she knew that this would never happen again. He was gone from her for ever, and it was just too much to take in. All her hopes and dreams were in tatters.

'Oh, *Mum*.' There was a great lump in her throat that was threatening to choke her but the tears wouldn't come. They were trapped inside and she felt numb. Penny hugged her tight.

'Why did this have to happen? Franky and I were perfect for each other. It's so unfair.'

'I know, love, I know,' Penny crooned as she rocked her back and forth. She gazed over the girl's shoulder towards the lake, her own tears hot on her face – and that was when she saw him; looking towards the house. Franky. It seemed that there would be yet another ghost in Feathermill from now on, and as Lou had always had 'The Sight' just as she had, it would be only a matter of time before she saw him too.

'You know,' she tilted Lou's chin and looked into her eyes. 'What you have to do is hold on to the fact that what you and Franky had was something very special. Now you have to go on for his sake and do all the things that he would have wanted you to do. Some people live their whole lives through and never have what you two had – and because of that I can guarantee that he will never be very far away from you.'

Penny's words had such a ring of truth in them that Lou was comforted. She rested her head on her mum's shoulder, praying that Penny was right.

'Is there anyone that we should contact? Any relatives that you know of?' Penny asked softly.

Now that she came to think of it, Lou couldn't remember Franky ever mentioning anyone, other than his flatmates. In fact, she realised now that she didn't even know where he had come from. They had always been so wrapped up in each other that their pasts had seemed insignificant. All they had cared about was their future.

'I don't think Franky had any relatives,' she answered.

'Oh. Well, where did he come from?'

'I asked him that once and he just told me "nowhere". Franky was just "the boy from nowhere".' And then, lowering her head, Lou finally gave way to her grief and wept for that boy, and for herself, and for all their lost dreams.

Epilogue

On a cold February morning, following the inquest into Franky's death, Zara paused at the door of the little flat she had shared with him and gazed around it for one last time. Lou's mother had phoned her late on Christmas Day, at Lou's request, to inform her of Franky's tragic accident, and since then Zara had found herself looking at life differently. What was she doing here anyway? Selling herself to anybody who had the cash to pay for her body just to exist? Suddenly the idea of an arranged marriage didn't seem quite so awful after all, and so she had made her peace with her parents, who had agreed to take her and Sunny in. They seemed to have mellowed since she had left home, and had promised her that she would not be forced into doing anything she did not wish to do. They had even been to visit her and billed and cooed over their granddaughter, which Zara took as a good sign.

The rest of her flatmates had said their goodbyes earlier in the morning and now she was all packed and ready to go. But oh, if only she had been leaving for a new life with Franky . . . She knew that she would never love anyone as much as she had loved him. He had touched her life and she would never forget him.

The sound of the taxi pulling up made her shift Sunny to a more comfortable position on her hip and snatch up her case. It was time to go home and leave the past behind. But as she left, her mind was full of what might have been.

★   ★   ★

At that precise moment in the small churchyard high on the hill in Devon, a couple gazed sadly down on the grave of their child. It would have been hard to recognise them for the travellers they had once been. But their dreams of going back to nature had died with their child a long time ago, and now they were the owners of a respectable hotel in Ilfracombe and had been for some years.

Twig and Fleur, or Brian and Donna as they were now known, had been gifted with two more children since Destiny's death, and not a day went by when they did not thank God for them. But no one would ever fill the gap that their little girl had left in their lives, and they made regular pilgrimages to the churchyard each week.

Echo was now a sturdy teenager and the only one of their children who did not live with them. As soon as he had left school he had returned to the life he had known as a child with his parents, travelling the roads with friends of theirs. Brian and Donna did not try to dissuade him, respecting his wishes, and he came home to see them whenever he was in the area. Their other two children, a boy of twelve and a girl of eleven, gave them constant pleasure and loved to hear the stories their parents told them of the time when they had lived from the land.

Now as they looked down at the tiny grave, Donna surprised Brian when she suddenly asked, 'Do you ever think of Franky? I don't know why, but I dreamed of him last night.'

'Funnily enough I do,' he admitted. 'In fact, a few months ago I was down in the town and I saw a young man who looked just like him. He's been on my mind ever since. I wonder what became of him?'

Donna shrugged, pulling her pure new wool coat more closely about her. Her hair was cut into a neat bob now and to look at her, no one would have ever known that she had once lived in the back of an old converted ambulance. Twig's long flowing locks had also been shorn and with his neat back and sides haircut and his smart suit he looked every inch the successful businessman.

'I don't know,' she answered. 'But I hope he found happiness in the end. I always had the feeling that the poor child had demons that he was struggling with.'

Brian placed his arm about his wife's waist now and told her, 'We ought to be getting back if your parents are coming for dinner.'

She nodded as, hand-in-hand, they walked away down the hillside.

In his penthouse apartment, Hugo was phoning round, trying to find a replacement for Franky. The man had not realised how much he had come to rely on him, and was not at all happy about his death.

'It'll take me months to find anyone as good as him,' he grumbled to one of his sidekicks. 'And now Zara has done a runner too, one of my best earners!'

The young man lounging on the Italian leather settee nodded. 'You're right, boss,' he agreed with a wry grin. 'It were right thoughtless o' the bloke to go an' die on you like that.' And Pickle then returned to gazing enviously around Hugo's pad. One day perhaps, Hugo would think he was good enough to take Franky's place. But at present that day seemed a very long way off.

In the tiny front room of her little cottage in Puddlesea, Mrs Golding sighed as she polished the ornament that had once belonged to Miss June. It was a Springer spaniel made of china that Miss June had bought soon after buying Bruno for Franky. She still thought of the lad and regretted the fact that she had been too old to adopt him herself when Miss June had died. She had married the gardener within months of the house being sold, and they had enjoyed eight happy years together until he too had passed away. She still chuckled when she thought back to the reactions of the villagers when they had learned of the forthcoming wedding.

'Getting married again at your age?' they had gasped.

She had held her head high and looked them straight in the eyes as she told them, 'That I am. If there's one thing I've learned over the last year it's the fact that life is too short so we should make the most of every minute of it.' And she and Mr Golding had done just that – and she did not have a single regret, except for Franky, that was.

He would be a grown man by now and she hoped that wherever he was, he was happy. The poor little chap deserved some happiness in his life after what that bully Jacob had put him through. Sighing, she placed the ornament back on the shelf and glanced at the clock. It was eleven o'clock. Time for a cup of tea, and maybe there were some of those ginger biscuits left . . .

Few people attended Franky's funeral that morning. Penny and David were there with Lou, and Mrs Dixon, who sat quietly at the back of the church, keeping herself to herself. Lorna was there too with Natasha, who had been reunited with her sister, with Penny and David's blessing. Lorna had gone to see them the week after Christmas and told them about Natasha, and Penny and David had been more than happy for the twin sisters to be reunited, but she had said nothing about the true relationship between Franky and Lou. The way she saw it, there was nothing to be gained by Lou knowing. It was far better that the girl should be allowed to remember him as the man she had loved.

At this moment, Natasha was wondering why Mrs Dixon, the cleaner from her father's surgery, should be there but didn't feel that it was the right moment to ask. There would be time for that later. For now, she was intent on helping her newfound sister through the ordeal ahead.

Penny and David had arranged it all because Lou seemed unable to cope with anything at the moment. Franky would be buried in the small pretty churchyard in Mancetter and David had made sure that he had the best casket that money could buy. It was the least he could do for his daughter, who seemed to be locked away in a lonely world of her own. None of them had the least idea what had made Franky go out walking as he had, late on Christmas Eve. They could only assume that he had felt the need for a bit of fresh air. He had been such a lovely young man, and for him to die so young in such a senseless accident was tragic.

The funeral service was short but poignant, and the mourners who followed the solemn-faced vicar out to the grave were heavy-hearted. Lou had been inconsolable in the days leading up to the funeral, but today she seemed to have drawn on some inner strength and was dry-eyed and dignified as she stroked the sparkling ring on her finger.

She listened with half an ear to the drone of the vicar's voice and then it was done and the rest of the mourners were walking away, leaving her to pay her last respects in private.

As she looked down on the shining brass nameplate she whispered, 'Sleep tight, my love. You will live on in my heart and I will work hard to become the best musician I can; just as you wanted. I promise to make you proud of me.'

Clutching her engagement ring, her tears sparkled like the diamonds within it, as she told him, 'I love you, Franky, and I always will. Rest in peace, and one day we will be together again.' And then she slipped away, leaving her love to sleep his eternal sleep.

Once Lou was out of sight, Lorna slowly approached the grave and looked sadly down at the coffin. Images of Franky at various stages of his life were flitting in front of her eyes. He had never been truly happy until he met Lou, and it seemed unfair that the one person who could have turned his life around was forbidden to him.

'I know why you did it, Franky, and I'm so proud of you,' she said, and her voice shook with grief. 'You wanted to cause Lou the least heartache possible. But don't worry; your secret is safe with me. She will never know who you really were. For her, you'll only ever be the boy from nowhere.'

Just for You

ROSIE GOODWIN

Just for You

Discover...
The Inspiration Behind *The Boy from Nowhere*

Find out...
Rosie's Favourite Things

Just for You

The Inspiration Behind
The Boy from Nowhere

It has always amazed me that the media seem to give much more press coverage to little girls who have suffered abuse than to boys. And yet, as a foster mum, I know that many little boys suffer abuse too. Before I started writing *The Boy from Nowhere*, I had the idea that I wanted to do something slightly different with my next book, hence I decided that I would focus this novel on a boy rather than a girl.

Soon after making this decision, I was lying in the bath one night when an image of a little boy popped into my head. He had huge, haunted, brown eyes and thick dark hair with a tendency to curl and immediately I knew that I had found the main character for my book. That very evening, I typed in the title and Alex was born. In no time at all he became a real boy to me and, as the story began to unfold, I grew to love him.

From the very beginning it seemed that the gods were against this poor little soul, but once I had set him on his path there was no going back. As with all my novels, Alex came to life and the story began to tell itself.

When writing my novels, I tend to start with a vague idea of what I want to do and then, once I have created my characters, they seem to take over. I suppose there is no right or wrong way to write as long as the end result is what the author hopes for, and every author writes differently. Once I start a book, it is very hard for me to leave it alone and if the story is flowing I am often to be found in my study tapping away, burning the midnight oil! No matter what I am doing, be it shopping, gardening or even spending time with my family, the next chapter of the book is always niggling away in the back of my mind, and my happiest times are spent at my computer getting down the ideas and the subplots that pop up along the way.

Poor Alex! From the very beginning he was destined to be unloved. First he was torn away from his family only to find himself with new parents who are not quite what they appear to be. His adoption is doomed to failure from day one and his torment ends in quite a dramatic way, although he does get to live for a time in an idyllic village in Devon, one of my very favourite places. He then goes on to have a happy interlude in his life but again it is short-lived and soon Alex finds himself back in care. But, as happens to so many children in the care system, by then he no longer trusts anyone and, asked where he is from, he will always say 'nowhere'.

As the story progresses further, Alex becomes very streetwise. He has no option if he is to survive and he ends up in London earning a living the only way he knows how. There are friendships made and broken along the way and more than a few tears, but Alex is hardened now and cares for no one.

But, of course, there is someone for everyone out there and when Alex meets the love of his life quite by chance, he truly believes that everything is about to change – for the first time his future looks bright. However, fate has yet more surprises in store for him and not all of them are good ones.

I won't give any more of the story away in case you haven't

read it yet. All I will say is that when you do read it, I hope you will come to care for Alex as I did. I shed many tears during the writing of this novel and often wished that I could snatch him away from the terrible life he was forced to lead and become the mum he so desperately missed. Perhaps you will too?

I shall greatly look forward to hearing what you think of it. It's so satisfying when a reader gets in touch to tell me how much they have enjoyed one of my stories. It makes all the hours I spend locked away in my study worthwhile.

With love,
Rosie x

Just for You

Rosie's Favourite Things

Family

Top of the list of my favourite things would have to be my family. They are the most important thing in the world to me, especially after recently losing my lovely mum and dad. My children kept me strong through this difficult period and made me realise that family is more important than anything else in the world.

Reading and writing

Reading and writing have always been some of my favourite pastimes for as far back as I can remember. I was christened 'The Bookworm' by my family at a very early age and nothing much has changed! I will read anything I can get my hands on – usually at least one book a week even though I am now writing full-time. Every evening I look forward to a soak in the bath with a good book before hitting the study to start work on my own novels. It would be very difficult to pinpoint one favourite. I enjoy any book as long as it is well written although I do love Dickens, Catherine Cookson's historicals and the classics. I can read them again and again and never grow tired of them.

My favourite comics as a child were *The Beano*, *The Dandy* and *Bunty*, which my granddad used to buy for me every Sunday when he came to dinner. He also supplied me with pens and writing pads to write my own stories even then. When writing my own books I love the freedom it gives me to go where I please and create characters that hopefully come to life.

Animals

As a child, I was privileged to always be allowed to have pets and my love of animals has grown from there. I have three Shih Tzus who are very much a part of the family and they come with us almost everywhere we go. We also have a pond full of Koi Carp but over the years we've had numerous animals as I'm a great one for taking in waifs and strays: rabbits, mice, guinea pigs, gerbils, cats, and a tortoise to name but a few. Of course, after the initial novelty of having the pets wore off for the children, it was always Mum who got to clean them all out and feed them – not that I'm complaining! My dream is to one day own a house with large enough grounds to start my own little animal sanctuary where I can care for unwanted pets, but my biggest fear is that they would probably never get to be re-homed because once I'd cared for them I wouldn't want to part with them.

Holidays

I suppose I'm very much a home bird and I've never been a great one for going abroad, mainly because my husband isn't overly fond of flying and because we hate to leave our dogs behind. Because of this we prefer to holiday in England. Last year, we bought a static caravan at the coast and now I love to escape there, although I never truly escape because I take my laptop with me. Our family often join us there too, so it's great fun to spend time digging sand castles on the beach with my little granddaughter, Charlotte.

Gardening

I absolutely love springtime when everything is coming to life. I always find it harder to write during the spring and summer in the daytime because I like to potter out in the garden. I tend to settle better to my writing during the evening anyway, but I especially love it in winter when I'm tucked away in my study with the wind howling outside and I'm warm and cosy with my characters.

I find it fascinating the way the garden changes with the seasons, starting with the snowdrops closely followed by the daffodils. We usually do far too many hanging baskets and tubs but have promised ourselves that we won't this year because we want to spend more time at the coast. Whether we'll stick to it or not is another matter entirely as it's so tempting when you wander round garden centres and see all the lovely plants – as any gardener will tell you!

Films and Music

I don't have time to watch a great deal of television and rarely get to go to the cinema anymore – being a foster mum and a full-time author does restrict the time I can spend in front of the box. I suppose I would have to say *Wuthering Heights* is one of my all time favourite films. A more modern day one I love is *Pretty Woman* – especially the bit where Julia Roberts strolls back into the dress shop looking like a million dollars after being insulted in there the day before!

And music! I get teased endlessly by my family because I'm a huge David Essex fan. In fact, my daughter bought me his Greatest Hits for Mother's Day. I love soul music and Tamla Motown too although I also find classical music very restful when I'm in the right mood!

Crying Shame

Rosie Goodwin

Claire Nightingale is haunted by the memory of childhood abuse and the painful choices she was forced to make. Longing to find peace, she knows she must first confront her demons.

Moving to Solihull with her adopted daughter Nikki, she tries to make amends with the family she left behind. But Claire is not the only one hurting: Nikki is scarred by her own abusive past, and their relationship, once loving, becomes fraught with tension and resentment. Struggling to come to terms with their pain, it is not long before ghosts from the past bring a new threat that jeopardises the possibility of any future happiness . . .

A heart-breaking tale of abuse, courage and, above all, the redemptive power of love.

Acclaim for Rosie Goodwin:

'A touching and powerful novel from a wonderful writer' *Bookseller*

'The all too rare skills of a true storyteller shine through Rosie Goodwin's writing' Gilda O'Neill

978 0 7553 4224 2

headline

Forsaken

Rosie Goodwin

The ultimate betrayal . . .

Born on a Friday, Sophie Winters has always been a loving and giving child, who'd do anything for her family. Yet her father, Bill, has always seemed to resent her. For her mother's sake, Sophie learns to live with Bill's animosity – until the night he drunkenly forces himself upon her.

Left pregnant and ashamed at seventeen, Sophie doesn't know where to turn. So when she meets the charming Ben Lewis and he offers her refuge at his mother's hotel, she accepts. At first it seems that Ben and his mother are quite the good Samaritans. But there is little goodness in the Lewises' hearts . . .

As Sophie begins to realise their dark intentions, a web of danger and deceit wraps itself around her. She knows that if she is to survive, she will have to fight for all she's worth . . .

Forsaken is a harrowing and compelling tale of triumph over tragedy that will not easily be forgotten.

Acclaim for Rosie Goodwin:

'Rosie's the real thing – a writer who has something to say and knows how to say it' Gilda O'Neill

'The tear-jerker of the season . . . [a] heart-rending tale' *Western Mail*

978 0 7553 3490 2

headline

You can buy any of these other bestselling books
by **Rosie Goodwin** from your bookshop
or *direct from her publisher*.

FREE P&P AND UK DELIVERY
(Overseas and Ireland £3.50 per book)

The Bad Apple	£6.99
No One's Girl	£6.99
Dancing Till Midnight	£5.99
Moonlight and Ashes	£6.99
Forsaken	£7.99
Our Little Secret	£6.99
Crying Shame	£6.99
Yesterday's Shadows	£5.99
Tilly Trotter's Legacy	£6.99
The Mallen Secret	£6.99
The Sand Dancer	£5.99

TO ORDER SIMPLY CALL THIS NUMBER

01235 400 414

or visit our website: www.headline.co.uk

Prices and availability subject to change without notice.

Reader Survey

**Your chance to win £100-worth of George clothing vouchers
and one of hundreds of free books!**

Simply complete this short survey and return to the following address by
8th January 2010:

Reader Survey
Headline Marketing Department, 338 Euston Road, London, NW1 3BH

Two hundred survey responses will be selected at random and a free
book will be sent to each respondent. The first survey selected will also
receive £100-worth of vouchers. The winner will be notified by post
by 25th January 2010. The adjudicator's decision is final and no
correspondence will be entered into.

Please tick the applicable box

1. Gender Female ☐ Male ☐

2. Your age?
☐ 18 or under   ☐ 31–45   ☐ 61–75
☐ 19–30   ☐ 46–60   ☐ Over 75

3. Occupation
☐ Housewife/husband   ☐ Manual
☐ Retired   ☐ Retail
☐ Unemployed   ☐ Middle management
☐ Student   ☐ Senior management
☐ Clerical   ☐ Other . . . .

4. How do you choose the books you buy? (Tick as many as apply)
☐ Friend's recommendation   ☐ Price
☐ From reviews in newspapers   ☐ Attractive cover
  and magazines   ☐ Set in my local area
☐ See them in a shop   ☐ Bonus material
☐ From adverts   ☐ Other . . . .
☐ I have heard of the author   . . . .
  or read their books before

5. Where do you usually buy your books?
☐ WHSmith   ☐ Bookclubs
☐ Bookshop   ☐ Internet
☐ Supermarket   ☐ Other . . . .
☐ I borrow them from   . . . .
  libraries/friends

6. Do you buy all of your books from ASDA? . . . .

7. How many books do you buy each year?
☐ Less than 5   ☐ 11–20
☐ 5–10   ☐ 20 or over

8. Name your top three favourite authors:
1. . . . .
2. . . . .
3. . . . .

9. Which region do you live in?
☐ Scotland   ☐ South-east
☐ North-east   ☐ South-west
☐ North-west   ☐ Northern Ireland/Eire
☐ Midlands   ☐ Outside the UK and Eire
☐ Wales

10. Which supermarket do you usually shop in?
☐ Asda   ☐ Tesco
☐ Morrisons   ☐ Waitrose
☐ Safeway   ☐ Other . . . .
☐ Sainsbury's   . . . .

11. Do you have internet access?
☐ Yes   ☐ No

If you answered **Yes**, please enter your email address here if you'd be interested in receiving email updates about forthcoming books, competitions and reader events . . . .

If you would be interested in taking part in further market research please tick this box ☐

Occasionally we may share your information with our affiliates. Please tick this box if you would prefer us not to pass your details on to third parties ☐

First Name . . . . Surname . . . .
Address . . . .
. . . .
Postcode . . . .